HARD ROAD TO HEAVEN

Jeanne Ann Vanderhoef

Copyright Jeanne Ann Vanderhoef
Published by Branchlands Publishing,
Charlottesville, VA 22901
ISBN 978-0-615-50676-0
August 2011

Dedication

To my three precious children, Craig, Lee, and Christy, who are all now grown-ups, you have my heart's joy, gratitude, and pride for what you were as children and what you have become as adults. I love and respect you more than, as Grammie would say, "more than tongue can tell." And though they have been gone for some years, I hope my parents, Janet and Kent Lambert, are paying attention up there in heaven. I owe them everything; Mum for her love, to say nothing of her 54 books that guided the youth of yesterday and still are popular today, and Pop who gave us (among many other wonderful things) the ability to see the world.

Most of all to my beloved, Dean (Vandy) Vanderhoef. There are no words! Just love and the knowledge that I was the most blessed of women.

Chapter 1
April 1945

Anna and I stand listening to the spring rain falling from the weighty, flannel sky onto the cobblestones. Like silver needles the drops stitch together the grayness of the buildings, the colorless cobbles, and the sky to create an ashen world. The drops bounce on the stones like the rattle of snare drums while my thumping heart provides the rhythmic bass in my ears. If we could only grab the handles of the basket that sits between us and run far from this dismal square in Poland and away from the cadence of those imaginary drums. My muscles tighten as if to obey my thoughts, but knowing that would bring us back into the very center of the nightmare from which we are trying to escape. We both stand motionless.

The basket holds my baby, Alexander. Protected by a screen made from the same willow and wrapped snugly in a blanket cut from my winter cape, he is, thank God, sleeping. Just a little while ago, as we gently piled potatoes on top of the screen, Anna whispered, "Schlaf in ruhe, Hertzlein." At the time I thought her benediction would protect him until we reached safety and beyond. Now, looking at the rain-soaked square, I see possible disaster for us in every sodden human who scurries from scantily stocked booth to booth.

If he were older, Alex would feel the same doubts and terrors that torment Anna and me, but he is only two weeks old and trusts anyone who provides him with the things that make him comfortable. I prayed through the long months before his birth that these decisions Anna and I have made for him are the right ones. We stand here now because we feel they are the only decisions we could make. When he is old enough, I will tell him about his father and he can then choose his own future.

The stench inside this sallyport is nearly unbearable. Hundreds of years of humans and animals have used the cobblestones and the stuccoed walls to relieve themselves. The rainy day coalesces and strengthens the odors, but there is no other safe place for us to wait. Besides, all building entrances in the city of Grudziadz smell the same. As much as I want to snatch up the basket and run out into the clean rain, the shadows in here give us what we need most. . . . .anonymity.

The clatter of a wagon's ironbound wheels and the slow clopping of a horse's hooves on the street passing the sallyport make my heart pound on my ribs as if it were trying to get out, but my unyielding throat blocks it. We've been waiting for so long and I feel inadequate to cope with the hundreds of anxieties that percolate in my mind. My legs seem made of spaghetti. I wonder if, now that the time is almost here, they will carry me out of this entryway.

Anna stands stiffly on the other side of our basket and stares straight ahead through the arched exit to the market place. She seems calm, but I know that her heart has to be drumming in rhythm with my own. The wagon appears and rumbles past, leaving only its echo.

"Oh." I moan and clutch her sturdy arm. "Anna, he's forgotten us. He's gone past." I whisper in German, her native tongue.

"Hush, child." The stoic woman's soft voice is so calm it makes me ashamed of my near hysteria. "Herr Breitski would rather forget his own heart than forget you. He's only behaving as he usually does on market day." Her generous mouth turns up in a gentle smile. "He doesn't want to arouse any curiosity by changing his routine, does he? I expect he's only taken old Bubbe to the watering trough. He'll be back."

She's right. This is no time to change an established routine. Ashamed of myself, I apologize. "I know I'm being foolish. It's all this waiting that's making me nervous. When we're safely on the

6

wagon and away from the square I'll be sane and sensible again, I promise."

"Well, if you ever plan to be sensible and not draw attention to us, I suggest you put your hands back under your apron and stop waving them around in the air like a ballerina." Though she whispers, Anna's voice is stern. It's so uncharacteristic that I know she is as tense as I.

"I am a ballerina, or I was," I'm trying to lighten her mood. "Shall I show you?"

Anna's brown eyes widen in alarm and she takes a step toward me with her hand out to suppress me if I should make any kind of move. I smile at her and hide my hands under my voluminous apron.

"Padded as I am with all these pillows you should know I couldn't dance one step." I look down at the obese, lumpy figure she has created for me. Hidden under a nondescript, brownish, dress, the pillows that bulge and billow over my rump and at my hips are almost eclipsed by the ones that create my ample bosom. Rags stuffed into the sleeves pad my thin arms. The whole unattractive torso is bound together with the only twine we can scavenge in this war-torn land. The string has been much used and often spliced, but this morning, before we left the village, Anna declared it strong enough. It must keep me together until we reach the small boat that is to take us up the north-flowing Vistula River to the Baltic Sea. Traveling only at night, it has taken two days to get to Grudziadz from Bydgoczc. Our nerves are tighter than the string.

As I look down at my outer shell, the real me is so lost under the weight of cushions and anxiety that it's doubtful I will ever find myself to dance again. At this moment, if I could only launch myself into a series of pirouettes or a Grand Jete, I know the tension would drain away. When I first joined the Warsaw Ballet, I had to prove myself before I was accepted. Even later, many found it strange and perhaps a little threatening that an American girl should become Poland's Prima Ballerina.

"Just wait," the newspapers said in my defense. "Just wait until you see her dance. You will understand.""

Yet because of Hitler and my husband who joined that little man's fearsome SS Corps in 1939, I can no longer dance for all those loving people. I, their ballerina, stand quaking in a dank, reeking sallyport beside the Grudziadz potato market. The people who loved me when I was a swan or Gissele or Aurora, who reveled in my fairytale marriage to the handsome Baron von Pawel, will someday understand my flight. If they survive this dreadful war, will they forgive me for taking my baby away to be brought up in another country? And I wonder if the time will ever come when I'll be able to dance for them again? And if it does . . . what if our two countries should . . . ? I can't finish the thought. My sigh carries no comfort. Of itself it is too heavy.

Anna, thank heaven, interrupts. She reaches over to pull the black crocheted shawl that covers my sagging, cushioned bosom a little tighter. The babushka hiding my hair has slipped back and she jerks it forward. If I were not wearing this drab scarf on my head, we would have no anonymity at all. My hair is a blending of my two grandmothers, one golden and the other copper. It is such an unusual color that the newspapers graciously named me Aurora for the sunrise. I have learned to answer to that nickname as readily as I answer to my real name of Carole, but my crowning glory is now my anathema. Anna and I debated cutting it off, but, in the end, it is only pinned and bunched under the dull babushka. My real body and my hair must remain a secret at least until we reach safety.

At the remembrance of the stranger's words last night, I feel a chill. He slogged along the muddy street of the village that has protected us these few last days. "She must move tomorrow," he had whispered as he passed Anna and our open door. "Her husband was seen nearby this afternoon."

Anna spoke through tight lips as she repeated the words. "The swine is no doubt in Grudziadz by now. Let's get our things together so we'll be ready before dawn."

"I wish we could take another route or leave tonight in the dark. Why didn't we go when Alex was born? We would be safe by now." I was almost spinning around the small room.

"Liebchen, remember the river was frozen until just the other day."

"Then we should have gone a different way." I knew I was being unreasonable.

"There was no other route as safe. You know that. Now be calm. We must prepare."

She assembled the pillows to disguise me. Everything had been ready since Alexander was born, but I understood it made her feel more secure to be busy. With a partisan friend we had crept into Grudziadz in the dark, spent the day in a cellar. The thing of most importance, to conceal my son. He arrived in this world with a thatch of my unusual hair and the wrinkled face my husband will have when he is an old man. If anyone should see him, there will be no doubt whose son he is.

My back hurts from the unaccustomed weight of the pillows and from the peculiar posture it takes to support them. As I shift to relieve the ache, the basket jiggles and I draw in my breath. "Please." I whisper to God. "Please don't let him waken." I close my eyes and listen for his cry. My mind races to find a way to protect my baby if he should make a sound that would expose his existence. For all these months we have kept my pregnancy and Alex's birth a secret from his father. How tragic it would be if we

9

were caught now that we are on our way to freedom.

There isn't a sound. He could be smothering. "We have to uncover him. Maybe he can't breathe in there." I bend over.

"He's fine." Anna catches my shoulder to stop me. "The basket isn't that tight. He breathed all right this morning, didn't he?"

"If he's hungry, he'll cry."

"He's not hungry. I'd be more worried that he can't move enough," Anna adds. "If he gets uncomfortable, he'll cry."

But the basket is quiet. Aware that I can't remove the potatoes and the screen to look at him, I give Anna a wan smile and we drift back into our own thoughts. When I look at her later, I see her expression is sad.

"Are you thinking about Meier?" I whisper.

"Yes, Liebchen. I was praying for him as I always do. If we only hadn't let him run to help that boy . . . if we'd been more alert, could we have saved him? But that's foolishness. My Meier was Jewish. They would have found him anyway." There is a hopeless finality in her voice. She shifts her position and rotates her shoulders. "We can only hope that, when the Americans finally arrive," she says, "they will march rapidly to the Baltic. I don't know that they'll find my Meier alive, but God is good, and we can pray. Only, please God, let the Americans be the ones to come and not the Russians."

The Russian troops are already over-running Poland on the way to Berlin. We've heard terrible stories of their behavior toward the women in the towns near where they camp. Anna is right to hope they never reach us. It is not like her to offer her feelings, much less her fears. Even when we saw her kind husband taken away, after her first heart-wrenching scream, she only set her jaw and swallowed several times in quick succession. No trace of tears today but, in the almost four years since Krystal Nacht, I have heard her often sniffling softly in the privacy of her bed.

"I wonder if my father is with Patton's Army?" I query softly. "Just think, Anna, he doesn't even know he has a grandson. Won't he be surprised when we are all together again?" My heart stops its steady drumming for a second. "I wonder if he knows we're still alive."

"Your father will always know in his heart whether you're alive or dead, Liebchen."

Her words soothe me. I believe if my father were dead, I, too, would feel it in my heart.

She says, "When we are finished with this terrible war, he will come. Perhaps we will already have found a ship to take us to America." She looks out at the square. At a faint sound from one of the entryways that open on each side of the sallyport, her eyes widen and her head jerks toward me. These doorways lead to the stairways that carry the residents upward into their apartments and to the courtyards behind. I am familiar with those stairways. When my parents and I first came to Poland in 1930, we lived in the apartment directly above where Anna and I now stand. The stairs have always creaked, but this strange noise is more a thump-thump-tap, thump-thump-tap. I strain to identify it. The only safe apartment in this building is the one we just left. These peculiar steps are coming from the opposite stairway.

Years ago, as my friends and I played hide-and-seek on these stairways and in the courtyards, approaching footsteps brought only a thrill of possible discovery. Discovery now brings dread. Whoever is creating the strange little sound may have heard our conversation, and he might be one of those who will, for his own gain, offer us up to the Nazis.

The German armies are weakened, and here in Poland there are few people left whom even Hitler might describe as a threat, but our disappearance from Ostatetcznie nine months ago brought back a fierce concentration of Sturm Schutztaffel and Gestapo from their enjoyments in the big cities. My husband is a possessive man. Nothing and no one he ever felt he owned escaped his grip.

Chapter 2

Partisans have told us the callused men of the S.S. will not be allowed to return to their pleasures until I have been found. That will most certainly keep them vigilant and willing to grant favors to anyone who turns us in. When the tapping reaches the cobblestones behind us, I turn my body to face the enemy and block the basket. Anna slides toward me. They will have to remove both of us to reach my precious baby.

The tiny, white haired lady who taps her way toward us with her black, silver-headed cane is familiar. She's no bigger than a sparrow, and I recognize her. She is a part of my youth. A Countess, she owned this building; perhaps still does. As our landlady in those early years when my parents first brought me to Grudziadz, on occasion she invited an eleven year-old me to tea in her apartment. She was aristocracy, something I knew only from books like The Three Musketeers or A Tale of Two Cities. Also, she was stern, formal, and I never knew whether I was behaving according to her standards.

Seeing her here in the dank sally-port, my first inclination is to curtsy as I did when I was a child, but then I realize, (and hope,) she will not recognize me in my disguise. Surely she'll recognize Anna? My heart changes its cadence. Surely as a refugee from East Prussia in the Russian revolution she cannot be a Nazi sympathizer. Still, being Polish nobility, if she hadn't collaborated with the Germans, wouldn't she have been arrested by now? Although it is only seconds before she comes around to confront us, can't seem to exhale as I turn to meet her. She stops in front of me and looks at the basket partially hidden by my voluminous figure and skirt. I want so badly to push her away that I find my hands straining against each other under my apron and Anna trembles where her shoulder touches mine. We move as one to grasp the woman's spindly arms.

As we propel her backwards toward the entrance, I accidentally kick the basket. Several potatoes roll off and there is a faint cry from the baby underneath. I am so frightened I let go of her arm and try to bend around my obstinate pillows to recapture the potatoes. When I feel my outer shell shift a little, I straighten quickly in dismay. Anna too lets go and drops to the cobbles. She kneels as if in prayer, a potato in each hand. We freeze when Countess Czeczelowa picks up the remaining potatoes and lays them carefully on top of the screen. When they are all in place except the two Anna holds and Alex has obviously continued to sleep, I look into the blue eyes behind the rimless spectacles and want to whoop with joy and relief when one of them winks.

"Carole," she says softly. She has recognized us. She is a friend. Taking the potatoes from Anna's immobile hands, she adds them to the pile. Neither Anna nor I comment on the scrap of paper she slides in with them.

Although I am sure they have recognized each other, Anna's expression is one of total disbelief. She struggles to her feet just as a man in a cassock walks by the sally-port entrance and looks in. He hesitates, stops. It is Father Stanislowski. I hold my breath as if that could make me invisible. The elderly Countess immediately begins to yammer in a querulous voice.

"I didn't want to go out in the rain and now it is too late to get potatoes for my supper. You have so many you can let me have a few." She bends again toward the basket. Anna plays the game and jerks her upright before she has a chance to touch the potatoes. "Take your hands off me," the little woman blasts. "I'm sure you brought these potatoes here to sell. Why not sell them to me?"

Anna, aware of the role the Countess is playing, answers the question in a polite, but firm voice. "These potatoes are for my brother's birthday tonight," she says. "We will, unfortunately, need them all. But look, there is one stall left on the square and see, the

14

rain has stopped. Here, let me assist you across the street. We'd better hurry, though, before that vendor decides to go home."

"Let go of my arm." The Countess jerks away from Anna and loses her balance.

I reach to steady her, but she shrugs away from me too. "I can get along perfectly well without your help, you selfish peasant. You farm women, you could let me have three potatoes at least." She mutters as she totters her way toward the entrance. "Good evening, Father," we hear her say. The priest bows slightly and walks out of our vision.

Even though she knows the Countess is only playing a part, Anna has reverted to the days when she first came to work for us. She starts to trail behind the imperious little woman as if she were her slave. Still a child when twenty-year-old Anna first came to us from the sugar beet fields, I remember that subservience. We had been taken to the beautiful estate of Friedenau to buy a horse for my father. When the von Wechslers, the owners, heard we needed a maid, they asked their own maid Lisa to send for her sister. Anna became part of our family. Over the years she has grown in confidence and stature.

Now she is my friend, my confidant, my guardian. In the twelve years since my parents returned to the United States, she has become closer to me than my mother. Though she always had an innate dignity, the self-esteem she lacked has become a part of her. It's painful to see her cowed again. Powerless to stop the tirade, I also know the Countess is right. Only by disparagement can she disassociate herself from us enough to help us.

I bend to remove the scrap of paper. "Anna's old room in the garret," the spidery writing tells me. "I hope it will not be needed. God go with you." Tears for the past fill my eyes, but they don't spill over. When I hand the paper to Anna, there is no one to

15

notice.

The scrap is small, but it seems to stick in her throat as she puts in her mouth and swallows it. She smiles and shrugs her shoulders as if to say, "Fine, but unnecessary."

Across the square there is only the one stall left. Farm wagons bearing poles, canvases and baskets from some of the others rattle across the streetcar tracks on the other side of the market place and disappear behind the buildings. The lonely stall belongs to Rudiger Breitski's wife. Only when Rudi feels the time is right will he and old Bubbe, his sway-backed horse, leave the watering trough and the gossipy old men who cluster around it to gather the skeleton of Gertrude's stall and the empty baskets. By then it should be almost dark and my baby's basket will be unobtrusive when it slides in among the empties.

"It looks brighter out there," Anna says nervously, "and people across the square are opening their balcony doors. I hope Rudi arrives before the sun comes out."

"Wouldn't it be better for him to delay until sunset? I don't even know what time it is, do you?" My watch was broken before we left Ostatetcznie. "It can't be much longer. It looks late."

"We can't wait. The boat runs on a schedule." Anna's whispered German words sound as if she's hissing. "We have to be exactly on time or the boat will leave. It's a good thing she's whispering because Father Stanislawski passes by in the opposite direction. I notice the tiny lady leaving Gertrude's stall with the potatoes in her green string bag. With her cane she moves surprisingly well, but stops and looks toward the sky. How many of my other acquaintances are a part of this wonderful Partisan chain? Anna's voice prods me to keep my mind on the business at hand.

"Rudi is loading Gertrude's stall parts," she says. "He's on his way. We have to be ready as soon as the wagon stops. Remember, child, if anything goes wrong before we are on the wagon, you take Alex and go. I will always find you, though it might take a while. Don't ever worry. I will be there."

"Dear Anna." I reach over and squeeze her arm.

Relying on her cane with the string bag bumping her leg, Countess Czeczelowa manages to create the impression that she is sweeping grandly into the sally-port. "Take care," she whispers as she passes, her nose in the air.

Anna makes a face at me. "She made me feel just the way I used to before your family came into my life. She should have been on the stage." Anna pauses again to look out at the square. Rudiger and Gertrude have finished the loading. In a moment the wagon will be ready to move. "I have to tell you, Liebchen, in case I never see another day, you have given me enough in the last fourteen years to make a complete and joyous lifetime. I have had a small part in helping you become a beautiful and grown up lady. You have made me proud and you have given me all the love--except for that which came from my Meier--anyone could wish for. Now you have blessed me with precious Alex. Although I would be satisfied if my life ended today, I hope that it doesn't. I do so wish to see him grow."

"Anna. You will be with him always, that I can promise you. I'm sure God intends us to bring him up together."

I am embarrassed that she thinks I have done so much for her. She guided me through my teen years. She applauded me in my career, and she stood beside me through my marriage. At the last she was my doctor, my mid-wife, and my protector. In the face of her selflessness, I have done nothing.

All the while we have been waiting for the wagon, streetcars have

17

been coming and going on the west side of the market place. We have watched each one. There has been nothing to alarm us. Now, as one halts in the middle of the block, two SS officers step down. I see the black uniform with the hated red and white insignia on the arm. As he takes off his cap and smoothes his hair, I see he's my husband's friend, Karl von Wagner. Before I fled, he was also my friend, but that can no longer be true. Anna clutches my arm when she recognizes him too.

"I hear Herr Breitski's wagon coming, child. Hurry and we will get away before he can see us." The wagon wheels scold the cobblestone as they roll over them, close and unmistakable. Once the wheels were encased in rubber, but Hitler has taken all Poland has to offer and now the wheels, bound only in iron, protest to each uneven stone.

We both stiffen. As soon as Bubbe comes near, we each take a handle of the basket and step out onto the street. Rudi and Gertrude sit side by side on the wooden seat. Behind them their baskets wobble on the wagon floor. The skeleton parts of the stall give off a low rumble as the posts that support the canvas roof jostle together from their position on the rack built into the wagon's side. Almost before it stops, Anna hoists her skirt and climbs aboard the wagon-bed. I lift the basket up to her and she nestles it among the others clustered there. As I position myself to override the hampering pillows, I feel a string snap somewhere underneath. My false body begins to slip away. Strangely, despite my panic, I think of a locust and wonder if it is as frightened when it loses its shell and is exposed naked to its enemies. Clutching the pillows to me, I try to climb aboard, but am unable to do either. Across the square the enemy has not moved.

In that moment the sun bursts forth. Caught in its spotlight, I jerk my head. The babushka catches on a hook that holds the stall's uprights in place and hangs there. Released, the hairpins fly and suddenly the Aurora is free to challenge the setting sun. Anna and I both see the SS troopers start their run across the square. With my only thought to protect my baby, I push her hands away and slide back.

"Go," I say softly. "I'll find you. You must save Alex." Rudi must hear the message because, with a slap of the reins on Bubbe's rump, the wagon rolls away.

Chapter 3

As I run, the unsubstantial string around the pillows gives way completely. They tangle in my legs and drop to the cobblestones, leaving a trail behind me. It's like struggling through deep water. Hesitating only long enough to fling the last of the red-ticked pillows onto a stairway entrance, I run on, hoping it will act as a decoy. With my flapping skirt clutched in one hand, I make it to the courtyard behind the building. An explosion of hard -heeled boots behind me sounds as if the entire organization of Hitler's storm troopers has gathered in this one town to hunt me down.

When we first came to Poland, we children played in this courtyard of number 10 as well as in the one behind number 9 where I lived. As a hiding place we used a small utility shed that held brooms, shovels, and things necessary to maintain the building. In the deep shadows I see the shed still hugs the wall. The door, loose on its hinges now, is partially open. It will have to be my refuge.

A deep bass voice yells, "She went up the stairs here." I recognize the voice. It is Kurt's friend, Karl. He was in our wedding, but now his boots no longer sound friendly. Led by the pillow, he storms up the stairway. The pillow has done its job.

Wriggling in behind a large wooden box, I'm caught up in a spider's web, an eerie phantom's touch on my face. I brush it away and pray its spinner is long gone. Jolting down on my behind, in my terror I hardly feel the cold, damp cobbles, but it doesn't matter because my head and body are now out of sight. I try to silently slide hide my legs behind the brooms and shovels lined up against the wall, but as I inch them forward there is a scrabbling noise and something brushes against my ankle. In the dull light a live creature quivers in the corner. It is larger than a mouse. Dear God. It's a rat. While we stare at each other, I see the same terror and anguish in his black eyes that must be in mine. He is safe from me, and, I hope he will return the favor. Neither of us relaxes.

I left the door ajar because closing it might have made a noise to give me away. Now, I hope it will act as another decoy. Maybe the SS men will think I couldn't possibly be stupid enough to hide behind an open door and won't search in here. At the same time I know Karl is well aware that I am far from stupid. Methodical and thorough, he'll search everywhere.

Heavy steps, just above me, descend the back wooden staircase. The rat hears them too and skitters across to hide behind a pile of burlap sacks in an opposite corner. It's too late for me to hunt another hiding place. Besides, there are no hiding places in the structures that hem in the other three sides of the courtyard. Once they were the stables for the horses and carriages of the apartment dwellers. As a child I used to dream about the beautiful horses that were curried and cared for by the men who lived above the stables and shared their space with the hay. It was all imagination because, by the time our family first came here, the low buildings had already been converted to garages, the haylofts removed. Here Hitler has successfully used one of his bribes to the German people, the Volkswagon, prohibitively expensive. Empty, neglected and forlorn, the garages are too open for me to use. I can't go over their roofs either. High wire fences on top, designed to keep criminals out, will keep me in.

The hollow thud of the boots hitting the wooden stair treads changes to rapid fire clatter on the cobbles and jolts me back to reality. Holding my breath, with my eyes closed and my hands covering my mouth, I wait. My two harriers are talking softly to each other as they open and close the stable doors. I can't understand their words yet, but the sounds are getting closer. The rat runs back to the corner just out of reach of my feet. My eyes are open now and, facing the same enemies, we no longer terrify each other.

Suddenly a flashlight plays around the shed's small interior. When they read my box, they will pull it out from the wall. I'm surprised they can't hear my bones rattling and my heart banging. The rat is startled enough to rush out the door. I can't see him, but I hear his scrambling feet, see the erratic vacillation of the flashlight's beam and hear a loud thump as a boot is stomped hard on the cobbles.

"Missed him." Karl's voice holds no regret, just a statement of fact. "Well," he speaks to his companion. "We know she's not in here. She's terrified of mice and rats. She'd rather be caught than be shut in with a rat."

He doesn't bother to close the door. I hear them stalk away. I'm glad my new ally escaped.

"Ach so. Where do we look now?" The voices come from near the sally-port arch.

"We'll search the apartments on the other side of the building."

"She could be on the roof."

"That's the last place she would be. She's more terrified of heights than of rats. She's even afraid to go near an open window if it's above the ground floor. Come on. Let's search those apartments."

I hear them clomping up the inside stairway of the sallyport. Karl has unwittingly told me how I must go if I want to reach help. Can I force myself to climb up on that roof? Baby Alex's face swims before me and I can almost feel him in my arms. Determined to try anything, I stand up. When the door bangs, I know they are inside.

Tearing off the cumbersome dress and shawl, I am left in Anna's godson's heavy black sweater and pants. Able to move more freely I dart out of my hiding place and race up the back steps of the building that's on the other side of the sallyport. Its roof will be my path. Rubber-soled shoes carry me silently up four flights of wooden steps. On the top landing I bump into a trash container. In spite of the gathering darkness, I see its lid fly loose and catch it before it clatters to the floor. After staring at it for a long moment, I noiselessly replace the cover. It's a stepping-stone to the roof. Again my heart changes its rhythm. I can't do it. I can't climb onto that can. I can't step on to that railing. I won't go up there.

Physically, after all my ballet training, I know I can do anything, but Karl is right. I cannot tolerate heights. Still, not even willing to look down, I know I have no other choice. Just a peek. My stomach lurches, my heart loses all rhythm and I'm dizzy. Clutching the rail to keep from falling, I drop to the floor behind the garbage can.

Below me a door opens. "All right," Karl's voice has grown hard, "now we'll tear this building apart brick by brick if we must. She's here, and we will find her." He slams the door with a sharp crack like a pistol shot.

There is no memory of climbing on the can, the railing, into the gutter or onto the roof, but I must have done all of those things, because here I am, like a timorous rabbit, only halfway to its burrow. The safety of a broad chimney is just out of reach. Seconds later, wedged between the chimney and the roof, I huddle next to its meager warmth. Against the warm bricks, my woolen sweater feels uncomfortably damp and clammy. Trying to warm myself, I push against the chimney and almost cry out. My breasts are sore.

Anna and I hadn't imagined that I would be the one parted from Alex. We were only happy that he would have a continuous supply of milk. Of course we had put in the two bottles in case of an emergency, but we didn't really imagine there would be one. Now, my painful breasts and the longing for my baby add to the despair that clings to me as I cling to the chimney. Already shivering in the early spring night, frightened, and forlorn, the tears come and run as if they will never stop. Still, they do lessen and there is a blankness left inside me like a pond with all of its water siphoned away.

23

My nose runs. My handkerchief is in my trouser pocket and, afraid of reaching for it, I wipe my nose on my sleeve. Mother would be outraged. I almost smile.

The clouds are nearly gone. A slim moon has appeared, throwing just enough light so I can see the river, but there is no little boat on it. Leaning away from the chimney a bit, I see an indistinct figure marching back and forth in the courtyard below. My arms automatically clutch the chimney tighter and the pain brings me back to the moment and the tears come again. A babble of raised voices precedes all the inhabitants of both sides of number 10 as Karl and his reinforcements push and prod them out of the sallyport and line them up in the street. I can hear the small children and crying babies. They squeeze my heart. I feel so guilty. I am the reason they have been rousted from their warm beds.

As scant as the warmth of the chimney is, I don't want to move. My eyelids, heavy from all the weeping, close. When they open again, I'm awake, alert and ashamed. How long have I slept? It must have been quite awhile because the people from below are gone and everything is quiet. Where are Karl and his henchmen? I need to move and if I don't do it before dawn the sharp-eyed SS will see me. The only way, of course, is across the roof to number 9 and then to the tiny casement window of the room once allotted to my dear Anna where the Countess now lives. Shifting positions, I face in that direction. Its roof, barely visible, appears to be higher than the one on which I huddle. Squatting on my haunches, I stare at what seems an impossibility. I see no way for me to climb that smooth, stucco wall. Although it is little more than a slight change of color against the dark sky, it seems to grow taller as I look at it.

The slender moon gives only a wan light, but out at the edge, where the two roofs disappear into the gloom, I can make out a pipe. I'm terrified and yet elated by my discovery. The pipe, from its apparent size and position, must be the drain from the building's wide eaves to the ground. I've never paid attention to drain pipes before and wonder if they have joints. This one is obviously beyond the edge of the roof on which I now hunker. Won't I be out into space if I try to climb it? I am amazed, acrophobe that I have always been, that the thought can even pass through my mind.

There has been no sound from below for some time. I stretch to see over the ridgepole. No patrolling guard. Peeking around the chimney, I can see no one in the courtyard, but the SS would never leave a job unfinished. They must be inside the sallyport.

Uncoiled, I take the first step. It's colder standing up. When my foot slips on the damp slate, I sit down hard. The cracking shingle sounds like a cannon. I hold my breath. There's no answering noise. I inch along, scoot by scoot. I dare not take my eyes from the roof until my shoulder touches the wall of building 9. Holding onto the edge of a fragile rectangle of slate for imagined security and, trying not to look down into the darkness, I let my other hand slide down the smooth drain pipe until it is stopped by the jutting lip of a joint. The flange is narrow, but so is my foot. It will make a tenuous foothold if I can force myself to let go of the slate and stand up to use it. Hoping there will be something on the other roof for me to grab on to, I rise to a shaky stand.

Against the night sky I see a radio antenna poking its spindly arms upward. I can't tell how it's attached, but it's the only possible handhold. But first I have to trust my weight to that pipe joint. In the silent night a loud, explosive sneeze erupts from the courtyard.

Another voice clearly answers "Gesundheit." I almost dive back up and behind the chimney, but when my heart starts eating again, and, once more with no recollection of the movements that put me there, I am on the roof of #9. And with a firm grip on the antenna's base. When I dare turn my head to look down, there is no one in the courtyard. I thank God for that and for the guard's incipient head cold. There is one more sneeze from below, this one muffled, a low rumbling laugh, and then silence.

What I think is the Countess' dormer juts out from the roof only a little to the right . . . But suppose I have the wrong window . . . My memory of Anna's window is that it's hardly big enough for a cat to go through. What if I can't get through it . . . but I keep going. For my son, I'm determined to try anything. Shivering in my milk sodden sweater and inching toward the dormer is frightening enough, but when I reach it I see there is less than a foot between it and the roof's edge. Doubling up, I let my feet slide into the gutter. It squeals. What if it breaks? I edge around to face the window. From the far side, already cranked open, a hand reaches out of the dark interior. Its owner grasps my arm and guides me with a whisper that is little more than an audible breath.

"Be as quiet as you can. Put your right foot in first."

Chapter 4

When my foot touches the floor I take a breath in what seems to have been hours. Tears of fear, anguish and, yet, relief spill over.

"Hush. There now." The sprightly little octogenarian closes the window. After she pulls the heavy draperies and turns on the light, she opens her arms and I fall into them. "I've been so worried." She pats me gently on my back. "I didn't know whether you had been caught or not, but I couldn't sleep until I knew." She backs away slightly and looks down at my damp sweater.

Before I can explain, her expression changes to one of comprehension. "Oh, you poor child," she says softly guiding me to a chair near the tile stove. "That was your baby in the basket."

I must have shown my surprise because she was quick to say, "Oh, yes. I heard it cry out when you jostled it. Then I watched from the landing window the whole terrorizing happening when the basket and Anna went off on the wagon and those dreadful men started to chase you. Until I heard you on the roof, I was so afraid for you. At least I hoped you were the one I heard." She bustled around while she talked. As she disappeared behind a heavy damask curtain, her last instruction was "Take off your wet clothes while I find something else for you to put on."

"I'm sorry to cause you trouble." Embarrassed, I pull the soggy sweater over my head. "Anna and I didn't anticipate this."

Her arm reaches around the curtain and she pulls me into her sleeping compartment. "It isn't something a young mother would expect. Though my clothes won't fit you, somehow we'll manage." She goes to a chest at the foot of her curtained bed and removes a white pillow cover. Made to fit the huge red-ticked European pillows, with its buttons closed it keeps the intractable feather contents from escaping. It's enormous.

While I'm washing myself from a bowl and pitcher in the tiny sleeping alcove, she cuts the case in two and folds it. "There now. You can take this other half with you for the future."

"Oh, dear, you've destroyed your lovely pillow-case."

"Someday the war will be over and you can buy me another one." After she pulls and tugs the linen piece around my chest one and a half times, she can button it. It's so tight it's hard to breathe. "It will stretch a little," she promises.

Breathing or not, dry and wrapped in a warm, wooly shawl, I return to my chair, which welcomes me into its embrace.

"You must be frozen." Countess Czeczelowa continues to bustle. "And are you hungry? Of course you are. Sit there and warm yourself while I fix you a little something and after that, unless you wish to sleep, we can talk."

As if the shawl she has wrapped around me has all the warmth and caring of the world knitted into its fibers, I begin to thaw. Then I begin to remember and the tears start again.

"Go ahead and cry," she says. "A little food will help you. Soon you will believe that your little one is not lost to you and we will begin our plans to get you together again." Her smile is confident and my heart believes her.

I watch her hang my sweater by the tile stove and hop across the room with her tiny, bird-like steps to pull apart heavy, rose-colored damask draperies. A graceful antique table, more suitable for a drawing room, stands supporting a two-burner cooking plate and a bread-box. Close beside the table, a lovely gilt étagère serves as a cupboard for the china and the few groceries she needs. These familiar pieces give me an added sense of welcome and security.

As she works I look around the room and become reacquainted. Of course, there is the samovar. King-like it rules the room. The Countess and the samovar have always begun and will always end each day together. As she pays homage to it by polishing its silvery surfaces, it serves her faithfully. Although the rest of the room is crowded with elegant treasures, it's the samovar that links the damask draperies, French furniture, Meissen china and polished silverware with the affluent past from which they came. The samovar surely has known all whom she has known and maybe, in its steaming, bubbling way has earned a title of its own.

Long ago I heard that the Countess originally came from East Prussia. If so, she must have suffered the hardships of the Bolshevik Revolution, the first World War, and now this terrible conflict. Something has protected her. Perhaps it is her breeding and fierce defense of her aristocracy that has brought her to this tiny bastion of gentility, but she and the beautiful, stalwart samovar are together, still living as decorously as possible.

While I ponder, my hostess covers the small inlaid table near my chair with a much-mended, embroidered cloth. She sets my table as carefully as if it were a state dinner. The silver is polished, the napkin, which she flicks into my lap, is well ironed, the salt and pepper comes in crystal and silver. Even with the ache in my arms where Alex should lie, it's hard not to bask in the attention and comfort.

When it's ready, the meal is beautifully arranged on the plate and smells delicious. How this tiny lady acquired white asparagus, venison, currant jelly and even white-flour rolls called Semmel, I can't imagine. Fed, as I have been for the past months on peasant fare, I try to eat with some semblance of manners. I hope I don't disgrace my mother.

The Countess watches me and, as if she reads my mind, she

suddenly says, "You are wondering where I get this food. I can see it in your face." She settles herself more comfortably in her chair. "Busso, our former huntsman from my husband's hunting lodge, lives in the forest not far from Grudziadz. He brings me fresh things—even eggs—whenever he can. The tinned asparagus of course, he gets on the black-market. Luckily, his wife comes too and does the little things for me that are hard for a woman of my age."

I savor my last bite, then stand to clear away my dishes. The Countess Czeczelowa puts her hand gently on my shoulder.

"Sit still, dear one," she says softly. "You must rest."

I can't argue. My work is not finished. I know I need sleep, but without Alex in his basket beside me, how I can ever sleep again? All my worries return. Is he cold? Hungry? Are the two extra bottles we packed in with him enough? Is the boat sea-worthy? Suppose something happens to Anna?

The Countess' voice breaks into my thoughts. "While I fix our tea," she says, "I want you to tell me why you and your baby are running from your handsome husband."

Her voice jerks me back from the little boat on the frigid river. It takes a minute to understand what she's asking and then I wonder how much I dare tell her.

She notices my hesitation and smiles. "Let me tell you a little of my story and perhaps you won't be afraid to tell yours." As she speaks, she turns the ivory handle of the samovar and its tea flows gently into gold and white Dresden cups. She hands me mine, puts the milk and sugar on the table beside me, then sits back. As we lean back with our tea, her expression grows sad.

"When the Bolsheviks revolted," she begins. "I was young. My husband and I lived with our two tiny daughters, Katya, who was four, and Marika, who was two and a half on our lovely estate near Koenigsberg in East Prussia. You remember them. On the first day of the fighting, the Bolsheviks stormed through our home and shot my husband as he stood by the foot of the stairs. Although my heart felt pierced and I wanted more than anything in the world to run to him, I could see, from the way he fell, that he was immediately dead. To protect the children I hid with my girls in a secret cupboard we had built to hide our silver and jewelry from thieves." She is quiet for a moment and swallows twice before she goes on.

"Late at night when it was safe and the noise of the ravaging and looting had become silent, I left the little girls asleep in the closet and crept out. Those hours of waiting had been agony such as I had never known, but I had shed my tears and now, wish to or not, it was time to go on."

I think of my crying on the rooftop and wonder if I have shed all of mine.

"My husband lay dead at the bottom of the stairway abandoned by all but me," the gentle voice goes on. "After I kissed my darling's lips for the last time, I covered him with a Persian carpet and turned away knowing the part of him I loved would be with me always.

"Once I had found my daughters' coats, thrown about on the floor amid the destruction, I wakened them. Little girls, sleepy and confused, gave no notice to the bumpy carpet at the bottom of the stairs, but as we went out onto the thoroughfare they kept asking me please to wait for Papa. I could only hurry them along. It was not the hour for explanations. Someday, I promised him in my heart, I would find him so that, at my ending, we will lie together again."

I couldn't help interrupting. "Did you find him?"

"It took many years, but he is now here in the cemetery in

Grudziadz." She was quiet for a long moment before she took up her story again. "A wavering line of newly created refugees struggled by us. Some, like me, had children by the hand or clinging to their coats. Some were alone and many pulled carts loaded with their belongings. I hadn't thought to save anything except the picture of the four of us when we were a complete family. Frame and all, it was under my coat close to my heart.

"Without acknowledgment, we refugees all became friends jostling along together, yet terribly alone. We didn't even have to speak. Someone lifted my children onto the back of a wagon with other small ones and we mothers plodded behind. Aside from elderly men and little boys there were no males with us."

"Suddenly, with the dawn, the Bolsheviks surrounded us again and I was shoved away from my babies. I fell and another wagon ran over my foot. The pain was excruciating, but it was nothing compared to the one in my heart. Two other refugees snatched me up and between them got me to the edge of the road. While I struggled to stand and to see over the heads of the crowd, the wagon disappeared. I was shoved aboard a little cart and the pitiable line shuffled on."

"Oh," I cry out feeling Pana Czeczelowa's anguish. "How did you find your children again? Please, please tell me." I leave my chair and hurl myself across the small space to end on my knees with my arms around the tiny woman. I knew she had found her lovely daughters for I had seen them coming and going from the building when I was a child, but the remembered pain comes through in her voice. It is the same as mine.

"It was three years later that a woman came to my door here in Grudziadz," she answers my question. "With her were two beautiful little girls, one seven years old and one two years younger. The woman had been searching for me and had cared for Katya and Marika all that time. She was a wonderful person, perhaps you

32

remember her? She worked here when you and your parents lived in the building. Ingeborg her name was. She died in 1938."

"I do remember her. She was always so kind to me. Where are your daughters now?"

"They are married and have children of their own. Katya's only son was killed early in this terrible war and she has only her one daughter left. Marika was luckier. Her son was too young to go, but is now old enough to work with the Partisans. They all live in Posnan and I don't see them as often as I'd like since the Germans have taken over. Still, I know where they are and that they are as well and as happy as possible. Now, tell me how you, an American girl, come to be in this terrible state. I already know why you cried out just now and why you felt my pain so acutely." She takes my face between her two hands and looks deeply into my eyes. "I was watching from the window in the corridor when the wagon rolled away and your disguise came apart. You are having to learn what agony a heart can bear?"

"Yes, Madame, that was my baby, Alexander—my Alexander." Tears I thought were all shed rise up to run down my cheeks. "He is only two weeks old and, though I know where they are trying to go, I'm so afraid I will never find him again." I reach for my tea cup in hopes that a few swallows will stop the tears. "How could you survive for three years without knowing your children were alive?"

"Dear child, you, too, will live from one day to the next as I did. In a way you are better off. You know that Anna is with your baby and will care for him as if he were her own. I saw her get on the wagon. And the potatoe basket there with her. You will find each other. Hitler's armies are exhausted; the Allies are coming closer and closer. It won't take long."

"Countess, with all my heart I pray you're right, but at this moment, I'm not sure I can bear it."

33

"You can bear it. You're strong." The Countess stands and takes my cup. "A lot can happen in a short time, that you have to believe." She walks across the room. "Now, I think you should get some sleep. After you leave here it will be a long while before you get any. As much as I would like to hear more of your story, that will have to come after the war is over."

"I'm not at all sleepy. I'd like to tell you how I came to be here unless you wish to go to bed. Please tell me what's best for you."

"Perhaps there is time for your story and a nap. Just remember you need to be clear-headed when we start you on your way toward your reunion."

"What time will that be?"

"Herr Major Metzgar will be waiting for you at the bottom of the stairs at two A.M."

Knowing the plan and seeing that there is a future excites me, and if it's the same Metzgar, he was a friend of my father's. "I couldn't sleep now." I breathe as I sink back into my chair. "Thank you, but how do we get past the guards?"

"There are ways," is all she will answer before I begin.

Chapter 5
1930

Nothing about the day we arrived in Poland was warm and welcoming. It was raining: a despondent kind of rain that made it seem as though the clouds, tired of holding the water, had simply drooped their edges and let it all run out. Electric lights from street lamps and stores barely penetrated the gloom. Even when the rain eased for a few minutes everything was blurred as though an artist, dissatisfied with his painting, had wiped across the wet canvas with a wadded rag. Gloomy was a synonym for the city of Grudziadz.

It was the fourth of July 1930. Back in the United States the sun would still be shining and, when darkness fell, my friends would run with their sparklers twinkling under a starry sky. I was homesick.

"It's hard to tell where anything ends or begins." Mother echoed my thoughts as the ancient taxi from the railroad station 'brumbled' over the cobblestones toward the city's best hotel. "Even people brave enough to be out on a day like this look drab and colorless. I can't see their faces under the umbrellas, but I'll bet they're as somber as their clothing. We may be the only spots of color in this whole town."

I looked at my parents. Dad, being in the U.S. Cavalry had been sent to Poland for two years to learn their methods of equitation, wore his olive-drab uniform. Mother's suit is navy blue. Dressed in my best beige skirt and jacket, I wasn't very colorful either. I wondered what mother saw that I didn't. The only flashy spot in the town was the bright, yellow English-Polish dictionary Dad had held in his hand ever since we'd crossed the border from Germany. Every once in a while he'd made pstch noises as he turned its pages and I thought if that were the Polish language, it must be no more than a series of sneezes. In my eleven years, I had seldom felt depression. Now, trying to get rid of its weight, I sighed.

"It's all right, darling." Mother took my hand in her gloved one. "I'm sure when the sun comes out, the world will be more cheerful. Come on. Let me see you smile."

"The sun probably never comes out here." I was reluctant to accept any cheer. "Suppose we have to stay here two years in the rain with these gloomy buildings and gray people who don't even speak our language. Suppose we never have any friends and have to be here all alone."

"Carole Pierson." My father's voice was stern. "Stop looking for trouble. Your mother told you to put a smile on your face and I suggest you do it. We're here for two years and you'd better make the best of it." There was a slight pause before he added, "Even if it rains for forty days and forty nights. If that happens, I'll build us an ark. All right?"

"Yes, sir." In spite of my dolor, I giggled at the picture of my father who, though an exceptional horseman, would have had no idea of how to build so much as a simple box. "I'll try."

The day seemed a little brighter. My father could do that. He was stern and demanding, but often, just when I thought I was in real trouble, he put in a small bit of nonsense. Besides, we were all painfully aware that the only possible thing he would hit with a hammer was his own thumb.

"Don't you remember those lovely pictures in the National Geographic of the young men and women dancing the Mazurka outdoors on the grass?" Mother's voice had brightened too. "They couldn't have done that if the sun never came out, could they? Let's just agree to be happy. This is our great adventure, remember?"

I did remember the pictures in the magazine. Though they were in black and white, it was certain that the sun shone on the young people dancing with ribbons flying from their costumed shoulders. At that time in my life I don't suppose I recognized what dancing would mean to me. I only knew it was a necessity. Even today, I must dance in joy or in sadness. Just as some people scream and yell and destroy things and still others withdraw into themselves, I am more fortunate. In dancing my unpleasant emotions float away. Only the joyful ones remain.

The conversation with my parents had taken place in the late afternoon. Now, in the Hotel Krolewski Dwor's dining room, it was impossible to dance away my wretchedness. I was seated beside a Catholic priest who, since he spoke some English, had offered his help when we first arrived at the hotel's desk. Daddy had immediately abandoned his yellow dictionary and had committed us all to sharing every waking moment with, what he considered, a male angel sent by God.

Here at a table covered with snowy linen, silver and an array of glasses, with hands folded in my lap, I was seated beside that "Angel." I tried to tell Mother before we came down to dinner that I found Father Stanislawski upsetting, but when, under questioning, I could offer her no specific reason for my feelings except that he was always patting me, she said, "Stop being so silly. The man is a priest."

"But he smells funny and has ugly teeth," I persisted.

"He can't help his teeth and your father and I didn't notice any smell. As for patting you, I'm sure that's just his way of being kind to children."

"He didn't get as close to you as he did to me," I muttered. Brought up to accept adults as always being right, I suspected it was wrong to be openly critical of one and particularly a man of God. It did seem to me, however, that from the first moment, when Father Stanislawski had joined us at the hotel desk, he had kept his hand either around my shoulder, on my head, or on my nape. Wherever he put that squishy hand, it pulled me up against the black cassock.

"Perhaps I may be of some assistance," he had offered in accented English as Daddy struggled with his dictionary at the registration desk. "I speak a little of your language. I am Father Stanislawski and I dwell here in this hotel. My church is but at the corner of the square." He waved his hand in, I presumed, the direction of the church and smiled. His teeth were tiny and discolored.

Startled, my father dropped his English-Polish dictionary. Knowing his dependence on it, I picked it up and tried to hand it back to him, but now that a rescuer had appeared, he was no longer interested.

"What a welcome sound it is to hear words I understand." My father had put out his hand to the tall, thin scarecrow in the black cassock. Man of God or no Man of God, I thought he looked like Ichabod Crane. The two men shook hands. It wasn't until my father introduced him to my mother and turned to me that my stirrings of revulsion began.

As soon as I had made the bobbing curtsy my mother required, my face was surrounded and pressed between two fleshy hands that didn't seem to fit with the priest's tall, lanky body. The kiss he planted on my forehead, made me shudder. From that moment on, as long as we were in the same room, the man kept one of those flabby hands on me and I began to feel a part of something disgraceful. Nothing in my life before had prepared me to understand why I felt so shamed but, because the priest was an adult and, because my upbringing demanded that I respect adults, I was powerless to even pull away. It was a relief when we were in our own room and the man had gone.

"What a break finding someone who speaks English," my father said when we three were alone in our spotlessly all white hotel room. "Father Stanislawski is going to have dinner with us. I invited him when we went back down to the lobby to see about the trunks."

"It will certainly be a big help having someone do the ordering for us. Won't that be nice, Caro? We won't have to guess what we're going to eat and your father won't have to struggle with that incomprehensible dictionary."

Mother was hanging our clothes in a big wooden wardrobe that seemed to take the place of a closet. One of its doors was mirrored and I could see myself in it. The reflected face was not happy. While my father was in the bathroom with the door closed, I tried to tell her my feelings about the priest. I know now that she was fighting her own depression, but then, when she brushed my feeling off as imagination, I felt even more debased.

After Daddy came out of the bathroom, I went in. At first I just looked. A strange metal tank hung above the bathtub. It was, I had been told, a gas heater for the hot water and I vaguely remembered having one in a house we had rented in Columbus, Georgia when I was four. Whenever we wanted a bath, my father lit it and because it made strange popping noises and smelled, it was frightening to me. A large box of matches for this one lay on a white wicker table across from the enormous tub. I knew I would never touch them to light the evil-appearing contraption.

The room was long and narrow and I wish I could say that all the white made it seem "pristine." Actually, it was just stark and cold like the bedroom. At one end next to the toilet was a tall window. The bottom half was of frosted glass, the top was clear. Like the window in the bedroom, it looked out on the fish market whose smell crawled in to permeate and foul the sterility of both rooms. The tub was extra long. The wash basin was large, made of marble and supported by a pedestal. The toilet had a wooden seat, a tank above and a pull chain. Between that and the wash basin, a strange appliance squatted on the gray linoleum floor. Perhaps a foot-bath.

At the end of the room, opposite the window, a door opened into the hall. The concierge had ostentatiously brought its large key inside, inserted it in the huge key-hole, and declared, according to Father Stanislawski, "Now you shall be in private."

Standing in the room alone, the sight of that key signified despair. It made me feel like a prisoner. With shaking shoulders, I sank onto the edge of the tub with my feet in the foot bath and my arms and head on my knees. With the first involuntary sob, I straightened and began letting water run into the tub to cover the sounds I couldn't seem to control. It wasn't enough. Mother heard and was sitting next to me on the tub rim with her arms around me before I even knew she was in the room.

"There, there my precious, I know."Her tender hands rubbed my back gently. "I think I understand what you're feeling because I feel the same way. It's all so different. But you know what, I'll just bet when we get used to it we'll find we're enjoying it just as much here as we enjoyed it at home." She laid her head on mine and continued her massage.

She was trying to make me feel better, but I didn't believe her. I couldn't even imagine that this peculiar country could have anything I could relish.

"No matter what happens, Carole, we have to pretend to be happy and interested." Her voice was soothing, but firm. "Daddy, I think, is feeling as discouraged as we are. He also carries the burden of being responsible for our being here, you know. That's a lot of weight. We shouldn't make it any harder for him, now should we? Come on, darling, wash your face and let's get ready for dinner." She stood up. "I know you won't let us down."

Understanding and feeling guilty for causing even the slightest added burden on my parents, I promised myself that I would accept everything that came my way from now on. I certainly didn't want to add to the family troubles.

We were a falsely cheerful trio as we changed our clothes and rode down in the ornate elevator. The lift had glass around its four sides supported by intricate, scrolled gilded metal panels. Through the glass, I could see Father Stanislawski waiting in the lobby below us and, though my heart seemed to sink with the elevator, I was determined to curb my imagination.

As soon as we appeared in the dining-room door, the Head Waiter, bowing obsequiously, led us into the crowded dining room. All diners stopped eating, some with their forks halfway to their mouths. I was conscious of, and hoped everyone would admire, my yellow crepe de chine dress with the pleated ecru lace collar. Proudly I thought it was our appearance that produced the interest. It was a long time before I recognized that it was because we were Americans. Not many foreigners came to this town in the Polish Corridor. Whatever it was, we were paraded the entire length of the dining room and by the time we reached a table by the large front window, we had been ogled and dissected by every eye. My consciousness had turned to self-consciousness and I could hardly wait to sit down.

Waiting beside the priest as the important Head-Waiter pulled the table away from the black leather banquette and ushered my parents onto it, I wanted to stop their sitting down. I had been hoping to sit next to Mother and let Dad cope with the priest, but found myself trapped in a high-backed chair between the man and the window.

Father Stanislawski stroked my hair as he sat down beside me. "Like a beautiful sunrise, it is," he said as he fingered a lock. Embarrassed, I tried to smile as I said, "thank you," but it was a wan attempt.

He continued to talk to my parents and, without looking toward me at all, lifted the edge of the long, starched tablecloth, covered my hands folded in my lap with one of his fleshy ones and let the cloth drop to cover them both. My face flamed and I hoped no one was looking. I tried to pull away, but his grip was firm.

Our waiter, whose name was Helmut, had been hovering behind the Head Waiter. He looked at me and smiled gently. I had a feeling he had noticed the priest's actions and my reaction. There was a great deal of discussion between my parents, Father Stanislawski, and Helmut as to the menu, but I wasn't consulted. After Father Stanislawski removed his hand to handle the large menu, I was relieved. I listened to the conversation for awhile then let my thoughts drift.

Deep in my memory of running with my friends under the dark star-studded night sky in Virginia, I involuntarily jerked my hands away when he again found them. Aware now, I looked at the man. He went right on talking to my parents while he took possession again. How could he dare? This time there was no drawing away. My hands were pressed tightly against my thighs and the covering cloth hid my feeble struggle. His thumb stroked ever so softly. Confused and afraid I might be reading something evil that wasn't intended, I sat motionless. My heart beat so fast I felt dizzy.

When the thumb stopped stroking my palm and found its way onto my leg, I stopped breathing entirely. When the whole hand slid along the crevice where my legs were pushed tightly together, I knew it wasn't my imagination. I struggled out of the chair and fled.

Chapter 6

Mother caught up with me at the foot of the broad stairway. "Carole, what's the matter? Tell mother, darling. Don't you feel well? Come, we'd better go up in the elevator. Does something hurt?" She pulled me into the open cage where the elevator man stood waiting.

Once the door closed I was afraid to look through the glass for fear my father and the priest might be following. Keeping my eyes up until we reached our floor, my heartbeat and breathing didn't even begin to return to normal until we were in our room.

"Now," Mother pushed the big eider-down comforter aside so I could lie down on the cot that had been brought in and placed behind a screen in one corner of the room. "Tell me where you feel bad. Are you sick at your stomach? Perhaps it's the excitement. Do you have a pain anywhere? I wonder if you have a fever."

She rushed to her makeup case for the thermometer, but even while the glass tube was in my mouth her questions never stopped. I wasn't sure she really wanted an answer and, since I had no truthful ones to give her, I was grateful for the thermometer that precluded lying. When she and the thermometer had proven I had no temperature and I had told her that I just felt queasy, she decided it must have been the excitement of the train trip and arrival. Since I didn't throw up, she finally consented to go back down to her dinner.

"I'll just rest a little while, Mum, and then when I feel better I'll come down." I needed to be by myself to figure out what I had done to precipitate such behavior by Father Stanislawski. He was a priest and, as such, I knew he could do no wrong. The fault had to be mine. I looked up at the crucifix hanging above my parent's bed. Daddy had said he was going to take it down as it looked heavy enough to kill them both if it should fall in the night. I hoped he would leave it. Maybe Jesus could help me comprehend my sin—whatever it was. I was puzzled as to how Father Stanislawski dared to behave as he did in a restaurant filled with people. What made him think that I wouldn't scream and expose him? But, he was safe because I was too guilty and ashamed to tell anyone. Curled up in the featherbed, covered with the down comforter was like being in a warm safe womb and after a time of self-doubt and abject abasement I cried myself to sleep.

Mother's solicitous "How do you feel, my precious," penetrated my cocoon and startled me.

Emotions are strange things. Sometimes those joyous ones we hold close to us as we go to sleep are still there when morning comes. We waken rested with that wonderful thrill of remembrance branching from our hearts to warm our whole body. But when I wakened to see both of my parents bending over me with anxiety born of love, the awful weight in my chest was still there. When Mother asked me later, as she did every night as she tucked me in, if I had anything I wanted to tell her, I said "no." It was almost the first thing I'd ever hidden from her. The only other time was when I was six and had filled my pockets full of those beautiful mothballs from the wooden keg in McCoy's grocery store. I knew I was committing some kind of an horrendous crime that would have to be kept hidden. When we got in the car and Mother's nose began to twitch I knew I was lost. But there was no odor to this secret.

"Jon, would you light that hot water thing in the bathroom?" Mother retrieved my pajamas and robe from the wardrobe. "I think Caro needs a bath after a night on that train."

"When you put it that way, I don't think a little hot water would hurt any of us." He disappeared obediently into the bathroom. In a minute there was a hiss and a small, dull phoom. "Thar she blows." Dad came bounding into the room like a sailor doing a hornpipe. I knew he was trying to cheer me up and he succeeded. I giggled.

"I'm hungry," I said. "Do we have some crackers or anything?"

"Goodness Gracious. That's right. You haven't had any supper." Mother looked at me in horror. "Jonathon, what can we do?" She turned to my father. "Do you suppose the kitchen would send something up? If we could make them understand what we want?"

"Don't panic. It's very simple. While you two get your baths, I'll go down and see if Father Stanislawski is still the lobby. He'll help us." He started toward the door then turned back. "Where is my dictionary? If he's gone to his room, I'll have to rely on it. Oh, woe is me." He flung the back of his hand to his forehead like an actor in a melodrama.

At the mention of the priest's name, something heavy dropped into my stomach. Mother reached over onto the table and picked up the small, yellow book.

"Here, you clown," she said, laughing as she handed it over. "If you don't go now there won't be anyone down there for you to practice on. Go." He went and the door closed behind him.

"Now, Lovey, the water should be hot enough for your bath in a few minutes." She looked at me and smiled. "We have time for a nice chat. Do you feel better now?"

My heart lurched, but, when I nodded with my fingers crossed in my lap, she continued. "We enjoyed Father Stanislawski. He is really a very charming man, you know, and your father and I learned a great deal about Poland. I'm sorry you weren't there. You are right about one thing, though. He does have ugly teeth. Still, I don't suppose he can help that. At least we can give him the benefit of the doubt, don't you think?"

I wondered why she brought up the priest. Did she suspect

something? Although I nodded again in answer to her question, the weight stayed. We went into the bathroom to test the water. It was hot, but Mother didn't know how to find out how much the tank held.

"I don't want to blow up the hotel by boiling too much of the stuff," she said. "Let's run the bath and see if we have enough. It's such a huge tub. If we can't get it deep enough for you to enjoy, we'll heat some more." When she turned on the hot water faucet, the water steamed.

Left alone I took off my robe and panties and climbed over the edge of the tub into the water. It burned my foot and I backed out. As the cold ran in, I bent over the edge of the tub and swished my hands around to keep it circulating. It became deeper and cooler. I thought I heard a noise at the hall door, but when I looked up I could see nothing except that the key lying on the floor. The gaping keyhole rang no alarm. My protected life had given me no reason to be suspicious or to hurry and I thought I'd put it back when I finished my bath. Climbing over the side of the tub I sank into the water.

Mother came back while I was putting on my pajamas and noticed the key right away. She hurried to the end of the narrow room. "My goodness," she said as she stuck it back in the lock. "I wonder how that fell out. You must always make sure it's in there when you're in the bathroom."

Before I could ask her why, there were sounds of a ruckus in the hall and one loud thump on the door itself. Mother ran through the bedroom and out into to the hall. Struggling into my bathrobe, I stumbled behind her. Helmut, with his tray balanced on his hand, stood rooted to the flowered carpet. He had a look of total incredulity on his thin face. With open mouth he stared at something down the hall. My father and the Catholic Father were in front of our bathroom door. The Priest was tall, but my father was taller and heavier. He held the clergyman off the floor and against the wall with his two fists entangled in the black cassock as if he were holding a pair of handles. With his magenta face close to Father Stanislawski's sallow one, he spat his words like missiles. Even in the dim light I could see the saliva spray onto the black figure. My father's voice was so low and throaty with fury I could hardly hear what he said.

"I know what you were looking at," he shot the words at the priest. "And I'll think carefully about whether I'm going to report you to the Bishop or whomever, but I'll tell you this. If you ever come near any one of the Pierson family again, I'll go as . . . high . . . as . . . your . . . Pope. Get out of here and don't let me see you again." He shoved Father Stanislawski away from him with such force the man stumbled over his cassock and fell to his knees. Struggling to his feet, he skittered down the hall and disappeared around a corner.

We all stood motionless staring at the space where he had been. Helmut recovered first and moved into our room with his tray. We followed. No one said a word while he set the table and laid out my supper of sausage, potato salad, milk and a huge slice of an unusual looking cake. When my father tipped him Helmut did bow and say thank you, but other than that there was a heavy quiet. Helmut looked frightened, my father remained angry, and Mother seemed confused.

"What did Father Stanislawski do that made you so mad?" I broke the silence.

Mother and Dad looked at each other. She shook her head ever so slightly. "He did something that he shouldn't have, something very bad."

My father was pacing back and forth between the bed and the table. "You don't need to know what it was. Just be sure you never have anything to do with him again."

47

Mother motioned me to the table. "I guess we really should have listened to you, Carole. You didn't think he was a nice man to start with, did you? Next time, if you try to warn us, we'll listen. Now, come on, Pet, the excitement is over. Sit down and eat your supper. It smells delicious."

I wasn't sure the excitement was totally over because my father continued to pace. It made me anxious. When I said so, he stopped and looked at me with such stricken eyes that I ran to him and reached my arms around his waist. Standing by the bed, his long legs bent, and, towing me with him, he sat heavily. We missed the bed and both slid to the floor. I saw the tears before he covered his face with his hands and great, wracking sobs shook his muscular shoulders.

I had never before seen my father cry and my anguish became equal to his. Mother dropped down on the other side of him and with her own tears streaming flung her arms around his neck and pulled his head onto her shoulder. Since he was so much taller, it was like an eagle being comforted by two sparrows.

"Don't cry, my darling," Mother kept saying over and over. "Oh, please don't cry. It's all over now."

"It isn't all over." His normally deep voice was little more than a squeak. "It's just beginning. It's because of me we're in this terrible place that's dark and backward. We can't even trust the priests. If I stay in the Army, we'll have to live here for two years. I don't think we can stand that. I'll have to resign."

"And do what?" She sat up straight. "Wait a minute here. We're not quitters. Just because it's a rainy market day and the hotel happens to be on the fish market doesn't mean it will always be dark and smelly. Let's go out tomorrow, even if it's still raining, and find another, more cheerful place to eat. That should help."

"This is all my fault." Daddy wasn't able to relinquish his suffering. Maybe, for the first time in his adult life, now that Mother had taken over, he found comfort in being weak.

"It's nobody's fault." Mother tugged his hands away from his face and looked into his wet, bloodshot eyes. She handed him her dainty handkerchief. "It's just too bad these things conspired against us all at once. We've had setbacks before, haven't we? This one isn't your fault. You don't need to resign from the Army."

She struggled to stand and to pull us up with her. Soon we all were sitting on the side of the bed. Daddy blew his nose on her handkerchief.

"Dear, God," he said as he crumpled the tiny linen square. "What good can anyone do with this little rag. Here, let me get a real one." By the time he'd fished in his pocket, found his own handkerchief and blown again, he seemed back in control. "You're right. We'll spend our two years here, like the troopers we are, and probably leave at the end with reluctance. Go ahead and get your bath before the "infernal machine" blows up. I'm all right. Sorry for being such a cry-baby. Forgive me girls?"

"You know there's nothing to forgive." Mother kissed him before she stood up and went to get her nightgown and robe out of the wardrobe. She kept talking all the time as she moved around the room. "Caro, your supper looks delicious. Almost, but not quite, like a fourth of July picnic. By the way, I have something for you. I almost forgot. Jon, fish out our surprise while I bathe, will you? It's in my cosmetic case." She disappeared into the bathroom and closed the door.

Daddy reached for the black patent leather cosmetic case, turned his back to extract something from it. I heard a match strike and when he turned back to me he held a spitting sparkler. I don't know that anything since has given me the same thrill or sense of security.

Here was a part of home.

"Oh, Daddy," I reached across the table for the sparkler. When it was in my hand, I could think of nothing more to say except "oh."

I've never dwelt on what happened in the hall. It was years before I knew what a pedophile was and recognized that my father was defending my innocence outside our bathroom door. In my hearing my parents never mentioned it again, but Father Stanislawski, in his warped use of the Catholic faith, would continue to cast shadows over my life.

Chapter 7

Stepping out the front doors of the Krolewski Dwor the next morning was like entering an irredescent bubble. Instead of the forbidding dark, wet gray of the day before, the feudal-style buildings stood proudly as they had for centuries, surrounding and protecting their market place in an appearance of benevolence. The balconies, even at the early hour of eight o'clock, already bloomed with red-ticked feather beds that hung over the railings in the fresh and tender air like giant, puffy peonies.

The only discordant note on the square was the orangey-red brick church that squatted menacingly on the corner. Among the weathered gray facades it appeared prepared to spring like a predatory monster. Father Stanislawski hovered in the entry as the faithful hurried past him with hardly a nod. To me, using Father in connection with him sullied the word. I shivered from my very inside out.

Trying to let the glorious morning reclaim me, I skipped close beside my parents past the ground floor shops that were opening up until he disappeared. Proprietors raised the heavy metal, telescoping shutters that covered and protected display windows overnight. As we passed, the owners nodded. "Dzien Dobry." My father answered with a facsimile of, "Dzien Dobry." Everyone smiled and I was filled with pride.

Daddy was tall and handsome in his uniform and each time he took off his military cap to say, "Good Day" in this strange language, a lock of his blond hair escaped to fall across his forehead. It made him look boyish. Of course, at that time, he and mother were young, but they seemed responsibly adult to me. In the light of that clear morning my mother seemed the most beautiful woman in the world. Her oval face was framed by golden hair. Wisps that escaped from under her fashionable, tight-fitting cloche shone in the sun. Where Daddy's eyes were almost gray, hers were large and so deep a blue as to be nearly purple. Her eyebrows made perfect light, brown accents.

While I seldom thought about my own looks, I was glad I'd inherited Mother's eyes and eyebrows. I wasn't quite sure they went well with my red hair, but I didn't care. As long as I had something of beauty to counteract my flaming hair and the freckles across my nose, I was content.

We had sauntered a quarter of the way around the square when Mother said, "Look. There's a café over there. In English, Breitski's Café. Let's hurry." She took my hand and Daddy's arm to tow us across the streetcar tracks that intersected the square.

Daddy was laughing as he pointed out to her that café was a French word.

"So now I speak French," she said as we reached the restaurant.

On tiptoe I could barely see over the spotless white curtains that covered the lower half of the huge front window. Long tables sat in front of high-backed benches that ran the length of one side of the room. Colorful steins and plates decorated the shelves high above them. Seated at other scrubbed-white tables, most of the patrons read newspapers. A recent arrival took a paper from the rack where more papers hung on long horizontal poles. How thoughtful of the café to furnish the morning papers.

My father shielded his eyes as he peered in. "It looks clean. Shall we try it?"

"Oh, let's." I was so afraid Mother might veto it as not being elegant enough. In New York, before we sailed, she had insisted we eat only in the finest restaurants. This place didn't look like the ones in New York, but it looked homey.

"Yes, I think we should." Mother hurried to the door. "How are we going to learn about this town unless we try everything. If we don't like it, we need never come back."

Daddy, dictionary in hand, opened the door into a haven of heavenly smells. A waiter in black trousers and white shirt with a long snowy apron, wrapped from waist to knee, was serving a table of eight men. Tall, thin and very erect, he looked as if he'd been starched with the napkins. A short, round-faced man with a bushy blond moustache and twinkly eyes hurried from a back room. He rattled off a string of unintelligible words as he led us to a table. Daddy began flipping pages in his yellow book.

Mother turned to Daddy in surprise. "I understood some of what the man said. I had one year of German, you know, when I went to Ferry Hall." She was so excited, but not as excited as the host. "He thinks . . ."

But the man had seen the U.S insignia on Daddy's uniform. "You are from America, yes?" In an obvious uncontrollable frenzy of delight, he bounced back and forth between Mother and Daddy, clutching their arms, explaining all the while, "I myself live for three years in die Oshkosh, Visconsin." He finally turned toward the back room. In a voice near hysteria he shouted,"Gertrude, Gertrude. Come here, schnell." Looking at us, he exclaimed, "My wife she too will be so excitement. She love so much your United States."

The proprietor seized my father's hand and pumped it up and down as if he were operating a railroad handcar. With every up or down Rudiger Breitski, as he introduced himself, beat on Daddy's shoulder with his other hand in his exuberance. Mother and I grinned. It was a genuine welcome. When Gertrude Breitski hurried in and her husband repeated his momentous news, she pulled my mother to her and embraced her as if they had had been lifetime friends. Mother melted into the older woman's arms.

"My English is not so good like Rudi's." The rosy-cheeked amply endowed woman held Mum away from her and beamed at my father. "I spend only one year in the Oshkosh, but I like very much there. We come home while father of Rudi is bad sick and die. That time since, we have father's café. Is good life, but is good life also too in America." She turned to where I stood and I found myself smothered in her billowing bosom. "Und this your child is? Ach, Liebchen, I your Tante Gertrude will be." She sat down and pulled me onto her lap. It had been a long time since I had sat on anyone's lap and I'm afraid I sat like an uncompromising stick. Caught unawares, I didn't know what else to do.

The other breakfasters watched our play unfold. At last, unable to stay off the stage themselves, first one and then another joined in with the two or three words he knew in English and soon my parents had a room full of new friends---all eager to help. When Tante Gertrude returned to the kitchen, I was allowed to sit on my own chair.

She must have ordered breakfast for us because it came, platter after platter. The warm rolls were the most delicious I had ever eaten. They were crispy crusted and I ate them with unsalted butter sprinkled with coarse-ground salt and slathered with currant jelly. Brötchen,Tante Gertrude called them. She made sure I repeated the German word for each offering, and, if I called her anything other than Tante Gertrude, I was quickly corrected. She was a German, she told us, married to, of course, Herr Breitski who was Polish.

By the time breakfast was over my life and the lives of my parents had been decided by the assemblage. I was not to learn Polish at first. "Too difficult it is," Tante Gertrude said firmly. "The child must to the school soon go. I call my niece, Trüchen. Only a year older than your Carole she is. She will good friend be, und Die Kliene." She patted my hand, "The German Sprache will learn schnell. The good German she will learn. Platdeutsch we not need."

From the inflexion and expression of distaste, I gathered Platdeutsch was something undesirable. She was so positive and forceful I began to worry that her niece, Trüchen, might turn out to be more an overbearing task mistress of some sort than a good friend.

It was hard to tell whether the other patrons of the café were Polish or German. Fluent in both languages, they used them alternately. When I asked, Tante Gertrude towed me to the huge front window.

"See there." She pointed into the square where a statue of a Polish soldier stood stalwart and straight on his high pedestal. "For many years upon there Kaiser Wilhelm stooded. Before that a Prussian it was. In two hundred years could from any Country be. Take down eins put up another. Everybody, Prussian, Austrian, German, Polish wish easy to the Baltic Sea to come. They fight. Who win for a little time this Polish Corridor have. Again fight. Another win. Statue change. People from many country now here live. Speak many language."

"Like America," I said. "Except everyone there speaks English. But you have so many languages. Don't you ever get mixed up?"

Tante Gertrude's laugh brought all other conversation in the room to a halt. Every face had a tolerant smile. "Manchmal , like today, we misch only Deutsch und Polnisch." And English, I thought. "Most time not. In zee home Rudi and I talk zee German. I sink all here do same," she fluttered her hand at the seven or eight diners left.

Even though I don't think they understood what she said they all nodded because she was nodding. Mother, Daddy and I also nodded like bobble-headed dolls. I couldn't help giggling. That produced an exchange of excited comments and I began to feel like a princess in one of my fairy-tale books. Just as in the books, whatever I or my parents, the King and Queen, did the courtiers were bound to applaud. I was glad when, at last, the other people went home or to work and we were left alone with the Breitskis.

Since my father's class at the Cavalry school would not start for a month, we needed someplace less expensive than the hotel to stay while we hunted an apartment.

"Zis not a problem be," Oncle Rudi stated flatly. You will go to Hel . . ." At Mother's gasp, Oncle Rudi laughed. "Hel is very beautiful island in gulf of Danzig. You will zere happy be." That would get us out of the Krolewski Dwor, he said. "Can also too visit towns of Zuppot, Danzig and Gdynia . "By time you come back in two weeks we be on vacation. You can live in our apartment above restaurant. Same time can hunt apartment for your own."

"My Schwester Hilde will to assist you happy be while we gone are," Tante Gertrude said to Mother. "She next door lives und the Conditerai owns. Her husband, he in the schule teaches, will your Jonasan Polnish learn." They seemed very quick to volunteer their relatives without knowing whether they would acquiesce. One, they said, lived on Hel and would be Dad's teacher while we were there.

Mother turned to me with a wink and said, "Well, it seems we're going to Hel."

Chapter 8

The resort village of Hel seemed to balance on the very tip of a long, skinny finger of land that dipped into the Gulf of Danzig. The gulf itself was no more than a drop of the Baltic Sea. Our two weeks there was like a pleasant, cultural bridge between America and Europe. Everyone we met, young and old, was eager to help. By the time we boarded the ferry to return to Gdynia I was fluent enough in German to start in the seventh grade in Grudziadz.

Herr Wolfmann, the teacher, over-awed by having a foreigner in his class, simply ignored me. After a few months my parents began to question why I didn't appear to have answers to any of their questions. When the truth came out, it seemed the school itself, thinking that the streets of the U.S.A. were all paved in gold, had no qualms about tripling the Pierson's monthly fee. Daddy, after trying fruitlessly to disabuse them of that notion, refused to pay it and I was withdrawn. Put in the hands of a tutoress, whose ambitions were to sing in the opera, during the next few months I learned, and we sang together, the entire opera of Samson and Delilah in French. Unfortunately she never gave me an inkling of what the words meant. My parents gave up, trusting that life in a foreign country would educate me until they could unearth someone of integrity to take on the job.

We rented an apartment in Nummer 9 on Grabowski Strasse and I began to become a little German-Polish girl. My life was routine, until, after a very short time, fate, as usual, took over its management. When Daddy started classes at the Kaserne, he needed a horse. On a beautiful chilly fall day we went to see one at the magnificent estate of Friedenau, and my fairy tale life began.

The estate was owned by a German Count, Graf von Wechsler. His title over-awed an impressionable eleven year-old and completely changed the course of her life. Met at the Friedenau station, their very own, by Zarotti, the von Wechsler's chauffeur, we were driven on cobblestone roads past field after field of dark, rich soil. Peasants, who lived in a village belonging to the estate, performed the backbreaking labor of harvesting sugar beets. Near an enormous barn, cows of assorted colors clustered together in the black mud. Zarotti told us the cow manure was used to fertilize the fields. The milk was sold.

The little village of thatched–roofed cottages was picturesque. Smoke curled from the chimneys, and there was a pond with water fowl, though I didn't see a church. Too young to recognize the importance of this, I didn't comprehend it until much later in my life.

Beyond the villiage, wrought-iron gates opened to let us roll up the drive to a Palace. Broad steps led up to a narrow veranda, centered on impressive double doors. A liveried butler emerged and hurried down to assist us. The massive structure seemingly spread out indefinitely. The single strip of grass between the drive and the building made the mansion appear to be springing from the earth like a commanding colossus. Scores of windows gleamed in the afternoon sun and I had the impression they were all staring at us in judgment. My eleven-year-old heart began to quail. A feeling of panic swirled through my body in a wave. I wanted to cling to Mother's coat as a tiny child might, but I knew better. Expected to behave as if I were accustomed to entering palaces, I had no idea how to go about it.

The men led and Mother, towing my trembling body, followed. Once inside, even the vast entrance hall with its deep, red, carpeting stretching like a mandatory path to a guillotine, intimidated me more. It pulled us toward the open doors at the far end where the von Wechsler family had gathered to greet us. When I saw they weren't wearing crowns, my heartbeat slowed.

A nice looking man, about Daddy's age, broke away from the

cluster and walked toward us with his hand out-stretched. "Good afternoon. I am Ernst von Wechsler," he said in accented English. "I welcome you to Friedenau."

Rittmeister Metzgar, who was our escort and who had been there before, took the long, thin hand, clicked his heels, made a small bow, and introduced the Pierson family. For once mother didn't have to put her hand on my shoulder to make me curtsy. Instead, she stopped me before I swooped nearly to the ground. The Count presented us to his wife, Elise, who, with her beautiful complexion and blond hair, was almost as pretty as my mother. I thought she must be about the same age too. His brother, Dieter, was young, handsome, and looked bored. He shook my hand like a robot.

"Come, let me introduce you to my Mother." The Count led us across the vast room to a massive, round table that dominated everything except the Grande Dame seated there. Surrounded by other chairs with cushioned seats and backs covered in petit point and a banquette along the wall, she appeared prepared to hold court.

Two lace-curtained windows gave the room light, but aside from a gramophone with a straight chair beside it and a beautiful floor-to-ceiling tiled stove in another corner, it was the only furnished part of the room. A huge Persian carpet under the table and chairs delineated that space, otherwise the highly polished floor was bare.

The Grande Dame occupied the only arm-chair. One-by-one we were introduced to her, a heavy lady with an imposing bosom upon which a pince nez would have hung like a trickling waterfall when not in use. But when we were introduced . . . it was scrutinizingly in use.

The Count turned to me once I was seated. "My goodness, I thought you were a grown up lady when you came through our door. Perhaps that was because you were wearing a fur coat." His voice and his eyes were kindly.

That, however, alleviated none of my terror, and, fastening on the words, "fur coat," I babbled that my Grandmother had thought that Poland would be cold, so they had my coat made from one of Mother's old ones. "It's only muskrat though," I added.

The minute the words were out, even my mother laughed. The hand, though, that clutched my shoulder had the strength of a falcon's talon and I'm sure she would have been happy to smack me with it.

"Sometime you must tell us what this muskrat is." The Count smiled at me before he turned away. Overcome with mortification, when the pince nez pointed to it, I slid onto the banquette.

Once established in the corner with mother next to me as a bulwark, the adult conversation flowed like a ribbon through my own thoughts. Beautiful music began in my head as it always did, and soon I was safely in my imagination dancing on that polished floor.

"Carole," my father's abrupt voice brought me out of my dream. Everyone else was standing. "We are going in to tea. Get a move on."

Forced back to reality, I slid out of my corner and trailed everyone else into the dining room. The table stretched before us longer than a bowling alley. Terror returned. At the far end eight places were set, leaving twenty-two empty chairs and a long expanse of snowy tablecloth. I know how many extra places there were because I counted them during tea. I couldn't even imagine what it would be like to sit there when every chair was filled with royalty. I could imagine how I would feel if I committed some terrible error in table etiquette that would call attention to me. My hands, underneath my napkin, clung to each other and, I was sure, would never come apart.

A little maid in black with a starchy white apron and cap assisted Rodczeck. I was seated last next to Dieter. We seemed to go by age, grade, and interest. Mother and Dad, as honored guests, were on the Gnädige Frau's right and left. Dieter and I were last in line. Eight people, though, hardly constituted a bud on the table's long stem.

Dieter didn't speak much English, though he tried. "What of age, you be?" was his first attempt.

"Eleven." I held up ten fingers, then added another.

"Do you schule go?"

"Yes."

We couldn't seem to keep the conversation going. I stared at my plate. Lisa poured the tea and Rodczeck passed the rich and delicious cakes topped with fruits and whipped cream. I managed not to spill anything.

Dieter tried again. "How you Poland like?" he asked.

"Very much." This time I looked up in time to see what an obvious struggle he was having. His expression showed definite signs of the strain the language and an unresponsive partner were causing. In spite of my feelings of inadequacy and immaturity, I smiled.

Dieter's expression lightened; dimples showed when he grinned.

"I'm sorry," I said in German and felt most of the tension in my body slip away. "I think I was just a little nervous. Let us speak in your language and perhaps we can understand each other better."

His noisy sigh made me laugh out loud. While everyone stared at the two of us, Silence descended on the rest of the table.

"She speaks good German," Dieter said as an explanation.

His parents immediately pummeled me with questions, when, where, and how I'd learned. They were most congratulatory that I had gone far enough to be able to go to a German school in just a few months. For the first time, the day became an adventure and I realized they were just people in spite of their titles and living in a palace. When I smiled at everyone, that smile reached my eyes.

"You asked how old I am." I turned to Dieter. "How old are you?"

"Nineteen. Old enough to serve my required two years in the Polish Army."

"Why don't you wear a uniform?"

"I take it off as soon as I get home." He made a face. "It scratches because it's rough wool and besides it doesn't fit well. Fraulein Goethe, our sewing woman, hasn't had time to fix it yet."

"If you're in the Army, how can you be here too? Don't you like it, wherever it is?"

"No, I don't like it, but every young man in Poland, when he's nineteen, has to serve two years. My friend, Kurt, who is also nineteen, and I pay a monthly fee to come home every night. Anyone can do it if he has the money."

"That seems a strange way to run the army, but then, our soldiers join because they want to, not because they have to. You don't like it at all?"

"Ach, izt alright, and we only have to do it for two years. Then I'm going to Heidelberg to college."

Gräfin von Wechsler signaled tea time was over and it was now time to look at the horses. Since that was why we'd come, I was ready to see what was on the other side of the high lilac hedge. As we went out through the front door, Graf von Wechsler made a teasing remark about my fur coat but, though an hour ago I would have disintegrated, I had enough courage to tease back. A little shyness remained, but even my shoulders relaxed.

The stables and horses were impressive. After much deliberation, Daddy bought a beautiful bay mare named Früling. Most importantly, we were invited back the very next weekend. On the train back to Grudziadz, I decided all fairytales must be written about Poland.

Chapter 9

Frau Elise led the way up the graceful staircase that climbed to the long, red carpeted hall of the upper story. My parents stayed below. At the landing I could see large double doors facing me from behind the railing. I wondered what could be behind them. Frau Elise explained to me that the first room we entered had been the playroom of many generations of von Wechsler children.

"Ernst and Dieter sought you were too old to play in ze nursery, but I sink you would like to be where zere older sister's toys are. Marta's toys."

This was the first I'd heard of a sister. "Where is Marta?"

"She married an Englishman and now near London lives. I wish she lived nearer." Frau Elise paused with her hand on the handle of the door. "We are such good friends and we only see each ozzer now once a year." There was another slight pause. "It is Marta who insists zat we all speak English and zat we must use ze good grammar." She giggled. "You see I still have trouble wiz your 't h' sound." she interjected as an aside before she opened the door. "Unfortunately, Ernst's mother refuses to learn, so wiz her, you must always speak in German."

The room was on the North East end of the house and as soon as we stepped into it I was uncomfortable. It was dark and spooky. Ashamed of being thought silly, to say nothing of being rude, I stiffened my spine to control its shiver. Still I wanted to know I was not to be alone on this endless corridor.

"Where is my parent's room?" I asked. Mother and Dad had stayed to chat with Gnädige Frau von Wechsler.

"Right next door. You won't be lonely." Frau Elise walked over to a magnificent doll house resting on a low table obviously designed for it. "Zis was Ernst's aunt's doll house when she was young. Is it not beautiful?"

It was. Victorian in style, it abounded with turrets, cupolas, porches and lacy carvings. If only it were in a brighter, more cheerful spot. I knew I would never stay in this room long enough to play with it. Now, though, I walked over and investigated the beautiful, small-scale antique furniture. The mother doll sat uncomfortably on a stiff velvet sofa and I couldn't resist moving her to a chair that seemed more suitable.

"Jah, zat really is better for her," Frau Elise commented. "How soughtful of you to see she was uncomfortable."

"It's a wonderful doll's house, Gnädige Frau. If I should play with it, I will be very careful." I spoke in German and hoped I sounded enthusiastic enough.

Apparently I did because Frau Elise laughed and said she didn't think Marta had been careful of it when she was small. She added that, though I spoke beautiful German, she would rather we converse in English because she needed the practice. When I agreed, she smiled, put her arm around my shoulder, and gave a little squeeze. I loved her from that moment.

"You and Ernst and Dieter don't sleep in this wing, do you?" I asked.

"Dieter's rooms are near zee stairway and zee ballroom. Ours are in zee ozzer wing. Ernst's Muttie lives downstairs right under where you are now."

It was hard for me to understand how Elise could use such an informal term for her mother-in-law. The Gnädige Frau was so austere. I couldn't imagine her imposing bosom as being a motherly place for any child to rest her head either in misery or happiness, but I lost my timidity when I heard the word "ballroom." In fairy tales every palace had one. That it really existed took my mind off my supposed isolation.

"Do you have many balls?"

"Not since Ernst's Vater died. He did love to dance." She looked sad and I thought she must have cared a lot for Ernst's father. "He did not pass his love of dancing to Ernst zough." She moved some of the beautiful antique furniture around in the doll house. "We don't know about Dieter's dancing yet, he's still young and ze Polish army keeps him busy. But if his friend Kurt has any say-so in ze matter, he'll learn. Kurt seems to like anysing zat involves ze girls." Again she giggled, but this time it was conspiratorial.

How pretty she was when she laughed. Her hair was very blond like Mother's and though her eyes were blue, they weren't nearly as large and beautiful. She showed signs, too, of someday becoming a little plump. Round now, she already had a very definite bosom. I wondered why she and Graf Ernst had no children. They certainly seemed the type to whom God would have given many. I thought when you got married, you ordered a baby and were provided with one at once. At least it was put in the mother's tummy to grow big enough to be born. Without siblings, I had no firsthand knowledge, but my friends who had brothers or sisters assured me that was the way it worked.

As if I had asked Frau Elise the question, she answered my thoughts. "Ernst and I had a little girl who would now be just ze right age to play wiz zis doll house." She ran her hand lovingly over the complicated roof and tears filled her eyes. "Gretti and her nurse played in zis room until our little one went away to live wiz ze angels. She was nearly two. Ze Doctor told us we must never have more babies. Even if we could," her voice grew thick and she swallowed. "It wouldn't be our Gretti." She turned away then and spoke abruptly. "Come. It must be nearly tea-time. I'll show you your sleeping room and zen we go down ze stairs."

I didn't absorb her last sentence. As I followed her across the hall, I was wondering what kind of a doctor could be so cruel as to tell people they weren't allowed to have any more babies, but I had found one more reason to be uncomfortable in that nursery. I was sure Gretti had died in there. I wasn't sure whether or not her spirit lingered there. If there were such things and if they had a choice, no child would leave this palace and such loving parents. Although I was sure Gretti would be a gentle spirit, I didn't want to meet her.

When Frau Elise opened the door to the small bedroom across the hall, sunlight spilled over into the corridor. The walls were a buttercup yellow, the furniture was white, and, with windows on two sides, there was no trace of gloom.

"She had a happy personality," I said aloud.

"Yes, she did." My new friend had recognized my timidity in the nursery and had brought me here to let her tiny daughter work her magic. I would never be afraid of Gretti, alive or in spirit.

At tea- time the evening's dinner party in my parent's honor monopolized the conversation. I listened to the guest list for a few minutes, but, since I had never been included in my parent's parties at home, I assumed I would be fed early or have a tray in my room. It came as a complete surprise then, when after tea I was told to be clean and ready in my yellow crepe de chine by 9:30. I was to be allowed to stay up for the party.

Because everyone else went to rest before dressing for dinner and I had not been given permission to explore, I went to my room too. I lay down on the bed to read Little Women, for the umpteenth time. The sun was warm when I went to sleep.

"Carole," Daddy's voice intruded on my dream. His second

"Carole," louder and more insistent, brought me fully awake.

 The sun had gone down and the one lamp he'd turned on wasn't very bright, but when Daddy said, "hurry up, it's time to dress for dinner," I jumped up in a panic.

"It's eight-thirty, Caro. Wash your face and hands, neck and ears and elbows (that was a family joke) and get ready to charm the Baron."

"What Baron?" Chills ran across my back and down my arms at the very words.

"Weren't you listening at tea time?" My father looked at me as if I were still asleep. "The Baron von Pawel," he answered. Before I could ask any more, he disappeared.

I knew from books that Barons were usually formidable, cantankerous people who thought all other humans were underlings. Trembling, I went down the hall to the bathroom. The door was closed. When I knocked timidly, Mother's familiar voice answered. Once inside I asked, "How did you know it was me?"

"Because we're the only ones in this wing and your father is already finished. It couldn't have been anyone else."

"Is there really going to be a Baron here tonight?" My voice quavered. "If there is, I don't think I want to come down."

"Why on earth not?"

"I'd be too afraid."

"Afraid of what? Barons don't bite." Mother reached over to get a wash-cloth and handed it to me. "Start washing. None of us has ever met a Baron before, you know."

Thinking to myself that if they didn't bite they probably ordered someone else to do the biting for them. "Aren't you scared?"

"No, why should I be?"

"I don't know how to behave with a Baron. Suppose I make a mistake. He might be angry. I might embarrass you and Dad."

Mother took my face in her hands and looked into my eyes. "Carole Pierson, you have never embarrassed me in your life. Just behave as you always do. A Baron is no different than anyone else. You'll do fine, my darling, and after the first time you'll never have qualms again." She let go of my face and turned to the mirror over the fancy marble wash-basin. After a minute she turned back. "I do understand. Whenever I feel a little shy about walking into an unfamiliar situation, and I will feel that way tonight, I say to myself 'I am the Grand Duchess Marie,' then I can sail into the room without a tremor. Think of yourself as the Princess Snow White and, I promise, you'll be quite comfortable because you'll outrank him."

I didn't quite understand how I could ever outrank a Baron, but it did help to know that Mother was sometimes a little insecure. It never showed. While I slipped into my dress, brushed my hair, and put on my patent leather shoes, I practiced being a princess. It wasn't hard. My friends and I often played "dress-up'" in our mother's old evening dresses with discarded curtains for trains. Well-rehearsed, my chin was high as I followed my parents down the great staircase and into the drawing room.

This room fit with my idea of a real palace. Here were the delicate damask upholstered chairs I'd expected in all the rooms. Here were the softly colored Aubusson rugs, the beautiful French antiques, and a room full of elegantly dressed people. I glanced around quickly, but didn't see a crown anywhere. Since nobility in fairy tales always wore crowns, he must not have arrived yet. I relaxed. Surely he would be announced with a fanfare of trumpets.

"And this is young Carole, the Pierson's daughter. Carole, may I present the Baron von Pawel." Ernst's voice broke into my inspection of the room.

I looked up into the kindly eyes of an elderly gentleman with white hair and a neatly trimmed goatee who stood with his hand outstretched, ready to receive mine. He was smiling. With no prompting from my mind, my hand found its way into his and my curtsy would have done credit to Pavlova.

"Tell me, little one, are you happy to be here in Poland? Do you like us?" His warm voice welcomed me once I had risen from a near swoon. His accent when he spoke English was so faint that he sounded almost British.

I hesitated, not knowing whether to address him as 'your royal highness', 'your grace' or even your eminence', all titles I'd read in books. Finally I blurted out, "Yes, sir, I like everyone very much."

"And what would you like to do while you are here in this country?" His eyes twinkled. In his expression I understood that he really cared about my answer.

"Most of all," I said. "I would like to learn to be a ballerina." As the words came out I wondered why I was confiding my dream to this perfect stranger. Even my parents had no idea what lay in my heart. I had never told them because back in small town Virginia it had seemed out of reach. Here though, as an actor in a fairy tale, everything was achievable.

"A ballerina. You want to be a ballerina," the Baron repeated loudly enough for everyone to hear and yet I felt no embarrassment.

"Yes, sir." I nodded my head at the same time.

"Then we shall have to see how to bring this about, little one. Everyone must have an opportunity to find out if what he wishes the most is, indeed, a possibility."

I smiled up at him, never doubting he would make it happen. Mother and Dad, who had overheard that last statement, stared at their errant child as if she had become some sort of gargoyle. Their expressions changed as they recognized the Baron's instigation. Then they beamed. All at once I truly became Princess Snow White.

When Rodczeck announced dinner, the Baron whispered to me that, though he would rather escort me to the table, his duty required that he take in his hostess. I giggled, knowing he was only joking and being kind to a little girl.

"Kurt," he said loudly in a voice of authority. "My new granddaughter requires an escort. Come," he ordered, turning to me. "Kurt is my son."

Chapter 10

So overcome with becoming an instant Baron's granddaughter, I didn't really look at his son. But once we were seated together at the very foot of the table, I found I was between the most handsome man I'd ever seen and Dieter opposite him on my left. Dieter introduced me to Kurt von Pawel. When my heart began to beat again, I could see his resemblance to the Baron. Was it the shape of his face, his mouth, or those shining blue eyes that made him so magnificent? Whatever it was my heart raced. Had I been Jo in Little Women, I would have swooned.

"What do you think of our American guest?" Dieter asked Kurt in German, of course. Before I could get my thoughts in motion to protest, Kurt, assuming I couldn't understand, answered.

"She certainly has red hair, doesn't she? Still, she might be pretty when she grows up."

With Kurt's eyes appraising me, I kept my eyes on my plate and blushed.

"She's only eleven. Who knows how her looks will turn out? She does have beautiful eyes though. When she stops staring at her food, that is." Dieter, still speaking German, had noticed my blush and seemed determined to make me uncomfortable.

This was going to go on until I found some way to stop it. I had been in awe of Dieter because he was nineteen years old. But at that moment he and his friend seemed exactly like the boys in my sixth grade class in Lexington. My timidity vanished.

"Dieter knows I speak German," I said in their language, looking into Kurt's startlingly eyes. "He is being very rude."

"Now, did you hear that?" Kurt looked across me at his friend in

72

mock horror. "Behave yourself. We shall have no more of this childish play. This is a young lady we have here and we must conduct ourselves accordingly."

Kurt's expression was stern, but he burst into laughter at the end of his admonishment. I began to laugh too. The dinner table quieted. All the way up its impressive length to the disapproving hostess at its head, faces turned in our direction. Even the ancestral portraits, on the wall, seemed to frown.

Gnädige Frau von Wechsler spoke. "Perhaps, since you now have involved us all, you would like to share your joke, hmmm?" She looked straight at me.

Snow White vanished leaving a quivering child who could no more have answered than she could have gotten up to dance Swan Lake on the table. Dieter, too, looked shocked, but Kurt, not in the least intimidated, rose from his chair, bowed, and said, "Our apologies. We were, I'm afraid, being rude, not only to you all, but to our young American guest. I am ashamed to say we were teasing this young lady. She was a good sport and took it very well. However, Dieter and I are indeed sorry. Young Carole owes no apology."

A knight in shining armor had just rescued the damsel in distress and had taken possession of her heart. For the rest of the dinner there was no more teasing. In fact she was mostly ignored.

With dinner over at last, the double doors opened and Gräfin von Wechsler rose. Like the Pied Piper she led the ladies across the sitting room's shining floor to the drawing room beyond. Most followed, but a few stayed in the sitting room. I was one of them.

Mother stopped to speak to me. "We're going to play bridge in the drawing room, Precious. You may stay up a little while longer," she said. "But up to bed before midnight. Don't forget to say your goodnights before you go."

I promised as I checked the ornate grandfather's clock to see how long I had. Dieter and Kurt had left the men and I saw them in their hats and coats, sliding out the front door. My knight had gone. With his disappearance the grown-up party lost its appeal. I might just as well go to bed. The men were coming out of the dining room and, thinking to start with the Baron, I turned to look for him. Someone put a record on the turntable and as the music began to charm me, I paused to listen.

"May I have this dance?" The Baron stood in front of me.

"Oh," I stammered, looking up at his great height. "I don't know how. I've never danced before. This kind of dancing, I mean."

"Then perhaps it is time for you to learn. A ballerina must know how to do all manner of dances, you know." He laughed as he took my hand. "What kind of dancing have you done, little one?" He asked as he stooped to put his arm around my waist. The best he could manage was a bit below my shoulder.

I stretched as tall as I could. "Not really very much. Mother taught me a dance she made up and I did it in a revue the college put on. Daddy was in it too." I chattered on. "He played a naughty boy in short pants. He looked so funny with his bowed legs. I did love being on that stage, even though I was scared to death before I got out there. Then I forgot there was an audience." Thinking I'd said too much, I stopped talking.

"Just relax, little one, and I will lead you. This is a tango and the steps are easy. After you grow a bit more it will be even easier. There now," he pushed gently to make my body do what he was doing. "Don't look at your feet, look up here at me. Tell me more about what kind of dancing you can do."

"Well, I can do the Charleston."

"I'm afraid I'm too old to do the Charleston, but perhaps after we finish this Tango you would show me how you do it." We continued to move with the music.

"Oh, no, Sir." Panicked, I nearly stopped moving my feet. "I couldn't do it now with all these people around. Perhaps some other time." I looked pleadingly at this tall, aristocratic man who had become my friend. From his smile I knew he understood. I have no idea whether I followed him in the tango or whether he just pushed me by brute strength, but I enjoyed every step and when he complimented me on my dancing, I was ecstatic.

The dance over and, having sense enough to know that an adult couldn't happily spend an entire evening with a child, I said my good nights to the Baron, forgot everyone else, and wafted up to bed like a leaf in a wind storm. The dancing had filled me with such joy I forgot about handsome Kurt in my dreams. I even forgot to be afraid of resident ghosts.

Sunday morning, long before anyone else was up, I tangoed the length of the hall carpet. The melody of the night before echoed in my head. Never mind that my first partner was an old man. What other little girl had an almost-prince teach her to dance? At last I had a grandfather and he was a Baron. Maybe that didn't make me a princess, but I was getting close. Besides, it was the dance itself that mattered. I floated down the stairs.

Rodczeck was watching and smiling in the hall below. "Guten morgen, Fraulein Carole," he greeted me in German. "You shall have your breakfast and then perhaps you would like to go out to see the gardens while everyone else still sleeps?"

"Oh, yes." I smiled back. "I would like that very much if you're sure the von Wechslers won't mind?"

In the dining room Rodczeck seated me at the end of the table where I had sat the night before. "Herr Ernst won't mind. And if he mentions it, I shall have to beat him up as I used to do when we were both boys. I was a little bigger and older, you see." The tall, thin man winked.

"Did you live here then?"

"My mother was then, and still is, the cook here." Rodczeck took a silver pot out of a little door in the top section of the tiled stove in the corner. "Frau Kieck is what she is called. When you have finished your breakfast, I shall take you down to meet her. She makes very good cakes, particularly for little girls. You have only to tell her what kind you like best." Rodczeck held the cocoa pot quite a ways from my cup and the rich, warm liquid formed tiny bubbles that covered the hot chocolate's surface. "Quickly, little one," he said, "take your spoon and scoop the bubbles into your mouth. That means then you shall have lots of money."

I smiled and started scooping. He watched with approval. It didn't take long and then, while he was putting the pot back into the warming oven I asked him about his father.

"He and my mother came here as cook and butler when I was only a baby so, you see, I have been here nearly all of my life. My father died a few years before I married, but my mother and I will stay with the von Wechslers as long as we can serve them. Graf Ernst and I grew up as friends and now, though our roles have changed, they are like our family." He poured another cup of chocolate and brought some warm, freshly baked rolls that he called 'semmeln, but with butter and currant jelly on them they were delicious. They weren't large rolls and I don't know how many I ate, but while I devoured them, I wondered how he had felt when he switched from friend to servant. I wasn't worldly enough to recognize that the class system made this not only possible, but expected. Rodczeck was of the domestic class and that would never change. He didn't seem to be bothered by it so I accepted it as well.

The draperies at the French doors were open this morning and I could see, even through the lace curtains that still covered them, that the sun was bright. A long porch ran past the doors and through the lace I saw shadowy steps that went down into, what I assumed, was the garden. As much as I was enjoying the semmeln, I wanted to explore and hurried through breakfast. As soon as I finished, at Rodczeck's insistence, we went down to the kitchen to meet his mother. The kitchen and scullery might be in the basement, but they weren't dark. Half of that story was above ground with high windows that let in plenty of light. The cook and her helpers had a private view of all comings and goings in the front driveway. A dumb waiter in the scullery took the hot food to the butler's pantry above. Upstairs, Rodczeck explained, warming ovens kept everything hot until it was passed for the second time.

Frau Kieck, Rodczeck's mother, was a cheerful, blustery woman who was shaped as though she enjoyed her own cooking. Two girls, introduced as Giselle and the Anna, helped in the kitchen. Anna, Rodczeck explained, was Lisa's sister.

"You come from America, yes?" Frau Kieck wiped her hands on her apron before she shook mine vigorously. I didn't know whether to curtsy or not so, rather than insult this nice lady, I did.

"Yes, I do," I said, then wondered what else I could add.

We smiled at each other. Giselle and Anna stood shyly by. Finally Rodczeck broke the silence.

"Fraulein Carole liked your semmeln, Mutti. She ate six."

I blushed. I knew how many I had eaten but wished he hadn't told. I blushed.

"A girl with a good appetite will grow strong and beautiful," his mother said. "Already such wonderful hair she has. See, it is like the morning sunshine. Come, Fraulein Carole, let me show you my kitchen." I was given a tour of the spotless expanse from the stone floor, white-scrubbed wooden tables, enormous stove and ovens, to the scullery and cooler where all perishables were stored.

"Thank you, Frau Kieck." I liked this motherly woman. "I think I must go now, but thank you for showing me your kitchen. Your food has been just delicious and I'm very happy to have met you."

"Whenever you like something in particular, you see that I hear about it and you shall always have it." The cook patted my cheek.

"That's very kind, but we are going back to Grudziadz this afternoon. I'm afraid I won't have any more of your wonderful food. Thank you very much."

Upstairs again Rodczeck brought me my coat and helped me into it. "It is very cool out there this morning, Fraulein Kleine."

I giggled at his new name for me. Who ever heard of anyone named, "Miss Little One?" Still, it had a tender sound.

"Thank you, Herr Rodczeck." I said as he opened the door.

"There is no need for the Herr,"Rodczeck corrected me. "The family would be very disturbed if they heard that and you might receive quite a lecture on the proper ways of address. Just Rodczeck is correct."

Not quite sure of the truth, I decided to ask Mother later and stepped out into the crisp autumn morning. Frost still lay on the shaded areas of the grass and parts of the high hedge that separated me from the stables and barns. I wanted to run around the hedge to see the horses and sheep, but time was limited. I thought I'd better investigate the garden first. Since we most likely would never be back here, I wanted to see everything. I skipped down the broad steps and onto the path that led toward the beds of shrubs and frost-tinged flowers. Around a bend, where no one could see me, I danced along, singing to myself, doing pirouettes and thinking about my dance with the Baron. I had no reason to believe he would ever remember his encouraging statements of last night and if he did, I had no idea what was involved in training for the ballet. Never having seen a ballet, I thought that one simply bought a pair of ballet slippers, stood up on them, and danced. Trusting the Baron, I also almost expected a teacher to materialize around the next bend.

Instead, the path bent suddenly to follow the shoreline of a small lake that, ringed with willows and leafless birch clumps, created the perfect frame for the reflection of a small chapel. It was all so serene and quiet it seemed like a painting. Following the path around the lake, I lost sight of the chapel for a few moments, but when I reached the other side, I saw that the chapel's double doors stood wide open. My heart leaped up to block my throat. Inside, a coffin, covered with fading flowers, occupied the entire entry. With no idea of who lay in the casket, I envisioned the lid slowly opening and a ghost rising out of it. It was a wonder my legs obeyed me, but they did and I ran. Chased by demons of my own imagination and gasping for breath, I followed any path not caring where it went as long as it was away from the chapel. Fortunately, all paths led back to the house, but I didn't even notice the Fiat parked by the front steps or Zarrotti, lounging against its fender. I ran up the steps, banged through the front door and catapulted into the entrance hall. Mother, Dad and I met abruptly at the foot of the stairs.

"Why, Carole." Mother grabbed me in her arms as I staggered in. "What on earth are you doing? You know better than to enter any house in that fashion, much less one that isn't your own."

With no breath to I answer her, I sagged down onto the steps. My father, still on the stairs, spoke sternly.

"Speak up, Caro. I have to get back to the Kaserne earlier than expected and you almost made us too late to catch the train." He stepped carefully around me. "Good Heavens," his voice softened. "You look like you've seen a ghost."

When I looked up he was standing on the floor in front of me looking so real and so safe my heart began to slow. I could breathe again and felt really foolish. How could I tell them that I'd run from a box covered with dying flowers? "I met a snake." The little lie sounded plausible. They knew my phobia well. Whether the feelings of revulsion and panic that filled my body whenever I saw a legless reptile was sensible or not, there had been enough occasions that my parents would understand my unceremonious entrance.

"I can't understand why a schlange would be out in dis cold wetter." Graf Ernst's accented voice reached out from the door of the sitting room. My heart gave a great thump. I was about to be found out. "Never mind, Carole. We shall see dey are gone before you come next week."

I looked at Mother.

"That's right, darling. Daddy has to go to Warsaw for a week and I can go with him now that Graf and Gräfin von Wechsler have asked us to let you stay here. Won't that be wonderful?"

The chapel and its eerie inhabitant vanished. I'd get to see the ballroom and maybe even Kurt.

Chapter 11

Yawning, Countess Czeczelowa tries, unsuccessfully, to hide her exhaustion. How hard it must be for someone her age to go so many hours without even a nap. There's no clock that I can see, but a small gold watch hangs from a chain around my protector's neck and nestles on her spare bosom. Like the samovar, the watch is an integral part of her life, and the way we'll know when two o'clock comes.

"I think perhaps you would like to rest until it's time for me to meet the Major." I raise my arms above my head to stretch, but the tight binder squeezes my breasts, a painful reminder of why I'm here.

"Oh, no. Let us finish the story first." The indomitable lady looks at the delicate watch. "I can rest when you've gone. It is already one o'clock. We only have one more hour--unless, of course, you are too exhausted." She carries my cup to the samovar. "My faithful old friend here has another cup of tea for us. He's a very good provider." I can hear the affection in her voice.

At the mention of tea I stand, but don't quite know how to ask what I need to "Madame," I am remembering when Anna lived in this very room. "I'm guessing there is still no plumbing on this floor."

"How remiss of me." She hops across the floor to pull back the curtains around her bed. "Here, dearest one, you will have to use this." She bends and retrieves a porcelain potty from the small door in the bottom of the night stand. "The little Austrian paper-hanger has certainly altered our lives, has he not?"

With the fresh cup of tea it is suddenly as if I have no past; as if only this present exists. Perhaps it's the late hour, the unfamiliar yet familiar surroundings, or the fear of the unknown future, but everything before, even baby Alexander, seems unreal. I know he is my very life and yet I am surprised that I no longer feel like crying.

As if I'm floating in some other dimension, the thought passes through my mind and is gone. Maybe I've run out of tears. When Pani Czeczelowa speaks, the deception shatters. I'm back on earth. Then the tears come to show me they are still available when needed.

"Let us go on with your story," she says in her twittery voice. "There is so little time left."

The tears stop and my memory obediently takes me back to my becoming a princess.

For the first time in my life I was alone. Not only was I isolated from everyone who loved me, I was in a room which was to be my retreat for a whole week. Nothing in it was familiar. If I needed comfort, where could I find it? Sitting on the edge of the bed, staring at my suitcase, I wanted to grab it from the luggage rack and run after the train that carried my parents to Warsaw. What had made me eager to sample a life so foreign to my own? The past week waiting for this fairy tale to begin stretched limitless. It had hardly begun and I wanted it to end.

A note from mother and a picture of my parents together lay on top of my clothes when I opened the suitcase. "My precious child," I read. "Don't waste time being sad." A small sob. "Daddy and I will be back in a week and this time apart will have been a dream or a nightmare, depending on you. You've spent many of your 'dress-up' hours pretending to be a Princess. Now here's your chance to find out how it really feels. Not many little American girls will ever have such an opportunity, so I know you will make the most of it. Here is a schedule of what you are to wear for dinner each night, but you may alter it if you wish. Just be sure to save the yellow crepe de chine for Saturday in case there are guests. Daddy and I already miss you. Remember the same sky is covering us all so we can't be very far apart, can we? Besides, we will have so much to tell each other when we are together again next Monday. We love you more than tongue can tell."

The promised list was attached, but it was the last phrase that increased the lump in my throat. That was my grandmother's favorite goodnight for me. Never before, when my parents were absent, had I been without her wise and tender love. I hugged the picture to me. When I thought about not seeing Grammie for two whole years, the tears flowed again. Unable to read the schedule, I poured a glass of water from the carafe on the night table. In a minute or two after a few swallows I was able to see my parents' faces and read the list. Beige and red silk, it said, was for tonight. Drying my eyes before I touched it, I hung the dress in the wardrobe. I began to feel better. It's only a week, I told myself. You can survive that. By the time there was a timid knock on the door I wasn't quite ready to sing, but I was humming.

Lisa's sister Anna stood diffidently in the hall. "Gnädige Frau has told me to come and take care of you," she said bashfully in German, but made no move to come in until I realized she was waiting for an invitation.

"I was just hanging up my clothes." I tugged her inside. Mother had given me a million instructions, but there wasn't one for being taken care of.

"Here, I will do that." She took my navy blue pleated skirt and middy blouse from me. "Such a pretty uniform this is. Sailors wear such, yes?"

"Yes, they do." I couldn't tell whether she approved or not. She hung the navy blue blouse with its white braid on the hanger. I'd never thought about it before, but it was rather like a regulation Navy suit with its sailor collar and two rows of braid on the collar and cuffs. In the time it took me to have the thought, Anna had everything put away. She explained that the Gnädige Frau Elise wanted me to meet her at the stairs. All of this in German, of course.

"I think she has a surprise for you." Her round eyes twinkled and she took my hand in her large, capable one to guide me out into the hall.

Anyone past thirteen seems ancient to an eleven-year-old. I wondered how old Anna was. She had no lines or wrinkles, but then neither did Mother and Daddy. Anna was sturdy, but not fat. Her light hair was in a heavy braid around her head like a crown and her eyes sparkled when she noticed me looking at her. We grinned at each other.

"Hurry, Carole," Frau Elise's voice called from the top of the stairs. "I wish to show you somesing zat I sink will please you. Anna," she ordered. "You must come too. While Fraulein Carole is here, I expect you will be a great part of this so you might as well know all there is to know about it." She led me toward the great double doors opposite the stairway. Anna hurried ahead to open them.

I gasped. Hidden behind those doors was the ballroom of my dreams. The polished parquet floor reflected each drop of the crystal chandeliers. Enormous mirrors in heavy gilt frames hung along opposite walls. They seemed to reach nearly from floor to ceiling and threw their reflections back and forth to each other so that the room appeared to go on and on into infinity. It was like staring into a magnificent, glittery tunnel. We three people, seemed to be standing in a long gallery growing smaller and further away each time the mirrors transferred our image from one wall to the other. Mesmerized, I stood in awe until my hostess spoke and brought me back into the room itself.

I looked where she pointed, but couldn't make sense of what I saw. The rest of the ballroom looked as ballrooms were supposed to look, but in this one a barre of about eight feet long looked out of place. Supported by two vertical iron pipes, it stood, stark and unattractive, in front of the enormous gold-framed mirrors. Several of the delicate gold and white chairs with their rose damask seats, crowded together to make room for the barre, looked like a group of gossipy ladies protesting their treatment. Even the gold and white grand piano appeared to shun the interloper. It was like a huge spot on a beautiful evening dress. But looks can be deceptive and because of Frau Elise's obvious delight in it I thought it must be something of value. I did my best to be enthusiastic.

"It's very nice." But I couldn't resist asking, "What is it?"

"It's your ballet . . ." She halted. "Do you not know what zat is?"

I was sure I had committed some unforgivable social error. I started to tremble. "No . . . I mean yes . . . Oh . . . I'm so sorry, but I really don't know." I whispered.

"Zat is your ballet barre. Did you not tell Baron von Pawel you wanted to be a ballerina?"

"Yes, I did. And I do, but I don't think I can dance on that."

Frau Elise started to laugh. "Have you ever seen a ballet?" she asked.

"Actually no. Our dance teacher in Virginia was just the wife of one of my father's Corporals. She didn't teach ballet. She just made up steps and taught them to us. But she's the one who said I should study ballet." The Baron must have left out the fact that I had never done any ballet.

"Now we know zat. But you will learn, Carole. Herr Rojanski, ze Meister, will come on tomorrow to begin. Baron von Pawel has said zat is your wish, and zis week is an opportunity for you to find out if it is truly zat what you wish." She started toward the barre, talking all the way. Anna and I folllowed. "We are also fortunate zat Meister Rojanski is recovering from an illness in Torun wiz his brüdder. We hope he will be willing to teach you. If he will, Zarrotti will fetch him every day as long as you work hard and do everysing he tells you. Does zat please you?"

"Oh, Gnadige Frau," I could hardly breathe. The fairy godfather had waved his wand, but who was Meister Rojanski?

"Of course you do not yet know who is Meister Rojanski. For many years he was the ballet Meister of the Polish Ballet in Warsaw."

He sounded important, but knowing nothing of the world of ballet, I didn't realize how important. Still, the lessons had to be costly. My parents had always said one never discussed finances with anyone outside of the family, but in this case. . . I swallowed hard, took a deep breath, and plunged.

"Such a famous man . . . Mother and Daddy haven't the money to pay for lessons from—" I quavered. I knew I was breaking the rules of etiquette and about to lose my dream. "I'd better ask them first."

Frau Elise knelt on the floor beside me so we were eye to eye. "You dear child." She put her arms around my waist. "You don't sink we have done zis wizout your parents' approval, do you? We discussed it ze morning after ze Baron told us of your wish and zat he wished to give you zis gift. Before you even went back to Grudziadz."

"Oh, but—" I started to protest further.

Frau Elise cut me off. "Ernst and I have no children, Liebling," she said. "and zis is such a wonderful chance for us to share one and to pretend she iz ours, is zat ze word? Your muzzer tells us you have dancing in your heart. Will you not let us have ze joy to help it come out?"

86

I flung my arms around her with such force that she lost her balance. We lay there, entangled on the floor and laughing almost like two sisters until I became aware that Anna, unaccustomed to this sort of informal behavior, was wringing her hands.

"Ach, Gott. Ach, Gott," She repeated over and over.

I sat up then so that she could see we were laughing. The sparkle returned to her blue eyes and a big grin spread over her pleasant Germanic face.

"Oh, Frau Elise," I said when Anna seemed all right and I had caught my breath. "How can I thank you? I promise I will work hard and make you proud of me. By next year perhaps I can be a real ballerina and can earn the money to pay the Baron back for my lessons."

"I don't sink your earning days will come quite so soon, child. In ze first place you will be only twelve years old and in ze second, ballet takes many years of study."

Such a thought had never occurred to me. I thought I would just learn how to stand up on my toes and that was all there was to it. That's what the barre must be for. To grab onto if I should start to totter before I had learned to hold my balance and to move around. What else could there possibly be?

"And one other sing. Perhaps since we now have rolled around on the floor togezzer it is time for you to call me Elise instead of Frau Elise and you must call Ernst und Dieter by zer first names too. Zat way we can learn to love each uzzer faster."

"But I love you already." Suddenly shy, I felt a little disloyal to Mother and Daddy as I said it.

"I sink you are only feeling grateful, but we hope zat love will grow as you become more comfortable wiz us. Right now, all is new and we are too, but we will give it time. I know it will come. Now, since it is yet early in ze day I sink we will get Zarrotti and he can drive us into Torun. We have some shopping to do, you and I. Ze Gnädige Frau has said she wishes to accompany us. So let us get ready and we will go, yes?"

"Oh, yes." I scrambled to my feet. Instantly glad my parents had taken the early morning train, I raced down the hall to get my purse. "For Torun," Mother had said as she tucked some Zlotys into it before she left. "If you should go there for lunch or tea, be sure you insist on paying the check. You won't forget?" With my arms straight out at my sides and my little purse swinging by its handle, I did my version of a pirouette down the hall. I would not forget.

The town of Torun was about the size of Grudziadz and looked much the same. With the sun shining I could remember the pictures of the Polish dancers in the National Geographic and hoped that now I would have a chance to become one of them. There was so much to dance about. If I had been with Mother and Daddy, I would have skipped along the sidewalks of Torun yielding to my joy. As it was, with Oma still in mourning for her husband, I felt obliged to behave, as Grammie always said, "with decorum befitting a young lady."

Chapter 12

The stores fascinated me. Elise bought wines and fruits and other things that weren't grown at Friedenau, but I kept wondering when we would get to the ballet shop as Zarrotti piloted the car through the narrow streets. When he stopped in front of an imposing hotel, I understood that we were to have lunch first. Much larger than the Krolewski Dwor, the hotel's marquee was of green glass instead of canvas and it had huge windows with draperies all across the front.

Well known there, the von Wechslers entered the dining room like royalty. Escorted to our table by the Hotel Manager himself, we found a smallish gentleman already seated. He stood immediately and bowed. Gnädige Frau inclined her head and held out her hand. Taking it gently by the tips of her fingers, he bowed again, stiffly. The performance was then repeated with Elise after which she turned to me and spoke in German.

"Here is Meister Rojanski, Carole. He has agreed to instruct you in ballet. I sink your German is quite good enough zat you two can understand each ozzer. If not, Anna or Lisa will always be wiz you to help. Now say hello." Elise and Frau von Wechsler looked at me expectantly.

From Meister Rojanski's pale face I suspected the man had been ill. As I put out my hand and made my curtsy, I wondered if he'd have the strength to teach me.

"Aha. She has some grace."

I heard him say under his breath as he took my limp fingers. What could he have seen in that peculiar little bow I had just executed? To be sure it was more than the tortured bob that used to emerge when Mother dug her nails into my shoulder back home. But something regal about the little man's carriage made me wish I had performed a great, sweeping gesture like the ones I had seen in period movies. Hopeful that I'd have another chance, I smiled into cold, gray eyes. There was no answering smile. Only appraisal.

Meister Rojanski was not a young man. His hair was streaked with white. His clean-shaven face showed the expectation and determination I was to come to know so well. It wasn't a gentle face. I was immediately intimidated. We were just sitting down, I with my back to the rest of the room, when I smelled an unpleasant, yet familiar, odor. Looking over my shoulder, I shuddered. There was Father Stanislawski, bowing obsequiously to the von Wechslers with his head coming very close to mine. His enmity was palpable. I couldn't move.

"How is Ernst, Gnädige Frau?" His voice carried as if from a great distance. It was hard to hear anything above the beating of my heart. The blood drained from my face. My hands were hard fists in my lap.

"He is fine, Father." The Gnadige Frau von Wechsler turned to Herr Rojanski and to me. "Ernst and Father Stanislawski served their two years in the Polish Army together." She looked again at the priest. "You must come to visit us sometime. I'm sure Ernst would be happy to see you even though you two always argue about your different religions." The Gnädige Frau gave a dry laugh at her own joke. If there was an answer, I was too frozen to hear it.

When she introduced Herr Rojanski and me to the Father, though I stood as good manners ordered, I couldn't look at the man. Nor could I offer my hand. Like an aspen tree, my spine shook so that I was sure everyone could see the limbs trembling.

"My goodness, child," Frau von Wechsler's voice penetrated my terror. "You're as white as the dead. Sit down quickly. Here, Elise, give her a little wine."

Despite the unwanted attention, it allowed me to sit down. I wilted into my chair and Elise, gave me her glass. I tried a sip and found it bitter, but sitting was like having a place to hide. I didn't have to face the enemy. The conversation that flowed back and forth between the adults, made no sense to my ears. It was only gibberish. Making a point of putting his hand on my shoulder, the priest excused himself to join his friends across the room. Trying not to cringe, I kept my head down. Knowing he would be in the same area and could reappear at any moment kept me from being a contributing member of our party.

Meister Rojanski asked me how much dancing I had done. When I, reluctantly, told him "none," all he said was "Good, then we have nothing to unlearn." After that, lunch was nothing more than an uncomfortable suspension in time. When I replayed it later, before I went to sleep, I realized with horror that I had forgotten Mother's instructions to pay.

Out in the sunshine, the air was fresh and cool enough to wash away my fright, my revulsion, and my guilt. I could tell the Meister had qualms about my stamina, but in the end, we walked slowly around the square and I convinced them that I felt up to going to the store for ballet slippers. The pink satin slippers with their ribbons trailing on the wooden floor of the small shop window drew me like a magnate. The tutu of my dreams floated above them from a coat hanger. I stood at the window until Elise pulled me away.

Once Meister Rojanski gave his orders to the proprietor in Polish, I was fitted with a pair of flat, black, ballet slippers with soles not even as big as the shoe itself.

"Where are the toe shoes?" I asked the Meister in German.

"They come much later. Perhaps in a year or two. If you have talent." He leaned over to feel the fit of the black slippers on my feet. "Those must be especially made." He nodded to the watchful shoemaker.

Hiding disappointment, I trailed Elise as she paid for the slippers and we all climbed the stairs to the Costumer's above. Instead of the luscious pink tutu I had envisioned, she bought a drab, black, knitted thing called a leotard with long sleeves and legs that reached my knees, discovered after I'd tried it on. Bulky, black stockings that were long enough to fit my tall father, strangled any further hopes.

"Tomorrow at nine o'clock. We start, yes?" Having already destroyed my dreams, Meister Rojanski's voice held no thrill for me as we let him out in front of his apartment building.

If my "yes, sir" was weak, he took no notice. He smiled but, it was as wan as his complexion and I wondered if he was as disappointed in me as I was in him.

"Until tomorrow then." He took off his hat, bowed to the ladies, and disappeared into a dim sallyport.

On the way home Elise was excited. She examined my slippers and leotard. "Just think, Carole, tomorrow you will get your wish and soon you will be a great dancer." Trying to be enthusiastic, I turned and knelt on the front seat so I had a better view of my two benefactors in the rear. Elise smiled at Oma, who smiled back as she stroked the slippers.

"So small, like our Gretti," she said softly.

Even Zarrotti got into the spirit. "The little one will someday make us all very proud. I am honored to be able to drive such a fine young lady. I hope I shall be able to drive her when she is grown and famous." He winked. It was hard to see that wink under his bushy eyebrows or the smile sandwiched between the mustache and the full salt-and-pepper beard, but I knew they were there and they lightened my heart.

Fear of Father Stanislawski faded. The black leotard with its flat leather slippers disappeared. All that was left was the knowledge and joy that every day I would dance. Someday, if I was willing to work, I would have the pink tutu and the handmade pink slippers. With no idea then of how far I would go or of how many slippers and tutus I would ultimately possess, I just wished Mother and Daddy were there so I could share my tomorrow with them.

Chapter 13

While I practiced my exercises in the ballroom, daily as the Meister insisted, Elise, as spokeswoman, reported to my parents what the Meister had said to her about my abilities. I arrived in the sitting room just in time to hear Mother and Dad's arguments being overridden one at a time. Finally, it was decided that, for the next week at least, I should remain at Friedenau. Mother would stay with me for that week while Daddy hunted for a rehearsal spot in Grudziadz. If Meister Rojanski was willing and if his health was now good enough, some weeks we would be with Daddy in Grudziadz, where luckily the Meister had another brother, and some weeks we would work at Friedenau. It all depended on Herr Rojanski's willingness to go along with the plan.

On Monday he said he would think it over. On Tuesday, he announced he was willing to try it. The week that followed was one of repetitious barre excercises, learning to stand in the various positions without the barre's support, and the introduction of the names and movements of steps like Entre Chat and leaps like Grand Jete. Almost too tired to enjoy the pitter-pat of my heart after dinner each night when Dieter teased me by grabbing my hair ribbon, I managed to rise to the occasion. He knew how it embarrassed me when he ran with it and threatened to give it back only if he got a kiss in payment. I never got the ribbon and he never got the kiss. Still I doubt he recognized the first stirrings of adolescence in a young girl's heart anymore than I did. When Kurt was there too, he joined the game. It created an extra thrill that nullified any exhaustion. It was a week of unalloyed joy.

By then Herr Rojanski and I spent each day alone in the ballroom. Even Mother, who, at first, insisted she watch, had learned that she was superfluous and a distraction. She returned to the more entertaining life of Friedenau. The next week, in Grudziadz, the plans were short-lived. Daddy had made arrangements for us to join the practice sessions with the ballet of the local Opera House as long as Meister Rojanski was my teacher. The "Powers" of the Grudziadz Opera Company were thrilled at having such a renowned Ballet Meister in their midst and it sounded like a perfect solution for everyone.

"You should have seen them," Dad had said to Mother and me when we got off the train in Grudziadz. "I could almost hear the wheels turning in their heads as they envisioned their Corps de Ballet in that shabby little palace of culture rivaling the ballet of the Paris Opera."

Although I knew nothing of the Paris Opera, it sounded like a worthy ambition. A theater, any theater, was glamorous to me. If the Grudziadz theatre was shabby, I did not notice it on the morning we arrived there. The idea of working among grown-up professionals at the barre was extremely scary. The Meister found no joy in it. Neither he nor my father had understood that he was to instruct the theater's corps de ballet as well.

"I do not get paid to instruct such a bunch of talentless cows." He raged to my father, to his brother, and to the manager of the Opera House. "My pupil and I must have the rehearsal hall to ourselves in the day."

"But Meister Rojanski, it is impossible. My dancers must also rehearse and there is no other place." The manager was tall, and except for the beginning of a paunch, thin. His hands as he waved them about in agitation were skeleton-like. I wondered if cranes ever had paunches.

My teacher was unmoved. "Those are my terms." His hat restored to his head, he reached for his cape. "Come along, Captain." He took my father's arm. "We go to find another more attractive place."

My father resisted and tried to pull away, but, aging or not, Herr

Rojanski's well-trained muscles were still strong enough to keep the two men attached to each other. "I have spent a week hunting for the proper place, Herr Rojanski." Dad was still trying to wrest his arm from the iron grip. "Believe me, this Opera House is the only suitable hall in Grudziadz. There is not another spot in this town." He finally freed his arm.

"There must be another place and I shall find it." The imperious man left the impression that only he had the intelligence to know where to look.

"Meister, we have looked and looked. I have asked everyone who might know of another place. We would not even have had this if it had not been that someone had a friend whose friend had an uncle who mops this floor. Please believe me. The entire Regiment of the Polish Cavalry swept this town clean. This, I'm afraid, is it." All of this, of course, was done with Dad's Polish soldier orderly, Meier, translating from Polish to German and for us, translating from German to English. Daddy was no linguist. I could only stare from one to the other in uncertainty.

Reticent and neutral, Meier seemed to be doing a good job. He had almost become a member of the family. When he first became Daddy's orderly, he went back to the barracks each night. Because the food at the apartment was better and the surroundings nicer, he slept on a sofa in our entrance hall. A plain farm boy before he was conscripted into the army, he had managed to learn Polish, German, Russian and a little English while he milked the cows. Mother said it made her ashamed that in our country only the most advantaged spoke a foreign language and that was usually French. We all thought Meier was remarkable. He had already become a necessary fixture in our home before the rehearsal hall episode arose. We all stood silently staring at one another while Meister Rojanski thought. At last he heaved an enormous sigh for such a slight body, drew himself to his full height, which came not quite to my father's shoulder, and pronounced his decision.

96

"We shall continue here for the remainder of this week after which, we shall see. It is perhaps better that we continue always at Friedenau, which, if the Captain and his Lady wish the daughter to become a ballerina, should be a necessity at least until we remove ourselves to Warsaw."

Although he spoke in German, I understood. Warsaw. For the first time in my life I was forced to look ahead. What would I be doing in Warsaw? If I had ever visualized beyond these years of learning here in Poland, I would have seen myself pirouetting around on an American stage. Would we all move to Warsaw? I couldn't imagine my parents would entertain the idea of their only child moving without them. They had been unwilling enough to leave me at Friedenau for a week. I looked at my father who, though he looked startled when Meier translated the Meister's message, said nothing for long minutes. When he finally spoke, he shrugged his shoulders.

"If you are willing to continue here for the balance of the week, perhaps we should leave all other conversation on the subject until Carole's mother and I have had a chance to converse. There seems to be more to this ballet business than I realized." The way he waggled his head told me he had accepted about all he was willing to accept. My heart sank. "Continue for today." He beckoned to Meier, kissed me on the top of my head, and left us abruptly. "We shall talk further."

Whenever that happened, I knew Dad was upset. He was never abrupt unless he was disturbed and could think of nothing to say. As a procession, Meister Rojanski, the theater Manager, the present Ballet Meister of the local ballet who had just arrived, Mother, Anna and I headed toward the rehearsal hall. The word Warsaw kept playing in my mind. There were so many questions involved with that word that I decided to think about it later when there were no other things of interest. If I was to have only this one day, and that was a possibility, I would put my utmost into it.

We climbed the steps to the quiet stage, a thrill to an eleven year-old who had only set foot on a stage once before. At the back of the stage, Georg, the Grudziadz Ballet Meister, parted the dusty, beige, background curtains to reveal the working parts of the theater. Meister Rojanski turned his back to Georg who, as was obviously expected, removed his superior's flowing cape and hung it, with the black Homburg on a hook near the door. Even, as inexperienced as I was, I saw the chain of command established. Feeling sorry for the young Georg, I lingered on the edge of the stage.

Suddenly, from somewhere beyond the rehearsal room with its long barre, dingy lights, and necessary mirrors, a clatter like a gaggle of disgruntled geese became audible and grew louder. The corps de ballet clomped into the hall. Their box toes were noisy on the dark wooden floor and almost overcame their babbling. Although some were only a bit older than I, they seemed so mature and self-assured. Not only that, they had toe shoes.

We were nearly finished with our time at the barre before I, at the end of the line with Herr Rojanski seated beside me with his stout staff, noticed how dirty and worn those once pink slippers were. Then I began to notice another thing too. The girls had great knots in their calf muscles.

My teacher spoke only to me. The corps de ballet followed his directions. I tried to believe it was not rudeness, only that they were professionals and needed no criticism, but I knew that was wrong. The Meister was again demonstrating his superiority. I felt sorry for the dancers and a little embarrassed for Meister Rojanski's incivility. When I smiled at the girls and boys at the barre, they never changed their blank expressions. I didn't blame them.

At last the younger Ballet Meister became angry. He spoke curtly to the pianist who had been sitting silent, but tense on his bench. In an attempt to re-establish his supremacy the music started with a crash.

Meister Rojanski's stick never missed a beat. "Faster," he yelled at the pianist. "Keep up your tempo. Follow my beat."

The staff pounded, the music filled me. At my Meister's order, I floated free of the barre and was dancing the steps as he called them out. Such joy. When the music stopped, I was surprised and abashed to find that I had been dancing alone. All others stood quietly watching, their backs to the barre. It was then I realized that it was true. Meister Rojankski would not teach the Grudziadz Ballet nor would he permit anyone else to interfere with his handling of me. It wasn't that I had such talent, but my teacher was the best and as such would accept no interference.

The arrangement by my father was not going to work. Since I could think of no other, when the Meister announced abruptly that we were leaving, I finished the day in misery and went to bed that night convinced my dreams were over.

Chapter 14

"This is impossible. I cannot proceed." Meister Rojanski's paced back and forth the length of our living room, flinging his arms above his head, his hands shaking like leaves in a hurricane. "I am not yet in the strength to instruct all those pitiful, poorly-trained stumblers."

Our second day in the Grudziadz opera house had gone no better than the day before.

"Their Ballet Meister is too young and knows very little," he shouted in Polish at Meier. "We must return to Friedenau at once."

"Impossible." My parents remained firm.

"It would be too bad to have such talent go to waste, but perhaps the young man at the theater could take your daughter as a pupil." Herr Rojanski looked sidewise to see if his words were having any affect. "Of course," he paused to make certain his next statement had a clear reception. "Of course he would probably cause the muscles to become knotted in her legs like those poor creatures in his corps de ballet." He moved toward his hat and cloak. "How sad, but whatever should be . . . will be."

"Now, Herr Rojanski, wait just a minute. There must be another solution to this." Mother jumped up and put out her hand to detain the departing man. "Carole seems to want it so much and you say she has talent." Mother turned to me. "That is true isn't it, dear? You do want to continue with the lessons?"

"Yes, oh yes. Please, Mum, can't we find a way?" I dropped to my knees beside her and looked up to see my father, ready to speak. "I want this chance so much, Daddy. More than I've ever wanted, or ever will want, anything in my life. If you'll just fix it so I can continue with Meister Rojanski, I'll never ask for another thing as long as I live."

Like a broken film everything stopped. Meister Rojanski didn't bend to pick up his hat. Mother's hand stopped stroking my hair. In the silence I could hear my heart. After the pause dragged out almost longer than was bearable, my father spoke.

"I'm not sure that last statement is true, but I'll call Elise to see what she says. After all, they might not want a child all the time. If she invites you, I guess we can get along with only weekends until you tire of your lessons. If she doesn't invite you that will end it, won't it? After all, many things can happen between now and the time we go back to the States. Does that suit you, Caro?"

Even if Daddy did think this was just a passing fancy, he was willing to give me this marvelous gift. He bent to pull me up from the floor. My face squashed into his uniform's brass buckle, but I hardly cared.

"Oh, thank you, thank you, thank you," was all I could say.

"Don't thank me too soon." He pulled away and went toward the phone. "Nothing is settled yet." Turning to Mother he asked, "I expect this is as good an hour as any to call Elise, don't you, Janice?"

It didn't take long to get the call through. With all of us sitting tense and quiet in the same room, not over-hearing Daddy's side of the conversation was impossible. He started out by explaining the situation and then Elise took over. Dad listened and, whenever his head bobbed, we eagerly wobbled our heads too.

"We'll talk it over," he said at last before he hung up. Then he sat, his hands hanging loosely between his knees. He seemed to be studying his riding boots.

Mother broke first. "Well, Jon, what did she say?"

Daddy looked at Mother and there were tears in his eyes. "She said . . ." There was a long pause. "She said . . . well, mostly she cried."

"Didn't she say anything at all?" From his behavior I was sure she had refused him.

"Yes, she did. She said a lot. She said—" My father's head came up and he looked straight into my eyes, "she said, thank you for giving me a child to love and to pamper if only for a little while. No one since my darling Gretti has ever given me such a great gift." He smiled. "So we will share you."

For a second I almost knew how Heaven was going to feel when I got there. It wasn't Mother's next words that brought me to earth. It was her tone.

"What are the plans, Jon? Are we to have any time at all with our daughter or has Elise completely taken her over?" She sounded almost belligerent. It surprised me. Jealousy was an emotion I'd never known in her. I thought she was going to refuse to let me go. My heart hesitated.

"Don't get yourself in a frenzy, Janice. You'll have almost all the time you want with Carole. Of course she'll be at Friedenau all week, but she'll come home on weekends. Or," There was a pause. "We can stay there at Friedenau whenever we want." He reached into his pocket for his cigarettes, which he smoked only when he was nervous. "Apparently the von Wechslers view us as a package deal, and for my part, I'd love to spend every weekend up there. That's the kind of life I can get used to very easily, how about you?" Without taking a cigarette from the package, he put his arms around me again and laughed. Even Meister Rojanski gave a genuine smile though Meier hadn't yet translated the conversation.

Mother didn't laugh. "I'm not in a frenzy," she said with a decided edge to her voice. "Since when have you ever known me to be in a frenzy? I'm just concerned. The von Wechslers seem like nice people, but how do we know what they're really like? For all we know we may be sending our child off to be sold into white slavery."

I wondered what that was. My father snorted.

"Oh, come on, Janice. Aren't you being a bit dramatic? After all she was there a week and nothing dire happened to her except that she was bitten by the ballet bug."

Mother shrugged her shoulders in a gesture I had seen before only when she was ready to fight. "If you don't care what happens to your daughter . . . I do."

Apparently Meister Rojanski recognized a sign of some kind. He broke in. "So, Vater, when do we start again at Friedenau? Shall we begin tomorrow?"

During Meier's translation, if the Polish man's reference to Daddy as 'Father' startled Daddy, he didn't show it. He seemed amused by it and perhaps even grateful. Mother didn't get huffy very often, but when she did, it usually lasted a while.

"Not so fast. Nothing's been decided yet." She still sounded petulant, but with Daddy on my side, I wasn't afraid. I hoped time and, what she called a "family confab," would change her mind. "We have to talk about this a bit more -- in private." She stood then and, almost roughly, pulled me away from my father.

With my head against her breast, I could feel her heart beating so rapidly that it made me afraid, but in a different way. What if my selfishness caused her to have a heart attack? What if Mother died?

103

My friend in Lexington's father had a heart attack and died, so it could happen. My friend had told me how hard and fast his heart had beat before it stopped.

I tore myself away from Mother and stood between the two of them. "Let's just give the whole thing up. I don't want to make anyone unhappy. I can get along perfectly well without ballet lessons. We were doing fine just the way we were." I knew the words weren't true and yet they were. I would give up anything in the world if it were in my power to keep Mother and Daddy healthy and happy. They would do the same for me, but this was a different Mother than the one I had always known and it was my willfulness that had created her. It was simple. I would give up the dancing.

All four of the adults in the room stood absolutely still. Each face registered a different reaction. Meister Rojanski's aging countenance showed disappointed resignation before he bent in defeat to reach for his hat and cloak. Meier seemed bewildered. Daddy looked at me in disbelief and in Mother's eyes I saw the recognition of what she had done. In less than a second, I was in her arms.

"Oh, my dear, dear child." She breathed with her lips against my hair. "Of course we won't go on again just the way we were. Why, how could we pass up this wonderful opportunity for you to learn from the very best. Two years is only twenty-four months and that's such a short time and . . . " She drew back her head and looked into my eyes. "Just think of all the wonderful tales we'll have to tell when we get home. I'm so sorry if I gave the wrong impression, Pet. For a minute, thinking of all the time I was going to lose with you, I was a little jealous. Will you forgive me?"

The Meister's voice broke into our happy moment. "I will see you then on the day after tomorrow at Friedenau." Meier translated as he helped the little man with his cloak. "I go now to prepare myself at home in Torun." He threw the cape grandly over one shoulder.

"Just a moment, Meister Rojanski." Mother's voice halted him before he could disappear. "We would like to have a full week with our daughter before we have to give her up." Her tone would have stopped a criminal in his tracks and before the man could utter his favorite word, "impossible," she continued. "We have acceded to your wishes and you shall have free rein from then on, but we demand some consideration. We will see you a week from today or we will not see you at all."

After he had ungraciously agreed and as he swept out, we heard him mutter, "She will forget everything she knows and her muscles will grow weak in that length of time. Too bad."

I vowed to make sure that would not happen.

Chapter 15

Mother was full of instructions, admonitions, biddings, and forbiddings. Other than that, my parents treated me more like an honored guest than a member of the family. "Be sure to leave yourself enough time to get your bath and to dress for dinner every evening," she said more than once. "Don't get in anyone's way," was another favorite. "Don't get on that motorcycle with Dieter. He drives like a wild man," came up often.

When Mother and Dad were just back from their trip, she'd been thrown into a state of shock when Dieter, with me behind him on the cycle, had come careening around the garden path and almost skidded into the steps. To be honest, I wasn't sure I wanted to risk my life again. On the other hand, riding with my arms around Dieter's middle had made my heart beat faster. Scared or not, I might have yielded to temptation. Mother, however, left nothing to chance. She made me promise that "never again would I get on the infernal machine with that boy."

Another promise she extracted was that I would never set foot or skate on the frozen duck pond. "I know it's tempting," she said. "But you never know how thick the ice is. Besides, you'll be too busy with your lessons. Promise me you'll stay away from the ice."

I was just learning to ice skate and thought it could have been a lovely substitute in the hours when I wasn't dancing. After a little resistance, I promised with reluctance.

"Next weekend is your birthday, Precious." Mother was rummaging around in the bottom of the armoire, or shrank as the Germans called it and her voice was muffled. "Oh, dear. I can't believe you'll be twelve years old. You're growing up too fast. I wish Grammie had put that brick on your head when you were little so you'd never grow up and leave us. Remember?"

When Mother recalled it, I could hear my precious Grandmother's voice. As a young child I had thought Grammie was teasing, but now, as Mother continued, I wasn't so sure.

"How can I bear to part with you for weeks on end?" Free of the schrank, she pulled me close. "I keep telling myself that it's what you want, but you know how we'll miss you. Everything will seem so empty if you aren't here to share it with us."

On the verge of offering again to relinquish my dancing and stay with them, I was interrupted by Daddy's timely entrance. His hug smelled of horses and hay and the clean, crisp air of late November, but he had heard Mother's last two sentences.

"I hope," he laughed as he took Mother in his arms, "that when Caro gets married you won't want us to go with her on her honeymoon. Ye Gods. You wouldn't make us go live with them forever, too, would you?" He ruffled my hair and gave Mother an extra squeeze so she'd know he was teasing.

I thought what he described might be the best of both worlds. Romantic that I was, I saw myself as a kind of Cinderella and had no doubt that someday I would marry a handsome Prince Charming. But how could I go off with some strange man, handsome or not? There could be nothing wrong with all four of us setting up housekeeping in a castle together. Once the moment passed I didn't renew my offer to give up the dancing.

Finally Saturday came. With all my clothes and possessions on the overhead rack and my parents settled onto the train's red plush seats beside me, I should have been content. Mother, however, kept taking in great gulps of air and letting them out in long, agonized sighs. With mixed emotions I doubted my ability and desires until I heard Grammie's voice again.

"Carole, this is your chance and you have to at least try."

Partially accepting her wisdom, I turned my face to the train window and was silent. With a heart still uncertain, my hands clenched in my lap, my tears were visible only to the hurrying passengers on the Bahnhof platform. Just before the train started, a tall, thin figure in a black cassock came abreast of my window. Father Stanislawski. His eyes seemed to search every compartment as he passed and slowed when he saw me. His yellow teeth showed briefly, he crossed himself and moved on. With a long shudder that left me clammy and apprehensive, I worried about that expression. I was glad there had been glass between us.

I looked quickly to see if Daddy had noticed. With a map of Poland spread out between them, my parents had seen nothing. If I told Daddy about Frau von Wechsler's invitation to Father Stanislawski, I was sure he would tell Ernst that there had been trouble with the man in Grudziadz. But suppose Ernst was a close friend of the priest's? I didn't really know what had gone on at the Krolewski Dwor. Ernst might come to the conclusion that I was a wicked girl who had caused the trouble. The von Wechslers wouldn't want me. It would remain my secret.

Maybe, if something terrible did happen, Dieter would become my rescuer. But he was part of the family. Kurt . . .? Kurt was such a tease he would only laugh or find some way to make me more miserable. I thought of those bright blue eyes and how they snapped and sparkled when he grabbed my hair ribbon and ran with it. Father Stanislawski began to fade.

Dieter had started the game, during the week Mother and Dad were in Warsaw. He and Kurt had quickly become allies. Once they saw how easily they could embarrass me, it became a ritual. As the ribbon flew through the air, while the most I could do was snatch, grab and miss, there was a lot of laughter. Even I laughed. In the end they usually maneuvered me into a corner.

"You can have it back if you'll give us each a kiss."

Aware that I could escape or that Elise would step in, I was always filled with a delicious kind of terror mixed with bashfulness. They never got the kiss and I never got the hair ribbon, but I did look forward to that after dinner hour. Anna, sometimes a quiet observer of the game, would be giggling when she brought the ribbon to me before breakfast, but she would never tell me how she got it.

Once the train started, it almost silently slid out from under the roof that covered the tracks and the station. We were on our way and the train window reflected the beginning of a smile. By the time we got to Friedenau's tiny station, I had forgotten the enemy was also on the train. After it stopped to let us off, started again, and began to pick up speed, that dreaded face was framed in its window. Father Stanislawski smirked, nodded, and was gone. All over so fast it was only a glimpse. I moved closer to Mother and Daddy, who stood, surrounded by luggage, in the snow on the shallow platform.

"Wasn't that the terrible priest from the Krolewski Dwor?" Mother asked.

Before she got an answer, sleigh bells announced Zarrotti's arrival. In the excitement of loading us into the back seat and the luggage into the front, I forgot my anxiety. "This is my first sleigh ride," I said to the Polish man as he tucked the heavy bear skin rug over our knees.

Zarrotti smiled at me as he climbed onto his perch. He had the considerable bulk and girth to match his heart and I considered him a friend. With a gentle slap of the reins on their rumps the two matched grays trotted away from the station.

"Zarrotti." I leaned forward as we jingled down the narrow road toward the barns and the big house itself. "How is Herr Rojanski going to get here in the snow?"

"On the train like you." He turned his head so I could see his face. "Griselda and Herman." He indicated the two horses with a nod. "And I will bring him to you."

I settled back, satisfied. Only the imprints of the sleigh's runners and horses hooves marred the softly undulating quilt that nature was dropping over our world. We were quiet as the trees on either side of the road slid by, each of us enjoying the beauty. The leafless trees, were decorated in puffy white as if for a wedding. Each branch and twig held its own thick icing that twinkled and glittered in the pale November sun when its moment came to star. The evergreens, like sentinels, towered among them and when a dark green branch became too heavy it shed its white burden with a soft plop. The silence was palpable. Beyond the trees the small rises and hollows stretched away over the fields that had so recently been filled with the laughing peasants harvesting Friedenau's sugar beets. Today, everything appeared ancient and yet newly created.

We smelled the cow barn before it appeared, but with all the beauty around us, it didn't seem as malodorous as usual. On our first trip to Friedenau, Captain Metzgar had explained that in Poland, as in a great part of Europe, the cow barns were never shoveled out. More straw was added on top of the old until, somewhere along the line, ramps were built so the cattle could get into the barn. No one seemed to know what happened when the barn was so full the cattle could no longer squeeze under the roof, but there were no abandoned barns near the large estates. Daddy said he guessed they either cleaned them out or burned them down to start over. Fortunately, it wasn't until later that I connected the milk and cream we used at the table with the cow barn.

On this beautiful day the stench produced hardly a gulp and a gag. As we turned in the gates, my eyes went immediately to the roof of the distant sheep barn where the stork's nest had, even in the fall, held the mother and father stork and their two young. Its occupants had now flown south and the nest should have looked lonely and forlorn perched on the ridgepole. Yet, covered as it was in soft white, to me it was a becoming crown befitting a palace.

The sleigh jingled past the duck pond with the frustrated ducks and geese waddling around on its frozen surface. We smelled the familiar odor of the stables, then rounded the high lilac hedge. The mansion came into view. It looked like a prima ballerina. All angles and edges were softened and the snow gathered around its base like a tulle tutu. Its wings spread like graceful arms and pure white defined the sills and mullions of its many eyes. In my imagination, it was the beginning, middle and ending of all fairy tales.

Above the imposing double doors at the top of the steps a large banner printed in many colors said "Frohes Geburtstag, Carole, and Greetings to Her Mother and Father. Wilkommen." The von Wechslers spilled through the front doors, the servants lining up on the steps below them. Suddenly, this was no longer a dream. Like all our moves in the Army . . . this was home.

Chapter 16

"This is a good place to have another cup of tea, don't you think?" Countess Czeczelowa, picks up her cup and toddles toward the samovar.

Aware that I have rattled on, guilt overwhelms me. Steeped in memories of the past, I have been oblivious to her needs and have kept this octogenarian from her rest. "Don't you want to go to bed?" Salty tears of shame sting my tired eyes and drain down into my throat. My voice is husky.

"No, dear one." She puts her cup down and stretches her thin arms above her head. "I want to hear it all. I'm just rearranging these old bones. If I don't move them occasionally, they won't move when I need them to. They are very unobliging in that way." She stands. "Come and get your tea. You need to move around a bit too."

Standing does feel good, but when we are again settled in our chairs she waves her hand like a queen giving an order and says, "Begin again."

I remember the gesture from days long ago and as my story of a happy past begins to overwhelm the fear of a concealed future, I accept the warmth, sip my tea, smile, and obey her command. "Where was I?"

"Your twelfth birthday," she smiles.

"That was a birthday to remember." Eyes closed I pause and see again Mother sitting on the edge of my bed in the pretty yellow room at Friedenau. So much has happened in these intervening years.

"I never expected such a birthday," I said to Mother as I was getting ready for bed. "My goodness, just look at all my presents." Carrying the doll Mother had made clothes for, I walked over to the dressing table and looked down at the monogrammed, silver-backed, comb, brush and mirror that the von Wechslers had given me. There were also two crystal pots, one large and one small, with matching silver tops. "What are these for?" Picking up the larger one, I carried it over to her.

"When I was young, ladies wore their hair long." Mother took the jar from me and stroked its glistening crystal topped by the silver lid. "Every evening it was given one hundred strokes at bedtime with the silver hair-brush. The hair that came out was wadded into a ball and put in the larger of the two jars."

"Why didn't you just throw it in the wastebasket?" I brush at my own hair. "Why did you save it?"

"Do you know, I'm not sure. It seems to me, though, I remember hearing Louise, our maid, discuss taking it—when she got enough—to someplace where they bought it from her to make transformations. That's what they called wigs and hair pieces in those days. Isn't it strange that I never questioned it before?"

It didn't seem so strange to me. Aside from answering my question about what the pretty jar was for, I didn't care where its contents had gone. I did think I'd try the one hundred strokes per night, but my hair being only shoulder length, I didn't expect to have much to put in the jar. Besides who would want to buy anything of such a strange carroty color? The pieces looked elegant and shiny lying there, but somehow they were a bit disappointing. They were the kind of thing more appreciated when one went from twelve to thirteen. I had the feeling that when my birthday came next year I would be expected to become an adult whether I wanted to or not. I dreaded it.

The doll in my arms suited me just fine. As if she could hold off the teens, I made her a silent promise I would always keep her near me no matter what the adults said. "It's been a lovely birthday," I said again to Mother when Gretchen, the doll, and I were in bed. "But do I really have to grow up when I'm thirteen? I think twelve may be my favorite age and I might like to stay here." If only Mother would tell me I could.

"Dear little birthday girl, you do find such funny things to worry about. If you will just enjoy each day, when November 30th comes around next year, you'll be just as eager to be thirteen as you were to be five or nine or twelve. We human beings grow in our knowledge, in our abilities, and in our desires. Even in our bodies without noticing the changes. Just as Grammie's promise to put a brick on your head wouldn't have kept you little, nothing else can either. You just go to sleep thinking about today and your tomorrows will produce everything they are supposed to. I know you'll be happy every year of your life."

Since it had never occurred to me to doubt her wisdom, I shrugged off my worries and turned back to the examination of my birthday gifts. Rodczeck had given me a pretty handkerchief. Frau Kieck had baked a beautiful cake. Fraulein Goethe had created an elegant coat and hat for Gretchen while Zarrotti, and Victor had made a little wooden bed for her. Anna and Lisa had crocheted a pretty blue and white coverlet and pillow case for the bed. Mother had included a nightgown and robe for the doll. When she was tucked under the coverlet with her brown eyes closed, I let my own eyes go to the night table.

One gift was impossible for me to put away. It was a Swiss music box filled with colorful hair ribbons and I wanted it always to stay on the night table beside my bed. Its tune was Strauss's Wiener Wald. Like its donor's voice, it lifted my heart. Kurt had come through the double doors just after Rodczeck started to serve the cake. I felt the blood rush to my face when he bent over my chair and kissed me on the cheek. "Frohes Geburtstag, Carole." He had set his package in front of me and slid into his accustomed chair opposite Dieter. Everyone was watching. I knew Dieter couldn't resist making some smart remark. He did.

"If Kurt gets a kiss, so do I. Just wait until after dinner, Kleine." When he leered at me, my already misbehaving heart thumped so loudly everyone at the table must have heard it. No one laughed, but it was a while before my heart got back where it belonged and developed a steady rhythm.

The hair ribbon game began as soon as we were released from the table and ended as Dieter had said it would. He kissed the top of my head. It was only a game and I knew it, but now in bed, I wondered why I was disappointed. In the middle of a possible answer, sleep closed my eyes.

Mum and Daddy went back to Grudziadz the next day and I was dreading Meister Rojanski's arrival on Monday morning. I had exercised during the week, but not enough to keep me in the shape he would expect. Although I was eager to get on with my lessons, I was not looking forward to the lecture nor the sore muscles that would follow. In the morning, since Anna had gone home with my parents to cook and clean for them, Lisa wakened me.

"Come look at how beautiful our world is. More snow fell in the night and now we are in a treasure-chest. See how the early sun makes all our earth's jewels sparkle."

Surprised at usually prosaic Lisa's poetic words, I jumped out of bed and hopped over the cold Persian carpet to the window. Ducks and geese grumbled to each other on a soft snowy plain where the pond should have been. Horses, like Christmas card paintings, stood in front of stables whose fluffy eaves almost met the marshmallow ground. The whole splendid stage twinkled in the sun.

"Oh, Lisa." I breathed as I turned from the window. "Help me hurry so I can go outside. It must feel like magic out there. Anything that beautiful has to be magic, don't you think?"

"It may be, but I don't think you're going to get outside to feel it. See, here comes Zarrotti from the railroad station and with him is his majesty Meister Rojanski. He is not coming here for you to play out of doors."

The sleigh had made deep cuts that destroyed the pristine vista, but I hardly noticed. A young German Shepherd dog sat alert and erect beside the Meister. "Look, he's brought his puppy." I hurried into my robe and slippers. "I wonder why."

"Rodczeck told me this morning that in weather like this he is to be given a room so he won't have to go back and forth by such an early train. I suppose arrangements were made for the dog too." Lisa, busy straightening the room, didn't look at me. "Mach schnell," she ordered as she left the room.

Getting dressed hardly took any time at all. Most of that was accomplished at the window while I watched the puppy scamper around in the snow. Victor, outside to bring in the Meister's suitcase, joined the game and even rotund Zarrotti leaped and bounced like a child while the pup ran from one to the other barking in joy. It would waken Ernst and Elise who lived on that side of the manor house, but my only concern was in getting down there to join the fun. Halfway down the stairs I saw I was too late. The Meister stood in the hall below, looking as if he would herd me back up and into the ballroom before I had a chance to meet his dog or even to have my breakfast. Ernst, in his robe and slippers was there too, sleepy, but smiling. Rodczeck came down the hall with a cup of coffee for Ernst and grinned when he saw me.

"Guten Morgen, Fraulein Kleine," he said as he marched by on the way to the front door.

I don't know exactly what happened next. When the door opened an enthusiastic, bounding, furry-body bounced off Rodczeck and caused the tray with its coffee cup to become airborne. The dog launched itself into my arms. Dropping to the floor, I closed my arms around a wriggling, tail-wagging, creature and heard Meister Rojanski's voice saying:

"Happy Birthday, Carole. My nephew brought your present to me only yesterday and already he knows where he belongs. May you have many happy years together." He leaned over to pat my head and the dog's.

"Do you mean he is for me? He is mine?" I couldn't believe it. "Oh, Ernst, is it all right if I keep him?" I turned to my host. "What will the Gnadige Frau say? And Elise? What if Kitty and Mennlein don't want another dog here?" Kitty was a cocoa brown Doberman that belonged to Elise. Mennlein belonged to Frau Kieck and was an ill-tempered Dachshund who really needed more love and attention and less discipline than he got.

In spite of the spilled coffee staining his robe, Ernst was still smiling. "Don't worry, Caro. Meister Rojanski inquired of all this last week and we are delighted that our adopted daughter has such a beautiful puppy. He tells us your gift came from the German-Polish border near Goerlitz where the Meister's nephew is a border guard. The dog is how old?" Ernst turned to my teacher.

"Six months and already had started his training as a border dog. I'm sure, Carole, that if you will just say "Platz" to him, he will sit down quietly and that will be a great improvement for all of us." Herr Rojanski was becoming a little edgy.

As soon as my birthday present heard the word "Platz" he sat down. His tail never stopped wagging.

"I think I'll name him Deupol for the two borders. Deutschland-

Polen. Don't you think that would be all right," I asked the assemblage? "I could call him Deu. That's short and to the point."

The Meister spoke up quickly, "I believe his name is Hans. I don't know if he will come if you call him by another name."

I walked away a few steps. "Here Deu," I said quietly as I moved toward the stairs. With no hesitation the puppy bounded after me. We belonged to each other no matter what name either of us bore. I wanted to wrap my arms around Meister Rojanski to thank him, but his austerity kept me from it. Instead I went to him, took his hand, made my required curtsy and found myself wrapped in his embrace. Surprised, a little embarrassed, and suddenly shy I started backing away, but when I looked up to see him smiling, I followed my first instinct. From then on, when we worked he was extremely demanding of me, but at all other times he was an adopted and cherished Uncle whose only thought was for my well-being. That is, as long as long as my well being didn't interfere with my dancing.

"Because of your birthday and because we are already a week behind and one day will make no difference, I think you should take the morning and get to know Deupol. Perhaps out into the beautiful sunshine and play awhile in the snow, yes? I will settle myself and this afternoon we shall begin again to strengthen the muscles."

It was one of the few times I ever knew my teacher to step out of character. I stammered my thanks to everyone. After Rodczeck brought my coat and boots, Deu and I raced out the door. It was the first day of a lovingly interdependent life together. After disturbing the powdered-sugar coating of the gardens, and passing the open door and displayed coffin of the chapel for the first time without nervousness, my companion and I turned toward home. The sleigh was just pulling up to the steps again. My heart stopped when I saw Father Stanislawski throw aside the fur robe and climb cautiously out. He reminded me of a cat shaking its wet feet as he moved prissily from step to step. I wanted to say to Deu, "Sic 'em." Of course I didn't, but he felt my unease and advanced with a fierce puppy-growl.

The priest stopped dead with one foot in the air, but once he had identified his enemy, he hurried to safety. Even though I wondered what the von Wechslers would make me do with Deu if he continued to growl, I wondered even more at a grown man who could be intimidated by a six month old puppy.

"Ssshhh. Or we'll both be in trouble." I said to Deu as the door opened again and Rodczeck signaled me to wipe my feet and to brush the snow off of the dog's coat. I tried to move slowly to give Father Stanislawski time to get out of the way, but Deupol stopped rumbling, shook most of the snow off for himself, and I couldn't stall.

Chapter 17

Deu's growl was only bravado, but he kept advancing a foot or two, retreating, then advancing again. Father Stanislawski, the object of the fierce display, behaved as if he were about to be eaten whole. Imagining Deu as the lion he saw in himself, I found joy in picturing the wild beast devouring the man cassock and all.

"Perhaps you had better wait for us outside," Elise said, softly jarring me out of my preoccupation. "I can't imagine why the dog is behaving this way."

I knew perfectly well why he was behaving as he was. "Maybe he needs to go to the bathroom," I said in his defense and hurried to the door even happier with my birthday present. "We'll meet you after a while at . . ." My words were cut off by the by the closing door and gave me the perfect excuse. I never said where.

Deu and I were out again and free. The sickening sense of fear and disgust that filled me whenever I so much as thought about Father Stanislawski was quickly buried in the virgin snow. Deu chased a rabbit under the laden bushes and emerged a marshmallow dog with two round eyes and a black nose. He shook himself as we ran and then rolled in the snow to cover himself again. I made snow angels beside him and threw snowballs for him to chase. By the time we reached the kitchen door in the back, I was thoroughly enjoying our liberation, but the delicious odors that escaped from Frau Kieck's kitchen had a very definite pull. I opened the door and we stepped in. The warmth of the room and the fragrance of freshly baked bread wrapped me in that special guardianship provided by familiar and loved things. I was safe here. Deupol, welcomed by everyone except Mennelein, was admired and petted. He behaved well and Frau Kieck gave us each a slice of warm bread with butter and applesauce.

Through the high kitchen window we watched Elise and Ernst

depart for a tour of the estate with the priest and my dancing Meister for a walking tour of the estate.

The Father still walked like a cat with wet feet. Happy at his discomfort, the cook and I continued to watch. The Maestro, ever the dancer, kept up with his host and hostess as they followed the sleigh's tracks. The priest held his skirts high and tried to keep his overshoes dry at the same time. Distaste showed in every line of his body as he minced along. With no sidewalks to guide him, he lagged further and further behind. Had Elise looked back, she would have recognized a reluctant follower, but she and Herr Rojanski were laughing as they floundered along, and Ernst was plodding ahead to break the trail.

When the group disappeared behind the bowed and breaking lilac hedge, Deu and I went upstairs to join Fraulein Göethe in the sewing room. She had volunteered to help me make a dress for Gretchen. With every stitch and tangled thread I knew that sewing was not to be one of my talents. To be honest, I hated it. Still, amid many finger punctures, the morning passed quickly.

Before luncheon every day there was time for gathering and conversation. I enjoyed listening to the grown-up discussions of everything from when the storks were due back to what that "ridiculous Austrian paperhanger" might do next. Even though the von Wechslers were German, there was very little conversation of a political nature. Because of the priest, I had thought to avoid the adult disucssion today, but the von Wechsler matriarch's rules were too rigid. Ida, Anna's youngest sister, had been sent to find me. With my dog at my heels, I entered the family sitting room as cheerfully as possible.

The warmth of the sitting room poured out into the chilly hall as soon as I opened the door. The tiled stove in the corner of the room rose from floor to ceiling and its radiating heat wrapped around me like a welcome blanket. Arranging my face in a smile as I turned from the closing door, I hoped I presented the picture of a well-behaved young lady of twelve as I made the obligatory curtsy. Across the sitting room, the family and their guest were gathered around the table. So afraid I'd see Father Stanislawski, I looked only at the window. The falling snow, beautiful a little while ago, now seemed menacing—as if it would bury me forever in this room. My eyes shifted, through no will of my own, and there he sat staring at me with an expression as cold and challenging as the weather. It made me rub my arms.

"Are you cold, Caro?" Elise pushed her chair away from the large table.

"Perhaps I should run upstairs and get a sweater," I said. It was a chance to postpone the inevitable.

"Ida will get it for you," Gnädige Frau's voice was firm and assured. "You come here to sit with us. You will soon be warm."

Not even the elements of nature would dare defy this overpowering woman, and I moved slowly toward her. Deu had stopped at the door, but now he bounced across the room ahead of me to put his forepaws in the dowager's lap and to try to capture the tinkling bell which she shook with great power.

"Nein. Nein. Nein." She shrieked. She raised the arm with the bell and swatted at Deu with the other. "This will never do. What is this dog? Take the beast away." She pushed at poor Deu as she shouted orders to Ida who appeared in answer to the bell's frantic ringing. "We cannot have this. We cannot have such confusion. Throw him outdoors." She pointed to the door. "How did he get in?"

Ida looked at me before she grabbed Deu's collar. I stood frozen while Ernst sprang to his feet. He spoke quietly and the maid stopped.

"Wait, Ida. Now Mutti," He turned to his mother and I wondered how he dared call this unfeeling old harridan an endearing name. "You weren't yet up when the puppy arrived this morning." He walked over to stand beside Deu, his hand on the dog's head. "Remember, Mutti," he continued. "Meister Rojanski talked with us about a birthday gift for Caro? This is the gift." The gift wagged his tail and Ernst bent to pat him."See how he already belongs to Caro. I have a feeling that if Deu went, we would lose his mistress as well." He looked at me. Afraid to move, I stared back at him.

"Ida," he directed, "take Deu to Fraulein Goethe. She will take care of him until we finish our luncheon. Will that be all right with you, Carole? Mutti?"

The room was absolutely silent. I had no power to stop my tears and, since I had no handkerchief, I sniffled as I nodded.

"Oh, my dear, dear Caro. I am so sorry." The authoritative voice was suddenly tender. "Come here, Liebchen. Come to Oma." She pulled me onto her lap where I could feel the stays and bones of her unyielding corset. Her capacious bosom was soft and welcoming as she pulled me against her and I sniffled again. She reached into the neck of her black, lace-collared dress and handed me her handkerchief. The scent was of lilacs, just like my Grammie at home. I relaxed against her.

"Yes, take the dog to Fraulein Goethe," the Gnadige Frau said to Ida. "She will take care of him." Frau von Wechsler continued to hold my head against her and to stroke my hair. "Poor little Carole. Oma was cruel and she is so sorry. Please forgive me."

Before I could answer, Rodczeck appeared to announce the midday meal. "Come child, let us go in to our Mittagsessen and forget all about Oma's terrible mistake." She took my hand and turned me over to Ernst. I had learned some protocol by then and knew she had to be escorted by Father Stanislaw. "Poor woman," I thought with some affection in my heart for the first time.

Ernst propelled me through the dining room doors and I was relieved to find I would be seated as far from the priest as our limited number would allow. He was on the matriarch's right while the Maestro, who fell somewhere between a guest and an employee, separated me from Elise. The conversation was adult and, if I gazed out of the windows at the snow, I couldn't see whether Father Stanislaw stared at me or not.

Deu was safely mine and would be waiting when we finished our meal. With a warm heart I pondered Gnädige Frau's use of the word "Oma". She had used it several times. Did she expect me to call her grandmother? Well, after all, that wouldn't be disloyal to Grammie, would it? It was such a different word. It was even a different language in a very different world. It certainly would be easier than Gnädige Frau. Besides, she smelled like a Grandmother. I wondered briefly about curtsying. Did one curtsy if she were only an adopted Grandmother? I decided I'd better ask Mother about that one. Wondering, too, why the Gnädige Frau had suddenly become a warm human being, I looked at her and when she smiled at me, a possible answer came. Perhaps she was missing the granddaughter she had lost and wanted to open her heart to a new one. Remembering the pain when my cat, Richard, died, I determined right then to provide all the affection she had been yearning for. I smiled warmly.

A change in the noise level brought me back to the dining room. Everyone else was standing. Luncheon was over and we were to move to the sitting room. I pushed my chair back quickly and followed, leaving as much distance as I could between me and the priest, who seemed to be trying to convert Ernst to Catholicism.

"I'm too old to change my ways." I heard Ernst say as he ushered the Father through the doors ahead of him. "But I do think you should plan to spend the night here. See how much snow has fallen.

Why, it must be more than a meter." The two men walked to the nearest window where Ernst pulled back the curtains. The pallid light reflected itself in the priest's face.

Only a shadowy boundary now, the wrought-iron fence set in the stone wall still divided the von Wechslers from the world. Their peasants, who tended the livestock and worked the fields were, I hoped, snug in their thatch-roofed cottages on the other side. If Father Stanislawski were to spend the night here, however, instead of the wall keeping the unwanted out, it and the snow lashed us all together as prisoners inside. With the thought came another fear. My room was at the very farthest end of the long upstairs corridor. The priest, no matter which of the guest rooms he had, would have me cut off from all help.

I had to share my fears with someone who could help. With the excuse that I had to find my dog, I made my apologies and left the room before the discussion of the man's overnight stay was even concluded. My first thought was to tell motherly Frau Kieck. But as a Catholic, wouldn't she believe the priest? And what would I say? The memory of that groping, flabby hand under the tablecloth splashed me with a wave of nausea. Grabbing on to the newel post, I slid down onto the carpeted steps.

Lisa found me with my head on my knees. Without hesitation she sat beside me and put her arm around my shoulder. In a whisper, interspersed with tears and gulps, my terrors, memories and the guilt that was in my heart poured out. If Lisa were shocked it didn't show. Her arms stayed tightly around my shoulders.

"You are not to blame, Kleine," she said softly. "If Father Stanislawski does stay overnight, I will see that Ida or I will stay upstairs with you. Don't worry, you will not be left alone. I will talk with Frau Elise."

"Oh, please, Lisa." I wriggled away from her. "Don't tell the von

Wechslers. They'll think I'm foolish. Oh, I would just die if they knew." In my agitation I jumped up and Deu, who had appeared from the sewing room, thought we were going out to play. He began to bark and bound around in the hall. The sitting room door opened wide and Ernest, followed by the others, emerged.

"What's going on out here?" he demanded. "Caro, you must keep the dog quiet. Everyone is going up for a rest and there certainly would be no rest with that racket."

Blocking the stairway, I froze. How long had he been standing behind that door? Could he have overheard any of my conversation with Lisa? He took me by the shoulders to move me away from the first step.

"There now," he said. "You and your furry friend had better rest too. Bring him up quietly after he has made a fast trip outside to attend to his business."

My shoulders relaxed. He didn't sound angry. Elise, followed by the priest and Meister Rojanski, passed close to me on the way up the stairs. When Father Stanislawski's cassock brushed my leg, I shuddered.

Before Lisa scurried away I managed to whisper, "Can't you just come without anyone knowing? You can have my bed. I'll sleep on the chaise lounge."

She shook her head and was gone. By the time Deu was finished and we were back inside everyone had disappeared. I had no idea which of the many rooms on that corridor housed my Meister and which contained the ogre in the black cassock. Too aware there was only one bathroom, I wondered, as the door was always closed, how I could ever bring myself to knock on it to see if it was occupied. My own door posed even more of a problem. There was no key in its lock and I could imagine the questions if I should ask for one. What excuse could I give? With my dog beside me, I worried myself to sleep.

When the door opened softly, I was awake at once. Deu, already up, was ready to bark or wag depending on who's face came around the door jamb. It was Lisa. She closed the door behind her, patted Deu's head, and came to sit beside me on the edge of the bed.

"Rodczeck says we are not nursemaids and that we may not sleep up here. He says you are a big girl now, you have the dog and that's all you should need. He was very definite."

My heart lurched. "Oh, Lisa. You didn't tell him did you? Please say you didn't."

"Of course I didn't. It was a little amusing though. He also said that you had the priest to protect you. Imagine. I'm afraid I did giggle at that and he wanted to know what was so funny."

"But you still didn't tell."

"No. I said I wouldn't and I didn't. I really wanted to, though. If I had told him he'd have slept up here in the hall himself. He and his mother are very fond of you. We all are, of course."

I reached out to hug her. "Thank you."

She jumped up and backed a step away.

"Why did that frighten you? I thought you liked me," I asked, bewildered.

"I do. Oh, I do, but you will soon be old enough for me to call you Fraulein and you must accept that such familiarity, even now, is not seemly."

"We can't be friends? In America we could be friends."

"In Poland we can only be sort of friends. If we were younger, we could play together while, perhaps, my mother was working for your mother. Still, we couldn't eat together or share a room together or even go to school together."

"Why not?"

"It's just something that is, that's all. Here." She held out her hand. "I brought you a key. Tonight lock your door and put this chair in front of it. Let me show you how." She tiptoed across the floor with the small straight-backed dressing table chair, slipped the back under the door handle, and pronounced the arrangement able to withstand the greatest of pressures.

She whispered in satisfaction, "No one can get to you. Of course, it won't keep the spirits out. Nothing keeps them out, you know."

The last sentence chilled me. On summer nights my father loved to scare the neighborhood kids while they clustered around him in the dark of our front porch. His tales were terrifyingly fun and exciting as long as we were in a crowd. Alone in an ancient mansion, it was different. Mother and Grammie had never managed to completely reassure me that ghosts did not exist.

"Do you think Friedenau is haunted?" I asked her.

"I'm sure it must be. We've have never heard of a spirit here. . . .but they do keep all those bodies out there in that Chapel. Their souls must be hovering around someplace. Anyway, I have no more time to talk about that. Some other time. I'm sorry I can't stay up here with you, tonight, but now you'll be safe with the key, your chair, and your dog."

She was so off-hand about the mysterious and frightening things called ghosts. I told myself Europe was an old civilization and they had lived with them much longer than we in the United States. Well, if they had survived all of these years, I could too. Except . . . while she had left me protected from the humans on my floor, what barricade did I have to keep a ghost from invading my room?

Chapter 18

When the door handle turned softly during the night, I must have been sleeping lightly because I heard it at once. At Deu's growl, I covered my head. Although the one tentative 'rrrfff' wasn't repeated, breathlessly I waited for the handle to rattle again. Still, what if the ghost hovered over me? Would it make a noise? Worse still, suppose the priest should be there?

The bed jiggled. Something cold and clammy probed around under the down-filled puff. It explored my face and neck before it clawed at the covers until I was exposed. When nothing else touched me, I opened my eyes. Deu's face was level with mine. No spirits shared our room. No humans either, but it was many shivering seconds before my heart stopped thundering and I could pull the quilt over both of us. Through the frosty windows, moonlight flooded the room. It was so bright I could read the clock without turning on a light. The snow had stopped, the clouds had passed, and it was Saturday. In a few hours Mother and Daddy would be here. All thoughts of priests and spooks were gone and, with the optimism of the young and my arms around Deu's warm body, I felt safe. My eyes didn't open again until the sun took over.

Standing barefoot on the cold floor to close the window, I scraped a peephole in the frost so the beauty of the day could shine through. Deu's tail wagged. "My goodness." I whispered to him. "Listen to that racket." Over the top of the lilac hedge I could see the ducks and geese flapping and stretching. A few waddled tentatively out where the water should be, but made protesting noises and grumbled to each other when they found it still frozen. Chickens, just released from their own houses, followed an old man with a pail of grain.

"Oh, Deu." I put my arms around his neck and hugged him to me. "Do you know that your human grandparents are coming? Isn't that exciting? You're going to love each other." His big, brown eyes

130

looked up at me in absolute trust. A wet, red-flannel tongue washed my face. Resisting a grimace, I reached for my clothes where Lisa had laid them out on the chaise lounge. My parents were coming and if they could get here from the station, Father Stanislawski would be able to leave. It was going to be a lovely day. Gathering my clothes, I marched down the hall unimpeded and knocked boldly on the bathroom door.

Across the hall, the priest opened his door. When he stepped out, I froze. Deu growled. With one hand on the bathroom door and the other on the dog's collar, I'm not even sure I breathed. Careful to avoid the dog, as if the bare boards might soil his shoes, the priest stayed on the carpet, but still came quite close. If he had touched me, I would have let Deu have him.

"Good Morning," he smirked as he passed. The odor was strong and his discolored teeth showed in a kind of evil leer. I didn't answer. He swaggered down the hall without looking back.

Inside the warm bathroom, I barricaded the door with the small chair and turned the key as well. When the trembling stopped, I hurried. Deu needed to get outside. But the entire time my eyes were on the door.

The awful man wasn't in the hall when we left, but we would surely meet in the dining room. If we were the only two awake, Rodczeck might seat us together. How could he avoid it?

After delivering the pup to Fraulein Goethe, I reluctantly opened the dining-room door. Everyone except Oma was at the breakfast table. My enemy and I were well separated. Once I said good morning, answered all questions about the state of Deu's and my night, and expressed my joy over my parents' expected arrival, the warm semmeln and cocoa went down in silence. Later, from the window in my room, I saw Zarrotti leave to drive Meister Rojanski and Father Stanislawski to the train that would be bringing Mother and Daddy to Friedenau. With all my heart, I hoped the four wouldn't meet. If they did, I prayed there would be no unpleasantness.

Herr Rojanski had left me with explicit instructions as to when, how and how long to do my exercises and I was hard at it when the ballroom doors framed Mother and Daddy like a portrait. Hurling myself into their open arms, I nearly knocked them down. Deu, following my lead, jumped on us all.

"Oh, my baby," Mother had tears in her voice when she could take a breath. "I've missed you so." Her hat was askew. Dad's was crushed under Deu's paws. They were both thoroughly dog-disheveled, but had never looked more beautiful.

"I've been lonesome for you too." Daddy returned the extra hug I gave him. "I thought the week would never pass. Why, is it when you're waiting for something like today or Christmas, time goes by so slowly?" He struggled to get his homberg out from under the dog. "C'mon, let's go down. We haven't even said hello to our hosts yet." He patted the dog and took my hand as he started for the door. "I assume this is your birthday gift from the Meister?" Deu, ready to go wherever there might be more fun and activity, frisked around him.

I pulled away. "You two go on ahead. I have to change my slippers. It won't take me long."

Mother hung back too. "I'll wait for Caro, Jon." She waved him away and gave him that look that meant she had something private to talk about.

My mind leapt immediately to the priest and I feared maybe there had been an altercation at the station after all. Once Daddy was gone, Mother put her arms around me again and brushed her cheek against my hair.

"When we got off the train and saw that Priest getting on," she said. "We prayed he hadn't been here at Friedenau. He wasn't, was he?" Her voice was insistent and almost accusatory as she straightened up.

"Yes, he was here, but he was afraid of the dog and Deu didn't like him either so I didn't see much of him." What did she think he might have done? "I kept my door locked and had Deu inside with me."

"Why was he here?"

"He came, he said, to see Ernst. They served in the Army at the same time. Also, to pay his respects to the Gnädige Frau. Because of the snow, they invited him to spend the night. To be truthful, I don't really know why he was here. He just was." My shoulders tensed and my face flamed with shame at the memory.

Mother didn't notice. She walked to the nearest mirror to take off her hat and fluff her hair. "Deu, is that what you've decided to name your puppy? What does it mean? It doesn't have a very pretty sound."

The dreaded conversation was over. My shoulders relaxed. While I finished changing to my shoes and putting a skirt over my leotard, I explained my choice of names for my pet. "If you don't like the name, we can change it." Disappointed I waited to see what she thought. Known for her good taste, I'd heard her funny little deprecating laugh when she and her friends discussed something of which they disapproved. I didn't want my dog made an object of ridicule.

It was a relief when she said, "Oh, no, darling child. He's your pup and now that you've explained it, I think it's a very appropriate name. He certainly is a beautiful young gentleman and he's obviously discriminating if he doesn't like that priest. I'll feel much safer about you now that he's your protector."

Anna, who had come back with Mother and Daddy, followed Viktor and the luggage down the hall. Eager to change the subject I walked over to say hello to her just as Deu bounded up the stairs and nearly bowled us both over.

"Ach, Liebchen." She was unable to do more than nod because of an armload of my parents' possessions. "Is this your present from the Meister Rojanski? He's beautiful." She regained her balance after Deu's assault. Without waiting for an answer, she disappeared into my parents' room.

 I traipsed after Mother down the stairs. Deu pushed ahead, panting and wagging at the bottom before we'd even descended the first step.

"I think we have a budding romance at home in Grudziadz," Mother said out of the blue. She gave a funny little laugh and I couldn't tell whether she was pleased or not. "Meier seems to spend a lot of time in the kitchen and he's always on hand to help Anna with the household chores when he isn't out at the Kasserne." She leaned toward me and spoke softly as if we were conspiring. I loved it when she made me feel like an equal. "Anna giggles a lot when he's around and blushes when your father teases her about him."

I could picture robust Anna grinning and twisting her toe into the carpet, but I wondered how Daddy made himself understood. He was no linguist and Anna's English couldn't have improved that much in a week. Mother must be kept busy translating, though her school German was barely adequate.

"How do they communicate?" I asked.

"She mainly titters and blushes. I manage to understand enough to

134

translate most of it for your father. I'm not sure it's always accurate, but they have to be satisfied. She's learning a bit of English too. You're missed in more ways than one."

It was hard to imagine sturdy Anna and spindly Meier in any kind of romantic attachment. Fairy tales always had beautiful, mistreated girls and handsome princes who saved them from lives of drudgery. Sturdy peasant-stock had never entered into it.

"Meier's always right there when Daddy teases her in case her feelings get hurt. But you know Anna. She takes teasing very well. She's quite cute about it. Do you remember the World's Heavyweight wrestler who was on the ship with us?"

Mr. Zabisco was a Polish giant of a man who had helped my father with the language while we were on the ship. They became friends. As gentle as he was forbidding-looking with his bald-head and bulging muscles, he spent hours telling me about Polish history and their customs. In a strangely graceful way, considering his great size, he had even taught me the Mazurka.

Mother's voice interrupted my thoughts. "Anyway, he's coming to Grudziadz and the posters all over town. 100 zlotys to anyone who will get in the ring with him. Anna thought that was a wonderful amount of money so your father asked her why she didn't volunteer. Poor Anna blushed. 'What, me with my paper muscles?' Proficient in the language or not, we understood." Mother stopped and leaned on the banister. "Daddy laughed so hard at her quaint way of putting things that even Meier smiled, though he tried to hide it. Anna was embarrassed."

"Do you think Meier likes her too?"

"Oh, yes. It's very obvious." The conversation ended as we reached the door to the sitting room, but I filed it away to think about later when I was alone. Even though they weren't a fairy tale couple, it was a romance.

"Of course you will come here for Christmas." Elise's voice was very assured as we opened the sitting-room door. Deu, who had been waiting by the door, naturally entered first.

Sitting around the table our hosts and my father had obviously been discussing the upcoming holiday.

"I'm sure we'd love to. If Jon can take that much time off." Mother crossed the floor and took her accustomed seat on the built-in sofa. I slid in beside her while Deu went immediately to Oma to put his paws and head in her lap. His tail never stopped wagging while she stroked his head and ears.

"Colonel Podhorski has suspended the school for the entire week starting on the 24th and continuing through New Year's Day." Daddy explained. "I'm sorry, Janice. In all the excitement of getting ready to come, I forgot to tell you." Then he turned again to Oma. "If you're sure you want us, we'll be here with bells on."

Everyone laughed except Oma who hadn't understood a word. While Elise translated, Ernst continued. "I trust you wear something more than just bells." He covered his eyes with one hand as if in shock. "After all we are going to a very fancy and elegant dinner party with bridge and dancing afterward at Baron von Pawel's. He is Kurt's father and the one responsible for Caro's ballet lessons."

Ernst turned to mother. "Ludwig entertains every year on December 24th. This is one party you shouldn't miss. It has always been the perfect start of the Christmas season except, of course, the day Ludwig was married to Atta."

Elise couldn't control herself and burst into Ernst's discourse. "Atta overdid everysing until it was cheapened. She was Hungarian," she added as if it were an explanation.

Ernst broke in again. "Even the castle, which has withstood several hundred years of onslaughts, couldn't withstand her determination. The old suits of armor that always stood guard over the grand staircase were relegated to the dungeon." Ernst paused for a breath.

Elise took over. "In zeir stead two life-sized electric Blackamoors sprayed zee guests wiz perfume as zey tried to get up to zee ballroom. People were coughing and wiping zeir eyes." She put her hand on Mother's knee and leaned forward as if the next weren't to be believed. "Ze walls were hung wiz gold lamæ and glitter. Ze tables looked like over-decorated birtzday cakes and ze servants were all dressed up in ridiculous wigs and livery. Zere was no sign of good taste during ze entire evening. Ze guests were shocked into silence."

Ernst wiped tears of laughter. "While everyone was eating the midnight supper, Atta tried to organize some kind of game with sexual overtones. Without fuss Ludwig stepped in front of her, thanked everyone for coming, and wished us all goodnight and a Frohes Weinachten. At the same time he and Gerhardt were ushering a screaming Atta from the room. The Ball was dramatically over."

"Sank God she left him and he divorced her before we ever had to go srough zat again." Oma, with Elise translating, was laughing so hard at the memory I could barely understand her.

"Who was Atta?" Mother asked when things had quieted down.

"Oh, I forgot you don't know zee von Pawel family history." Elise reached for a cigarette as she settled more comfortably in her chair. After Daddy lit it for her, she continued. "Atta was Ludwig's second wife. He married her after Gretchen died having Kurt. Our little girl was named for Gretti. We were zee dearest of friends even

137

zough she was older and already a great friend of Oma and Opa von Wechsler." She smiled at Oma. "Anyway, we sink Ludwig was just lonely and wanted companionship. He also needed a mother for Kurt. Well, his choice was, how do you say it in America, lousy. Atta would have been a better show-girl zan a companion and muzzer." She puffed on her cigarette. "Ze marriage lasted a very short time after she found out Ludwig had a feudal castle, lots of land and peasants, but very little money. We've never known whezer she was found out or left of her own accord. Maybe boz."

"Who brought up Kurt then?" Mother, though she loved good gossip, was more interested in the present than the past.

Oma answered and Ernst interpreted. "There was a succession of nurses, governess and tutors. Until last year, that is, when the Polish Army required he and Dieter serve their two years. When they finish in May, I expect they will both go away to the University at Heidelberg."

I listened avidly to this analysis of the von Pawel family. My heart cried for the poor little boy who had to grow up without a loving mother. From then on I would see only good in him and it was easy to make excuses for what I considered very tiny flaws.

When Elise jumped into the conversation I snuggled up against Mum.

"Actually, Kurt was a handful, wasn't he Oma? His friendship wiz Dieter caused us all a lot of worry at one time."

My back stiffened in protest and I wondered how anyone could find fault with a young boy who had so little.

"Oh, yes." Oma answered her. "Particularly when the boys grew to adolescence. Kurt was wild and Dieter thought he should be allowed the same freedoms. Fortunately, Vatti was still alive and could control Dieter. I spent many sleepless nights when they were out riding around on those motorcycles chasing the wrong kind of girls. I hope we've passed the worst of it." She was quiet for a minute.

"It would really be a help if the Polish Army demanded more of Kurt," she went on. "He could use a little stiff discipline. We've tried to give him some standards, but Ludwig hasn't been bothered much by the necessity of being a father to the boy. Kurt, while he can be polite and charming when he sees a requirement for manners, seldom listens to his father. I'm not even sure their paths cross that often."

They were being critical of Kurt and I wanted to change the subject. "Does the castle have a moat?" I interrupted.

Everyone looked at me. "Don't be rude Carole," Daddy said."The Gnädige Frau was telling us about Kurt's family."

"I don't mean to be rude. I apologize, but I do want to know more about the castle. After all, I'm not going to get to see it."

"Of course the child is interested in Ostatetcznie." Oma looked at me with compassion and understanding. "What is this moat you wish to know about?"

"It's a place around a castle. . . ." I began in German.

Daddy jumped in. "It's a wide ditch filled with water that surrounds a fortification for protection . . ."

I translated. "Ach, eine Festungsgraben."

Ernst caught on at once and turned to his mother in explanation, then said to me in English, "No, Caro, there is no moat there. I don't know if there ever was one."

"There was." Oma leaned back in her chair. "Ludwig's brother drowned in it when he was but two, before Ludwig was even born. The old Baron had it filled in. "Her large bosom rose and fell in a sigh. "It hasn't been there for sixty or seventy years and I doubt many in their village would even remember it." Oma smiled as if those memories of old were pleasant, though how the death of a baby could have been that, I didn't understand.

"Is there still a drawbridge?" I asked. While my German was pretty good, these were words I hadn't met.

Ernst figured out the logical answer.

"Zugbrücke." He said emphatically. "Sie meint eine Zugbrücke."

I'd learned two new words. Everyone except my parents said "Ahhh."

Oma frowned as she thought, "I don't believe there's a Zugbrucke now, is there Ernst?"

"There'd be no reason to have one." He took a cigarette from the silver box and explained the prior bit of conversation to Mother and Daddy.

"Where is Dieter," I asked.

"He's gone to pick up his girl for a party the young people are going to." His girl, Sybilla, will be spending the week-end here."

I was crushed. I'd never imagined Dieter having a girl and before I could recover came the second blow. Elise was saying that Kurt and his girl were going to stop by so they could all meet the Americans. I hoped the girls would be fat and unattractive like the daughters of a wicked step-mother. Still it didn't matter that they'd be ugly and ill-bred. Like Cinderella, I'd be left at home.

Dieter and Sybilla didn't come in until it was almost time for tea. Once I met dainty, blonde Sybilla, I was captivated. She was no child of a wicked step-mother and I didn't care.

"You have to be Carole," she said in perfect English when the introductions came around to me. "Dieter has told me all about you." She turned to him. "You were right. She does have beautiful hair. I'm jealous," she said to me. "Wouldn't you like to trade your hair for mine?"

I didn't know how to answer her and fortunately, Deu bounced in to make his own introductions before I had to.

"Ach," she said and knelt on the floor to take the dog's wriggling body in her arms. "What a beautiful puppy. When did you get him?" She looked up at Ernst.

"He belongs to Carole," Ernst smiled. "He was a birthday present from her Ballet Meister."

Sybilla stood up when Deu ran over to greet Oma. "Now I have two reasons to be jealous---no, really three. You have hair like the sunrise. You take ballet lessons, which I have always wanted to do, and you own the dog of my dreams. And, how old were you on this birthday?"

I told her I was twelve, wishing I could have said at least eighteen.

She bent a little, put an arm around my shoulder, looked me in the eye and said as if she had read my thoughts. "Age doesn't make any difference. I predict we shall be great friends."

Accepting the words as gospel, I was instantly her disciple. Once she and Dieter were dressed, they appeared again in the sitting room. Sybilla floated in buttercup-yellow chiffon and Dieter, in tails, was as handsome as any man could be. At least that was what I thought until the doors opened again. Kurt, framed in the doorway like a portrait, was lighting a cigarette. In perfectly tailored tails, he smiled and snapped the lighter shut. With a casual inhalation, he blew the smoke into the air. Even I recognized that he was quite aware of his affect and that his smile exuded superiority. Tall, lean, with dark hair and eyes that could have mesmerized Merlin, in an instant he took permanent hold of my romantic heart.

His date was pretty enough. But overwhelmed by my own feelings, I hardly noticed her. By the same token, she barely acknowledged me. Before the four of them left, Ernst announced that he thought the next weekend would be the perfect day to go in search of a Christmas tree. Everyone except Oma and Kurt agreed. Oma said she'd hunted a lot of Christmas trees in her day and she hoped we would let her stay at home where it was warm and dry. It was hard for me to understand how anyone would prefer a boring day at home to the hunt for a perfect Christmas tree, but I didn't say so. Kurt said he too would have to miss the fun because he had a previous date. It took some of the edge from my excitement, but I would have to be alone before I could sort my thoughts.

Much later, with my thoughts still jumbled, loud voices outside my bedroom door awakened me. Deu growled once.

"Ilse," Elise's voice was firm and disapproving. "I shall have to tell your mother that you were found behaving in a very unladylike way with Kurt in the backseat of his car. Whatever made you do such a thing?"

"I had too much champagne. Besides, it's my business not yours and Mother won't care anyway."

"Whether or not she cares doesn't matter to me. When you are in my home, you will abide by our standards."

I could almost see Kurt's date tossing her long, mousy-blond hair in defiance. My mother would have said "true to type." Even at my age I thought I knew that "ladies" didn't drink too much. I had guessed that Ilse was no lady and here was the proof. Kurt could only love a lady and I intended to be the one. While I thought this over, Ilse slammed her door and, I hoped, eradicated herself from Kurt's life and mine. I no longer considered her a rival.

Chapter 19

Another glorious morning, crisp and cold with a sky unbroken by clouds, it seemed as though God had drawn a heavenly, blue paintbrush from horizon to horizon and had covered the earth beneath with a white drop cloth to catch the drips. I asked Deu what he thought as we looked through the window, but he was too anxious to get out into it all to answer with more than a tail wag. After breakfast I went to the ballroom to practice as I had promised, but it was hard to keep my mind on exercises. Even Deu was restless. When Mother and Daddy stopped in on their way downstairs, I asked Daddy to take him outdoors.

Mother sat down on one of the pink and gold chairs, "Jon, would you ask Rodczeck to bring me some coffee, please? I think I'd like to stay to watch for awhile."

Daddy agreed, stumbling over Deu who frolicked around his feet and nipped at his shoe laces. When they were gone, Mother wound the phonograph and put on a record of 'Wenn Die Elizabet Nicht So Schöne Beine Hät', a new tune from a musical that had opened in Berlin. "I thought it might be easier, since Herr Rojanski and his stick aren't here, if you had something to give you a little rhythm. What do the words mean?" she asked.

"If Elizabeth didn't have such beautiful legs," I translated as the German voice sang on.

"Now what's he saying?" Mother settled herself as she spoke.

"She'd be much happier with the new, longer dresses."

"It certainly rhymes better in German, doesn't it?"

"Yes. And it has a great beat for my exercises. I'm glad you brought that record." My feet flew to the lilting tune. It was faster than the

Maestro's stick, but I felt my muscles must be stronger because I had no trouble at all.

When the record ended, Mother put on another, but she didn't turn the machine on. "Caro, we need to have a little talk." She seemed to be embarrassed.

Her hesitancy to begin made me apprehensive. I knew I hadn't committed a crime or she would have used my full name, but I stood waiting with muscles tense.

"Darling," she finally began. "You're twelve years old now and we have to have a chat." She'd already said that. "What I mean is that when little girls start to become grown up there are changes in their bodies and . . ."

Here it comes, was my thought. The birds and the bees. A girl in Lexington, whose mother was about to present her with a new sister, had told Ginger and me how the bees pollinated the seeds and the birds spread them around everywhere. One seed got inside her mother and a baby was growing in her tummy. She would have to go to the hospital to get it out, Molly repeated. Ginger and I determined not to get too close to any birds and we already avoided bees.

When Mother hesitated, I broke in. "It's all right, Mums," I said proudly. "I already know all about the birds and the bees. Molly told Ginger and me before Emily was born.

"How did Molly know?" Mother asked.

"Her mother told her."

"Well then, we don't have to go through it all again, do we?" Mother's sigh was one of relief. "Do you have any questions about it?"

I shook my head.

"Then I guess I'll go down stairs and join the others." She stopped by the door. "One more thing . . . Everybody knows you have a young girl's crush on Kurt. Don't let him touch you." She went out and the door closed.

What did she mean by 'everybody' and couldn't I even shake hands with him? After a while with no better understanding of her intent except that I was too young for a boy to touch me, I put another record on the gramophone and, with Kurt as an imaginary partner, tangoed around the ballroom. I thought it was all right to let him put his arms around me in my dreams. When the record ended, I spoke out loud to my reflection in one of the mirrors. "I wonder how old I will have to be to go to a real ball. Just imagine, balls and castles. Counts and Barons. Christmas trees and Dieter and Kurt and Sybilla and me. Oh, I do wish it could be tomorrow." My heart fluttered until I faced the present and Anna's face in the mirror. Her voice made me jump.

"Don't worry, Kleine, someday you will have everything you dream of, and when it comes you will be of just the right age," she said. She put her strong arms around me. Wrapped in her 'no nonsense' embrace I wondered if she ever had dreams like mine and almost laughed when I remembered her statement about her paper muscles.

Still, she must have had dreams of her own to understand mine so well. Though I might have chosen someone more romantic looking for her, I was happy she and Meier had found each other. I tightened my arms around her ample waist and gave her a hug. Here in the ballroom, as if she were embarrassed to have been caught in a soft moment, she untangled herself from my embrace.

"Your Mother says it is time for you to come downstairs. Lunch will be very soon and they are having a conversation she thinks you will enjoy." She crossed to the chair that held my clothes. "Schnell, schnell, here are your shoes and your skirt. Put them on while I pick up the music records." She busied herself straightening up the small gilt table. "Such a messy girl you are," she mumbled, smiling.

Dressed in record time, I was opening the sitting room door before Anna had time to pick up the leavings of my musical morning. The first words I heard were my father's.

"Caro will be beside herself with excitement. After all those fairy tales she's read and reread, to be invited to a real ball. I suppose she'll agitate for a long dress. Well, that's going too far, don't you think? After all, she's only eleven."

"I'm twelve, Daddy," I said as I raced across the room and slid onto the banquette beside Mother. "And that's almost the teens. Am I going with you to the von Pawel castle? Am I really invited? Oh, it's so thrilling. Isn't it thrilling, Mum? To think, I'm going to get to see the castle. I can hardly wait."

"Whoa, Lovey," Mother hugged me to her. "You are not invited to the Baron's dinner party. But Oma and Elise and Ernst are going to give a ball here in their very own ballroom. To that one, you are invited."

Oma smiled at me. "We decided, child, even though you weren't here to contribute to the conversation that we have been in mourning for Vatti long enough. We think a ball is the way to announce that we are ready to have some joy in our lives again. You will agree."

Since it had never occurred to me that they were still in mourning, I agreed. Not getting to see the castle was disappointing, but other things were going to happen and that was enough.

I must have sighed, though, because Daddy said, "Watch out there,

Carole. It appears to me, you have more than any little girl of twelve has a right to expect. Be satisfied with what you have."

"I am Daddy, I am. I guess I just needed to let out some of the excitement. I nearly can't hold it all."

Elise reached for my hand. "Not only zat," she said giving it a squeeze. "But one day zis next week you and I must go into Torun to do our Christmas shopping. Are you ready for zat? Do you have your list made?"

Before I could answer, Mother did. "Oh, I do hate to miss the fun of shopping with my little girl."

"Actually, we'll have to go tomorrow if we want to get the invitations to the ball mailed as nearly on time as possible. Could you stay an extra day or two, Janice? I could call Herr Rojanski tonight and if he will let Carole go one more day wizout a lesson, we could pick him up on our way home. We could get to Torun, shop, have lunch, shop some more and be home in time for tea." Elise stopped for a breath.

Without hesitation Mum said, "Just try to stop me."

"You'll have to go without me." Either Oma had understood the word Torun or she understood more English than she pretended. I had suspected it before and wondered why she wouldn't admit it. "I've already ordered all of my gifts from Berlin and I don't have to depend on the three stores in Torun. I'm surprised at you, Elise. I thought you'd have done all your shopping before this."

Looking up just in time, I caught Elise winking at Oma. She was going to Torun just for me. She answered her mother-in-law hastily. "I zought I was finished, but I have a bit more I have to do and besides we must get zose invitations."

"May I stay up for the supper," I pleaded, knowing from my fairy tales that the magic always came at midnight.

When Mother looked at Daddy who shrugged his shoulders and raised his out-stretched hands in a gesture that had always meant, 'it's all right with me.' I knew I'd won. Through it all I listened and wondered how I could survive until the magic night came. I could hardly tear myself away from the table to take Deu outside or to go to bed. When I did go, my dreams, waking or sleeping, were all of waltzing around the floor in Kurt's arms. Graciously I planned to relinquish the tango to the Baron who had taught it to me after all. In those dreams I whirled around in my white ankle socks and patent leather slippers. Maybe they'd let me have silk stockings. But what I wore hardly mattered. I was invited. I would be there.

Daddy went back to Grudziadz alone on Monday while Mother, Elise and I went to Torun. Elise said the Meister yelled at her when she called him.

"How do you expect even one with such talent to become a professional," he screamed. He was a bit mollified when she told him we'd pick him up on the way home so he wouldn't have to ride the train. That might keep him from being too much of a bear on Tuesday. Hard as it was, I gave up dancing around the room to practice my exercises so nothing could add to his fancied burdens.

Chapter 20

The excitement bubble came near to bursting when, while we were in Torun's largest department store, Mother and Elise steered me into the fabric department. There they helped me pick out a pattern with puffed sleeves, a rounded neckline finished with a tiny pleated ruffle and a wide blue satin sash. The pattern picture showed the pink dress reaching the floor with the same pleated ruffle at its hem. I would never be allowed to have it that long, but I did ask, "Is that for me and if it is could I, please, have it below my knees?"

"Um Gott es Willen, Kinde, you can't wear a short dress to a ball. No. Fraulein Goethe will make it just ze way it is in the picture. Don't you sink so Janice?" Elise was sympathetic. What else could Mother say but yes?

My dreams that night were disjointed and senseless. Sometimes I was running away from something on the edge of a moat so indistinct that one foot was almost always over the edge. At other times I was trying to get out of a dark, windowless room that stretched into infinity. Even there the moat still ran beside me, but I could no longer see it. I just knew it was there. To add to my terror I wore something long that tangled around my legs and made me move in slow motion. I had to keep running or something would catch me. When a horrible warm, wet thing hit me in my face, I screamed.

My eyes popped open to daylight. Deu's nose and slathering tongue were just approaching for another lick. It was several minutes before I could disconnect from the nightmare. When I did, I wondered from where it had come when I'd had such joy the day before. There was nothing in my life to parallel it. Surely, even with the moat and the long, tangling garment it could have nothing to do with the ball or my lovely new dress. It was just a bad dream.

Deu wriggled onto the bed beside me and we lay there until the aftermath of the dream had been exorcised by the morning sun. Only then could I take the coming wonders out of my memory to examine them. First, of course, came Christmas. Before we could have that, I had been told, we were to go into the forest and select a tree. Because I had never been on such an excursion and never had so many other wondrous things on my mind, I dwelt on it a very short time.

Christmas at Friedenau involved so many people that my hoarded weekly allowance had barely stretched enough. I brushed that aside too. I'd done all my shopping in Torun the day before, except for Mother's gift. I hadn't been able to get away from her long enough to select anything. Anyway, because I still had almost two weeks . . . and another allowance, it was only a fleeting worry. That brought me to what had replaced Christmas as the main event, the ball. This time my daydreams took me into the familiar ballroom where I saw myself reflected in the mirrors. I hoped I would look pretty, but would the pale pink taffeta they had selected make my hair, seem redder? Although the dress was going to be all I could wish, the mental picture of me in it worried me. The neckline made my neck look like a turkey's and it hung on me like a sack tied in the middle by the blue sash. Why, when yesterday had been so perfect, were my thoughts today so negative?

Although I complained about those preliminary exercises at the barre, I loved even those hours. My legs and body always responded to the rhythm of the stick. On the days when the pianist came and there was music, my whole body became weightless and the notes seemed to lift and move me with their rhythm like a carefree zephyr.

"Everything must be real," the Meister had told Elise when he insisted on hiring the young man from Torun. "A gramophone is something that is ersatz." Whatever provided the rhythm, dancing was like breathing for me . . . a very necessary part of me.

The days crept by. Kurt was there nearly every day after they left the Kaserne in Torun and their teasing was incessant. It was hard, sometimes, not to take offense at the intensity, but when I once complained mildly to Daddy he pointed out that, at least, they noticed me. Once, after a long day of plies, jetes and entre chats in the ballroom, Kurt offered me a ride on his motorcycle. I was ecstatic. My conscience heard Mother's voice forbidding both Dieter and me to "ever do such a thing again," but I rationalized What she had said. "Not with that demon" had meant Dieter. She said nothing about riding with Kurt and so I went willingly.

Thrilled to be sitting behind him, I was too shy to even grab his jacket, but when we turned out onto the slippery cobblestone road and the speed increased, without thought, I clung.   "Could we, please, slow down a little?" I shouted in his ear.

I felt him laugh and the speed increased. Like a fierce, infuriated beast, the machine roared and belched. We flew.

"Please, Kurt. Please slow down." We skidded across a patch of ice. My breath hung in my throat. As the skid continued, I grabbed his jacket tighter and felt him laugh again as the bike righted itself.

He yelled something, but the cold wind that stung my cheeks and forced tears from my eyes carried the words away. Our speed increased again. He turned his head to make sure I could hear him. "Now you'll see what fast really is," he shouted.

I closed my eyes in terror and buried my head between his shoulder blades as we accelerated toward an inevitable death. I wished I had listened to Mother. Just when we were about to hurtle into oblivion, the machine slowed a little. We made a reckless u-turn and skidded until my foot rested on the cobbles. The heavy machine pressed against my leg. Thoughts like 'what can I do with my life if I can no longer dance,' made me recognize the reason for Mother's orders. I wanted to be safely at home so I could tell her I understood.

Rodczeck stood waiting at the bottom of the steps. "The Gnadige Frau expects to speak with you before you go home," he spoke to Kurt.

"Good," Kurt was taking off his gloves. "I was planning to stay for dinner anyway." He swaggered up the steps.

Just inside, three furious women surrounded us both. Ignoring me, they each had a turn at Kurt who, because he was older and should have known better than to take a chance with my life, was the true culprit.

"There will be no dinner here for you tonight." Oma shook her finger under Kurt's nose as she finished her castigations. "If you ever want to be welcome here again, come like a gentleman in your automobile. Now go. I don't ever want to hear the sound of that awful machine on my property again." That last was a useless statement as both he and Dieter went back and forth to their military duties on motorcycles. But I knew when he had offered a laughing apology and gone home, I would have my turn. After Oma and Elise left us, I waited.

White-lipped Mother uttered only one statement. "You worried me." With that she burst into tears. My heart broke.

That was punishment enough to discourage disobeying her again. I understood that the reason for her anger was not that I had disobeyed her, but that she was so frightened.

"Are you going to tell Daddy? He'd be so disappointed in me."

"I don't see any reason to." She looked me in the eye. "After you've spent time in your room instead of skating on the pond in your free time, you'll remember. It's too bad Deu has to be punished as well when he's done nothing wrong, but sometimes the things we do

153

have far-reaching consequences and innocents are punished too. How do you suppose Daddy and I would feel if you'd been seriously hurt? Or killed? Think what the rest of our lives would have been like."

I couldn't imagine it but, while she cried in the knowledge of how it might have been, I cried in abject remorse. My punishment was small payment for the pain I had caused everyone. Still, it was in those hours, alone in my room, that I began to make excuses for Kurt. Soon I had exonerated him completely. Thank heaven Daddy wasn't to be called in as judge and jury. At least, when Fraulein Goethe continued work on my dress, they weren't going to deny me important things like the ball, but no one had mentioned hunting the Christmas tree.

During the night we had a snow dusting and before dawn the sun was out sprinkling diamonds on its surface. Zarrotti and I went in the sleigh to pick up Daddy from the station. On the way, he and I had our first real chat.

"Do you have any children, Zarrotti?"

He smiled at me through his heavy beard and handlebar moustache. "Five. All grown now."

"Do they live here at Friedenau?"

"Some do, but the two boys are in the Polish Army. Wolfie is in Krakow and Ziggie is in Zuppot up on the Baltic Sea."

"I know where Zuppot is," I spoke up, delighted that I could contribute my knowledge. "We spent the night there when we were coming back from Hel. I remember they sold such beautiful pieces made of the amber that comes from the Baltic Sea. Did you know that sometimes there are even petrified bugs inside the amber?"

He said he knew. "Krakow is nice too. It is in the mountains. Both boys are very happy."

"Your other three children must be girls and they must all live here. Am I right?"

He grinned broadly. "You know them all. Lisa, Ida, and Anna are my daughters. Does that surprise you that I could have three such pretty daughters?"

I wasn't surprised they were pretty, only that I hadn't known Zarrotti was their father. I wondered how I could find out who his wife was without being rude. He saved me the trouble.

"Their Mother died of lung disease, four years ago. She was a wonderful woman." He turned the car into the little station just as the train pulled in. "Her name was Lisa too."

Daddy hardly had one foot on the platform when I began to pour out the story of the chauffeur's family. "Whoa, now. Don't I even get a hug before I have to digest the lineage of every soul at Friedenau?"

I hugged him, but hardly stopped talking on the way home. I had so much to tell him about going to hunt for a Christmas tree, Christmas itself and, most of all, the plans for the ball.

"You have had a busy and exciting week, I can tell. You must be exhausted thinking about it. I am just listening to it. I think I'll go back to Grudziadz and hide until after Christmas."

I was stunned at his reaction until I saw the twinkle in his eye and the uncontrollable twitch around his mouth. "Darn you, Daddy. You're making fun of me again."

Chapter 21

The two passenger sleighs, followed by the long wagon sleigh, slipped quietly into the trees. All of the occupants, lulled by the silence and beauty of God's green cathedral, rode in companionable silence.

"Tannenbaum. O Tannenbaum." Ernst's baritone voice erupted so suddenly in loud and boisterous song it shattered the peace of the dense forest. Startled winter birds screeched and flew. Globs of snow plopped from laden tree limbs with muted oomphs and I'm sure the faint sounds of hooves were those of fleeing deer. The horses broke into a trot while the stunned humans remained dumb.

As soon as reason returned, even the two men in the wagon-sleigh sang. Their voices, deep and strong, gave substance to the impromptu choir. "Wie treu sind deiner Blätter," rang through the woods. Mother and Daddy rode in the lead sleigh with Ernst and Elise. Zarrotti drove two plump gray horses named Tristan and Isolde. As if aware of their operatic heritage, the horses shook their heads and jingled their harness bells. The two who pulled us, Georg and Busso, though not gifted with such musical names, jingled their bells as well.

"Carole must ride with us, mustn't she, Dieter?" Sybilla had insisted when seats were being portioned out between the two sleighs. When I hesitated, Dieter shoved me roughly into the smaller of the two. Without a word, he helped Sybilla in next to me and slid in on the other side of her. He looked grumpy, but once we were all wedged together on the narrow seat and covered with the fur robe, his expression became one of satisfaction as he took the reins. I couldn't imagine what had caused the change, though it was welcome.

In the forest where the light was dim, I saw Dieter reach under the robe to take Sybilla's mittened hand. He brought it out from under

156

the fur, carefully removed her mitten, stuffed it into his own pocket and returned the two clasped hands to their hiding place. Sybilla smiled. As naive as I was, I thought that holding hands meant they were almost engaged. There was a small flash of envy in my heart and then a twinge of discomfort when I thought I might be the odd-man-out. As if she recognized my feelings, Sybilla reached over under the bear skin and covered my mittens with her free one.

"Halt," Ernst ordered loudly. The drivers pulled on their reins and everything came to a stop. "Look in there." He pointed to a small clearing in the woods where a full and symmetrical fir dominated the surrounding trees with its beauty.

"A little too tall?" Daddy asked.

"If we choose it, we'll take it home and the boys will cut it to the proper height. The rest can become firewood." Ernst jumped out of the sleigh. Everyone except Elise and Mother followed.

"Aren't you coming?" I turned to them before I floundered through the deep snow behind Ernst, Daddy, and the two men with the axes.

"We can see just fine from here." Elise laughed. "Ernst and Dieter wouldn't listen to us anyway. We'll just sit here quietly and wait for tea."

Although I had seen the basket and the samovar on the floor of the sleigh beside Zarrotti's feet, in my excitement I hadn't made a connection. A picnic in the snow added another special quality to the day. Behind me Dieter and Sybilla didn't give me much time to contemplate this development. Dieter pushed on my back, shooing me in front of them.

"Come on, or you'll miss getting to vote on the tree," he said. "That will mean you can't have any Christmas."

"What do you mean, I can't have Christmas? Of course I can."

Sybilla nudged Dieter with her elbow. "Stop teasing, Dieter. You know she can have Christmas. Everyone can have Christmas."

"Well, maybe she can but, she can't have it under this tree unless she votes for it. That's the way it is in America. If you don't vote, you don't get what you want. Isn't that right, Carole?" He looked at me.

"Perhaps, but we're not in America and Elise will let me have Christmas under this tree or any other tree. Besides, I'm not so dumb. I know when you're teasing. Hurry up or you won't get to vote either."

By then we were at the foot of the perfect tree. When I walked around it and looked up, I thought what a tragedy it would be to take it away from all of its friends and relatives in the forest. Everyone else voted for cutting it, but no one saw that, alone on the other side of the tree, I didn't cast a vote. The axes made their first cut. The tree trembled and gave a soft groan. I had never seen a tree cut before nor had I known that it would react when it happened. I wanted no one to notice the unexpected tears that stopped just short of overflowing. Alone, I floundered back to the sleigh where Zarrotti was starting to serve the tea to Mother and Elise. The sounds of the murderous axes rang through the forest.

"Stop hurting it." I wanted to scream. And even though Frau Kieck hadn't forgotten my hot chocolate, I couldn't swallow it nor could I swallow one bite of cake.

Mother, knowing how I tended to ascribe feelings to even a lowly pea left alone on a plate, guessed my thoughts. "Don't you think that tree is going to be proud to stand in the beautiful ballroom all decorated, adorned and admired?" she asked. Everyone was gathered around the sleigh with the samovar in it. "What honor it will feel as it sees itself reproduced over and over in the mirrors. Why, it will be as if it's reflected forever into eternity. Isn't that wonderful, Carole? All the trees around must be very envious, don't you think?"

Looking around quickly I nodded, but only Dieter had his mouth open to speak. Sybilla must have pinched him because he shut his mouth and looked at her quizzically.

She smiled at Mother. "What a glorious thought. I've been worrying about it going so far away from its family. Thank you for giving this story a happy ending."

I took a piece of cake.

The peasant's houses at Friedenau all had oil lamps shining through their windows as we drove through the tiny village. It gave me a cozy feeling to see the warm glow reflected on the snow outside. Smoke curled from the chimneys and scented the crisp air. It seemed to wrap around us in affection. Maybe it was because I felt so fortunate to be a part of these formerly unknown rituals. As if in a dream, I gathered this moment into myself to remember for the rest of my life. The village children were skating on the duck pond near the road and waved as we jingled by. I wondered if I might be allowed to play with them someday. I suggested it to Dieter.

"That would be unseemly," he growled. "You're better than they are, and besides they wouldn't want to play with you."

I looked at Sybilla. "What makes me better than they are?"

"It's hard to explain." She gave my hand a squeeze. "Believe me, it just wouldn't work very well. They, as well as you, would be uncomfortable. I'll tell you what. I have a cousin almost your age and one day, when you're not having a ballet lesson, we'll bring her over to play with you or maybe you can come to us. Would that be all right?"

Grateful to her, but still not understanding, I nodded. I would ask Mother what made me better. I was sure she could explain it.

When we arrived home, Oma was resting so the adults didn't stop in the sitting room. After they gave up their hats and coats, they went right upstairs to rest. Since dinner was usually around nine and it was only six, Deu, Kitty, Menelein and I went back outside under the stars. I was searching for that euphoric feeling that could wrap me in dreams. It seemed that kind of magical night. The feeling came, but not in the same way.

I heard the horses snuffling and chomping on their hay as I passed the stables. The fowl, in a structure of their own, chittered, clacked and peeped as they pushed and shoved for more and better room on the perches. The sheep barn was nearly silent except for an occasional soft baa when one of them had something to say. The cows were far away across the road, but they, too, would be lying on their bed of hay chewing contentedly. Even the three dogs stayed sedately beside me as the snow crunched under our feet. These clear, crisp, feelings of this day were etched in my memory. I wanted never to forget. Very few American twelve-year olds would have the chance to live this enchanted life. Mother had once reminded me how very lucky I was. Standing with the mansion cradled in the snow and with the sparkling sky above me and the comforting smells and sounds of contented animals around me, I raised my arms to embrace my world and said a very heartfelt "thank you."

That wonderful feeling of euphoria stayed with me as I watched the tree installed in the ballroom, then helped with the decorations. It presided over the very center of the room. Every one of the eight mirrors threw its reflection back and forth into infinity.

At last it was Christmas Eve and time for the party at Ostatetcznie.

Dieter and Sybilla came down the stairs while I was playing solitaire in the sitting room. Men in penguin suits, as Daddy called their formal tails, all looked alike so I gave Dieter only a glance, but Sybilla was even lovelier in pale blue than she had been in yellow. As she pirouetted and bowed gracefully to me, the rhinestones in her hair sparkled and my enchantment grew. One by one the household filtered in, my own mother coming last. She dominated the room like an empress. Her simple dress of black velvet was adorned with my great-grandmother's pearls. They hung in the low, rounded neckline, paying obeisance to her beauty. The dangling pearl earrings framed her face and trembled as she moved her head. She outshone the jewels and everyone else. All I could say was, "I'm so proud of you." It was a phrase she had said to me so many times.

She smiled and pulled me to her for a kiss. "And you are so beautiful," she said in return. I knew I wasn't beautiful, though people did remark on my hair, but she never neglected to reassure me. "Puppies and kittens are cute when they're young, but they grow into their beauty as adults. People do that too. Don't worry, Pet, you'll be a beauty when the time comes for it."

While they rushed into hats, coats, capes, muffs, and galoshes, I heard Elise speak to Mother. "I hope you remembered to wear your long underwear under zat stunning dress. Ostatetcznie can be very cold in spite of zee huge fireplaces."

Mother laughed. "I suspected that. I'm very warmly dressed where it doesn't show."

"Where's Kurt?" I asked. I had expected him to bring his date to Friedenau as he had the last time.

"His date will go directly to Ostatetcznie wiz her parents. After ze party he will bring her back here for the rest of the weekend. Since his home is inhabited by nothing but men you know, she couldn't very well stay zere, could she?" Elise stepped out into the snow before I had to answer.

"Goodnight, Lovey." My handsome Daddy gave me a kiss on the forehead before he helped Mother down the steps. The two cars started off, chains clanking. I waved until they were out of sight and Rodczeck pulled me inside the hall.

"Your dinner will be ready as soon as I bring it up from the kitchen, Kleine," he said. "Wash your hands and then go into the dining room. I'll be right there." He started down the stairs to the kitchen.

"Rodczeck," I called after him. "Couldn't I come down and eat with you?"

"The Gnädige Frau would be very angry when she heard about it." He continued on. "You sit in your place at the table and I will come in a moment. But don't forget to wash."

Here it was again, the same incomprehensible thing. Why would Oma be angry? At home in Lexington, Lena, our cook, and I had often eaten together in the breakfast room when Mother and Daddy were out and she was even from another country, different customs, different skin. As I washed my hands in the little lavatory huddled under the stairs, I wondered if Oma would be upset to know I used the same cramped space the servants used.

"Don't you dare tell, Deu," I said to my constant companion. His tail wagged. He often stayed in the sitting room with only his head across an invisible line from the dining room when I went in to eat. Alone, in my usual spot facing an endless length of table and a wall of portraits, I wished I could have his protection beside me. The room was dim with only one candelabra at my end of the table and the lights under the portraits of Count von Wechsler, his father, and his grandfather on the wall at the far end. The lights, small as they were, made the paintings the dominant feature of the room and I couldn't take my eyes from the man whose body was in the closed casket in the chapel.

One day, after gathering some wild flowers, Lisa and I had decided to put them on the Count's coffin. Once we'd tiptoed inside the chapel, I saw steps going down. Courageous because there were two of us and we had Deu, I said to poor Lisa, "Let's see what's down there."

"Oh, no, Carole. Rodczeck says there are only more dead people down there. I don't think it would be safe. Their spirits might get out and into us." She tried to pull me away from the steep steps.

"But it's day time. They can't come out till dark. Let's just peek."

"Well. . . . ."

She didn't get to finish before I pulled her with me. We were only halfway down when we saw the generations of von Wechsler's coffins, scattered helter-skelter on the earthen floor under the chapel. It sent us stumbling back up and out of the building. As we passed the Count's casket, I was sure I heard a moan. Now, staring at his painted face, I thought the old gentleman would have his chance to punish me. I was relieved when Rodczeck came with my dinner, though he didn't stay. The Count and I stared at each other. When I moved the candelabra in hopes of distracting him, his eyes followed me. When I sat down again, his frown seemed to have deepened. He looked angry. The candles flickered and the shadows grew closer. The man in the frame moved. Gripping my knife tighter, I slid my chair back a little. My eyes never left the painted face. My hands shook. The eyes continued to bore into me while the frown became a real scowl. I was frozen. Suddenly he winked at me and I screamed and ran. The heavy chair fell over as I pushed past it on my way to the door.

Anna, Lisa and I collided as they raced from the sitting room while

Rodczeck burst in from the pantry. With the chandeliers fully lit, the portraits became just pictures. Deu put his paws on my shoulders to slather me with wet kisses.

"What happened?" The three of them asked.

When Anna pulled me into her strong arms, it was as normal, easy and safe as coming home.
"Tell Anna what frightened my Kleine." Her hand, roughened by years in the sugar beet fields, smoothed my hair back from my face. "Everything is all right now. Anna is here. Tell her what it was."

Ashamed to have been so silly, I blamed it on the big, dark room and some vague imagined noise. "Please let me eat in the sitting room," I begged. "I promise I won't spill or make a mess in there. This room is just too big for one person." I turned to Lisa. She would understand.

Before she had a chance to intercede for me, Rodczeck picked up my plate and motioned to everyone to follow. In single file we marched to the sitting room. Deu led the way. Anna and I were still there when Lisa burst in to tell us to come quickly.

Gypsies sang outside with a dancing bear. There was such a scramble to get my hat and coat I was ready to go without them. When we stepped out the door, the bear was twirling slowly on his hind legs. A young gypsy girl of about my age played a lilting tune on the concertina. As he lifted first one foot and then the other, I felt a terrible pity for this enormous, brown, beast. He could have killed any of us with one swipe of his huge paw, but harnessed and muzzled, he was tethered to a dark man with spangles on the hem of his jerkin and a red bandana over his black hair. Under his drooping mustache, he was extremely handsome in a swarthy way. When the concertina stopped the bear stopped.

The girl came up the steps, a small linen tablecloth in her hands, for sale. Even in the dim light that came from the windows of the house, I could see that the open cut work and embroidery was carefully and beautifully done. Sure it would be too expensive for me to buy for Mother's Christmas present, I was desperate enough to have Anna ask. The price was only five zlotys. Not only did I have that in my coat pocket, there were six so I gave her all I had.

"Anna, please tell them the extra zloty is for the bear, a treat. After all, he's the one who danced.

Chapter 22

Tiny putt-putt noises come from Countess Czeczelowa's lips as she exhales. My ramblings have put her to sleep. A tiny slit in the curtains shows me an inky-black sky without even a star for relief. I'm desperate to know what time it is. Moving quietly to her side, I try to read the watch hanging on her bosom, but its face is upside down. I reach carefully for the lovely, jeweled time-piece.

Her eyes pop open. "It's almost time for you to go down, Carole," she says.

We hug each other for only a moment, but as I remember the terrible things she has survived I feel some of her indominatble courage flow into my body. While she is pinning the extra binder under my sweater, I try to tell her what she has meant to my life, but she won't listen.

"If it becomes necessary, God forbid, just pass on to others in need what you found here. That's the only thanks I want. Now, Herzlein, it's just two o'clock," she interrupts. "You must go quickly and quietly. "God willing the Major will be waiting."

We exchange a final kiss, little more than a gesture in the air, then I am alone on the landing outside of her closed door. My cautious steps follow each other from the attic to the second floor. Stopping, I peer over the railing. Nothing. I listen. No sound. For all I know I can be dropping into the depths of hell and my body, stiff with apprehension, almost refuses to obey me. The thought that moves me on is that somewhere, at the end of this nightmare, are, I pray, Anna and my baby.

For a while, upstairs in the reliving of the past, Alex has become only a treasured dream. Now he is real again and I feel the terrible pain of his loss. My downward steps are more hurried. I pass the first floor and round the last landing. On the dim cobblestones of the sallyport no figure moves. Slowly, tread by tread, clutching the banister and straining to see even the slightest movement, I descend. Almost at the bottom, lights blind me, hands grab my arms and there is an unpleasant, but familiar, odor. Father Stanislawski stands grimacing. The flashlights reflect on the shiny black boots of the SS men beside him. They are the ones holding my arms.

"I knew the Lord God would grant me my revenge someday." The priest spits out, the spray hitting my face like a curse. I try to raise a hand to wipe the spittle away, but both arms are so tightly held I can only duck my chin. He laughs, his cigarette stained teeth darker than ever. I square my shoulders and raise my chin.

"God doesn't deal in evil," I say through clenched teeth. "Only Satan directs you."

One of the SS men jerks me around . "Don't speak that way to a priest, you American heathen." He hisses the words like a snake. Glaring at him, I can't help retching.
He takes it as a sign of defiance and pulls his gun. "Put handcuffs on her and take her out. We'll deal with her there."

Metzgar is already out there. His clothes are torn, both eyes are swollen almost shut, and blood runs down his face from a wound on his head. I want to cry, but won't give these Nazi vermin the satisfaction. We are bound together in pain, despair and silence as we wait . . . for what? Soon another SS trooper, followed by another, comes carrying a slight body in his arms.

"Herr Major," he stammers to an officer who is obviously the leader of this detail. "She did not answer the door and when we broke it down there was a shot . . . "

My beloved Countess. I had so recently drawn my warmth from that courageous body. Now I wish I could give it back to help her live again. But her last choice was, perhaps, the best way. With no hands free to touch her in love or even to cover my own face, I close my eyes and thank God that her generous soul has escaped. She is free. She has cheated them. These Nazis will have no more pleasure at her expense. Somehow I must let her daughters know that her end was of her own choosing although, in anguish, I accept the ultimate responsibility for her death.

I expect Kurt at any moment. If he is in this town, he will not resist the temptation to be a part of my degradation. Whether he takes me back to Ostatetcznie to torment me further or sends me to a concentration camp, I will have no chance at all. Under my breath I say "Goodbye my precious Alex. I guess we'll meet again in Heaven."

"What's that you say?" The SS man jerks me around to face him. In the street light I recognize him as a friend of Kurt's.

"Only a prayer for the Major and the Countess." I answer him politely, though my choice would have been a kick in the right spot to maim him for life.

"Don't worry about that Polish dog and the bitch." His short laugh is more like a grunt and suits his swine-like features. "They'll get their reward when they get to Hell." I hear a shot and Metzgar's body falls to the ground. "You see," the delight in the voice is obvious. "They're both already on their way. Let that be a lesson to all of the Resistance."

My prayer comes too late for Metzgar. I look at the SS man and wonder how a man, born to a civilized family, can become an animal, only because a madman wills it.

"You're lucky to be married to von Pawel" The pig-faced man rattles on. "I'll bet you'll get to go to that nice, pretty concentration camp over near Auschwitz. Treblinka, is that it's name? They'll do wonders for your beauty over there. No one will call you Aurora

after they shave your head." With his face close to mine, he reaches for my hair. "You're a pretty thing now, but not for long."

I had heard of Auschwitz and Treblinka from the Partisans. As resigned to my fate as I think I am, the mention of them still provokes fear. As jealous of his possessions as Kurt has always been, I can't believe he would allow even another SS colleague to behave as this one is behaving toward me. I jerk as far away as his hand in my hair will let me. It hurts. I might be going to die, but I will no longer be any man's plaything. And, oh, dear God. Please. Please don't let anything like this happen to Anna and my tiny Alexander. Oh, gracious and forgiving God, please don't punish my innocent baby for my mistakes.

The SS man in charge grabs another handful of my hair.

"Let go of me, du verücktes Nazi schwein," I yell loudly for the benefit of the other SS troopers within hearing. Knowing my insult will get back to Kurt, I wish I knew something more vicious than 'crazy Nazi pig.'

A command car drives up. Even in the near dark I recognize my husband's walk. As he comes toward us, I wonder how I could ever have thought of his stride as proud and commanding. It is nothing more than arrogant and haughty. He stops in front of me and takes my chin in one gloved hand. When he jerks my head, I feel my neck pop and a terrible pain shoots the length of my body.

"Throw the bitch on the train." Without even looking at me, he sentences me to die as coldly as he sentenced his father.

Perhaps I will be given time to make my peace with death, but, oh, dear God, I did so want to help my Alex grow up. My hatred is painful. How could I have loved him so and now be so filled with nothing but the deepest loathing? Being wrenched from one guard and handed off to another puts an end to my wondering. Kurt has

*heard of the insults. At once he begins assaulting the trooper who
pulled my hair. My husband may hate me, but in his mind I am still
his possession. No one touches anything of his without permission.
With the riding crop he always carries, he rains blows on the man
with no concern as to where. Too late the victim shields his face
with his arms. I can't help pitying him. His shirt tears . . . red welts
and blood show through. The other subordinates watch silently
and, at the end, when Kurt's anger, never abated is at least
satisfied, he marches back to his car without a word or glance at
me. I no longer exist for him. At least I have one thing to be
thankful for.*

*The bodies of Metzgar and my dear Countess are thrown onto a
farm wagon just like the one that carried Anna and Alex away.
Hoisted up, I am left to kneel next to them on the uneven flooring.
My shackled hands make it impossible to rearrange them so they
can be more comfortable. Even knowing that they are beyond
caring, it's strange how mentally disciplined we are. My head
hangs down as if in submission. Actually, I am praying. God has to
be still out there somewhere.*

*The freight train waits on the very track that brought me to
Grudziadz a lifetime ago. From Kurt's descriptions I know what
will happen to the pitiful people in those overcrowded boxcars. It
was when Kurt laughingly told of his father's last humiliation
before he was led into the gas chamber that any feeling for him
shriveled and drained away. It was the next day that Anna and I
began our work with the Partisans. Kurt had told our dinner guests
how, as Ludorf stood naked before him, his pitiful manliness
shrunken and wizened, he, Kurt, had laughed and held his father up
for ridicule in front of all the other prisoners and SS officers. He
would surely find a way to shame me as well.*

*Thrust into an overcrowded boxcar, because of my hair, I suppose,
I am recognized immediately. "Here is Aurora," someone says.
They all examine me. "Yes, it is our Aurora." Someone near me*

touches my arm. "Why are you here? Is your husband not with the SS?"

"But she worked with the Partisans," another voice, another hand on my arm. "She helped my brother get away. Thank you dear lady, I wish I could help you now."Questions come from every side. "Is that why you are here? Did you get caught? Why won't your husband save you? Why did you give up dancing?" The questions went on and on until at last someone says, "Tell us about your life in the ballet. Something beautiful to hold us together."

While I recognize one or two from having seen them backstage or in the ballet audiences, how different they look now that the stylish evening clothes and jewels are missing. Yet, breeding, kindness, and education cannot be erased even in this squalid boxcar. What is necessary now is the same thing I was privileged to give them in the theater. Entertainment, that will keep them from thinking of what they were, where they're going, and what their end will be. I'm grateful to have something to give.

Trying to get my thoughts back to those special times before Mother and Dad reluctantly went back to the United States without me is difficult. "I have already told a part of my story this evening," I say. Tears start again at the memory. My voice becomes nothing more than a squeak. At once understanding arms come around my shoulders and soft, sibilant noises meant to soothe ripple through the car. When my throat is clear, I try again. "Two people are dead tonight because of me."

"Not because of you, Aurora," a man's voice from the back of the rattling car is so soft I can hardly hear it. "Because of Adolf Schickelgruber. He alone is the criminal of all time." The voice is rough with hatred. I know the man is right and yet, I'm sure the guilt I feel truly belongs to me as well as to the Austrian paperhanger. I must try to help these people and maybe that will expiate some of my sin.

*With only a slight quaver, I begin where I left off. "There was a
Ball at Friedenau . . .*

Chapter 23

Christmas morning didn't start early because the Baron's Ball ended late. We'd hardly finished opening our gifts, when it was time for lunch. Everyone was delighted with their presents, especially Mother, but the coming ball, my pink dress and the possibility of being in Kurt's arms while we waltzed, far over-shadowed everything in my heart. I was sure I must be truly in love with Kurt because nothing, not even my dancing lessons, had replaced that picture in my reveries.

Overnight, with my help, gnomes had set up huge tables in the ballroom and filled them with gifts for the estate's peasants. Our beautiful tree with its hundreds of lighted candles glittering over and over in the ballroom mirrors would watch the holiday festivities with pride and benevolence. Viktor's duty for the day was to see that the candles didn't burn too close to the branches and to replace them before they did.

While Lisa had explained that on Christmas morning the peasants would be coming to receive their gifts, I had no idea what an impact that would have. The eager, but subdued peasants showed me a system that I, as a free American, found incomprehensible. Dressed in their Sunday-best dirndles, the people gathered outside in the cold. Even the excited children stood mute. When Rodczeck threw open the front doors, they filed in quietly, lining up the carpeted stairs to the ballroom where long tables had replaced gilt chairs. Stacks of warm winter underwear, shawls and heavy hand-knit sweaters covered some of the tables. For each child in addition to clothing there was a toy. At the last table, smaller than the others, the father of each family received an envelope from Ernst. Money, I had been told.

Oma sat smiling and nodding like a queen beside the exit door and spoke briefly to each person who curtsied or bowed to her as he or she left the room. I didn't know until later that these were the only

Christmas gifts many of them, no matter what age, would receive. The rapt look on the children's faces when they first saw the resplendent tree shamed me. How, when I had so much, could I have held the thought of a ball above the joy of giving at Christmas?

The peasants curtsied to Oma or bowed to Dieter as he handed out the long underwear and warm jackets for the men, and to Elise, handing out the shawls and sweaters to the women. Most embarrassing of all was their obeisance to me who, with Mother's assistance, was giving out the toys and candy. When one little boy refused to bow, his apologetic father escorted him quickly from the room without his toy. I remembered the day the same little boy had thrown a snowball with a rock in it through the fence at me. It was deflected, but I now understood why he hated me. Although I wanted to leave the room, it would have done no good. Like the boy, I was frozen in my position in life.

A male voice from the back of the boxcar interrupts,"If I had the space I would bow to you now." The cultured voice speaks in accented English. I can barely see him squashed in over by the sliding door. Bearing no resemblance to the boy who made the scene in the ballroom, he now appears to be a gentleman. "I wish to thank you," he says, "for the toy and candy Zarrotti brought from you. He also told me how kind you were and how hard you worked on your ballet studies to become someone special. It made me hate you more for those things that, as a child, I considered the privilege of your class. That hatred became envy as I grew older, but it made me work to be something other than what I seemed destined to be. I was successful. When, at last, I felt gratitude and understanding, I brought my wife to see you dance. Now, I thank you for the pleasure and joy your dancing has given to us. Above all, though it might have been unintentional on your part, thank you for lighting a spark. Perhaps you and I have both learned that one's position in life can be changed. Now, sadly, here we are as equals."

Standing on the other side of the swaying car the speaker has a tenuous hold on a wooden box nailed to the side near the locked door. As he sees me look at him, he smiles and tries to bow. The box breaks away and its contents scatter. A cold wind, streaming in through the cracks in the sides of the boxcar, blows the papers it contained. We all snatch and grab as they flutter around us. It takes time to get each paper to its proper owner, but dawn has come and we have a dim light filtering in with the wind.

They are as much of our life's history as the Nazis allow us. Mine says:
>"CvP; Number: 7694169
>Sex: female
>Verätor"

I am not a traitor and I also know what those numbers are. After they tattoo them on our arms and into our very souls, we will no longer have names. Have those who are pressed in here with me heard rumors of these spirit-robbing numbers? Do my numbers mean that 7694169 human beings have been annihilated? It is such a terrible secret that no one I know, except Kurt, has ever spoken of them. He found the papers amusing.

At the moment it's as if, by each holding our own paper close to our bodies, we will be allowed to remain human. Are these nearly blank sheets really all that is to be left of us? How will my baby ever know his mother? I wish I could cry, but the thought rises out of a crater too deep for tears. The boxcar is hushed. I make myself speak into the silence.

"Let me tell you about the ball."

With all the excitement, you can imagine that by the time the night finally came I was afraid I was going to be sick and wouldn't be able to go. Alone with me in my room, Anna assured me there was nothing wrong with me and I would be fine as soon as I had something to eat.

"Here, Kleine." She handed me a plate of delicate tea sandwiches. "Frau Kieck says these are the ones you didn't eat at tea time. If you don't eat them now, she's going to give them to you for breakfast. She also said what you just told me, 'If you don't eat you'll be too sick to go to the ball.' Then you won't have a chance to dance with Kurt."

I'm sure my mouth must have dropped open. "How do you know my feelings for Kurt when I like Dieter just as well?" Daddy would have called me an Alibi Ike.

"Um Gott es Willen, Kinde." You talk about him all the time. Do you think I don't notice? And I don't think you like Dieter just as well. He's more like a brother?" She analyzed my face for confirmation. "Well, I won't say anything to anyone else and maybe they won't notice. Although I don't see how they can help it if they listen to you."

Horrified, I was determined never to mention Kurt's name again. "Do you really think everybody knows?"

"So what does it matter if they do? You're a child and will have a thousand crushes before you are grown and married. They know that. They've been through it themselves. Time to put on this beautiful dress."

Knowing full well I was not merely a child and would never have anything as childish as a 'crush,' I finished the last sandwich before I raised my arms for the pink confection to slide over my head. Anna's revelation made me feel gawky and uncertain but, once the sash was tied and the pink slippers were on my feet, I began to feel better. She fastened the pearls Elise and Ernst had given me for Christmas and led me into the hall to let me look in the full-length pier glass. The reflection showed a girl, confident and lovely in her youth. No queen in diamonds and full regalia had ever been happier. The hall chandeliers highlighted her so the red hardly showed in her hair to disagree with the pink of the dress and bow. Looking at that girl, I admired her as if she were a total stranger, which she was.

Mother and Daddy were nearly dressed when I opened their door. "No grown up aliens allowed in this room." Daddy threw up his hands in amazement. "Darling. You look so lovely."

Mother spun around on her dressing table bench. "Oh, dear. Daddy's right. I can't bear to have my little girl grow up. You are truly going to be a beauty and we're going to be so proud. Come, let me just fix that bow. It's a bit lopsided."

Mother's thoughts and dreams for me seem to have entangled the present and future together. I wasn't sure whether she was pleased or not. I moved closer to her to have the bow in my hair fixed and it only took her a second to adjust it before she turned back to the mirror. When she and I looked in it together, I wished I were as beautiful as she was.

"Come on, Janice," Daddy, handsome in his dress-blue uniform, waited by the door. "You're gorgeous enough. Bring this young lady and let's go before we're late. She is going to do us proud."

Mother winked at me in the mirror. "Just hold your horses, Jonathon. I'll be ready when I'm ready and it will be in plenty of time. You scoot along now, dear one, and Daddy and I will see you in the ballroom."

I exited, hopefully like a princess.

By the tree in the center of the room, Viktor was lighting the last of the candles. The small orchestra, ranged around the piano, was tuning up. The sparkling, crystal chandeliers lit everything while each mirror captured the tableau. Reflected in there too, it was as if we were all waiting for the curtain to rise. I was awestruck.

Kurt's voice from below penetrated my reverie. "Well, isn't anyone going to greet us? Come down," he yelled up the stairs. "You have guests here."

Forgetting to behave in a manner befitting my appearance, I almost galloped to the stairs. Tripping on my skirt reminded me. Daintily I held it and trailed my other hand along the broad banister as I descended step by step with dignity. His reaction was all I could have wished.

"See what we have here," he said as if genuinely astounded. "A vision of beauty and grace."

My heart bounced up, flipped over, and left me weakened and flustered. Still, conditioned by my father not to let my emotions show, I smiled graciously and continued slowly down the stairs while Kurt watched.

"You've grown up overnight." He stepped forward as if to help me down the last step. If he touched me, I knew I would swoon. (They always did that in books.) Instead he drew his date forward to introduce us. While my heart settled, I stayed above them on the last step. His date was no girl with a big nose. This one was beautiful and very sophisticated.

He first turned to her and then to me. "This is the little American girl I've told you about," he said. "Carole I'd like you to know Gisella von Knopf. She lives on the estate next to Ostatetcznie. We've known each other since we were little."

The proprietary way in which she took his arm caused uncomfortable stirrings in my chest. They were clearly more to each other than friendly next-door neighbors. I forced a smile and put out my hand. She ignored it. Her off-handed, "Guten Abend," hardly acknowledged my existence.

"You're to go straight to the ballroom." I waved the ignored hand vaguely toward the upstairs.

Kurt resisted her pulling long enough to turn his head, shrug his shoulders and laugh. "You look very pretty and grown up, Kleine. So pretty, in fact, that I must do something about it so you won't collect any hearts other than mine." His hand darted out, snatched my hair-bow while the other hand tousled my hair. The very thing that had brought forth his compliments was destroyed.

As they passed me on the stairs, I stood horror-stricken. In that moment I hated him with my entire being. Tears stung my eyes before I turned to race behind them up the stairs toward help and comfort. Kurt's voice stopped me on the landing.

"Now we are back to our usual after-dinner game. You are a little girl again. This time, however, there is a difference. Before you get your ribbon back, I will claim my kiss."
But by the time I had wiped the tears and turned my head, they had disappeared.

For a twelve year-old girl that statement was the height of romance. I was torn between repairing the destruction and staying in an unfinished state. In the end, because for one night at least, I had outgrown the child in me, I went to find Anna in Mother's room. With more ribbon and a hairbrush, the damage was obliterated.

"Who did this?" Mother questioned.

"Kurt," I answered reluctantly.

"I shall have to speak to him. He has no right to tease you this way at your first big, grown-up party."

Anna hugged me to her and shook her head. "It's all right, Kindchen," she said. "Those tears have washed your eyes clean and they will sparkle more than ever.

Mother caught up my hair and pinned the new bow in place a little higher and more beautifully than before. When Daddy came in from the bathroom, she told him of Kurt's insult. Daddy looked grim and I knew he, too, would speak to Kurt. I was wretched knowing that they both would be hard on him for something I was sure was just a joke. I tried to tell them I had reacted badly. They ignored me and said Kurt was too old to be so cruel. Cruel? I thought that too strong a word.

Once I was by myself in the hall again and the door had closed, I leaned against the wall in misery. I wanted to climb into my bed to make this nightmare go away and yet, I was eager to see if Kurt meant what he said. I heard Elise and Ernst leave their room and start toward the ballroom. Without another thought, I hurried to join them.

Like Mother and Daddy, they were effusive in their praise. My heart rose though now it didn't seem to feel as weightless and fluttery as it had. I had heard the word euphoric a few days before and had recognized the feeling. I liked it and thought Christmas a very euphoric time of year as we three entered the ballroom together.

When the guests began arriving in a beautiful array of silks, satins, velvets and sparkling jewelry, there was no time to think about my own troubles. As at the dinner table, Dieter and I were last in the hierarchy and on the end of the receiving line. He introduced me and I curtsied to each guest. Many remarked on how pretty I looked. That required a smile, a Danke Schöen, and another curtsy. It also pumped up my fragile spirits. The child in me still lurked somewhere behind those mirrors, but in their reflection I thought I looked quite grown up and belonged.

The first tango brought the Baron. He bowed and took my hand to help me from the chair. He needn't have bothered. My knees had grown springs and I nearly knocked us both over when I bounced up. When everyone nearby smiled, I was a little embarrassed, but forgot all about it in my concentration as we started the tango.

"Are you enjoying your ballet lessons, Gnädige Fraulein?" My mentor asked while, in spite of the difference in our size, we glided smoothly around the floor. "Meister Rojanski tells me you have so much talent you will soon graduate to those special slippers ballerinas wear. What do you think of that?"

"Oh, your highness, did he really say that?" Flattered by his formal address to begin with and excited by his revelation, I stumbled. "Oops." From the way the Meister yelled at me in classs I thought I was the clumsiest pupil he'd ever had. Day after day as my feet followed the beat of that vicious stick, I had longed for a sign that I was doing well. The only positive indication was when I was allowed to leave the barre and we had real music. Then I sometimes felt light and free the way I had when I had danced in this ballroom alone before Herr Rojanski came.

"Yes, he did," my partner looked down on me. He stared at me for what seemed forever before he apparently came to a decision, nodded his head slightly, and continued. "He also told me he hopes to sit in the front row of the Opera House one day and watch you become the star Pavlova was. That's a very high compliment, young lady. If you continue to work hard, perhaps I will live long enough to see you reach that stardom."

I forgot where I was and who he was. In mid-step I stopped to throw my arms around his waist. With my face against his white silk vest I don't know how many grateful words poured out or even what they were. I just knew I had been handed a tremendous gift.

"I don't know how to thank you," I said finally when I had exhausted all my words.

"Well, Carole," he was chuckling. "You've certainly tried. The only thanks I really want, however, is your hard work and your success. Now the music has stopped, let us sit down."

Sure that I wouldn't be in Poland after another year, I asked him how he would know if I became successful.

"We'll worry about that when the time comes." He bowed to Oma and again to me before he left us.

One by one some of the older gentlemen at the ball steered me around the floor, but it was almost time for the midnight-supper before Dieter came near Oma and me. My excitement over the Baron's revelations alternated with Kurt's promise of a kiss, which seemed more likely and might come sooner. Besides, though he had seemed positive, what the Baron had said was probably stretching things. By the time Dieter appeared I had convinced myself that it was most likely an old man's fairy tale for a child.

"Well now, ravishing one," Dieter said with an elaborate bow as he took my hand to lead me to the floor, "You seem to be cutting quite a swathe. How does it feel to be almost grown up?"

"I really don't think I'll be all grown up until I'm thirteen, Dieter," I answered him. "But I certainly am having a wonderful time. Everyone has been so kind."

"Don't let it go to your head, Kleine. It's only because you're an American and a pretty one at that. Just go on being you. With that hair and those eyes, little sister, we'll have to sweep the young men away from the door."

"Thank you, Dieter." I smiled up at him. "That's the nicest thing anyone under seventy has said to me this evening."

"You deserve it." The music stopped. "I hope you don't mind when Kurt and I tease you." He looked down on me and I realized how much he had grown in the past year. A little taller than Kurt, he must be over six feet. His blond hair curled and one curl always fell over his forehead like Daddy's, which gave him a puckish look. I realized that I liked his looks. It felt nice to have a handsome brother.

"No, I don't mind. Only sometimes I think Kurt really likes to upset me."

"Don't let him. It's just his way." We reached Oma as Rodczeck announced supper. Oma took my hand and we led the way down the stairs to the dining room.

"Now you wait until all of the grown people have served themselves from the buffet before you serve yourself." Mother found me in line. "Sit right here, on this chair until it's time. After that, you must say goodnight to everyone and go to bed."

"Must I say goodnight to every single person?"

"I don't think that's necessary. Just to Oma to thank her for a lovely evening and to Ernst and Elise. "

When she started off to find Daddy, I ran after her. "Can't I even say good night to the Baron and to you and Daddy?"

"Of course you may and I'll come up to tuck you in."

I sat down on the chair. I hadn't seen Kurt and Gisella for a long time, but felt that they would pass me pretty soon. They'd be almost at the end of the line. I was used to the protocol by then. As another young couple, friends of Dieter and Sybilla's, were moving along the buffet table filling their plates. I couldn't help overhearing their conversation.

"I don't care," the girl said to her escort. "Even if they are drunk they have no business out there necking in Kurt's car. They deserve to be sent home."

"Well, they were, so you needn't worry."

"I don't blame Kurt, he's a man. But my mother says a lady can get as drunk as she likes, but she should always stay in the middle of the floor." She took a heaping spoonful of a horrible, fishy stuff called caviar. "My mother is always right," she continued defiantly. "I'm a little tipsy myself, but you wouldn't catch me out there in the cold in your clutches."

The young man laughed. "Now, you've spoiled my fun. Why couldn't I have figured that out? No more champagne for you young lady." Still laughing, he steered her on down the table.

I'd been hoping Kurt might ask me to dance, or try to collect on my ribbon or at least say hello. Now I knew why I hadn't seen him. He'd been banished like a naughty boy. I couldn't blame him for ruining my evening, it was too special for that. But I couldn't seem to get rid of the feeling of dissatisfaction. I had imagined what my first ball was going to be for such a long time and, in spite of the Baron's compliments and expectations, something in the evening had gone awry. I wondered what I should have done to make it the ball of my dreams. Where was the glass slipper?

Chapter 24

"Zis would be good for you to hear." Elise and Mother were in the hall when Deu and I came in from our morning walk. Elise spoke as Rodczeck took my coat. Dieter was already in the sitting room, standing stiffly in the middle of the floor. I recognized, immediately, what this was to be about, but didn't think Dieter and Sybilla had been drinking too much at the ball.

Mother pushed me ahead of her to the table and took her usual place on the settee. When she patted the cushion beside her, almost positive I had done nothing wrong, I tried not to be apprehensive. Still, it all seemed ominous.

"I would hope," Elise's tone challenged Dieter to dispute her words. "I would indeed hope that you would never insult your hosts as Kurt insulted us last evening." Elise stared at Dieter to see if her words had any affect.

His 'here-we- go-again' expression didn't change.

"Thank God his father was here to send him home," she continued. "Of course driving them there caused a hardship for both Zarrotti and Johann. They said the "betrunkenen" young people slept all the way home and they had a hard time getting Gisella out of the car when they arrived at her house. Kurt, fortunately, continued to sleep. What a mess they created for everyone." Elise stopped, her eyes on Dieter. "I do hope you would never behave in such an unseemly way."

"You know—" Dieter began.

"I'm so glad to hear you say that," she said in obvious relief without letting him finish. "That's all. See that you always behave well and are a credit to us." She looked at me as well as at Dieter.

Since I couldn't conceive of being drunk, much less necking in a car, I wondered why I was included. It seemed that Dieter, Deu and I had been excused. We left the room as if under orders.

"Let that be a lesson to you," Dieter laughed when we were safely in the hall. "Poor Elise. She's not quite old enough to be a mother to someone my age and she's so nervous. Did you notice? Too bad Mutti wasn't up to taking the responsibility of lecturing these two miscreants." He snickered again. "Since we hadn't yet committed the crime, it did seem a bit premature, didn't you think?"

Nervous myself, I hadn't noticed Elise's anxiety, but Dieter bounded up the stairs and was beyond the landing before I could consider how to answer him.

Soon Meister Rojanski and I were hard at work. Elise's admonitions were forgotten and what the Baron had confided to me seemed impossible. Nothing I did satisfied the little man. The faster my feet flew, the more irascible he became. Finally he stood up, leaned the stick against the chair and, with folded arms, faced me as if in a fury. Reflected in all the mirrors, even though he wasn't much taller than I, it was terrifying.

"The Baron told me what he said to you last night. I am distressed. It is not yet the time you should be told such things. I shall take care not to confide in him in the future. No," he began to pace back and forth in front of me, "I am furious that your parents plan to remove you from Poland when they leave. How dare they waste my time in such a manner." The last was not a question. He came closer and peered into my eyes, resembling my mental image of Svengali.

"But Meister Rojanski," I was so frightened I hardly spoke above a whisper. "We thought you understood that we were only to be here for two years."

"That was before I saw that you had such a talent." He was working

186

himself into a frenzy. He stalked away, tromped back, threw his arms in huge circles as if to disengage them from his body, all of that with the utmost grace. I was so mesmerized it nearly overrode my fear. I had never seen anyone behave in such a way before.

Anna who was chaperoning my practice hours got up and left the room in a hurry. I was abandoned.

 "How can they defy me in such a way? I have plans for you." He ranted on another round trip. This time he looked at me and pointed to his stick where it had fallen on the floor. Afraid to pick it up, but more afraid not to, I crouched down without taking my eyes from his angry face. "That was awkward," he shouted, not removing the pointing finger. "Put it down and do it again." When I had done as he demanded to his satisfaction, he allowed me to sidle forward, my arm extending the stick to its fullest. He then grabbed and swung the rod around. I cringed as if I'd had reason to cringe all my life. Herr Rojanski froze and for a long minute I watched as his face lost its anger.

"I'm so sorry that you have found reason to be afraid of me, Carole." He fumbled for the chair and sat down heavily. "It's just that I have such plans for you and now your parents are going to ruin all that. They should have known that ballerinas leave their homes and train only for the ballet when they aspire to become dancers." He put both hands on the stick in front of him and leaned his head on them. "She could have been my final memorial," he said so softly it was nearly a sigh.

Daddy's voice came from the doorway. "Because Carole loves to dance and wanted to learn ballet, we thought that it would be nice to take this opportunity for her to have lessons. We never thought of having her make it a career." My parents came quickly to stand beside me. Anna was behind them. "Apparently you had a different understanding." Daddy put his arm around my shoulders, which still quivered from the emotions of the past few minutes. "Are you

187

cold, dear? Anna would you get the Kleine a sweater please."

I wondered if that nickname was going to follow me all the days of my life. Once she'd gone, Daddy spoke to the Polish man and I was required to translate. "Suppose you present your plans. After all we, as her parents, whether we agree or not, would like to know what you have in mind."

Without skipping a beat, the Meister rose and advanced upon my father like a threatened animal. I could almost see the smoke and flame of a tiny, infuriated dragon exuding from his nostrils.

"Do you intend to waste my time in such a way?" Though his voice was not shrill, I could hear the frustration. "To give me such promise and then remove it . . . to show me a young Pavlova and then to take her away as if I had no feelings . . . That you should not be allowed to do." Like a fencer, he lunged at Daddy with his stick.

At least a foot taller, my father backed away. "Now, now," he said soothingly, "I don't know what you're talking about. Who is going to remove whom?"

"You want to remove Carole, the most promising pupil I have ever had. The most promising pupil anyone has ever had. Surely you cannot consider such a thing. "

It was hard for me to keep up with my translation. No one seemed to notice when I stumbled over a few words. Confused and scared as I was, I don't believe I even heard the import of any of them.

"My goodness," Mother's voice had a quaver in it. "We had no idea. Jonathan, we really should have observed these lessons more closely." She turned to the irate little man. "Do you mean she is really good?"

"Madame," Herr Rojanski's tone was one of defeat. "She is more than good. And someday, if I had been allowed to mold her, to keep her working, practicing, she would have been great." There was no hope in his voice now.

"Oh, dear. I don't think I could give up my baby. No, no, no. It's out of the question. She must come home with us when the time comes." Mother ignored Herr Rojanski and shook her head with vehemence.

Herr Rojanski, his stick under his arm, picked up his street shoes, elbowed my father aside and walked toward the door. "Then the lessons will end now."

"Now wait one minute." My father could sound very military and forbidding when he issued an order.

Herr Rojanski turned and waited. Later, Daddy said he had seen the expression on my face at the thought of losing my ballet studies.

"Yes?" Herr Rojanski waited.

"Please understand. This is a very sudden announcement for Carole's mother and for me. It is something we must talk over and it deserves a great deal of thought. If a career in dance is something my daughter thinks she must pursue, as parents we can do nothing other than consider her future. Carole will be thirteen next November, and though it is unusual for a girl of that age to be included in such a significant decision, she must be allowed to have her say."

Daddy looked at Mother for affirmation. When she nodded, he went on. "It would not be fair for us to decide her life for her. Why don't we continue as we are? The decision-making process will be ongoing and you will be included in it all the way. The answer must be a clear "yes" or "no". There can be no "maybe." Now or ever. Will that satisfy you, Meister?" Daddy walked toward the man where he stood by the door.

"You are a gentleman, sir." Herr Rojanski turned and bowed from the waist. He held out his hand as he came back toward my father. "Of course I can understand how it would be hard to give up one's only child. Particularly to give her to a career which takes so much time and energy. A career that can break a leg, break a heart, or make a star." He paused as he and my father shook hands. "I assure you, however, that your young lady, whom I love already as my own, will be a star that shines more brightly than the legendary Pavlova. She has everything the great ballerina has and she is also beautiful. If she is trained correctly, the world will fall at her feet."

"Couldn't she be trained in the United States?" Mother joined them near the door.

"Perhaps, Madame. Perhaps she could, but I have seen the results of training which has progressed too far too fast. The leg muscles are knotty, the movements are often angular and unfinished. Ballet is still too new to your country for anyone to know how it will be by the time Carole is ready to step on the stage. I beg you to let me continue with her." He paused hoping, I thought, for a reply.

"I don't think we could even consider leaving her here." Mother seemed to have definitely made up her mind. "Couldn't you come to the United States?"

"I'm sorry, Madame, but I fear I am too old and too unwell for that." He, too, was definite. As his voice continued, I heard it as if I were in an exciting nightmare. "When she is fourteen," he said, "she can join the Warsaw Corps de Ballet where I assure you she will stand out. She will almost immediately start to become known. After that I will have done all I can for her and it would be her decision as to whether she remains in Poland or dances for the whole world in Paris or New York. All of that is, of course, depending on whether she loves it and how hard she is willing to work. I will demand a great deal of her."

"Oh, no. Not all alone in Warsaw at fourteen." Mother's words were breathy and faint.

I barely heard them. The whole conversation and my father's reaction was so unexpected that it hardly had any reality. The thought of leaving the Meister and the wonders he was holding out to me against separation from my parents filled me with a tortuous ambivalence my heart couldn't accept.

Daddy again took charge. "Let's just let things ride for the moment, shall we? We have almost a whole year to decide. One, what Carole's wishes are. Two, how she is progressing. Three, what we feel we can do about it. And four, what arrangements have to and can be made. Does that sound satisfactory to everyone? In the end it will amount to someone losing of course, but in situations like this that is inevitable."

Mother began to cry as if she already knew the outcome. After Daddy led her from the room, I was left alone with Anna and Meister Rojanski. He changed back into his ballet slippers, motioned me to the barre. Once Anna returned to her chair, he banged his stick on the floor and we proceeded with our lesson. His satisfied expression would have told the world that he, the former ballet master of the Imperial Polish Ballet, had just won a great battle.

I wanted to cry. While my feet followed the beat of the stick automatically, I knew that when we arrived at the moment of decision I would choose to stay behind and dance. On the other hand how could I bear to leave Mother and Daddy? My heart and mind fought each other all through the exercise part of the morning.

After lunch, at which I ate little, the pianist came. "And what kind of music would the Meister select for this session," he asked as he settled himself on the bench and put his music books on the candle stands of the Bechstein. He was a pale young man with long skeletal fingers and an obsequious manner. His name was Herr Langer and he played beautifully. My parents and the von Wechslers said that, with another personality, he might have become a concert pianist. As it was, he did this and gave lessons for a living.

"Masquerade," the Meister said. "Do you have the music?"

"My dear sir, I am never without the music of Chopin or Khatchiturian. To me they are the greatest. Give me a moment." He shuffled through the stack on the piano.

"Sit down, Fraulein." My teacher indicated a chair beside his. "As we always do, first we will listen to this music together and then you will begin to dance to whatever story you hear in it. Do you agree?"

The "Fraulein" startled me. Usually he didn't care whether I agreed or not. We did what he wanted. Now I know that he was trying to draw me to his side more firmly than I was drawn to my parents. At the time, however, I saw none of that. I was simply confused. Still I answered, "I think so."

The title Masquerade sounded ominous to me. While it wasn't hard to translate, I had a vision of masks, strange costumes, and all manner of dreadful creatures. I didn't think I would like it. In the chilly room with only my black leotard and my ballet slippers on my feet, I was prepared for failure. The first notes sounded. Before even a minute had passed I had left my chair and the ballroom. I was somewhere inside the music, becoming a young tree on a hill being buffeted by high winds. Great gusts would come and the tree, wishing to float in the air, tugged at its roots, but the earth held it while it waved its branches and swayed its slender trunk. The powerful music was always there when, time after time, the gusts blew the tree nearly flat. After each of the blasts, when the sound softened, the tree settled back into the earth until, at last, the unrelenting wind wrenched it free. The little tree skipped and twirled over the earth that had nourished it until the capricious wind left it behind, close to the spot from which it had sprung.

There was only silence around me. Then I heard a soft sigh and the Herr Rojanski's breathless voice. " Beautiful . . . beautiful. Never did I think to see such feeling from a twelve year-old. Tomorrow we order your toe shoes. You must stay, Carole. You must stay with me. Such beauty and such talent belongs to the world."

Seated on the floor, still with the feeling that my branches were above my head and my roots were exposed, I now understood that my parents, like the earth, would always be there. No matter how far apart we were, they would never abandon me until I was safe and ready. They were my support and I could always come home.

I was not yet prepared to answer Herr Rojanski's plea. Mother and Daddy would have each other and could get along without me, but would I be ready to get along without them?

Suddenly, the sensitive musician filled the ballroom with the tuneful strains of a Strauss Waltz. As always the music invaded my heart and my soul. As if the past hour had never happened, I danced joyously into the romantic, cool and shady Wienner Wald.

Chapter 25

I halt in the middle of my tale as the freight train slides to a stop. These Nazis are certainly masters of mechanics. Even our passenger trains at home do not stop as smoothly, but it seems everything the Nazis do is arrogant, secretive and silent. Hitler has greased the squeaking doors, wheels, palms and minds of the Germans and the grease he's used is improved schools, autobahns, Volkwagons and fear. The beginning was easy because, for generations, parents and schoolmasters have denied children the right of free thought. They're taught by the "believe it because I say it's so" method. No wonder the people follow the leader who makes the most noise. By the time the terrible truth has become obvious, it is too late.

Before I can search for any better answers, the doors of the freight car open. No one inside moves. On the platform are the soldiers with their guns at the ready. The humanity pressed together in front of those guns are the actors who have no other choice than to continue the play as it is being written. There are faces behind the guns. Some are expressionless. Some grin derisively and dare us to do so much as blink. Only one or two within my range of sight tries to avoid my eyes. Inside the car there is a hushed rustle.

The scraping of heavy boots and shots disturbs the unnatural silence. Some foolish soul has tried to escape. Or was he the wise one? What's coming may well be worse than his death, but I won't easily give up my life. I will bear whatever comes because, someday, the Nazis will lose this terrible war and, if I still live, I will hold my baby in my arms. Looking at the faces of the guards, unbidden thoughts crowd in. But are Alex and Anna already suffering or dead? I shudder. It's better not to think. I can do nothing, but continue to believe they are safe on Hel. The doors are closing. The train is moving. Not for long. Almost immediately it slows and stops.

"Why are we stopping again?" A frightened voice asks. I see a tiny little lady cradled in the arms of a younger woman. The old one's face is lined and frail like those of Kurt's father and the Countess. Like them, she will probably not live to escape this hell.

The doors open again and beyond the blank-faced guards there is barbed wire. Lots of barbed wire. Smoke is coming from chimneys inside the wire and I know what it is. Kurt bragged about the efficiency of these awful camps. I am terrifyingly aware that, like his father, on Kurt's orders I am about to enter a death camp. I never thought a living body could grow as icy cold from its very core as mine does.

"Hieraus." A guard in front of the door raises his gun and gestures with it to get us going. "Raus, raus, raus."

We move, not like the proverbial cattle, but more like cowardly kittens. We stagger along as, poked and prodded with guns instead of lion-tamer's chairs, they make us do our tricks and move faster. We drag up and support the old and frail who stumble, but it might be better if we let them lie there and die beneath the shuffling feet. Although I try not to notice, I am aware of emaciated nude and semi-nude people who watch us as we pass. Once in a while an expressionless face changes and there is an almost happy sign of recognition. But, before a hand can reach out or a word framed, reality returns and the face is again impassive.

At the entrance to another barren-looking building we are told to shed our clothes and to march, in single file, through a trough of fetid liquid.

On the other side, while the number 7694169 is tattooed on my arm, I am too debased to even be embarrassed or angry. When the seedy tattooist is finished, a hand grasps my arm and I am pulled roughly aside. I am surprised to see Eduard, a friend of Dieter's, in an SS uniform. His expression is one of unconcern, but his head shakes almost imperceptibly as he hands me a suit of striped clothes and presses something into my hand. When I am dressed, he marches me through this building of degradation and, without a word, deposits me in a tiny cell-like room at the end of another long barracks. A bucket sits in one corner. Filthy sawdust clumps around it on the floor. The stench is terrible. I see regret in Eduard's expression. Without a word, he locks me in my tiny compartment and disappears.

"D has managed to influence where you go,"is all the note says but it tells me that Dieter's keeping the promise he made at the Ball. It's a small scrap of paper. I put it in my mouth, chew and swallow.

My traveling companions file into the barracks. They pass my door and, through a small barred opening, I see that women and men alike are dressed in the same striped clothes that I wear. Would they give us clothing if they were going to burn us? I hope not. Still, their heads are shorn and they shiver. Is it from cold or fear?If Kurt has his way, the gas furnaces will warm us into extinction. I lay my head against the small barred opening so they can see my hair and know I am still with them. Aurora, I hear one of them breathe. They know I'm here and I feel less alone.

It's night. We've eaten watery soup. Was it potato or cabbage? Who could tell?Thank God, though the smell of the bucket is still strong, it's dark. No light comes from the one naked bulb that is supposed to light this whole building. I hear a whisper.

"Aurora", the unknown voice whispers, "Aurora, are you here?"

"Yes," I whisper back. "I'm here. Are you all right?"

"That depends on what you mean. We are alive."

"I'm glad of that," I say though I don't know whether I'm telling

196

the truth or not. "Are there any guards still out there?"

"No."

"Will you tell us some more of your story?" Another voice chimes in. "Maybe then we can sleep."

"I'll try, but I shall have to speak so softly perhaps some of you may not be able to hear."

"If you speak slowly we can pass it along," the masculine voice holds confidence. It is encouraging. They may die, but they will not give up.

"All right, here we go. Where was I?"

"You were about to get your toe shoes. "

My thoughts go back to that wonderful day. I was so young, so innocent and so excited. But I didn't yet know my baby and, thankfully, didn't know how empty my life was going to be.

Chapter 26

It took a whole week for my toe shoes to be made in Torun. By the time they came I was almost too excited to try them on. My muscles were strong by then and when my toes were wrapped in lamb's wool and those beautiful pink, satin slippers with their glossy ribbons were on my feet, I rose to their boxy tips as easily as if I had always danced in them. The meaning of ecstasy paled beside the thrill in my heart.

Although nothing was said during that waiting week, it was as if Herr Rojanski were determined to get as much knowledge into me and as much effort out of me as possible. Svengali wanted me thoroughly bewitched in case my parents still thought they were going to remove me from Poland. The slippers tied me to him as surely as a wedding vow.

Every morning at nine the lessons started with limbering up at the barre. After the toe shoes came, however, when it was still very cold outside, I was already there doing my exercises before the Meister arrived. Herr Langer also came in the morning now and we had music all day long. Even the routine exercises were a pleasure.

My teacher never again mentioned whether or not I had talent. We just exercised until Mittagsessen, ate, rested while the Meister regaled me with stories of different Ballets, then learned the steps of those ballets until tea-time. I never asked, and Meister Rojanski never said, whether I was learning a specific part or whether I was in the Corps de Ballet.

Staying on in Poland or going home was something I tried to avoid in my thoughts. Although Daddy said I would be a part of the decision-making, what Mother wanted would be the ultimate anyway. Since dancing was a part of my being, even if it were in Warsaw, Berlin, Paris, or New York, would I be living with my parents? And how could I bear to go far from Kurt?

Infrequently, in the late afternoon, Dieter stopped in to watch or ask questions, but Kurt, when he came, only made jokes to try to embarrass me. Because the Meister so obviously disapproved of him, I found it a distraction when he was there.

"See," Kurt would say to Dieter or even to the Meister. "Our girl is growing a figure. Soon she will be of marriageable age. Which one of us will get her?" Then he would laugh as if it were the biggest joke in the world.

The first time it happened I tried to grab something to put on over my leotard, to hide what he called my growing "figure," but that only made him tease me more. I told Mother how embarrassed I was, but she said, "Just ignore him, darling. Young boys think that sort of thing is funny and if you pay no attention he'll stop."

I didn't see him as a young boy. To me, he and Dieter were grown men. Time after time I wished I could sink into the floor to escape his taunts and every day I hoped he'd come. The Baron came once a month to give the Meister his check and to see how we progressed. Sometimes he and my teacher held private conferences, but all the old gentleman ever said to me was. "Don't worry, Kleine, you will stay here with us. You will be our gift to the world of ballet." In my heart, I hoped it was so.

In spring the days were longer. In my free hours after teatime while Deu and I were in the garden, the music that ran constantly through my head set my body free. On the greening grass, I leaped and twirled and let my arms float in joy on the gentle breezes. Even the chapel lost its terrors for me and I passed the open doors and the exposed coffin without a quiver or a backward glance. I even once said, "Good evening Graf von Wechsler," to the casket. It did feel creepy and I never dared repeat it.

Anna married Meier in the Friedenau village chapel in July. Of course, the entire von Wechsler family was there. Afterwards the villagers, in their Sunday-best costumes, celebrated in the square. It was thrilling to me to see the dancing. The girls' white skirts, with many rows of multi-colored ribbons around the bottom, swung gracefully. More ribbons floated from the shoulders of their gold braid-bound, black jerkins. Flowered wreaths encircled their head. They looked just like the magazine pictures I had seen in the National Geographic. Had that really been only a year ago? My life was so changed.

Today, Fraulein Goethe had dressed me as they were dressed and with urging from Anna, Lisa and Ida, I danced joyfully with the throng of revelers.

I am so deep into that sunny memory that I pause while I wait for the imagined accordion music to start again.

"I remember that day." A young man whispers from the dark. I recognize it as my new friend from Friedenau. "I think I began to really regret my ill-behavior toward you as I watched you twirl and dance with my friends. You looked so happy."

"I was happy. May we all be as happy again."

A soft "tak" (yes), then silence.

"Continue, please," begs an old reedy voice. "We so badly need a bed-time story."

I recognize him too. He was crippled and, though prodded and mistreated by the guards, had maintained his dignity as he hobbled along with the help of a younger man. Quickly, I continue my tale.

In the Fall, Meier got out of the Army and found a job as an electrician. He and Anna seemed happy living together in her small room in my parents' Grudziadz apartment. After the sofa in the hall, I suppose even a small room was an improvement. On the weekends when they all came to Friedenau, Meier was able to electrify all of the outbuildings for the von Wechslers. They, of course, insisted on paying him well, though he tried to refuse. It was probably more money than either he or Anna had ever seen all at once.

"I wonder that all of those straw-thatched houses don't burn to the ground at least once a week," my father had said as we had driven past the village one winter night.

"They are very careful people," Mother had answered.

The soft, yellow lights of the coal-oil lamps and candles were shining dimly through the small windows and the snow, like puffy down comforters, covered the steep thatched roofs. I thought they looked cozy. I'd never been inside of one, even on Anna's wedding day.

When summer was over, the storks flew away. Snow came to cover their nest for the winter and in November I was thirteen. I didn't feel any older, but got to stay up an hour later.

Mother, Daddy and I went to Paris for Christmas that year. Deu stayed at Friedenau. I missed him. Meister Rojanski asked us to deliver a letter to the Ballet Meister of the Paris Opera Company.

"He will ask you to dance for him, Carole, so take your leotard and slippers with you. I just want to be sure."

"Sure of what," I asked.

"I know I am not making a mistake, but I just want Monsieur Chandon to tell me so. Perhaps I just want to brag a little about my good fortune."

"What good fortune," I asked, but he would say no more.

Monsieur Chandon was a graceful, imperious and rather pretty man. With no preliminaries he read the letter, then ordered me to change my clothes and to audition for him. It was terrifying to be closeted in the dressing room with many of the girls of the Paris Opera ballet. Some weren't much older than I. They were curious, friendly and smiling, but chattered to each other and me in French, which I didn't understand. I smiled at them, and some recognized my fright and crowded around as they steered me toward the stage. It was as if they were saying," don't worry, we've been through this. We understand." They gave me courage to step beyond the already open curtains alone. They were my audience and sat in the very front rows.

"I want you to improvise." The Ballet Meister's voice commanded in English. He sat just out of my sight in the center of the opera house. "Start the music."

The first few notes were from a Straus waltz and I immediately forgot where I was. As always, caught up in the music, I danced through a field of flowers, bending to gather one here and there. A burbling brook ran beside me. Holding up my pretend skirts, I crossed it by dancing from rock to rock. In a forest I circled the trees and when the music stopped I was just about to dance happily down a wide path and out into the sun again.

There was a silence before the corps de ballet girls applauded. Monsieur Chandon hurried down the aisle.

"Tell Meister Rojanski he is not wasting his time." He spoke to me as he would have spoken to a grown-up. "If you ever get tired of the Polish Ballet, you come directly to me and you will be welcomed. If I were not his friend, I would be pleading with you to stay in Paris now." He spoke to my parents in flawless English and in front of everyone, "To be truthful, I am finding it very hard not to sign her to a contract right this instant. I have never seen any dancer, young or old, with the body-control this young girl exhibits. And with such absolute grace. It's as if she is floating on the music notes. I have never seen such ability in one so young. Not since Pavlova and perhaps even she didn't have it at your daughter's age. One can ask for no more than that. You must be very proud. I will also say that you have found the finest to train her. In all the world there is no one better that Gustav Rojanski."

We left and after a long silence on the way to our hotel I began to wonder if my parents had heard Monsieur Chandon's words at all. Finally Mother said, "If she's really that good, she can be just as good in the United States."

Daddy paused, took off his hat and rubbed his forehead. "Where, in the United States, do they have teachers equal to Herr Rojanski and to Monsieur Chandon, aside from possibly New York." He put on his hat. "And we won't even be stationed in New York, Janice. Are the teachers there as good anyway?" He seemed to be thinking out loud. "Even if they were, she would have to live away from us no matter what. Maybe we'd better rethink our priorities."

"I don't want to think about it right now," Mother began to cry. "It will spoil our vacation. Please, Jon. No more."

"We will have to talk about it soon. Still I'm willing to wait until we get back to Friedenau where we can talk with the von Wechslers too. You know they will have to have a say in this because they will have to be the ones on call, even if Carole is in Warsaw. And how will she be cared for in Warsaw? There's a lot to be thought of. But . . . this decision cannot be delayed forever." He frowned as he turned to look at me. He studied my face as if we had never met before.

I wanted to put my arms around them and say it was all right and I would rather go home with them, but I couldn't do it. Monsieur Chandon had given me the final encouragement to know that dancing was my life, more than a goal. It was a wonderful chance. I wanted to take it. Mother didn't answer. Sitting between them in the taxi, looking at Daddy's set jaw and Mother's tear-streaked face, my heart was breaking. How, when I loved them so, could I hurt them like this? Where could I find another way? In that moment I hated what the two Ballet Meisters had called my talent. Why couldn't I have been a normal girl?

"I'd rather go home with you," I blubbered. Somehow I had lost control. No matter. I had to make it right for the two people who loved me so much and whom I loved with all my heart.

They both turned, wrapping me between them like the filling in a cream puff.

"Whoa, now, Caro. This isn't a decision that can be lightly made, and not in the throes of emotion. It's too important." Daddy's voice was tender. "Let's go home and your mother and I will each do some unselfish thinking. You've just shown us how generous you can be. Now it's up to us to decide what's truly right for you." He knocked off my beret when he tried to stroke my hair.

In the confusion I did see that Mother was almost smiling. She thinks she's won, I thought with a small feeling of resentment. It was the first negative feeling I could ever remember having toward either of my parents. I was ashamed.

Back at Friedenau after the New Year, though 1932 arrived, my routine resumed. Meister Rojanski and Herr Langer continued to discuss in what month I would be ready to transfer to Warsaw while Mother, Daddy and the von Wechlers said nothing. I just danced and tried not to think that soon—one way or the other—I would have to leave someone I loved. Every night, tired as I was, I wished upon the first star I saw and found good omens in every unusual thing that happened in my life. Exhausted, I went to sleep with a heavy heart. In my dreams I was always fighting some unknown adversary. What I wanted so much had to be wrong. I was ashamed.

Spring enticed its first daffodil out of the ground about the same time the ice began to break up on the Vistula River. At Friedenau, the baby lambs arrived. The storks came back and my heart lightened. I realized I could find pleasure in other things in life whether I danced in the ballet or not. Self-important as I'd become with all the compliments, I thought perhaps I could get along without a Meister when we were back home. Perhaps I'd learned all he could teach me and it would be all right to go home with Mother and Dad. While I'd grown to love him almost like a grandfather as well as a teacher, I decided he could come to America, marry my grandmother, and we'd live happily ever after while I danced there. The von Wechslers and Baron von Pawel, had grown to be family too. I loved them all and didn't want to part with any of them. And Kurt. . . . . as much as he sometimes hurt me, I couldn't bear to think of leaving him.

"He'll get over being so mean when I'm grown up," I told myself quite sure that it was true. "If I'm going to marry him I'll just have to come back." While I was fighting myself in my heart, the grown-ups were working out my life.

On an afternoon in early May, one by one they all drifted into the ballroom where Meister Rojanski and I were hard at work. Deu came with them as if his presence was an absolute requirement. Even Meier and Anna were there.

"Carole," Daddy began. "We have something to say to you. At the end of my announcement, if you disagree, you may speak up, but first hear us out." He scared me.

"We, with no exceptions," He looked at Mother who nodded her head and smiled. "We have agreed that you must follow the talent that God has given to you, though only He knows where you got it. It certainly didn't come from my side of the family." Everyone laughed as he hoped they would. He told me afterward he felt it would be easier on everyone, mainly Mother and himself, if he could keep it light. "Next month you, Anna, Meier and Meister Rojanski will move to Warsaw."

My mouth must have dropped open because Daddy said. "Ah, Ah. Don't speak yet."

"Deu too?" I couldn't help asking.

"Yes, Deu too." Again everyone tittered. "Meister Rojanski has a cousin who has a large apartment across from a park and near the Opera House. You four plus Deu can live there in safety and comfort. You can come to Friedenau on weekends when you want to and every July you will come home to us for a month. Christmas, we will always come here and, Meister Rojanski tells us, as you grow to be more famous, you will be invited to dance in Opera Houses the world over. Your Mother and I will always be there to watch you even if I have to leave the Army to do it. How do you feel about those plans?"

By then I was crying too hard to answer. I didn't even know whether it was from joy or homesickness.

Chapter 27

May was a very hard month. When Mother and Daddy were at Friedenau, I wanted to spend every minute with them, but my lessons interfered. At night when I went to bed, I cried myself to sleep, trying to imagine the years without them. When they went back to Grudziadz during the week, I wanted to go with them, but . . . as always . . . when dancing again filled my soul, I knew they had made the right decision. When I weakened, they stayed strong and if they weakened, I never knew it.

Everyone at Friedenau recognized the changes that were tormenting me. Elise and Oma were always there to offer an ear or comforting arms. Ernst offered his shoulder and Dieter even stopped stealing my hair ribbon. The day the decision was announced and after my parents had left for Grudziadz, riding home from the station with Zarrotti I tried not to cry. As soon as I was in my own room, I let the flood begin.

Elise tapped gently on the door, but entered without waiting. "Caro," she murmured, sitting down on the edge of my bed and putting her arms around me. "I know you are feeling frightened about being wiz out your parents for such a long time, but more zan zat, you are feeling disloyal. You are doing what you have to do, you know. Zat's not disloyalty." Her gentle hands smoothed the hair back from my forehead.

"They will be lonely without me."

"Your parents have tried to bring you up to be an independent person." She rocked me back and forth as if I were a baby. "Zey have always known zat someday you would move away from them. Zat is the way life is."

"But . . ." I started to interrupt.

"Zis change is, perhaps, a bit earlier and unexpected, but in ze United States you wouldn't have been able to live wiz zem and continue your ballet anyway. Don't you remember your fazzer saying zat in Kansas, where he will be stationed, zere would be no teacher for you. You would have to live in New York and zat's, zey tell me, a long way from Kansas."

"But I could see them more often." I remained unconvinced.

"Anysing that changes your life is apt to be hard," she continued. "Even when you fall in love and marry, you will probably feel disloyal to all of us and to your dancing as well." She sighed. "Right now I expect you are regretting ze talent and desire zat makes you have to choose one way of life above ze other. Don't ever regret, Liebchen. Soon you will be in a position to give pleasure to sousands of people and you must never blame yourself for taking ze pas God chose for you. He knows what he's doing even if we don't."

She laid her cheek against my head and while the tears dried on my cheeks, we leaned back against the pillows together. My heart was still heavy, but bearably so. A few weekends later, my parents, the Meister and I traveled to Warsaw together to be sure his cousin's apartment was suitable for four people and a dog. Of course, everything hinged on whether the Polish ballet would accept me. The apartment building was modern enough to have a fancy elevator that took us to the fourth floor. It stood in the center of the vast lobby looking like Cinderella's coach. Glass and gilt abounded.

Aboard and ready to rise, we waited and we waited. There was a jarring thump and we rose abruptly.

"I'm not sure about this," mother said clinging to the brass railing that ran around the inside of the glass cage. By then we were swaying in a gentle, almost circular motion. "Do you think this contraption is safe?"

"I think it's been behaving like this since the day it was created which must have been pre-Cambrian." Daddy chuckled. "I noticed it was driven upward by a huge piston." He looked at me. "That's a round steel shaft that pushes the cage up from below. I don't think God himself could break it."

Mother let go of the bar to put her hand quickly on Daddy's arm. "Don't blaspheme, Jon," she almost lost her balance. "You might give Him a reason to try."

Daddy winked at me. The "contraption" finally swayed to a stop on the fourth floor. The doors remained closed until Herr Rojanksi stepped forward and slid them open.

"Aha." Daddy said. "Automation extends just so far I see."

To spare the Meister's feelings, I didn't translate. We exited directly into a small hall. In front of us a mirrored, Victorian hat-rack reflected four expectant faces. Beside it, a stand allowed room for a large collection of umbrellas. The locked front door to the apartment opened from this little hall into a larger one. Both had oriental rugs and the larger room seemed crowded by a huge, bow-front chest of drawers and opposite, a schrank for coats.

It was a huge corner apartment with plenty of room for everyone. Heavy green velvet drapes and Biedermeier furniture liberally adorned with anti-Maccassers, made the living room seem dark. The living room, library, and my bedroom were on the front of the building and a wide balcony ran from corner to corner in front of them and overlooked a lovely park. The bathroom was around the corner, and I assumed, beside the elevator shaft. The dining room joined the large corner living room while the pantry and kitchen came behind it. A long hall on the inside led to two more bedrooms and a bath on the back of the building.

Before a room could be assigned to the Meister, however, he asked if we would mind if he lived with his cousin instead. There was a silence as Mother and Daddy stared at him. My teacher hurried to explain.

"Since I will not be dwelling in a different city, it will not be necessary that I be a part of the household. To be honest I would really prefer to live with those of my own age and my cousin and his wife are just around the corner."

"That would certainly be all right, wouldn't it, Jon?" Mother looked at Daddy who nodded.

"I would be near enough should I be needed and yet I would have more freedom. I do not mean to insult you, but I would enjoy that freedom." He gave one of his rare smiles.

"It's settled then." The two men shook hands.

"That will also give Anna and Meier a little sitting room and a private bath for themselves."

Most of all, I was pleased. From the time it had been agreed that Anna and Meier would be in loco parentis, I had wondered how I could survive having Herr Rojanski as a third parent.

"I will pick Carole up to go to the theater each morning and in the afternoons she will be under the direction of the great Meister Masaela, he continued. "There is no doubt he will accept her into his corps de ballet, even though she has not yet danced for him. That will come tomorrow morning, as you know."

"What about at night? Surely she won't be allowed to walk home alone after the performances." Mother worried.

"I will escort her home nightly, Madame, but to be truthful, I do not imagine my services will be necessary much longer. As soon as she is well-established, I shall return to Torun. Anna, Meier or Meister Masaela must then take over those responsibilities."

"Yes," Daddy seemed satisfied.

Mother nodded her head. Only I was shocked. It was impossible to imagine life in the ballet without my irascible teacher. We had been so bound together at Friedenau. Was I to lose everyone who gave my life stability? In the hotel that night, I told my parents how I felt and asked them to beg him to stay.

"Caro dear." Daddy took both my hands in his and pulled me onto his lap. He hadn't done that since I had become almost a teen-ager. He looked seriously into my eyes."Even your few years of living in the Army should have taught you that life is a series of hails and farewells. When the Meister decides it is time to go back to his own life, he will go, but he will never leave you. The things he taught you and the memories you share will always be in your mind and heart. And, as you know, as long as you both live you can always meet again." Daddy paused to hand me his handkerchief.

"But . . ."

"But me no buts." Daddy smiled. "Herr Rojanski is not a young man. Remember when he came to us he was trying to recover from an illness? He was retired then. Should we not let him have his own life back?" He moved and I teetered on his knees. "He has given these two years to you and probably will give almost another one. Even when he goes he will, I'm sure, be here on every opening night to applaud for you. Caro, please be as generous to him as he has been to you. Don't make him feel guilty for leaving when the time comes." He took his handkerchief from me and put it up against my nose. "Blow," he said.

I did and we both laughed. The next morning I auditioned for
Meister Masaela. This time the music was The Rustle of Spring. At
once the leaves and flowers hidden in me opened and, in the soft,
fresh breeze under the placid blue sky they fluttered and twirled in
the joy of awakening. In July I would become the youngest member
of the Polish Imperial corp de ballet. The train ride back to Torun
was filled with plans and admonitions.

Except for the weekends when we were at Friedenau, I spent the
month of June in Grudziadz. Herr Rojanski thought we should
move to Warsaw at once, but he lost the argument. Every day of
that last month was a mixture of torture and joy. On the first of
July, Elise and Ernst traveled with us to Bremerhaven where we
watched my beloved parents get on an Army Transport. As they
sailed away, apprehension that I wouldn't be able to uphold
everyone's faith in me dropped over me like an onus. I found no
way to justify all the sacrifices everyone else was making.

I think Elise was afraid I might jump into the Atlantic and swim
after them because she put her arms firmly around my shaking
shoulders and turned my face into her bosom Tears ruined her new
silk dress. Still, you can't cry forever and though my heart was
often weighty, by the middle of the month when we moved to
Warsaw, there was excitement in having new surroundings. There
was even more when I was able to dance again.

Each time I got into 'the contraption' Mother and Daddy stood
close beside me and I smiled with the memories even as unshed
tears clouded my vision. Deu found the park less enjoyable then the
gardens at Friedenau. To begin with he was on a leash and then,
too, he could never go out alone. The ducks on the small lake
chased him rather than letting him chase them and a mean swan
pursued us hissing and flapping. There were a lot of children too.
He liked children, just not in such great numbers. They scared him,
particularly when he broke loose, waded in, and grabbed one of
their toy sail boats. One little owner snatched his boat and hit Deu

with it.

After a few days we ran across a part of the park where dogs were allowed to run free. There he found some friends and so did Meier. One of Meier's new friends led to a job with an electrician who allowed him to take Deu to the park for an hour or so in the afternoons. Anna took him with her in the mornings when she went to market so he got plenty of exercise.

On the few times I had more than one day free, we rode home to Friedenau on the hard wooden seats of the third class carriage because that's where dogs were required to ride. Thinking I should be unselfish and let him stay at Friedenau, I left him once. After we both had grieved and whined for three days, Ernst had Viktor bring him home to me.

During that first time Dieter, Kurt and I were walking around the Friedenau gardens with Deu, the dog flushed a rabbit. I described how unhappy he had been on his leash before we discovered the section where he could run free. When I revealed that he was taken there several times a day Kurt was infuriated.

"You spoil that dog," he raged. "He's an animal. He should be taught a lesson and he'd get over his restlessness in a hurry. Let me have him for a week and he'll be adjusted when you get him back."

Dieter muttered something I couldn't understand and even though I recognized no wrong in Kurt, I wasn't sure his way would be my way.

"Thank you very much, Kurt," I smiled at him. "He seems to be getting along fine now and Meier and Anna have made friends too, so I think the problem is already solved."

Kurt started to argue, but shrugged his shoulders and turned to Dieter. "Come on, smart guy. Let's get on the bikes and go to

Torun for some fun. Leave this child to train her dog if she thinks she can." He whirled around and started down the path toward the house.

"Sorry, Kleine," Dieter patted me on the head despite how tall I had grown for my age. "Too bad you're not old enough to go along."

In a few minutes I heard the roar of the motorcycles and listened until the sound faded away. They weren't back before we were ready to leave the next day. No one seemed concerned. I supposed they had stayed with friends overnight. When I said so on the train going back to Warsaw, Meier snorted and said something in Polish I didn't understand.

"What did he say," I asked Anna.

"He said he was sure they were quite friendly."

I turned my attention to the window. The train followed the Vistula River all the way to Warsaw. Villages perched on its banks like birds on a tree limb and as we rolled by, peasants in the fields raised their hay-forks to wave. One young couple was having such fun throwing great forks of manure at each other and laughing so hard they didn't even notice us. Two years before I would have been disgusted by the straw and manure festooning the girls head and shoulders. Now I laughed with them and accepted it without a shudder. I hoped the Polish balletomanes would accept me as well.

Chapter 28

Loud voices waken me. I'm shaking with the cold. It's very dark and I must have gone to sleep huddled here against the door. I trust those poor souls in the barracks understand why my tale ended. I hope I put them to sleep too. What's that saying that Grammie used to quote to me? "Sleep knitteth up the raveled sleeve of care." In this frightening and desolate time, I can't remember the rest of the quotation. Whatever it is, whoever wrote it was wrong. I've slept and I still care that I'm separated from my baby and I'm still afraid. How close am I to those gas chambers Kurt described in such awful detail? Am I to hold my baby again only in Heaven? So many questions crowd my mind and heart. Only Kurt could answer them and I already know what his answer would be.

Footsteps shuffle past my door in a long stream. It's too dark to see to whom the feet belong, but a soft rap on the door now and then tells me they're friends. Shivers rattle me to the very bone. Are they on their way to those gas chambers? By virtue of suffering the same, strong, fearful emotions we have become like family. If I'm still alive, and those footsteps never shuffle back I will mourn for them too.

 I crawl the few feet to where I think my straw-filled mattress must be. Under the dirty blanket there is no warmth, no relief. Even my tears are cold. The faltering steps come to a silent end. I wait for the guards to come for me. There isn't a sound. Am I to stay forever alone in a building steeped in evil tragedies. Even on the rooftops in Grudziadz I'd managed my terror, but here? Here I have to depend on the compassion of these Germans, and they are not human beings.

There isn't even room to pace. Something is shoved through a slot in the door. By the bit of wan light coming through the grating, I can see something floating in the liquid in the bowl. It looks like a mouse. My stomach heaves. Where are the others? They haven't come back. Are they going through fear and torture or are they now at peace and with their God? If it weren't for Baby Alex, I could almost wish I were one of them, but I have to fight to the last to be able to give my son a mother.

Only three days since Anna, Alex and I waited so eagerly in that sallyport. I try to pretend I'm hugging Alex to me. My breasts are still sore. My clothes are wet and clammy. Why doesn't this useless milk stop? I work at the edge of the blanket until I can tear a piece that's long enough and narrow enough to bind me tightly. Wishing for a pin I look at the pail. In standing up to reach for it my arm brushes something that tears at my sleeve.
There is nothing sharp on the pail, but a nail is sticking out of the rough lumber wall. It doesn't stick out very far and it isn't loose. I work at it with my finger nails. After a long time it comes out of the board.

Fearful that someone may come and shivering with cold, I rush to take off the clothes above the waist. When I have the binder in place I pin it with the nail. It's a thick nail but it works. Tightly bound, I'm not comfortable, but without wet clothes next to my skin, I'm warmer.

A thin strip of light reveals a crack in the wall. Putting my eye to it I can see guards emptying pails of what must be meat on the ground. One piece lands quite close to my peephole. Dear God. It is a baby's arm with the tiny fingers still attached. It is bigger than Alex's arm. Some other mother has given up her child for a dog's breakfast. My heart is almost too heavy for my body to carry it.

Boots stop outside my cell. When the door opens, it is the same man who brought me to this cell. He reaches for me, his hands surprisingly gentle. Perhaps he is just being kind to "one who is about to die." My heart flutters.

"Kommen Sie," he says as he propels me from behind with his

hands on my upper-arms, I'm marched like a marionette to the door of the barracks. An army truck stands beside the steps in the rain.

Hoisted aboard, there are six or seven others already sitting on the board seats that rim the truck. I think they are all men. Two new guards replace mine. Both scramble aboard. When a canvas curtain shuts us all in, we roll away. After awhile I begin to relax. The two men by the tailgate have put their rifles beside them on the side away from us "criminals."

"Perhaps there is a hope of escaping," the man beside me whispers in English. "Can you run, Aurora?"

I peer at him in the dim light. It is a man from the cattle car. For the first time since I was taken I feel almost warm and am about to answer when . . .

"I can hear you. It is not necessary that you think about that," my guard says in perfect English. "We would shoot you quite dead. Don't talk. Enjoy the ride. You will not be in such bad shape once we get where we're going."

"Where are we going? Please tell us that." I ask

"You have no need to know."

"Where were we then?" I have heard about Auschwitz and Birkenau, but Kurt never told me in what part of Poland they were. I want to know if I'm getting closer to the Peninsula of Hel.

"I will tell you only that you are fortunate to be away from the place where you spent last night."

The other guard kicks his companion on the boot. "Wass sagst du?" he demands.

"Nichts. Wichtig," the English speaker answers. To us he says, "Enough." And lapses into silence.

Left to our own frightening thoughts, we rattle along in semi-darkness hour after hour. The guards nap one at a time and we stop only once for food and for a bathroom. The driver brings us each a hard roll and a tin cup of water. For the bathroom---they hand me a bucket and cover me with a blanket. In the brief seconds that the rear canvas is raised, we try to see out.

"That's Bismark Strasse." A man on my right whispers excitedly. "We're in Poznan. That's my home. Maybe they're taking us home."

I would be happy for him if they were, but not for me. I had hoped we were going North toward Hel. I pray that Alex and Anna are there. If they're taking us home, I'll be taken back to Kurt. Poznan is to the south and west. The Hel I want is far north. The other hell will be wherever Kurt is.

We're rattling over a road much bumpier than the cobblestone roads we've been traveling. None of Hitler's fine Autobahns here. When we stop and are ordered out of the truck, we are in a cluster of small thatched cottages. After years in this country I know that these simple dwellings belong to an estate and they all look alike. I can't see the Manor house, but it will be large and imposing. A few of the cottages are surrounded by barbed wire and we are marched inside the enclosure as if we were criminals.

With no preliminaries the Nazi guard says, "You will work for the Baron who lives on this estate. Do your work well and you will live to see Germany rule the world. Heil Hitler."

"Hah," the man next to me whispers as the gate is closed. "Germany is losing the war fast now that the Allies are closing the scissors. They . . ." He doesn't get to finish.

Our two guards raise their arms in a salute to the man who has brought all of this criminality to pass before they climb in the truck and trundle away. But we are not alone. New guards have appeared, one of them a woman. Two of them prod the men prisoners into one hut. The woman shepherds me into another. Inside, the earthen floor is covered with straw. Straw pallets lie about in the three rooms that comprise the downstairs. A ladder leads to a loft above and I assume there are more pallets there. At this hour the other occupants must be at work. The hefty woman and I stare at each other.

"Tomorrow you will go to the fields," she says. "Take off your jacket." She wrenches it from my shoulders and drops it on the floor. "You do not look strong enough for field work, number . . ." She pinches my arm. She is pushing back my sleeve. "Where is your tattoo?" she demands.

Maybe if I don't say it out loud I won't lose my identity. "On the other arm," I whisper.

She sees my sweater, wet where the milk has soaked through again. "What's that?" She begins to tear at my clothes.

"I had a baby," I try to protect myself.

"Where is it?"

"It died." I feel dishonest and disloyal saying those words and only pray they are not true.

"When?" Is it my imagination or has her voice grown softer?

"The day before I was taken."

"You poor, poor child." She busies herself gathering supplies. All the time she works, she talks. "I lost a baby once." She rinses my breasts with clear water. It's cold, but it feels good. The woman winds a new strip of flannel cloth so tightly around me I can barely breathe, but it is better, less sore.

"Only three days old she was. Just a tiny mite when Gott took her back." A safety pin holds the binder in place this time. "And then my husband---he too died working for Hitler. They told me der Furher was sorry and gave me some money, but it bought no love from me."

"Don't you like the Nazis?"

"We'll talk about that no more," she says with finality.

 A warm petticoat comes next, then a shapeless peasant dress. Even though it's spring it's still cool, but it feels good to get out of those striped clothes. I feel as though I've worn them a lifetime. The sweater she hands me is heavy wool. I stick my arms into its embracing sleeves and absorb its warmth and thank her.

"Do you hate Hitler?" Her voice penetrates my cocoon. "Most of the women who come here to work hate Hitler. He's been good to me. He gave me this job." She stirs something in a huge cauldron that hangs in the open fireplace. I wonder why she asks me the question and answer cautiously.

"No, I don't hate Hitler," I say, out loud. I go far beyond that, I assure myself.

"Where's your husband?

"I am divorced,"

"Where did you live?"

Be careful, Carole. "In Krakow", I say.

"Ach, my sister lives in Krakow. Maybe you know her, Jashi Gronika."

"No I don't think so."

"What street did you live on? She lives on Gorski Strasse."

Good heavens. What are the streets in Krakow? "Bismark," I say hoping this town is like all others.

"I don't know where that is. Is it in the high part of town or the low part?"

Because I don't know what she means by that, I say the only thing that comes to mind." I don't feel very well. May I sit down?" I sidle toward a straight-backed chair. She rushes to help.

"Perhaps you aren't strong enough to work in the fields," she says. "The Baron here is very kind. If I ask him, maybe he will let you work in his dairy."

I was sure that if she did favors only for me among the workers I would have more trouble than pleasure. "I'll be just fine in a little while. I'm really very strong."

"That may be, but I shall tell his wife anyway. They both are kind people even though they are Polish. I am from Germany, you see. So was my husband."

She keeps rattling on and I hardly listen. My mind is too busy. Is what the man whispered to me true? Is that why she's being so kind? If the owner of this estate is Polish, there must be a reason the Germans have let him stay here. Most, if not all, other Polish or Jewish owned property has become the possession of the Third

Reich. Why has this farm been left in Polish hands? Does this owner play along with the Germans? I go from feeling warm and almost friendly to the chilling cold I felt on the rooftops of Grudziadz.

"What kind of farm is this one?" I hope my voice doesn't quaver.

"Oh. This is a very special farm. On it we grow sugar beets, but the Baron's cows also produce the best milk in Europe." She straightens her shoulders and raises her chin proudly. "Our Baron, even if he is Polish, went to the United States of America to study about milk cow farming. Our cows are clean and our barns don't smell. We get much money for our milk."

If she had run around the table waving an American flag she couldn't have given me joy more quickly. Could there be more than one Polish Baron who had studied dairy farming in the United States? This man could be my father's friend, Baron Donimierski. "Tell me more about the farm," I say. "I have always liked cows."

She hasn't even started to answer when the door opens and a stream of women enters. Two guards shove them along with their rifles. As they stumble over the sill, the delicacy of some of their faces intrigues me. These are no farm-women accustomed to laboring in the fields and from the widening of some of their eyes, I see that they recognize me or, at least, they recognize my hair. While the male guards and our woman jailer jabber with details of the women's behavior during the day the new arrivals and I look at each other in mutual interest and misery. There were eleven of them and each stands at the foot of one of the straw mattresses like an exhausted soldier.

When one of them mouths the name, Aurora, I grin. I want to hug her like an old and valued friend.

The woman guard sees the grin and, leaving the men, turns toward me.

"Well then, we have friends among the elite, do we? Never mind. We will soon become all of one class. You." She points at me. "Step over here. I think ladies must be properly introduced to each other, is that not so? What is your name?"

My heart does several flips. I had hoped to hide my identity in this new place. I hesitate.
I have just decided to give my name when the door opens. Standing in the doorway was the giant of a man I know as Oncle Karol Donimierski. Even though his glance sweeps me and goes right by without recognition, my heart leaps with joy. I understand.

"Good evening, Frau Kleitz," he speaks to our jailer. "I hope you have had a pleasant day. I am here because I am in need of a woman to work in the house. The Gnadige Frau wishes to have it especially clean for some highly placed visitors who will be coming soon. Can you recommend some of your field workers for the job?"

" Herr Baron." Not quite used to a position of authority, Frau Kleitz, makes a little bobbing curtsy. "This new woman, number 7694169, does not appear strong enough for field work. Perhaps she would be right for you." Her hands are clasped under her apron, but her elbows stuck out freely. She uses one of them to indicate me. "She should be just right for your household."

"I'm sure she will be fine." He hardly glances my way. "Well, number 7694169, you bring your belongings if you have any, and come along with me." He starts out the door, stops and turns back. "Oh, yes, Frau Kleitz, we shall require that she stay in the house until the work is done. Perhaps even longer if the visitors extend their visit. I shall see that she does not escape and trust that this will not deplete your field work force."

"No sir, Herr Baron, I will still have plenty, but I thank you for your concern." She speaks to me as she closes the door behind us. "This will be even better than the dairy work."

I follow my savior down the path in silence, swallowing a smile. Inside the splendid house the draperies are already drawn. Once in the Library with the door closed, Oncle Karol envelopes me and says tenderly, "My dear little Carole. Jannina and I have been so worried. Dieter von Wechsler sent us a message that you had run away from Kurt and been caught and were in Auschwitz. He said he would try to get you released to us. With your husband's temper we prayed you would make it before Kurt knew you were out of Auschwitz. I don't know if you have heard, the war will soon be over. The Germans are almost too weak to fight as we speak." I draw my breath in quickly and hold it, afraid to believe that what he says.

" Not all Germans have a love for Hitler even when they appear to work for him. Jochin, for instance, is supposed to be spying on me, but he is the one who delivered Dieter von Wechsler's message. I suspect he works with the Polish underground, though I dare not ask."

My heart skips. Here's a chance to find out if Anna and Alex were still alive. Maybe I could even escape and be guided to Hel by the Partisans. My thoughts sing until reason takes over and I know I can't put Oncle Karol at risk by running away from his kindness. Tante Jannina steps softly into the room and opens her arms. Like a child coming home I walk into them and for a second am safe. Then, in my heart I hear my baby's cry of loneliness. I can never be safe until he is safely in my arms again.

Later, when we are sitting by the fire Oncle Karol says, "Now Caro, for heaven's sake tell us, first, why you married and then had the nerve to run away from that egomaniac Kurt von Pawel. Of course his egomania is reason enough, but how did you tolerate him for six years?"

"I didn't know you knew him?" I was surprised. "You lived so far apart."

"I didn't know him at all until he brought what seemed like the whole army of his SS friends here to search for you. With no apologies, they tore this place apart. That's when I knew you had disappeared and when I understood why. I guess he thought that since your father and I were friends, you'd come to us. Well, he was wrong and now the Germans are weak, but we'll still be careful. He might come back."

"Excuse me, Karol and Carole, Tante Janina interrupts with a laugh. "The servants will be back from their Sunday holiday soon and one never knows who can be trusted. So even if we have to break off abruptly," she turns to look at me," we have to know what's happened to you, Carole. Besides, we can keep you safe now and tonight I'll let your parents know you are with us. According to my hidden sources," Onkle Karol winks at me, "your father is just on the other side o f the Elbe River with General Patton's Third Army about now. Because I furnish them with the best milk in all of Europe, I'm allowed by some Germans and lately by the Russians also to hear things I'm not supposed to hear. They both say, that crazy Austrian is not able to take over the world and it won't be long before we get to march him to Auschwitz."

"Who are the guests who are coming?" I ask. "Should I hide while they are here? Might any of them be apt to recognize us?"

Oncle Karol stretches and grins. "Perhaps," he says in an off-hand fashion. "As soon as Hitler surrenders, perhaps Jonathon will come. When he knows you are here, not even your President will be able to stop him."

'Time is so short," Tante Nina reminds us "and it is late. Caro please tell us quickly of your life with the ballet and your years after your marriage. Just the highlights please."

"Don't leave out your marriage to Kurt. I'll never understand that."

"It doesn't make sense to me now, but I do remember how much I loved him." With more of their questions and prompting I start my tale at my first solo performance with the Warsaw Ballet.

Chapter 29

Between 1932 and 1935 I remember only my trips home in June, daily practices, matinees, evening performances and, because there was always a Christmas day matinee for the children, post-Christmas celebrations with my parents and the von Wechslers. As promised, I crossed the ocean in the summers when there was no ballet to spend a month in my own country. Although I loved having that time with my parents and thrilled to the sight of each Stars and Stripes that flew from Fort Riley's flag poles, I was really more comfortable in Poland.

The American girls' conversations centered around boys, clothes, dances and other things that were outside the sphere of my knowledge. At first they were interested in my ballet, but once they had asked a question or two and I had answered, we no longer had anything in common. I missed Deu and Anna and was always ready to go back before the end of the month.

Among many good friends in the Corps de Ballet, my closest friend was a Russian girl from Vladivostok. We became like sisters and when I wanted her to come to live with us in the apartment, Anna and Meier agreed. Katya wasn't pretty in the traditional sense, but her hair, a thick, glossy black, framed a face that, though pleasant, was almost plain. Two years older than I, she joined Anna in alternately coddling and teasing me because I was the youngest and smallest in the Corps de Ballet. On stage, when we were all made up, I thought I looked as grown up as the rest. Still, at home, Katya and I reverted to teenagers, giggling and behaving like the adolescents we were.

I talked to Katya about my feelings for Kurt. He was a part of a dream that I knew would never be fulfilled so I told her how I allowed him to thrill my heart. She understood because she had a crush on Meister Masaela's assistant, Vladimir. We made up romantic scenarios with ourselves, of course, as the heroines.

Because I spent my days steeped in something I loved and because I was young and nothing except my separation from my parents marred my life, the nights were filled with happy dreams.

Each time I saw Kurt on my rare visits to Friedenau or when he came to Warsaw with Dieter, the dreams became more exciting and he became the hero of any ballet we were performing. That kept the Corp de Ballet's endless practice sessions from becoming mechanical, but when there was music I was, as always, only what it made of me.

When the Corps was posed around the stage as background for the soloists, I watched carefully and studied each of her movements. Often, although the steps and positions were firmly dictated, I felt the dancer could have been more free and graceful. I practiced at home in front of my mirror to see if such freedom were possible. In the end, without recognizing what I was doing, I had learned each soloist's part.

Sometimes too, I watched the people in the front row. There was the haughty, big-bosomed woman in sable and diamonds accompanied by a spindly little man whose lifetime occupation seemed to be to pick up the things she dropped. The poor man spent nearly the entire evening bobbing up and down picking up her fan, her program, her glove, or her handkerchief. The only thing he never touched was her purse, which, I assumed, held the money. That hung by a gold chain from her bejeweled wrist. I felt sorry for him.

Then there was the little girl with her governess who came often to the matinees. She sat as still as a tiny mouse, except for her feet that twitched with the music and hands that clasped each other tightly so that they could not rise above her head to follow our positions. She was about eight and I think I recognized her from the beginning children's ballet classes.

Once in a while there was a familiar face. Seldom the one I hoped to see, but some of Dieter's and Kurt's friends were there from time to time to come backstage and to invite me to supper. Anna always chaperoned of course, but the visits broke the routine. Some of the young men were fun and even handsome. A few, in a moment of privacy after Anna had left us at the door, declared their love, but none replaced Kurt in my heart.

Truchen came once with two friends from the earlier years in Grudziadz. They spent the night with us and we giggled and talked so much we hardly got any sleep at all. Those visits, my parents' letters, trips to Friedenau and the down-to-earthiness of Anna and Meier kept me in touch with reality. Mostly, I followed the daily routine like an automaton except when I was actually dancing. Then I became someone else.

Being under sixteen I had school lessons in the mornings and ballet from one until six. There were performances every evening except Sundays. On Thursdays we also had matinees. Holidays were rare, but there was no ballet during the month of July, which gave us all the chance to go home. This year, Deu and I were to celebrate his fourth and my sixteenth birthday together in our usual way, I on stage, he in the dressing room with Anna. My sixteenth birthday. Three years with the ballet. I can't say I didn't aspire to more than dancing with the corps de ballet, but when I mentioned my hopes to Anna or Katya, they reminded me of how young I was. Sixteen sounded much more grown up than fifteen. Perhaps now I could begin to think about advancing to even as small a part as one of the mice in the upcoming Nutcracker.

Waiting for the usual celebration after the performance on my birthday evening, it seemed to me was going to be a little too inadequate. Meister Maseala would congratulate me in front of the entire company, then we would all go home. Anna, Meier, Katya, Deu and I would celebrate there with one of Anna's special cakes. We'd done that every year since we'd moved to Warsaw, but the sixteenth birthday should be a little different. If not yet a woman I was, at least, no longer a child.

When the curtain calls were over, the theater was empty of patrons, I waited expectantly. Nothing happened. The Meister was not in evidence. I tried to hide my disappointment as I changed into my street clothes and was almost out the door when he called us all onto the stage.

"I wish to honor our little American girl on her sixteenth birthday," he announced when we were clustered together. Everyone smiled as he separated me from the bunch. I'd expected that, but he held up his hand to stop the polite applause that came from the assemblage. "As a birthday gift to you, Carole, I now, with my magic wand, turn you into the Sugar Plum Fairy." He waved a wand, which he brought out from behind his back, over my head with a flourish. "Do you all not agree with me that she is the perfect ruler of the Land of Sweets?"

I held my breath. What did that mean? He couldn't mean to give me such a large part. There was applause and I looked around in bewilderment, not sure what it was for. A crowd of people stepped from behind the curtain. When I recognized Mother and Daddy, my heart gave one giant, choking thump before everything disappeared.

Kurt's voice made me open my eyes. He held me in his arms. I closed my eyes again. "Where shall I put her?"

A dream? Then I remembered what I thought I had heard.

A folding chairs scraped across the floor. "Here. Here's a chair." Arms set me gently onto it.

"Head down." Someone bent me double. Blood flowed to my brain and life began to become real again. I tried to sit up but the hands held me down.

"We shouldn't have tried to surprise her. It was too much for her." Mother's voice came from right in front of me. I opened my eyes into her beloved face as she knelt peering up into mine.

"I'd like to sit up, " I mumbled with my lips against my knees. "What's happening?"

"You fainted," Daddy's face appeared with Mother's.

" I don't know how to faint."

"It doesn't take practice." Daddy answered. "Here. Let her sit up." A wet cloth replaced the hand on the back of my neck.

This wasn't the way they treated heroines in movies when they swooned. They're never put in this undignified position or hit with clammy wet rags. Why didn't they leave me in Kurt's arms. Kurt's arms. Was that just a dream? Is he here? What's going on? I struggled to sit up.

The stage was full of people, but I almost fainted again when I saw all of my closest and most loved surrounding me. The von Wechlers, the von Pawels , Anna, Meier, Katya, Deu and Mother and Daddy were all there along with the entire ballet company. Tears rolled down my cheeks as I hugged each one. There wasn't even anything I could say. My tears had to say it all. I hugged everyone even Dieter, he was a sort of brother, but when I came to Kurt he took care of the situation.

He grabbed me and pulled me to him. "I think I have just become a balletomane put under a spell by a beautiful Sugar Plum Fairy," he whispered before he let me go.

I wished I knew how to faint again, but my attention was being claimed by so many at that moment I had no time to dwell on what he had said. The rest of the evening was a wonderful kaleidoscope of warmth and friendship. If I'd been the real Sugar Plum Fairy, my wand could have produced nothing more perfect. So perfect it couldn't be true. It had to be fantasy.

But the realities unfolded. Mother and Daddy would stay till the New Year came. Everyone was proud of me and happy for me. Kurt had said something which, though he could have meant something quite different, I hoped it was meant in the way I chose to take it. At last he saw me as someone grown-up.

On the first morning of our rehearsal for the part of the Fairy, when the music started and without waiting for direction, I began to dance.

"Halt," Vladimir, Meister Masaela ordered the accompanist. He shouted so loudly that everyone in the rehearsal hall fell silent. All eyes turned on the two of us. "What do you think you're doing, Carole?" In definite agitation, the man was pounding on the floor with the ever-present staff.

My heart started to knock against my ribs and my breath came out in such soft gasps my voice must have been barely audible. "I thought the Meister made me The Sugar Plum Fairy." I was terrified that it had really all been a dream. "Was I wrong?"

"Of course you weren't wrong, but you don't know the Fairy's part."

"I think I do. May I show you"?

"Pani Vladimir," Katya's voice came from the auditorium. "Carole knows all of the steps of every ballet we've ever performed. She could dance any part. While the rest of us scan the audience for friends during a performance, she studies the ballerinas. She is even more attentive during the rehearsals. Please let her show you."

232

"Yes, yes," chorused the rest of the corps.

Vladimir adjusted his glasses, looked at the floor, stared at Katya, then said to the accompanist, " Play." He looked at me with something akin to a sneering disbelief.

The music started. I began to dance the part of the Fairy when the Nutcracker Prince and Clara arrive at the Land of Sweets.Suddenly I felt as though some wonderful forces were carrying my weight and as if my toes were barely skimming the floor as lightly as the fairy's. When the music stopped there was silence, then there was applause. The Meister stood beside Vladimir. Even Tito, the accompanist was clapping his hands together, gently so as to not damage his livelihood.

Saying nothing else Herr Masaela simply instructed Tito to, "Play one of Aurora's solos from Sleeping Beauty." To me he ordered, "Dance."

I did, though not as lightly as I had danced the Fairy. Now I was apprehensive. Why was he having me do this?

When it was over he walked to me. "That was not quite as good," he said. "It needs work, but you will be ready by the time the Christmas season is over and The Nutcracker is finished." He started to walk away.

"Please, sir. What do you mean?" I must have looked like an idiot, flat footed in my pointe shoes with my mouth hanging open. His words made no sense to me.

"Can't you understand the Polish language?" he asked. A big grin brightened his face. He became almost handsome. "What I mean is that our dear Prima Ballerina Krajinski is to be married and has accepted an offer from the Metropolitan Ballet in America. It seems only fair in such a case that the Americans should allow us an exchange Prima, even if she is a young one. If you do well in the Nutcracker and are well liked, you shall be Aurora in Sleeping Beauty for the winter season. Is this something you wish to do? You will not also go flying off to America?"

For the second time in my life I fainted.

"I don't dare offer you anymore parts unless you break this habit." The Meister held me, bent almost double with my forehead nearly touching the floor between my splayed legs. "It would be terrible if you should fall in a faint during a performance."

"I promise I will never do that." I twisted from his grasp until I was kneeling in front of him. "Oh, please, sir. I will never do it again."

"I seriously doubt you did it on purpose this time," he smiled and pulled me to my feet. "But," he said as he walked away, "see that you don't. Warsaw needs you."

On opening night of The Nutcracker, and forever after, the theater was packed. I was glad to have had that small part to lead me into the success that was to follow. They were again all there for me, the von Wechslers, the von Pawels, all my friends from Grudziadz, Torun, and Warsaw. Most importantly, peeking from behind the curtain to see if Kurt was there, I saw Mother and Daddy in the center of the very front row between Oma and Baron Ludwig von Pawel. Although I didn't see Kurt, he must have been there too. Instead of making me more nervous, knowing they were there to support me, calmed me.

Once more that magic force bore my weight and I felt as if the Sugar Plum Fairy floated above the stage. The applause and curtain calls told me it was a success and that I would be Aurora when the Sugar Plum Fairy had gone back to her Land of Sweets.

Chapter 30

On New Year's Eve 1934/35 Aurora captured the heart of the city of Warsaw. Meier brought in the newspaper while we were at breakfast the next morning. While Anna read the review aloud, I sat at the table almost afraid to listen. A usually caustic critic by the name of Langer had reviewed The Sleeping Beauty and I was sure he would leave nothing more than tattered shreds of what I had dreamed would be my career.

"The American ballerina, Carole Pierson, who danced the role of Aurora last night, has, indeed, proven herself to be the true Sleeping Beauty," she read. I couldn't believe it as Anna read on. "One did not expect to see such perfection in a girl so young, but one was thrilled beyond measure as intricate step followed intricate step with all the weight of a feather on a cloud. Add to that the beauty of the girl with hair like the aurora of the sunrise. She gave to one and all this miraculous evening. One can only say, thank God she is now ours. However, I do predict . . . our Aurora will soon belong to the world."

We all sat too stunned to even converse as we listened to Pan Langer's unexpected words. Katya recovered first.

"Why are we surprised?" she asked. "We knew we lived with Aurora and that she dwelt in the clouds. Oh, Carole, I am so proud to be your friend and, to be truthful, a little envious too. I hope that's all right because I love you more than I envy you," she added.

Anna pushed her chair back and came to put her arms around me and to embrace me. "I wish your Mutti und Fatter could have been here to see, as we did, the wonder of your dancing. Even Deu sat up straight to watch. Of course," she held me slightly away from her and looked into my eyes. "There was never any doubt in any of our minds that you could outshine even the famous Pavlova." She pushed me back down onto my chair. "Still," she said pouring me another cup of cocoa, "you must not let this man's words go to your head. He can be wrong, you know."

Everyone laughed. We all knew Anna took her job as mother, father, and disciplinarian seriously. She would not allow me to have an inflated ego for even one day.

When the doorbell rang, Meier went to answer it. Kurt, his overcoat draped in sheets of the newspaper, crossed the dining room in a few determined strides, gathered me up, stood me on my chair and dropped to one knee in front of it. No one had time to absorb what was taking place, least of all me.

"Princess Aurora," he said in a pleading voice looking up at me, "say you will become my wife to love, honor, and obey me and to dance only for me all the days of my life."

There was an almost tangible silence while we all stared at this formerly always correct and conceited man as he knelt, newspapers fluttering from his shoulders, at my feet. I didn't even absorb his words before the others all began to laugh.

"I hardly expected laughter," Kurt stood up and tore the papers from his overcoat. "Is that all you can say to an honest proposal of marriage?"

I couldn't speak. Anna stepped around the table to confront him. "If I thought for one second you were serious, I would have a great deal to say." She looked up at him and her expression was almost fierce.

His shoulders stiffened and his voice was very cold. "Then speak, Anna, if you have the right to do so. If you don't have the right, let Aurora speak for herself."

"It's true I don't have the final right, but since her parents aren't here—and if you are serious—I shall tell you what they would say to that proposal and we will mention the subject no more until they are here. Carole is only sixteen years old," she began. "Just sixteen," she reiterated. "She is starting a promising career in dancing which she loves. Whether or not she thinks she loves you like an adult, she isn't old enough to make that judgment. Let us just say in this instance that you, a grown man, were carried away by the glamour of the ballet and were only making a joke. At least, to most women on the brink of a career, some of your words must have been meant as a joke. If, however, you were not being witty and if you care to pursue the subject in a few years, everyone might be willing to listen." She turned to me, "Carole, get down from that chair."

Kurt, no longer gentle, lifted me down and almost dropped me on the floor. His words had not had the affect he'd expected, I said to myself, and he had been embarrassed in front of, what he considered, menials. That's why he was so abrupt, poor man. Then my heart, with a great thump, began to beat rapidly when I realized that he had actually asked me to marry him.

"Can't you speak for yourself, Carole?" His voice was harsh.

His original actions had been right out of one of my dreams and I wanted to say, yes I'd marry him in a few years, but I, too, had thought he was joking. I had to be careful not to let my secret feelings show because I was sure he would use my own words to tease me.

"Why, of course I would marry you," I said. "Except I have so many suitors that I'd have to ask Anna or Mother which one would be most suitable for the Princess Aurora." I thought that treated the whole thing lightly. "So you're welcome to come around any time you have a moment free." I kept my voice light and waved my hand airily as if to dismiss him.

I don't know what would have happened next because the doorbell rang again to interrupt what, from the expression on Kurt's face, I was afraid, might have been a tantrum. His father entered the room. Anna made a bobbing curtsy.

"Good morning Herr Baron," she said.

"Good morning, Anna and everyone," The Baron continued to stride toward me. "Ah. Here is my beautiful protegée. Come, little one, and let your Grandfather hold such a tremendous talent in his arms for even a moment."

I moved toward him and, as we reached each other, I curtsied. His arms enfolded mostly air and my head. Laughter again saved us all from a moment almost too tender to bear. This gentleman had poured concern and money into me for almost six years. Without him I knew I would probably be taking tap and ballet from a small town teacher in the middle of Kansas. I owed him every moment of my joy in this day and the days to come.

"Now that did not come out the way it was intended. Let's try again." His arms folded around me. I felt warm and at home. Having no other, I had grown to love this man as my revered and adored grandfather.

"Herr Baron," I tried to speak, my voice thickened with tears of gratitude and my words muffled in the lapel of his suit coat. "Without you there would have been no Aurora in Warsaw today." I drew back to look up at him. "In Kansas, where Daddy is stationed, probably no one has ever heard of the ballet Sleeping Beauty. It's possible that no one has even seen a ballet at all. You are responsible for my being in this time and this place and I will love you for it all the days of my life. When I dance, it will always be for you whether you are there or not." I managed to free my arms to give him a great hug.

"The honored title is now Opa and do I not also get a kiss?" He bent to offer his cheek. I kissed him just beside his ear in answer. If his whiskers prickled, I didn't notice.

"This is a fine state of affairs," Kurt's voice was sharp. "Here I propose marriage to the beautiful Aurora, and do I get a kiss? No. All I get is laughter."

The Baron turned from me quickly to look at his son. "Were you serious?"

"Indeed I was. You've always told me never to let a worthwhile thing escape my notice. What could be more worthwhile than an American Princess who is bound to become a Queen? Would that not be a beautiful addition to the von Pawel crest?" Kurt's chin lifted and he looked almost smug, though I knew my idol couldn't have such covetous emotions.

"And what did she say?"

"If it's any of your business, she didn't get a chance to say anything. Anna answered for her."   Kurt was being insolent. I wanted to tell him not to speak to his father that way. My father would have told him if he'd been there.

"And Anna said?"

"Ask Anna."

"I don't need to ask Anna. I know what she would have said. She is a wise woman. But, let me tell you that if Anna had not intervened and if Carole, at the age of sixteen, had accepted and if you, God forbid, had married this child, there would have been no money to support you. Since the only work you have ever done was your two enforced years in the Polish Military, Carole would, no doubt, have danced for your bread and butter. "

"Mother left me plenty of money, if you remember." If a man could be said to flounce, that was the impression Kurt gave. I was ashamed for him.

"To be managed by me until you are thirty-five years old, if you remember. But enough. Let us air no more linen in this company. The worst did not happen. Carole is free to follow her career and to make us even more proud than we are today. Instead of this disastrous bickering, let us celebrate. Come, our heroine, since it's the first day of the New Year and there is no performance, let's all go to the Excelsior Hotel to luncheon and to celebrate. The von Wechslers had to take the early morning train because the Gnädige Frau felt ill. Ernst is sure she will recover, but it seemed best to take her home. At least they got to see and applaud your performance last night. Elise said they will telephone you tonight. In any event, we will pick you up at one-thirty."

When Anna and Meier tried to refuse, the Baron insisted. He said that if they didn't go, none of us would go. They finally agreed. He and Kurt left us. I never heard what was said between the father and son on their way back to the apartment the Baron kept in Warsaw, but when we were all together again, everything was as light and celebratory as it should have been.

People who had been to the ballet the night before recognized me for the first time. It was such a thrill to have them whisper to each other as we passed their tables, and to have the little children bring their menus and even napkins to be autographed. At first I didn't know what they wanted, but Kurt made sure I fulfilled, in his words, my duty.

He treated me like a Princess and he, my advisor. He made sure that everyone who came hesitantly to our table knew that I was Princess Aurora and not Carole Pierson. Familiar with Tchaikovsky's music, the chamber orchestra played excerpts from the Ballet and again there was applause. I was forced to stand and bow while my dinner cooled on its plate. I happily ate it cold. At last it was quiet and it was then Kurt reached over to take my hand in his under the tablecloth.

My shock was almost the same as it had been when the awful priest had done the same in the Krolewski Dwor, but revulsion was replaced by the deepest thrill I had ever felt. I looked up at him and knew he would recognize the love in my eyes. I didn't care.

When everyone else was busy talking, he leaned over to whisper, "I'll keep asking until you say yes." I thought what I saw in his eyes was love.

The day was so important and my excitement so great I can almost remember it minute by minute. When we had said goodbye to father and son at the station and the train had pulled out, Katya and I were left alone on the platform. As we walked back toward the cabstand, we hooked arms.

"I'm so proud of you," she said again. "You behaved all day like a real grown-up lady. Wasn't it fun??"

"Oh, Katya," I turned to hug her in love and gratitude, "it would have been so much less without you there. How can I ever thank you for being my only "sister"? She murmured something in Russian. I couldn't understand it, but it didn't matter so I continued.

"As it was, with Mother and Daddy absent, it must have lost some of its luster though, to tell the truth, I don't know where. Maybe it would have been more wonderful if I had been able to say yes to Kurt, but I still don't know whether he was serious or not. Besides," I sighed a blissful sigh as we walked on arm in arm, "I feel too young. I think, if he truly means it, it would be better to wait until I learn more about how to be a grown up."

My parents called at eleven and between Anna, Katya and me, they were left in no doubt about the glamour and success of the beginning of my 'new year'. The dawning of my unintentional career. In bed that night I tried to relive again the wonderful New Year's Eve performance: the applause, the standing ovation, the curtain calls, the flowers, and the name that has stayed with me until this very day. Rarely has anyone ever called me anything but Aurora since then except Kurt who always put the "Princess" in front of it. Snuggled under my down puff, I found it hard to differentiate between those thrills and the thrill of Kurt's warm hand under the tablecloth. I slept the dreamless sleep of the truly happy.

Chapter 31

At the theater the next morning I was briefly celebrated again as a Princess. Everyone had read Herr Langer's revue and I was congratulated over and over. Reality, however, quickly returned when we lined up at the barre and the daily exercises began. From then on, by night and on Thursday and Sunday matinees I got to be a princess. But Anna made sure I remembered that Aurora was the dancer. Carole Pierson was the American.

When Kurt came to Warsaw I was Aurora all of the time. Sometimes he came with Dieter, but more often alone. He never called me anything other than Princess and he treated me like one. When he was there and when I had time, he insisted on shopping with me and even advised me in my clothing selections.

"That isn't right for you," he would say when I picked something out for myself so I always let him choose first. Frequently I thought his choices made me look too old or too sallow, but it hurt his feelings if I said "no" and I loved him too much to do that. For the first year, when he couldn't be there, he filled my dressing room with flowers. By the second and third years, when Aurora became known all over Europe no matter what role she danced, his appearances were fairly regular on the weekends. Afterwards we always went out for a late supper. Anna sat at another table well removed from us, but always within view.

When Aurora danced by invitation in Paris, Kurt was there in the front row. In Milan---there he was. There, also, was Anna. Soon, Kurt began bringing a friend for Katya and we four went together. Sometimes they got up to dance and we had a little time alone to talk. Our chaperone, be it Anna or Katya, did allow us a few minutes of privacy at whatever door was ours for the evening and, of course, we could converse out of her hearing and even hold hands under the tablecloth in the Cabarets. In other places where there were orchestras we danced every dance just to be in each other's arms. No matter where we were, his conversation always centered on our inevitable marriage.

"Herr Gott, Princess," he exploded one late night in our few allotted minutes at the front door. "Are we never to have more than this snip of time alone?" Aurora had signed endless autographs at the table, which had kept us from dancing and, though proud, Kurt was angry. "I want you and I guess I'll have to marry you to get you. Marry me. You need taking care of and I want to be the one to do it." He seized me so roughly it hurt and kissed me with such ferocity that he bruised my lips. "I've seen the line-up of men at the stage door and one of them might steal you away from me. I can't go on leading this sort of life."

By then I had loved him for eight years and, over the tables in nightclubs and restaurants, had told him so. Now, thrilled at his words, I didn't question what he meant. Although he'd never said so, I knew he loved me and, to me, that meant he wanted what I wanted. He knew the ballet was the very blood that coursed through my veins and probably was my only strength. I told myself that "this sort of life" must have meant being together only in cabarets. His kisses at the door had become more and more ardent and demanding. He had crushed me against the wall with his body and my own feelings told me the time was coming when I would defy Anna and my own morality.

I was 19 years old on the day I held his adored face in my hands and whispered, "Yes, my darling, I will marry you."

The ring he slipped on my finger held a diamond as big and as bright as Venus in the night sky. He said it had been his Grandmother's and his Mother's and that was the only time I ever heard him mention her.

"What was she like?" I asked him.

His reply was to kiss me quickly and leave. I wondered why he was never willing to talk about her and decided it must be a subject that was too painful for him. Poor little boy, I thought. The fact that Kurt had asked me to marry him and I had accepted was too much for my heart and brain to comprehend. Also, there was something that didn't quite let me have the joy I should have been feeling. So sure of my love, it was something else, unknown, unwanted and incomprehensible. I didn't even tell Katya my news. Although she always stayed awake until I got home, I wasn't ready to share. Mother and Daddy were coming the next day for their Christmas visit. Maybe that's what's I was waiting for. To her usual query as to whether I had had a good time I answered "of course," slid into bed and spent a nearly sleepless night.

Strange feelings soared when I dwelt on the pressure of Kurt's eager lips against mine and the hardness of his body as he pinned me against the front door. Those, I was a little afraid of, and they were accompanied by that weighty feeling that something was wrong. I wanted to understand it. Morning dawned before I slept without even a dream.

When Mother and Daddy arrived and we were back in the apartment, Kurt was waiting. He hardly shook hands with my Father before he stated flatly. "The Princess and I are to be married at Friedenau on January 1st. We do hope you will come."

The statement was met with open-mouthed silence. Fresh from the railroad station, still in our heavy coats, boots and hats, we must have resembled the frozen court of Sleeping Beauty. All heads whipped around to look at me.

Mother found her voice first. "Is that so, Carole?"

I looked at Kurt who stood relaxed and smiling. "I've accepted his proposal," I admitted. "We haven't discussed any of the plans."

"Without talking to us?" Daddy said.

"I didn't know I was going to say 'yes'. I couldn't help myself. Truly I couldn't. It just happened last night. You must have known I've always loved him."

Daddy slowly shed his coat then he turned to Kurt. 'Have you discussed this with your father? If not---you should before you discuss it with us." He put out his hand in dismissal. "Perhaps it might be wise if you go do that now while we have time to talk about this . . . . privately . . . as a family. It's been a shock as you can imagine."

Kurt made a funny sound almost like a snort. I was embarrassed for him. "Perhaps a surprise. But a shock? That I cannot imagine. After all, she will gain a title. A real one. What more could a parent want?" He left and the door slammed behind him.

"Her happiness," Daddy said softly to the closed door. There was a long pause.

"We will bring coffee," Anna took Meier's arm and they started to walk stiffly to the kitchen.

"You belong in this conference too, Anna, you and Meier. Mother dropped her coat on a hall chair. She started into the living room still in her fur-topped boots, hat and gloves. "Bring the coffee and we'll all sit down together."

"Gnadige Frau," Katya's soft voice stopped her. "Allow me to help with boots. Please to sit here and I will the unstringing do." She gestured to a Biedermeier chair that dominated the space between the living and dining room doors. Her English was improving, but was no more grammatical than my Polish.

Mother smiled at her and sat. "Did you know about this?" She

246

asked. We all knew what she meant.

"I know Carole love him much." Katya removed one boot.

Mother took off her gloves. "Do you think he loves her?"

"I think, yes. He come Warsaw much often. Sit in theater. They go to cabaret. Anna go. Daytime walk in park. Sometime I go. Anna, Meier go also. Have lunch in café. Carole talk with me how much and long time she love him. I happy for her. I only hope he not hurt Carole. He more selfish, I think."

"Thank you Katya, you're a good friend. What will you do if they marry?"

"Carole will not leave the ballet. We still live, dance. He come like always. I sleep in back room."   Katya had it all worked out in her mind.

"What?" Mother's voice rose in horror.

"Katya doesn't mean now." I hurried to interject. "It's just a mistake in her English."

Mother breathed a sigh of relief. "I only hope he agrees with your plans, but it would be out of character," she said softly as she walked into the living room. Daddy, Katya and I followed.

I would have been too uncomfortable to curl up next to Mother even if the stiff sofa had been less austere, so we four sat like wooden puppets on a shelf until Meier and Anna returned with the coffee and brötchen. Mother directed everyone to places and they perched on the edges of the heavily carved chairs. We had never sat in the living room under tense conditions before and I had no idea how unfriendly the furniture could be. As if no one knew how to begin, we sat in silence for several moments. Finally Daddy cleared his throat.

"Tell us your feelings, Caro. Are you sure this is what you want to do? Have you thought of all of the problems you will be facing?" He leaned a little forward so he could touch my clenched hand. He took it in his and uncurled my fingers one by one. He stroked them and looked into my eyes. "I know you think you love Kurt, but will that be enough to make you live forever so far from us? Will you be willing to give up your citizenship . . . perhaps even your ballet?"

I started to interrupt to tell him that Kurt knew how much both of those things meant to me and that he would never ask me to give up either one, but Daddy continued on.

"Yes, you'll be a Baroness someday, but does that mean anything to you? Your children will be brought up as Germans. The world is growing edgy right now at Hitler's antics in Europe and you have to remember that they have always been a combative nation. Do you think you could ever be happy cut off from us and the land you love?" Daddy looked deeply into my eyes. "Think carefully, my dear child, before you answer."

I had heard the von Wechslers and the Baron discussing Hitler and, what they called, his shenanigans. They didn't like him. I had tried to broach the subject with Kurt, thinking I would impress him with my knowledge of the affairs of the world, but he became furious.

"You don't know what you're talking about," he'd growled, so I'd never ventured into politics again.

I did know that Hitler had withdrawn Germany from the League of Nations while improving the schools, the roads, and the economy. The people of the Vaterland were singing his praises. I did not know that most other Nations, with few exceptions, remembered WWI and were neither laudatory nor comfortable with his growing influence.

Ernst, Elise, the old Baron and Sybilla's family were also not confident. "He has improved the schools in Germany, maybe. But the teachers still preach the 'believe it because I say it's so' theory," the Baron said sadly. "The youth, boys and girls, are marching to his cadence and no one, adult or child, asks questions. They just close their minds and obey as they always have. What a pity, and what a danger perhaps for all of Europe."

I had heard all of that, but love came first. Like the Germans, I didn't want to listen. I was sure Kurt would never let me face anything unpleasant. He would take care of me and my life would go on more wonderful and complete than ever. All of the things Daddy had mentioned would never happen. Eventually, after Kurt's father died, I was satisfied he and I would move to the USA with only trips back to Europe in the summer. I would dance at the Metropolitan. We would have children (though how I could do both never occurred to me) and life would follow the fairy tale happily ever after.

"You don't need to worry about all of that, Daddy," I spoke with the confidence of an all-knowing nineteen year-old. "If things look bad over here, Kurt and his father would send me right back home until they got better. Why even Meister Maesela wouldn't let anything happen to me. They love me too, you know."

"You're sure of that?" Mother took my other hand in hers.

"I'm so sure."

"Well then, there isn't much more to say. We both need some rest while we digest the unexpected fare of this morning." Mother stood up and I waited for the joyous words that would give me happily into Kurt's safe keeping. They didn't come.

"Aren't you happy for me?" I asked following them to the door.

"My dearest girl." Mother turned and took me in her arms. She laid her head on my head and I felt her tears on my forehead. "I know what you want and need from us and we want so much to give it. It just takes a little time. It's not an easy thing to give your child away. We always knew—hoped—that someday love would come for you, but we just want to be sure it's the right love. The love that will make you happy all the rest of your days. You're very young, Precious, and very self-sufficient and wise, but this is a big step. Don't be in such a hurry to take it." She let me go and started off. but stopped again. "We love you so much," she said, tears running down her face. And then they were gone.

Anna was crying too as Meier led her away. Katya and I stood alone.

"When I meant to make everyone as happy as I was---how could I have made them so miserable?" My own tears started.

Katya put her arms around me. She was crying too. "They will be happy for you, Aurora. It's just they can't face losing you. You will see. When you all back together, your Mother and Father will have thought it out. They will smile again. Anna too."

I felt better. We went into our bedroom and my excitement grew as we discussed plans for the wedding. It never occurred to me to change Kurt's plans or to ask for more time. I was sure Fraulein Göethe would make me a beautiful wedding dress. Mother was here to help. Daddy could get a day or two more of leave so he could give me away, and on the first day of 1939 I would belong to Kurt forever.

Katya was right. When we met again at lunch time, everyone seemed cheerful and ready to discuss the wedding plans. If there were sighs or if the conversation seemed strained from time to time,

I didn't notice. I accepted each thought, plan, or idea with joy.

The Baron and Kurt joined us at teatime. If there had been any struggle between them, it didn't show. Daddy and the older gentleman were closeted in the library for a little while, but came out arm in arm. I've never known what they discussed, but before we went to bed that night Mother and Daddy came into the room to, as they said, tuck us in one more time.

Sitting on the side of my bed, she took one of my hands. "Understand, Caro, that we love you more than words can tell." She leaned over to kiss me on the forehead. "We want only the best for you. Daddy hasn't said much to you yet and now he wants his turn." She traded places so my father could sit down.

"Caro," he joked. "I knew that first night in the Krowlewski Dwor that coming to Poland was a mistake. If we had run then, perhaps we would never have lost you." He smiled at me. "On the other hand, you would never have had the chance to become Princess Aurora or Giselle or any of the fantasy people whose bodies you have imbued with reality and grace. You would never have had the joy of giving pleasure to thousands as you have done. But . . ." he paused. "No man is easy to live with, just ask your Mother. I have a feeling Kurt may be more difficult than most. He's very sophisticated, which you are not. He is extremely sure of himself and I suspect will be demanding. You may find yourself torn in many directions. Don't become too giving, my darling, or you will find you've lost your own identity. Please, please, please, even when you dance, remain Carole. Carole is the one we love." He, too, kissed my forehead. "Having said that, if you're sure this marriage is the one you want, we give you our blessings. Goodnight girls. We can make more plans in the morning."

They turned out the light as they left the room. Lying there in the dark, I wasn't sure what he meant about my identity. How could I lose that. I would always be me. How little I understood.

Chapter 32

At breakfast Mother insisted Anna and Meier join us at the table. Anna giggled and refused. Daddy insisted, both Meier and Anna bashfully refused. Mother explained that they were now in a different position in the household. They were family. They still refused. At last Daddy issued an order. Meier, the ex-army-private, saluted and perched on the designated chair like a bird eyeing a cat ready to spring. Anna followed suit. We had gone through this same tussle for seven years each time my parents visited.

Meier was still ill at ease with them. Unless spoken to directly, he seldom entered the conversations. When we were alone and he and Anna were in charge, I had gotten to know him as a kind, funny little man who loved my Anna with all of his heart and who would have given up his life to protect either one of us.

Mother opened the conversation. "Is the chapel at Ostatetcznie just a burial plot like the one at Friedenau or can it be used for a wedding?" She looked at me.

Before I could answer, Meier cleared his throat. "It is permitted that I speak?" He asked in halting English.

The forks already traveling to our mouths stopped in mid-action. We all stared until Daddy said, "Why, Meier, you speak our language. When did you learn?"

Meier, blushing and struggling for each syllable, cleared his throat again. "Anna and I learn in night. We . . . how to say?" He stopped and looked at his wife for help.

"Hope?" She questioned.

"Hope," he repeated. "We go wiz die Fraulein to America one day."

Daddy smiled. "You are doing very well and we are proud of you both. Yes, someday you will come to America."

Meier's repetition of "someday" was so soft as to be almost inaudible as he stored it away in his vocabulary. "Sank you, Herr Major. We be happy come. Now no more speak the English." He started again in Polish.

"He says there is a chapel at Ostatetcznie which he would assume Kurt plans to use. He saw it once when he went there with Zarrotti to deliver something," Anna translated. Her English was by now almost as good as mine. Meier nodded vigorously.

I said, "It's a lovely old stone chapel. I don't think you have to worry about that part of the wedding, Mum. Kurt will have taken care of that."

"Is he Protestant or Catholic?" Daddy asked.

"Come to think about it," I answered, "I don't know. It's something we have never discussed. If he were a Catholic, wouldn't he have gone to church on Sundays?"

"Possibly." Daddy spread jam on his brötchen. "It seems there are quite a few things about this man you plan to marry that you don't know. Some rather important things."

"I know we love each other. Isn't that enough?'

Daddy just looked at me. I knew he was right. I would have to find out at least what religion Kurt was. But, when he and his father returned in time for tea, it seemed Kurt was more interested in the reception than the wedding. We all sat silently while he told us briefly how and where the ceremony was to be conducted. It would be in the huge entrance hall at the foot of the stairs and then everyone would go to the ballroom for the reception. We would spend our wedding night at Ostatetcznie, after which he and I would spend two weeks each in Paris and Berlin.

"But. Kurt," I felt I had to interrupt. "I'm not sure whether I can take that much time away from the ballet. I'll have to ask . . ."

"You'll be given the time." Kurt looked at me with a slight smile. We were all seated around the table in the dining room and he was holding my hand. He squeezed it so hard I inadvertently jerked it away.

"But what if I'm not?" The smile made me think he was teasing.

"Don't worry about it, Aurora, I will work it out. You just enjoy the fact that you will soon be a real Baroness. Wait for January first. We'll make 1939 sing." He took my hand again under the tablecloth as he turned to his father. "I presume I can depend on you to order the proper kind of supper for an evening wedding reception." As he talked he squeezed my hand again, too tightly, but this time I managed to show no reaction.

"I'm so pleased to be allowed to be part of these festivities to take place in my home." I thought there was a slight sarcastic tone in Opa's statement. "Perhaps you could think of some small task for Janice and Jonathan. After all it is their daughter's wedding you're planning." This sarcasm was real.

"Yes, Kurt. A mother looks forward to sharing in her daughter's wedding plans. While we realize this is different because we are the strangers in your land." Mother leaned over to put a hand on Kurt's sleeve. "Please allow us to help in some way."

"Why, naturally, Mother. As soon as there is something, I shall be overjoyed to let you know."

"Well, at least we can help choose the wedding dress and since

Katya will be the attendant she will need a gown too." Mother turned to Katya with a smile.

"Dieter will be my attendant and Sybilla will honor Aurora," Kurt said with finality.

The wedding dress was forgotten. I found my voice. "Kurt, dear." I stood up and went behind his chair to put my arms around his neck. "Katya is the sister I never had and I don't think I could feel married without having her there close to me. Sybilla can be in the wedding party too. It only means you will have to have another friend to escort her down the aisle."

His expression darkened and then---like the sun coming out---- he grinned at me. I went back to my chair. "Of course, my darling Princess. I didn't think. Of course it should be Katya. I will ask Karl. He will be delighted to couple with Sybilla." Again there was stunned silence.

Karl had been a friend of Kurt and Dieter's. He had been in love with Sybilla ever since I'd known them. Eventually there had been trouble between Dieter and Karl until Sybilla had chosen Dieter. Karl had moved away. Kurt hadn't mentioned him in several years. Wherever he was, to have him in the wedding could only bring disruption. Kurt couldn't have given the matter any thought or he would never have suggested such a thing.

"But," I lurched into the breach. "Have you thought of Dieter and Sybilla? That would ruin everything for them and most certainly for us too. We don't want any unhappiness at our wedding."

Kurt squared his shoulders and raised his chin imperiously. It was not one of his gestures I liked. He spoke to the room. "I think it would add spice, don't you? After all, who wants a bland stew? We possibly could even stage a duel to amuse our guests." His face held the expression of innocence.

How could he think this was a time for joking?

Katya, who obviously took him seriously, broke in. "It won't hurt my feelings not to be in the wedding, Caro. I can find another job to do." She came around to give me a hug.

"He's kidding." I patted her arms. "You'll both be my attendants and Karl won't be here, will he, Kurt?" He shrugged. That indifference made me uncomfortable, but I thought we could discuss it if we ever had some privacy.

"As to the wedding dress," Mother crossed the room to sit beside me. "Do you have a seamstress here or would you like Fraulein Goethe to make it?"

Kurt spoke up. "She will wear my grandmother's wedding dress." He was emphatic. "Oma was married at Ostatetcznie in 1859. The gown is quite suitable for today."

"Now hold on," his father chimed in. "Kurt, you can't tell the bride what she is to wear. It's her wedding." He looked at me. "It is indeed a lovely gown, but you must have the one you choose. I will have my mother's delivered to you this coming week, my dear, and then you can decide. Wear it only if you love it above all others. Is that agreeable with you, Janice and Jonathon?"

Mother nodded. "That way the groom will not know what she has decided until he sees her coming toward him down those curving stairs." She sounded satisfied.

"Coming toward me?" He pushed his chair back and stood up. "I shall escort her and we will come down the stairs together."

Daddy jumped up from his chair and stood almost face to face with his soon-to-be-son-in-law. "That is my job and my right to give her away. I don't mean to argue with you, but I will insist on that part of the American ceremony being properly carried out."

"If you intend to ruin everything, we will do it your way," Kurt conceded.

I wished he had been more gracious in his concession. Apparently, so did my father. He took a step forward. I had only witnessed my father's anger once before. That was when he had cornered the priest in the hall at the Krolewski Dwor. He was slow to ignite, but now I saw the same expression on his face. Kurt shifted his feet and balled his fists.

My father's lips disappeared into a straight, grim line. "If I should wish to destroy the ceremony, I can do that easily. I am in a position to say there will be no marriage at all. To take my daughter and my wife and walk out of this room." His voice was flat and firm.

"Try it. Aurora will not go with you." Kurt sneered.

"Aurora may not, but Carole will."

Frozen in my chair, unaware that I was holding my breath, my heart beat furiously enough to break. I had never defied my father and knew I could not do so now.

"Apologize." The Baron strode across the room to face his son. "This is an American girl you wish to marry. You may not dictate how the ceremony will be conducted."

"It's my house." Kurt was defiant.

"You're wrong. As long as I live, it is my house and I say that it is the bride's right to have things as she wishes. You may offer suggestions, suggestions only. And understand me well. There will be no Karl in the wedding party."

Kurt's hand came up as if to push his father away, but in the next second there was a complete metamorphosis. He became as gracious as I had ever seen him. His hand dropped to clasp my father's clenched fist. He smiled. "Of course my father is right. I am overstepping my bounds. Do forgive me. Everything will be as you wish."

I was so proud of him. Daddy allowed his hand to be vigorously shaken and even managed a wintry smile. With a continuing gracious smile, Kurt motioned for everyone to sit.

"Now that that's settled, let's sit down and have more tea. Anna, do you think you could heat some more water? Would anyone like some torte?" Kurt passed the cake plate to his father.

"No, thank you." The Baron passed it on. "I think, Kurt, that you and I must be running along. We have many things to do at Ostatetcznie. There's the seven o'clock train." Opa came around the table to kiss me goodbye. "Expect the gown on Monday or Tuesday, but remember, don't wear it unless you really and truly love it. For this important day, the dress must be exactly the one you want."

I already knew that, beautiful or hideous, the one Kurt wanted would be my choice too.

After they were gone, Daddy put his arms around me and said softly, "Caro, I love you with all of my heart and want to do whatever will make you happy, but I am not sure that your young man and I will ever develop a bond of the kind you might wish us to have. I will try, but guarantee nothing."

"That's all right, Daddy," I was so sure the recent disagreement was only because of timing and tension. Surely Kurt would never be rude to my father again once things settled down. "You'll grow to be the best of friends. I can almost see you both now playing with your grandchildren. Laughing and enjoying them and each other."

Children. That was a new thought and one I thought I'd better ask Mother about. Still, some time after that first 'birds and bees' attempt, she had realized I didn't have a true picture and we had what she called "a talk". Actually, it was more like a lecture. She explained in a vague way about monthly periods so that I was left with the idea that something like a punctuation mark was going to be imprinted on me, but there was no what, where, how or why. Whatever this dot was--- it would purify my blood. When the real thing arrived at age thirteen, I was terrified. "I know it's scary at first," Mother had said, "but it's one of the things females have to put up with so they can have children." That was as far as the conversation went. The period came relentlessly every month, no babies followed. Now I needed to know how the two were related and I didn't want to ask Mother further. She had been so obviously embarrassed.

I was ashamed to be nineteen years old and to know as little as I knew. When the girls in the ballet talked about their romances I listened closely. Some of it I understood, some I guessed, and some was incomprehensible. I had seen statues and paintings, which had taught me the anatomical differences. My chaperoned life certainly left me no way to learn anything on my own. It wasn't something I worried about though. Kurt would know how everything worked.

In the next weeks when I wasn't on stage, I gave much more thought to the wedding itself. Not until Mother and Daddy had left for Ostatetcznie could I bring myself to even ask Katya about making love or having a baby. She did know. I was horrified at her description, but Katya said she had been told the act was supposed to be a beautiful part of life and that if I didn't find it so to begin with, she was sure I would later. When I tried to come to grips with my feelings, I became so tense and confused that I had to put my mind on the wedding plans and forget what might come later. Besides, Kurt was too much a gentleman to behave as Katya had said some men did.

The night after Kurt and his father had gone and before Katya and I had our talk, when we were all in bed I thought about the gown. Having studied the Civil War through every grade in the southern schools of Virginia, I thought 1859 must surely be close enough to 1861 to embrace the hoop skirt, my favorite of all fashions. It was so romantic. I hoped Kurt's grandmother's gown would be of that period. It was. Delivered in a small dome-topped trunk by the Baron's butler, Gerhardt, himself, the gown was of ivory and gold silk brocade with a low round neck, elbow-length puffy sleeves, and a tiny waist. The hoop with the petticoats and pantaloons that came with it were all of the finest creamy nainsook and perfectly preserved. Kurt's grandmother might have just stepped out of her finery an hour before. There was no veil, but Gerhardt produced a black velvet box.

"My very best wishes, Fraulein," he said with a low bow from the waist as he opened the box in which a diamond tiara twinkled like a tree at Christmas. "The Baron said that if you should wish to have a veil. . . " Here he consulted a piece of paper which he took from his pocket. "He will procure one of Chantilly lace from the nuns who create such cobwebs." He looked up at me. "Those are his very words, Fraulein Pierson. He said also, "His mother did not wear a veil and Kurt's mother did not wear this dress.""

"Thank you, Gerhardt." I said as he put the box and its treasure into my hands. "If the gown fits me, I will wear it. You may tell the Baron I said, thank you and yes, if it fits, I will happily wear this dress and no, I don't believe I will need the veil." I turned to my mother who seemed able to read my mind. She nodded in agreement. "Now let me try on the gown so you won't miss the return train."

While Mother helped me slip into the hoop, the petticoats and finally the dress, I thought about the young lady whose name I didn't even know and her thoughts as she dressed to marry Kurt's grandfather. Did she love him as much as I love her grandson? Was her life happy? I thought about Ostatetcznie, its cold entrance hall, its stone columns, and its wide staircase flanked by figures in armor. I pictured the "Hall" itself, decorated with battle flags and portraits of the von Pawels. I remembered the portrait of Kurt's grandmother and knew she would be watching as I came down the staircase, in her dress, to marry her grandson. Would I, an American girl of nineteen, be adequate? Could I be equal to the duties that must be required? The grandmother, I had been told, was seventeen when she married the fifth Baron. If she could do it, I could do it. Kurt would help.

Only a little too long, the beautiful dress fit. Mother put the tiara on my hair and we went out to show the audience gathered in the drawing room.

"You may tell the Baron I said "This is my happy choice."

Chapter 33

Even though I'd had to give up being the Sugar Plum Fairy when, given bigger roles, I missed doing a Christmas show for children. But this year I was grateful. I needed the freedom to be at Friedenau for the month of December with my real family and my adopted one. Although life with them was not really ending, I knew that relationships would somehow change. I would continue ballet in Warsaw so, of course we would live there. Kurt understood dancing was a necessary part of my well-being and, though he was a little jealous of my love for it and would rather I danced in Berlin or Paris, he was willing to spend most of our time in the city he called provincial. I thought that was sweet and generous of him. Mother and Daddy would continue to come each Christmas and we would go to the USA every July. I would still have two homes, but was sorry Friedenau wouldn't be one of them.

I'd never thought to question what we would live on. Barons and their sons seemed to have unlimited resources without having a job as we knew it. Our lives, it appeared, would go on just the same with one significant change. There didn't seem to be anything we needed to do for the wedding at Ostatetcznie. I savored every minute I had to spend with those I loved. Kurt hardly came to Friedenau. Although I missed him, I was satisfied he was tending to the wedding plans which he, himself, had made.

The surroundings at Friedenau tied me to my youth. I repeated old memories and collected new ones with as much care as if they had been priceless Fabergé eggs. Rodczeck even fixed my tea parties in a basket when I wanted to share time with the wooly sheep in their warm barn. Once I was an old married lady that sort of thing would never come again.

After Meister Masaela extracted a promise that I wouldn't chance a fall by ice-skating, Deu and I circled the pond on foot. The geese honked at us and the guinea fowl greeted vociferously. Oola, the goose girl, said they were overly noisy because they had missed me. I preferred their kind of noise to the din of the city, and had missed them too.

I wanted all of my human friends from Friedenau to be invited to the wedding, but Opa von Pawel and Oma von Wechsler talked me out of it.

"They would be uncomfortable," they said. "Even Anna and Meier wouldn't be comfortable as guests."

"Oh, but—" I started to argue.

The Baron broke in. "Instead of engaging outsiders to assist my staff, since we are combining the two households anyway, if it's all right with you, Louisa, we'll use your servants as well. That way they will have a reason to be there and it will be a help to our household." He waited for Oma's agreement.

"The gardener and the goose girl, too?" I asked. They were important to me.

"That might be a little more difficult. But, yes, the gardener and the goose girl too." The Baron laughed.

"I'm sure Caro would invite the entire village if she thought it possible," Oma beamed. "We can send a reasonable number over there. Before you leave today we'll speak with Rodczeck as to how many should come."

How easily everything was done in this gentle life. One wished and it was done.

For our part of the wedding festivities, my parents and the von Wechsler's would give a New Year's Eve Ball at Friedenau. Katya and I were overcome with excitement. Since I hadn't seen Kurt in almost a week, and because, except for the mandate to appear on the day, I had nothing to do with the wedding itself, the ceremony had very little reality for me.

Mother had seen to it that Katya had all the proper clothes for the ball and had taught her all she needed to know to be a part of the family. She learned quickly and, the night of the ball, she was so beautiful and gracious I thought she was perfection.

Kurt was supposed to be in the receiving line with me, but was not there when the guests began to arrive. When he appeared, Karl was with him. The receiving line edged together to repel the enemy. The Baron's "No" must have been audible to everyone in the vast room.

Daddy stood next to me and I heard him say quietly to Kurt, "You can't do this."

Kurt shook my father's hand vigorously, the smile I disliked wide and confident. "It's done is it not? Short of making a scene . . . what will you do about it?" He grabbed me and kissed me hard enough to bruise my lips, then took his place beside me, his grip on my hand too tight once again.

For the first time, I admitted to myself, I'm about to marry a man who can be hateful. As we stood side by side, the flutterings of my heart won out over the anger in my head, and I let the warning fade.

"So nice of you to invite me," Karl leaned forward and kissed me on the cheek. "Best wishes for your upcoming marriage." As he passed Kurt, he raised his eyebrows and shrugged his shoulders as if to say the whole affair was a waste of time. In seconds he had a glass in hand with the other men clustered around the punch bowl.

Once the receiving line broke up and one obligatory dance during which Kurt stared over my shoulder and we didn't speak, he left me standing alone. I didn't lack for partners, old or young. While Dieter and I were waltzing, he said in my ear. "Unless I'm wrong, Karl is truly smitten with your friend Katya. Look at him. He hasn't taken his eyes off her. It serves Kurt right." Dieter laughed and swung me around so I could see them better. "This time Kurt's strategy has turned on him. Did you know Karl was going to be here?"

"No. Kurt's father forbade it. I never thought Kurt would disobey Opa. Will you mind?"

"Not now. Look at Katya dancing with Johan while Karl follows them around the floor." His voice was jubilant. "At least that means Sybilla's part of his past."

At the end of the waltz Dieter started to walk me across to Kurt. Tomorrow at this time he would be my husband. When I looked at his handsome face, I was sorry for even that one moment of doubt. The musicians were shuffling their sheet music. Conversations filled the silence. Hidden from Kurt's view for a moment, we stopped behind the potted plant.

"Daddy says I don't know enough about Kurt. Tell me the things I need to know. Please, Dieter."

"By now, you know the man is unpredictable." Dieter dropped his hands, but his eyes stayed on my face, "He and I have been friends a long time. Or maybe "playmates" is a better description. Even I'm not sure what he's thinking. Believe me, Kleine, I'd help you if I could. You're like my sister, you know, and I love you. And if you need me, I'll always be here."

Staring back at me, our reflection with the miniature tree in the mirrors repeated itself around the walls of the room in those gilt-edged frames. Between us, like a third person, there was the feeling that someday I would remember this moment as one of tremendous importance. Yet I only whispered, "Thank you, Dieter." We both scanned the room for Kurt. "One more request. Promise me there won't be any unpleasantness between you and Karl tomorrow?" I wanted to believe that the events of the past no longer clouded the future. "I can't ask him to leave now that Kurt has led him to believe we invited him. I don't know what to do except get the whole thing over with as quickly as possible."

"Kleine, Kleine, wait a minute." Dieter put his comforting arm around me and led me toward the balcony door. "Let's get out of the limelight."

In the mirrors in front of us Kurt appeared, but before we could turn to greet him, he grabbed my shoulder, spun me away from Dieter, and flung me roughly toward the wall. I stumbled against one of the chairs. My face, as I scrabbled to catch myself, to comprehend what had just happened, came into focus in the reflective depths of mirrored wall. It was that of a complete stranger. When I finally looked away, Kurt and Dieter had disappeared onto the balcony. Ernst was right behind them. The French doors closed.

Still gasping with shock, I ran across the immense room and out into the hallway. Mother, and Katya found me in the bathroom. None of us spoke. There were no words to say. We huddled together in misery like sheep in a blizzard.

"He misunderstood," I said weakly at last.

"He seems to do a lot of that." Mother's voice was grim.

"Dieter and I were talking. I was only trying to understand the man I'm going to marry." I took the handkerchief Katya offered. "Was that wrong?"

"Of course it wasn't wrong." Mother backed up a little to look in my eyes. "If you marry him, you're going to need a lot of understanding. Do you still want to marry him?"

Although I was frightened and embarrassed, not to marry him when I'd loved him so long was incomprehensible. "What can I do?"

"It isn't too late to cancel tomorrow. Most of the guests are here and we could simply make an announcement. They will understand."

"He's overwrought because of the wedding. I shouldn't have danced with Dieter. I've made him feel insecure. He doesn't understand Dieter's like a brother to me."

"Overwrought? Kurt is never overwrought." Katya muttered.

Knowing how protective she was of me, I ignored her. After I wiped away any evidence of tears, I repaired my lipstick and combed my hair. "I'll go out and explain it to him right now."

In the ballroom Ernst and Elise were dancing. Despite his bland expression, his steps were jerky and stiff. Elise looked miserable. Daddy and the Baron conferred by the punch bowl. Kurt was not in sight. I found Oma sitting along the wall where my barre had once stood. She clutched my hand and pulled me down onto a chair beside her.

"Did he hurt you?" Without waiting for an answer, she almost hissed the words, "You must not marry that boy. He will not keep you the happy girl you are. He is too terrible. I forbid it."

"Oma, he is not . . ." I didn't know what to say. The night before my wedding should have been a joyous occasion. Instead I had managed to make Kurt so angry that he had alienated my first and second families in their entirety.

When Daddy and the Baron saw me, they came at once to sit with us. Sybilla, Mother, Katya joined us and. when the dance ended, Ernst and Elise pulled two chairs over as well. Like the Great Wall of China, they had constructed something to protect me from evil. was grateful, but someone had to straighten out the mess. When Dieter came inside from the balcony, Kurt followed. They looked amicable enough. I sighed with relief. Dieter joined the seated row while I rushed to Kurt in the warm glow of the Christmas tree.

"I'm sorry," we both said at once. He kissed me briefly. Everything that had been opside down righted itself. When he laid my hand over his arm to walk, his fingers were loose and gentle. He was again the enamored suitor of the Warsaw nightclubs, proud to be seen with me.

It was only during a restless night that I wished he had apologized to my family too. It was their party and their daughter. I drifted off and wakened early, wondering how I could fix everything. Reliable Deu stuck his nose in my face and insisted on going out. I dressed quickly. Rodczeck had not yet turned on the dining room lights. Deu and I tramped through the gardens until we came to the little chapel. I had long since made my peace with the Count's portrait and now I went in hoping this man I'd never known could understand the turmoil in my heart. Standing by his coffin, I told him the whole story: the dance, the conversation with Dieter, Karl's appearance, Kurt's temper, and Oma's warning. After the guests departed, my parents, the von Wechslers and Katya had tried to explain why I should cancel the wedding before it was too late.

"It's already too late," I said to the silent mahogany casket. "The habit of loving Kurt has grown into my heart. I can't see my life without him."

If the Count disagreed, he gave no sign. With a sprig of the Christmas wreath from his resting-place as a talisman, Deu and I went out. The heavy door closed behind us.

At the breakfast table everyone was cheerful. They were full of plans. I began to believe I had dreamed it all. As the weight in my heart lifted, the little thrills of excitement came back. The endless day of preparations dragged, but a nap helped. Teatime came at last. I was so nervous I only managed a bite or two before we were loaded into sleighs. Tucked under cozy, bearskin rugs with my parents and Deu, we left Friedenau for Ostatetcznie behind my favorite horses, Tristan and Isolde.

As we jingled out through the gates of Friedenau I looked back to catch a last glimpse of the girl, Carole Pierson. She would never come back here the free happy little girl who, as a shy, unworldly eleven year old, had first climbed those beautiful entrance steps. Growing up, that I understood. The von Wechslers had made her believe she had brought warmth and life back to Friedenau. Now, as an adult, could she bring warmth to the austere, gray stones of Ostatetcznie? She would try.

The wedding party gowns hung, pristine and glowing, in the splendid bedroom suite that was to be mine. Sybilla and her maid were already there. Hilde had come to help Anna.
Kurt would dress in a separate suite, his since childhood. My parents and surrogate parents had always shared my rooms. I assumed after the ceremony Kurt would share this huge bed in this beautiful room with me, a new beginning. Every time the doors to the suite opened, I could hear an increasing volume of voices from below. They were all friends, I told myself. My stage fright was worse than an opening night at the ballet. This was no dress rehearsal and I knew there would be no way to rectify an error in my performance. Could I forever keep the marriage happy?
It never occurred to me that Kurt would have any responsibility for our happiness. The burden was mine.

Once the same small orchestra that had played at the ball began to play the light operatic love songs like Because and One Alone, I felt lighter and happier. Even better when Daddy appeared in the door. I took one last look in the huge gilt-framed mirror before taking his arm. The stranger there in a magnificent ivory and gold brocade gown looked like a Meissen figurine on a wedding cake. Because of the hoop skirt, the dress accented her small waist and white shoulders. Her hair almost outshone the sparkling tiara. She was beautiful, but, though I was aware that her Grammie's lace handkerchief was tucked inside next to her heart and the Count's snippet of his Christmas wreath was hidden in her bouquet, I had trouble recognizing her.

The prelude to the wedding march began and Ernst came to get Mother. As we kissed each other on both cheeks, I choked up. "I wish Grammie were here."

"She wishes so too, dear heart, but she just wasn't well enough. She loves you. Be happy."

When Mother was gone, I saw myself running after her, sitting by her side, and watching someone else get married. The vision was so clear, I wondered why. I took Daddy's arm as Sybilla, blond, and Katya, dark-haired, went down together. Although I couldn't see them, I knew that the elegant trains of their soft green velvet dresses would trail gracefully behind as they descended the magnificent curving staircase. They would be beautiful. A happy Dieter and Karl would meet them at the bottom of the stairs while the spirits of the Knights in the ancient suits of armor stood stiffly at attention on either side.

The Chapel had never been a possibility. Kurt wouldn't hear of it. In the Great Hall below, guests sat on gilt chairs arranged so they created an aisle. The minister instructed us to walk with 'stately tread' and that he would be at the far end. I depended on Daddy to get us wherever we were supposed to be. My body was trembling so. Afraid I would break the stems of my bouquet, I was only reassured when Daddy volunteered that he was shaking too.

"This is worse than going into battle." he muttered and then squeezed my arm close to his body. "I don't want to give you away, Caro," He blurted just before it was time to take our first "stately tread." "Not to any half-finished, petulant, little boy. But if Kurt makes you happy, that's all any father can ask of him." He patted my arm with his other hand. "If he doesn't, you come right home to your loving Daddy." He kissed me quickly on the cheek and it was time to go. "Right, left, right," he said with a little laugh as we started easily down the long staircase to Kurt.

If the kiss lasted too long and if Kurt forestalled my stopping for a second to hug Mother and Dad by hurrying me back down the aisle, at least the terrifyingly formal ceremony was over. We were married. After a long string of toasts the supper was finally over and the guests and my family departed. Carole von Pawel was alone in that sumptuous bedroom, waiting for her new husband.

I had tried not to worry about it, but now I had time to wonder what the words "wedding night" really meant. Katya's explanation of how one made babies made it a little scary. Still I reminded myself how Kurt's kisses during our engagement had roused in me feelings that I didn't understand and made me not a little I ashamed. I was sure Mother would have considered them horrifying and less than lady-like. I was determined to keep them controlled. Kurt had told me often enough that he loved me for my grace and beauty. I didn't want any strange sensations to destroy that love. From now on when we would be spending the nights in each other's arms I hoped those feelings wouldn't come. Even though I preferred my familiar pajamas, I put on my new satin nightgown and filmy peignoire and sat down on a rose velvet chair to wait.

Chapter 34

A full orchestra playing The Triumphal March from Aida would not have seemed out of place when Kurt in his long velvet robe arrived in the bedroom. His butler, Gerhardt, followed with a champagne bucket and two maids, each carrying a tray of sandwiches, desserts and fruit. Kurt's valet, Otto, supervised the installation of a table near the kachelofen where the room was warmer. Like a magician, he waved his hand, the parade vanished and we were alone.

Kurt insisted I share the champagne. Not being used to more than one glass, after my third and with no control remaining, I did not protest when he carried me to the bed and tore off my peignoir and night gown. My body responded even when he proved Katya's description correct. If I should have been ashamed of my ecstasy, I knew only joy that Kurt and I were truly one. At last, after all my dreaming, we belonged to each other. As he rolled away from me, I whispered, "I love you." There was no answer. My lover was asleep.

It was one o'clock in the afternoon when Otto wakened us. "Your train to Berlin leaves in two hours, Gnädige Herr and Madame." He drew back the heavy draperies and put both of our robes within reach.

When I saw that my nightgown lay on the floor in full view of the man, I covered my flaming face and slid down under the covers. Kurt laughed. "Come up, you silly little girl. Otto is quite used to women in my bed, though you're the first who has a legal right to be here." He jerked back the bedclothes and left my nude body exposed. If Otto's glance was longer than it should have been, at least he was moving toward the door.

Something heavy buried those beautiful feelings from the night. Who were those women? Did he love them? With my new awareness, I couldn't imagine making love as we had last night without love.

"Shall I send Anna in to you, Madame?" Otto asked.

"Send her in a half hour," Kurt ordered.

My head was spinning, and I missed the import of what he'd said. I wanted a bath. I had to dress so I would look beautiful for my new husband and our trip. We'd missed breakfast, but were we to have no lunch either? There must be time to eat, to say goodbye and to thank all the people here. Mother, Daddy and the von Wechslers would be at the station in Torun. If we didn't start getting ready now, how could we have enough time for those we loved and were leaving.

Ready to make my point when the door closed, before I could move, Kurt crushed me to him. It was a sensual half–hour in which I found that right or wrong, proper or wanton, I had no control and was more in love than ever.

At the Bahnhof the goodbyes were tearful, but my parents and I had had so many partings over the years. Each one since I had joined the ballet had been a terrible wrench, but this time Kurt was opening another new life for me. My tears dried as soon as we left the station and, with the shades drawn in our compartment Kurt again took me in his arms. We never had lunch.

The Paris I had known when I danced there was not the Paris I found with Kurt. We stayed out late, and were in bed until noon. We danced. We drank champagne. Kurt took me to the most famous of the couturiers and had to approve each design himself. I often felt the things he liked were too sophisticated for me, but he listened to no criticism. We met many of his friends, most in SS uniforms, and their ladies who seemed to be on vacation. Often their companions were heavily made-up girls. I didn't think they were wives. Their behavior bothered me because I suspected the officers were married, but Kurt told me not to worry about it. They were just "being boys on vacation."

"Would you have a girl if you went on a vacation without me?"

Kurt didn't lie. "That's the way men do, you naïve little creature." He turned away to light a cigarette.

"Even though we're married?"

He laughed.

"Even though we love each other?"

Kurt whirled around. He grabbed me by the shoulders and shook me roughly. ""Listen to me, Carole. At this moment with you picking at me like a hen in scattered corn, if you continue this inquisition I'm not sure I will continue to love you. Stop before I walk out of this room and find myself a girlie who is not a lady and who knows how to have a good time without asking questions."

My heart almost stopped beating. We'd been married only a few days and I'd made him angry enough to want to leave me. I'd thought we were close enough to discuss even the most private of topics, but this was one I would avoid in the future. Later, when I had time to really think about it, I was sure I would have no worries. We were married now and Kurt would never go on a vacation without me.

When our time in Paris was over, we moved to Berlin. That city seemed to me to be populated with military. They were everywhere. "I'm glad you are no longer in any military group, German or Polish," I said. "I love you so much I don't want you away from me even for one hour." It was easy now to open my heart.

Kurt smiled. "I'm going for a haircut and a shave" was all he said, but his kiss was warm on my lips as I let him go. He loved me, he would come back.

The Ballet Meister of the Berlin Opera Company had been in our suite the night before. He had come to beg me to dance for the Berliners at least once during our stay.

"She's out of practice," Kurt had said flatly, with a stern look in my direction as he left the room.

I recognized my orders. "I'm so sorry, Meister. My husband is quite correct. We must go back to Warsaw in a few days and that would give me no time for rehearsals. I'm afraid I would disgrace you." At his protest, I put a hand on his arm. "Please. I did so enjoy my guest appearance here last April and I know you and Herr Masaela are friends. Wait a few months and then invite me again. I will come, I promise." Later I raised the subject with Kurt, trying to explain how I felt.

He interrupted. "It's simple. I don't want you out of my sight. You're mine and I don't want to share you with anyone."

"I'm glad because I don't want to share you either."

Now, as he left for the barbershop in the hotel I was reassured that I had no worries in the world. Hours passed. I read and napped, then dressed for our scheduled evening with his friends at Berlin's most extravagant cabaret. When he came finally, it was late and he wore a uniform, the dark brown uniform of the German SS. He was also very drunk.

"Why are you dressed like that?" I asked. "Is it a joke?"

"You have eyes. You're not stupid." His words were slurred and he wobbled a bit as he swaggered across the room to stand in front of the full -length mirror. "It fits well, don't you think?" When he turned to look at the back, he nearly fell over. "I had it tailor-made."

"When?" All I could think was he hadn't been away from me long enough to do all this.

"The last time I was in Berlin." He staggered to the bed. "I'm tired. Get out and let me go to sleep."

"What about your friends waiting in the cabaret?"

"To hell with you and to hell with them. Go."

Feeling like a dismissed slave, I backed into the sitting room and closed the bedroom door. All this time, while he made me love him more and more, he had been doing the very thing he had assured me he would never do. Or had he assured me? Had I just taken it for granted that, because he loved me, he would never do something that might take him away from me? Either way, I felt betrayed.

In the taxi to the cabaret to make apologies to his guests, I worried about how long I would have to stay to not seem rude. With the help of the of the head waiter I found their table, introduced myself, told them Kurt was sick and we hoped they would forgive us. They didn't seem surprised. Two of the flashy girls were the only ones who even showed any disappointment. With their painted eyes they examined me as if I were a figurine brought in for appraisal. Ignoring them, I apologized to the officers again, fought off their uncalled for advances and escaped. It was not the place for me.

In our suite Kurt lay on the bed in his shiny new black uniform with the hateful swastika on the sleeve armband. I felt disgust for this stranger. For the first time I glimpsed something of what was beneath my husband's handsome façade. It was impossible to explain it away. As I stripped off the hateful coat, hoping that some of the tarnish would leave him as well, but it was tenacious. Years of idolatry don't fade in one moment of clarity. The discovery was painful. I threw myself on the pink sofa in the sitting room. If tears stained its damask, I didn't care. I cried for Kurt's betrayal, my feeling of inadequacy, the awful pall of disillusionment, and the unattractive picture of Kurt in a drunken stupor. At last, exhausted, I slept.

In the daylight, I woke in a panic. I rushed to the bedroom to apologize, eager to be taken into my husband's arms in forgiveness. He was gone.

"He's at breakfast and didn't want to waken me," I said aloud as I ran the bath water. Dressed in my most beautiful new suit with the sable collar and cuffs, I sat on the sofa waiting for my lover to come back. He didn't come. He didn't come all afternoon. He was not there at teatime or dinnertime. I didn't know whom to ask or where to call so I sat and waited. I castigated myself for being such a fool. I wondered how I had managed to make him hate me so much.

As the sun set, I stood and stared out the window as if I could penetrate the buildings and see him inside. I debated whether to call the hospitals or the police, but was afraid to for fear it would infuriate him if he found out. I did call the desk a dozen times to see if there was a message. There was none. I ordered a dinner I couldn't eat and finally went to bed.

At last I recognized the extent of my husband's anger and understood I was being punished. It was obvious even to me. I had wanted to deny him the right to play soldier. But what was it really? There was no war, no battles. It was a game that gave him authority and put him in no danger. Well, if that's what he wanted, I would deny him no further. If I couldn't openly admire him for this, I could at least be quiet. Except for being married, life would go on as it had. Kurt would come and go. I hadn't planned to give up the life I loved for him. Why should he give up his life for me? Still, reviewing all that, why couldn't I make my feelings accept my thoughts? I had always known our marriage wouldn't be like my parent's marriage unless I gave up my dancing. And I couldn't be that generous.

Every squeak of a floor board, every closing of a door on the hotel corridor made me hope that he had come home, but it was almost morning when he did. The first I knew, he slipped into bed and took me in his arms. "Are you going to be a good girl now?" He breathed in my ear.

The alcohol smell was strong, but so were his arms. I gratefully gave him his answer.

Our last two days in Berlin were dreamlike. At times he treated me as if I were the queen of his universe and at others, like a child. We explored the fabulous shops on Unter den Linden where he bought me a diamond bracelet to "show how much he loved me," he boasted. He insisted we buy some shoes with very high, thin heels and then made me wear while we shopped and even scuffed through the snow in the Tier Garten. As we sat at an inside table having tea, I thought the animals in the nearby zoo were suffering less than my misshapen ballet feet in their dainty fashionable stilts.

There was a nice string orchestra and Kurt loved to dance. We did and though it was agony, I had learned my lesson. To have said my feet hurt would have been a criticism of his taste. When I managed to squeak out they were cold, he bought me some velvet galoshes with fur around the top to go over my high-heeled shoes. My toes were warmer, but just as painful.

In the evenings we went to the theater, had late suppers, and traipsed home to our suite to show each other how much love we could give. At least that's what I thought. The last morning after breakfast I had nearly finished packing when, with Kurt's clothes still in the armoire, I asked him if he would like me to do his packing for him.

He didn't even look up from the newspaper. "I'm staying here," he said as casually as if he were remarking on the weather.

"Why?" My brain was unable to comprehend.

"I have a job here now, you know. You did understand that, that it was a job?"

"I thought you'd be posted in Warsaw."

"What would the German SS be doing in Poland? Mein Gott Carole, you are stupid. "

"I'm sorry, I just thought . . . I don't know what I thought."

"That's the trouble with you, you don't think. You're such a baby. I should have married someone with more sense." He shook the paper as he turned the page in such a way as to let me know he was getting mad.

I was dangerously close to having gone too far. "I suppose I just couldn't imagine we could be parted so soon. When will we ever be together?" I asked timidly.

He threw the newspaper down as he stood up in obvious anger. "If you were a true wife, you would give up the ballet and be wherever your husband wants you to be. It's not my fault that you won't behave as other women in your station behave. Someday you are going to be a Baroness, you know. But you'd rather be a cheap toe-dancer deforming your feet and making a spectacle of yourself."

With each sentence, he grew more irate. He grabbed his overcoat and cap in a fury. When he stalked out and slammed the door, he left me standing, mouth wide-open and hands pleadingly outstretched, beside my bags.

When the boy came to get my luggage, I put on my coat and dutifully followed him to the elevator like an automaton. In the lobby Kurt was nowhere in sight, but a young page handed me a note. "I've paid your bill," it said. "Go back to your dance hall." No signature. No endearment.

On the overnight train my thoughts alternated between what have I done and what can I do. There was no rest. I couldn't even cry. I was to be discarded like a shoe that had been tried and didn't fit. Since his clothes were still in the suite, he would continue to live there. Would he be alone? Unlikely.

When the train finally pulled into the station and Anna smiled her greeting, I wanted only to be home with her where I knew somebody loved me and that I wasn't worthless. Her loving words and warm arms couldn't repair the part of me that was a wife, but she gave me back the confidence and value of a ballerina. Within a week I was Odette in Swan Lake, aptly swimming in her lake of tears.

I felt I danced heavily and without inspiration and I must have. Even Herr Masaela, though he understood part of the reason, scolded me for it.

"You must get your emotions under control, Aurora" he said lovingly. "That selfish man is gone. You are a dancer and, as such, owe those of us who love you your heart. Forget him and know that you can be everything to us as we are ready to be everything to you."

I tried. Day by day without a word, with my hours filled with practice and rehearsals and friends, it got easier to go to bed at night with Katya instead of Kurt beside me until, one day, I found I could laugh and find joy in dancing again. As if he were clairvoyant, Kurt appeared in my dressing room when I came off-stage that night. I had no questions, no criticisms, no anger. I simply opened my arms.

He offered no explanations, but he was there. He never mentioned his work. I never asked. When his time was up, he left. In my heart I knew he would come back. Months passed. I was unaware that Hitler was gobbling little bites out of Polish defenses. At the ballet we noticed a decline in our audience. There were fewer Poles and more Germans. As I paid more attention to the radio, and began to question Meier about what he thought was happening, I discovered how unaware I had been. His fear, though not articulated in details that would frighten us women, chilled me. The newspapers told us the Polish high command seemed to be growing more powerless.

On September 1st the German Luftwaffe disabled the Polish Air Corps. On September 3rd the Germans stormed through our streets. They terrorized everyone and left the Jewish Ghetto a barren waste. Truck after truck after truck loaded with human beings, men, women and children, rolled past our apartment.

When Meier went to the corner to buy cigarettes, we watched from the balcony helplessly as he was prodded onto a truck. Anna shrieked "Meier" as she raced out the door. He waved at the balcony once, but he did not come home. When the word Jude appeared derisively on buildings and sidewalks, we understood. Meier was a Jew. The walls were inscribed in derogatory filth. The ballet was cancelled. There was no audience.

"Kurt will come," I tried to soothe Anna. "He will find Meier and bring him home. Then we will all hide at Ostatetcznie." Despairing, I hoped it was true.

"Caro," Anna's tears streamed down her pitiful bereft face, "Meier ist ein Jude, he has gone for always." She threw her ample apron up over her head and we cried together. "Kurt will not help us," she whispered through the cloth at last. "He hates Jews."

And she was right. After night fell Kurt swaggered in. "I know, I saw him taken. It's too bad, but he was a Jew and our noble Furher intends to cleanse the world of such scum. I'll do what I can, but I can't jeopardize our lives for a—for him."

"Heil Hitler," I said sarcastically. "Perhaps the little paper-hanger will overdose on wallpaper paste."

"Caro." Kurt gripped my shoulders and shook until I thought my brain would burst. "Don't ever say such a thing again. It's my job to turn traitors in and I wouldn't want you to be one of them, rolling away from me on one of those trucks. You will make an enviable Baroness and I know that you will never be so foolish again."

His references to me as a Baroness struck me as odd. Opa had many years to live before Kurt would inherit the estate and the title. The lesson in all this was that I should never reveal my thoughts again.

With the ballet shut down, we gave up the apartment on September tenth and prepared to move to Ostatetcznie. Katya's brother, Igor, appeared before we left Warsaw and insisted she go home to Vladivostok with him. She wanted to go with us, but Igor said, since Europe was so unsettled, her parents wanted her at home. Russia was in league with Germany at that time and it seemed safe. She agreed to settle me at Ostatetcznie and then they would go on to Gdynia to catch a freighter.

When we got to the von Pawel estate, Kurt was already there. He met us in the Great Hall.

"Where is my Opa?" I asked Gerhardt who stood beside the stairs waiting to take my coat.

"He is no longer here, Baroness." Gerhardt looked at the floor.

"Where is he? When will he be back?" I didn't understand. And why did he address me Baroness?

Kurt interrupted. "Don't badger him, Baroness. The man you called Opa was a traitor. He's gone where all traitors go. To hell, I imagine."

I stared at him as if I'd never seen him before. Without more I knew who had arranged the arrest of the gentle old man. His own son. This stranger was not my husband. He had never appeared in my romantic girlish heart because I had always clothed him in the costume of a lover with the mask of a hero. I was to blame, not for what he was, only for not allowing myself to see the truth.

I touched Gerhardt's shoulder softly. Although I wanted to run to Anna's arms, I forced myself to walk quietly up the stairs to my suite. With every step I told myself I couldn't cry away my burden on Anna's willing shoulders because Meier's disappearance was part of that burden. That Kurt had turned Meier in as well was my fault. If I had opened my eyes sooner, could I have prevented these tragedies? Maybe not for Opa, but Kurt would never have come in contact with Meier, were it not for me. I would have to atone for these sins without burdening Anna.

Chapter 35

In my bedroom with the door closed, I leaned against it as if my weight alone would keep out my husband. My husband. For so long I had dreamed those words with love. Opa had given his son everything except a conscience and the ability to love anyone except himself. I had given him everything I had to give, but all was never enough for him. The realization of what kind of man he was, what he was capable of doing, and what he had done brought a nausea so intense I ran for the bathroom. As I knelt, clutching the commode, moments of our past played their scenes.

Unlike anything I had known in my own loving family, the malevolency had been unrecognized, excused, and explained-away. Now, like machine gun bullets from a bandoleer, the scenes flashed by in all their deadly malignancy and demanded to be faced. Spent, unable and unwilling to stop the repugnant scenes, I let go of the commode and slid to the floor.

Never could I accept Kurt again and perhaps never again could I see myself as a worthwhile human being. I was alive though, and it was clear Anna and I would have to get away. She was in the bedroom putting something in the armoire.

"Don't unpack," I said. "We have to get to the American Ambassador in Warsaw at once. We can't stay here."

She put her hand over my mouth. "Hush, child," she whispered. "These walls may be listening. Your heart may be breaking, but until he leaves for Berlin . . ." She didn't have to say his name, or maybe she couldn't. "It's important that we behave as usual." She turned to the bed, plumping pillows, and turning on lights.

She didn't touch me again. It was a kindness I didn't deserve, now that I was fully cognizant of the kind of man I had married. She must have known long before this. She had been born just before

WWI, when her family, part German, part Polish, was suspect by both nationalities. Because I was an American and my country was not at war with Hitler, I wanted to argue with her, make it all go away. She just shook her head and put her finger to her lips.

Normal behavior would be hard with all the loathing that festered inside, but Kurt was leaving this afternoon. Once he was gone we could get away and I need never see him again. I plunged into a chair, my head buried in my hands. What if he changed his mind? God knew he was mercurial. I might be able to keep up the pretense during the day, but what about the nights? In his arms I wouldn't be able to hide my revulsion. Even Shakespeare couldn't have written such an incongruous scene.

He did stay home. Gerhardt told us when he brought up the bags. Relentlessly the earth turned. Dark inevitably followed daylight.

"I can't let him in here," I whispered to Anna before she left me that first night. "I'll scream. Or something worse if he touches me. He'll know."

Anna's round face was furrowed with worry. "I wish I could do this for you. I could so easily shoot him before I'd have you live through this. But we don't know who is on his side, who to trust. You're a good actress, keep that in your mind, and soon you'll be on your way to others who love you." She stopped whispering and raised her voice. "Good night, Carole," she said with her usual cheerful tone.

"I won't go without you." I choked the words back when Kurt swaggered in without knocking. As soon as I saw that arrogant face, I wanted to fly at him, to bash that handsome mask, to finish his worthless life before he could do more harm. Anna's eyes flashed a warning, her back to him. So instead I became an actress with smiles and appropriately lady-like demureness in all the proper places.

"You wouldn't what?" Kurt demanded.

"I wouldn't think of dying my hair." It was the first thing that came to me. It was the wrong thing. It started Kurt on a tirade aimed at poor Anna. I would have to be more careful or she would disappear like Opa. He was still writing the script.

When we were alone, he did touch me, more than touch me, and I surprised myself by uttering my usual terms of endearment. With closed eyes, I recited the words as if they were a printed script. Conceited and intent on his own pleasure, he missed any mechanical intonation. He heard only the words. I was learning.

When I was sure he was asleep, I tiptoed into the bathroom and soaked in a bath as hot as I could stand it without crying out. Still, I didn't feel clean and spent the rest of the sleepless night on the sofa in the sitting room.

It was hopeless to wish he would just tire of me and let me go. Kurt von Pawel never let go of anyone unless that person could no longer serve his purposes. When I was of no more use to him, he would destroy me as he had destroyed his father, just to acquire that cold title Baron.

During the daylight hours before he went back to Berlin, he stayed out on Hitler's business. Anna and I had walked in the snowy garden while Deu frisked along beside us. We did our talking there. It all seemed so simple to me.

"You and I will go to Warsaw. And Deu. Ambassador Bishop will put us on a ship and we'll be home before Kurt even knows we're gone."

Anna snorted. "That sounds simple enough, Carole. Except Kurt has spies and will have us arrested before we even get to the train.

Deu will be shot and maybe we will too."

"How will he know? He'll be away. I'm an American. The Ambassador will protect us." I had no inkling of real intrigue.

"Think, child. Why are we having this conversation in a freezing garden even though the Baron is not here? Otto and Gerhardt have their instructions. Their eyes are on us every moment." She stopped walking and bent to a branch of berries to keep up the pretense we were enjoying the outdoors. "Your husband is still here. In the person of every one of his servants. They wouldn't still be employed here if they weren't loyal. Think, Caro, think."

"Then how can we do it? How can we ever escape?"

"There must be other ways. All will be dangerous, but the Poles are forming an underground. Give them a little time and they will be able to help us."

"A little time? How long is a little? How do you know about this underground?" I Struggled to keep up with her on the snowy path.

"Zarotti whispered it to me when he brought my coat over the other day."She strode ahead without looking at me. "He and I agreed some time ago that the Baron was not for you and that the time would come when you would have to leave Poland. So the time has come, though you may have to leave alone. Zarotti gave me hope. Now we just have to wait."

"I won't go without you. How do we know who is in the underground or how to contact them?"

Anna jabbed me with her elbow. "Smile," she whispered as Kurt strode out the conservatory door, leaving it open.

With a wide forced smile in his direction, I ran to close it so all the plants wouldn't freeze in the below-zero weather. He caught me as I flew past him.

"Where are you going in such a hurry? I expect a kiss when I come home." He jerked me into his arms, the kiss so violent that his teeth cut my lip. When he let me go, Anna handed me her handkerchief with head bowed. Kurt only laughed. "That will teach you not to ignore me when I've been away."

I handed the handkerchief back to Anna. "I was just going to close the door. The cold air, the plants . . ."

"To hell with the plants. Gerhardt can always get more. I have something to tell you."

With a silent wish he'd freeze to death, I concentrated on his face as if I were interested in anything he had to share.

"The German High Command has ordered all the landowners, German and Polish, to provide horses for the German Cavalry." He spoke as if he were the one in charge. "They've requisitioned everyone from Sybilla's father and Ernst von Wechsler." He looked so smug. "Too bad they bet on the wrong team. Favoritism has to be cultivated," he bragged.

"Is that why you joined the SS? So you could receive favors?" I was interested in his information. What would this do to the von Wechslers? To Sybilla's family? They both had been outspoken against Hitler.

"I'll gain prestige by giving them the horses I don't want and I won't lose the good ones."

I knew enough not to answer. You've lost me was my only thought as I hurried inside.

While he was at home this time, he did allow me to have a barre set up in a basement room. He wouldn't "let me ruin the ballroom" to "satisfy my childish hobby." I didn't debate the point with him, that was too dangerous. I did keep up with my exercises so that, when I was free finally, I'd be able to earn a living. I wrote long letters to Mother and Daddy, but worried about their reactions and the possibility of censorship, I didn't our troubles. There would be time enough for explanations when we appeared at their door.

The nights were worse than any nightmare. But each time Kurt left he had no idea he was anything less than my master. Each minute of each hour without him I counted as a blessing.

One morning while he was still with us Sybilla and Dieter burst into the breakfast room. It was the firs we had seen them since Opa had disappeared or since Kurt's boast about the horses. I had been afraid to use the telephone to call them. I was also afraid something had happened between Friedenau and Ostatetcznie.

"Get up, you lazy people," Dieter said, pulling Kurt to his feet. "I can't have a uniformed sloth as the best man in my wedding. Congratulate me. Sybilla finally agrees that life is too short to wait any longer." He beamed at me.

Ignoring our breakfast, we jumped up and hugged all around. For a second my problems and the necessity for pretense were forgotten. I was genuinely happy.

"Where's Oncle Ludorf? I want him to hear the news too."

After an interminable silence Kurt signaled Gerhardt to pull out a chair for Sybilla. "He's gone to Dresden on business," he lied.

Sybilla sat next to me with a quizzical look. "I know it sounds silly to ask. You will be my Matron of Honor, Caro? Please say yes quickly so I can start telling you all the plans." Her eyes glowed with happiness.

Not knowing whether I would still be here, I forced myself to answer with enthusiasm. "Yes, yes, of course." With Kurt pounding Dieter on the shoulders and accepting for both of us, what else could I have said even if I had wanted to?

"We were in such a hurry to tell you, we haven't eaten yet. We weren't sure how much longer you would be here, Kurt." Dieter sat down beside Sybilla. "Do you suppose you can find something to feed two love-sick beggars?" He looked pitifully at the butler.

Gerhardt smiled. He had already taken the coffee pot from the warming oven and was pouring it into cups. When everyone had coffee, he disappeared into the pantry.

"Because of the war, it has to be a small wedding. In the chapel at home." Sybilla bubbled. "Your pink chiffon dress, the one you wore to the New Years eve party, will be perfect."

Dieter cut in. "We'll have a short honeymoon someplace. Since I've been drafted as the Procurer of Food for the German armies here in the corridor, I'm not allowed much time off. It does mean that, despite being gone a lot, we'll live at Friedenau."

"Sometimes," Sybilla chimed in, "I can travel with him and that will be more honeymoon."

Kurt teased him about not joining an outfit where "real men are doing a real job."

Ignoring him, Dieter smiled wryly. "That's exactly why I'm glad we will be living near each other forever. I really need you to keep me humble."

Gerhardt didn't know I was watching him as he set heaping plates in front of our guests. He appeared to turn a secret smile at Dieter when he moved the crystal jelly pot toward the couple. April and the wedding seemed a lifetime away. Positive as I was that Anna and I would no longer be here, I also knew Sybilla would understand.

Chapter 36

After our midday meal, Anna and I religiously walked around the estate. Never following the same route, we went out of our way to speak with the goose lady, the sheep man, and whomever else we passed so it appeared we were walking simply for the exercise. If there were eyes following us from the windows of the house, we never saw them, though we were always conscious that they might be there. As we discussed ways to escape, we were careful to laugh now and then or playfully chase or push each other as if we were enjoying life.

Isolated at Ostatetcznie as Kurt forced us to be, we heard little news. The bits we did hear from the German-controlled radio only told us that times were becoming more ominous. It wasn't until the Nazis had already invaded France that we learned Britain and France had entered the war. We reasoned that in time, just as it had in World War I, the United States would come to Europe's rescue. We were surrounded by the enemy and didn't know whom to trust.

We thought we knew where the von Wechslers' sympathies lay, but who could be sure? There had been no contact between the two houses. Sybilla must be busy with the wedding plans. We heard nothing from anyone outside of Ostatetcznie and sometimes speculated that we were alone in the world.

Other than Zarotti's passing furtive reference about "the partisans" to Anna, we had no way to communicate with him about possible assistance. The telephone, Anna pointed out, was the most dangerous of all. We had only questions, no answers. Kurt appeared and disappeared without a hint of where he was going or how long he'd be gone. The only surety was that he expected me to be there when he came home. In his weeks way I was sure we could have found an escape route if only we had known how to go about it.

And there was another worry. Since the cable from my parents reporting their safe arrival home after my wedding, we had no further word. Each morning I held my breath when Gerhardt brought in the mail and each morning, with pity in his eyes and voice, he'd announce, "nothing today, Madame." He never said more and I was afraid to push. A million things could have happened. I thought of them all, each thought worse than the one before. Only something dire would keep Mother from her typewriter. But if they'd been dead that word would surely have reached me.

Here it was late March. Sleeping little and eating next to nothing shadowed my eyes and hollowed my cheeks. Anna tried joking and even scolding. "Unless Meister Masaela had a part for a skeleton, he wouldn't let you near the stage. You'll have to fatten up or you won't be able to earn a living." Still, she was worried about my parents too.

"This isn't like them," I said to Kurt when he was briefly at home. "I've always had at least one letter a week. Maybe I should go to Warsaw to Ambassador Bishop. He could find out for me." Oh, how I hoped he'd let us go.

"You will go no place." His voice was sharp. "They're fine. You're just being stupid. You belong to me now and they know it. You don't need them any more so why should you have to hear from them? You Americans have a phrase, 'cut the apron strings.' Do it."

"You can't mean that I can't write to them anymore? That's not fair." I felt tears welling in my eyes.

"Write all you want, though I don't see why you'd want to. They're obviously happy to be rid of you."

"They love me no matter what you think." No matter how much he hurt me and turned my love for him to hatred, I wouldn't let him damage my love for my family.

"Maybe the letters were never delivered," he growled and stalked out to the hallway.

Anna came in from the bedroom. "I couldn't help overhearing," she whispered. "That man will never accept accountability. He runs away. He's a coward."

"Is the word disgust an absolute or is it possible for it to grow?" I wondered aloud instead of just agreeing with her.

She put up her hand to silence me as the door opened. Otto came in without knocking. I hadn't heard him coming and it startled me. He didn't bother to speak, but went straight to the tile stove and filled its firebox with briquettes from the scuttle he was carrying. I don't know whether the look he gave me as he left was a sneer or a leer. When Kurt roared off in the car after lunch, Anna and I departed for our daily walk. It was an unusual March day with a sun that was trying its best to wash away the winter snow. If I hadn't been so tense and miserable, I would have thrown my arms wide to draw the warmth to me. As it was I scarcely noticed.

"Why haven't they written?" I asked Anna as we walked in the garden?" I'd questioned her so many times that there was no need to say "who."

"Here's a thought. Kurt could be collecting the letters, yours and theirs to you." Anna's frown made me feel nauseous. "If he likes what you say, he probably sends yours on to them. He knows they would be over here in a minute if they didn't hear from you. Have you said anything in your letters about the troubles here? He does read them."

That startled me. I tried to think what I had written to my parents. "I've been as cheerful as possible. I want them to think life here is idyllic. Time enough for them to learn the truth when we can tell it face to face. Fairy tales, that's what I've written, nothing but fairy tales."

"Well, if you hadn't, Kurt would have had us done away with before now. As it is, he thinks he has the same docile girl he married, which is why he continues to treat you as he pleases. I wish it didn't have to be this way. We have to play the game he's set up until we're free. You know the Major and your mother love you. They have to be writing."

"If they weren't getting my letters, Daddy would send Ambassador Bishop or somebody to find me, I'm sure." I accepted her explanation. It was the only possible one. "So who's delivering the letters to Kurt?"

"Maybe Gerhardt, maybe Otto, maybe the Postmaster. Maybe we'll never know." She had turned us around and we'd started back to the cold, forbidding, fortress of Ostatetcznie.

How could I have ever have thought it romantic? I had been told there were dungeons beneath a part of it, but I'd never been down there. I could visualize the enjoyment on the face of one of Kurt's handsome ancestors as some pitiful innocents were tortured or released in death in its cold grasp. If others in the family had been like Kurt, those things could truly have happened. As for the letter thief, I remembered the pity in Gerhardt's eyes when, each morning, he told me there was nothing. He couldn't be the one. I wanted to stand in the middle of the garden and scream, "Who can I trust?'

The answer was clear. No one. Just as we reached the spot where the draw -bridge had once been, it was clear to me. "It's Otto," I whispered. "He has shifty eyes and he adores Kurt. It has to be Otto." We had arrived back at the house and stepped back into our fragile, distressing lives.

One afternoon, just a week before Dieter's wedding, the whole of Ostatetcznie, could have heard him thundering up the stairs and yelling. "Kurt. Kurt, du schwein, get out here."

When I emerged from my suite, Gerhardt was pleading at the top of the stairs, "He isn't here, he isn't here. Please come down, sir, the Madame is resting."

"What do you mean not here? He was in Torun last evening." He whirled to face the butler. "He damn well better be here."

I ran down to stop my livid friend before he assaulted Gerhardt. "He isn't here, really. If he was in Torun, we didn't know it. We haven't seen him for two weeks."

"Well, he most certainly was in Torun. H accosted Sybilla's mother on the street and now they've taken her."

"Who's taken her?"

"The Gestapo came a while ago and loaded her into a car and drove away with her."

"Why would they take her? Magda isn't the kind to cause any trouble. Maybe you'd better tell me the whole story."

"Kurt told her he'd heard a rumor Hitler had been shot, she made the mistake of saying 'God be praised, the pig is dead.' She should have known better. Mein Gott he's in the SS. But now they've taken her away."

"Do you think Kurt can help? I don't . . . "

"Help? Of course he won't help. He did it deliberately. He's been mad ever since she criticized his behavior at the ball all these months ago."

Gerhardt interrupted us. "Madame, may I suggest you both go out to the garden. It's a warm day for March and perhaps the air will allow you to think over the situation more clearly. If you sit in the summer house, I will serve tea there."

Nodding in instant understanding, I led Dieter to the conservatory door and out to the gazebo. How could I be so careless? The butler winked as we passed and my heart quickened. We did have allies, one here and more at Friedenau. Two days after our meeting in the sun-warmed summer- house Anna and I became a part of the underground and gave the first of many refugees a stopover in Ostatetcznie's dungeon.

Chapter 37

The memory is so strong that for a moment I am back in that snow-covered garden at Ostatetcznie. The incredible feeling of relief I had felt at Gerhardt's wink and Dieter's presence again covers me like a protective blanket. I sit silently, wrapped in remembrance.

Tante Nina's voice jerks me back to the present. "Is that why you stayed in Poland? Couldn't you have gotten home before the Americans declared war on Germany?"

Safely curled up on the familiar sofa in Karol and Jannina Donimerski's small sitting room, I answer her. "Getting away from Kurt was harder than getting away from Poland. Besides, the dungeon at Ostatetcznie was a perfect place to hide the refugees. Once we became involved, we couldn't abandon those people. That's just the kind of people we are . . . and you are too. Don't you remember the day the old man came towing the mule? You bought it because it was left over from WWI and had the U.S. brand on its haunch. It had had a hard life for those fourteen years and we all determined to keep in the lap of luxury for the rest of its days. Bless its heart. It lay down in a warm stall that night and died in its sleep. Even if you had known what was going to happen, could you have abandoned it?

Oncle Karol picks up the samovar and starts toward the kitchen. He stops in the doorway. "Do you remember the baby buffalo that came with those Russian Gypsies?"

"Oh, yes, he was so sweet." I smile at the kind man who loves anything American after his years in Wisconsin. "He used to come right into the kitchen, didn't he?"

"Yes, and no one ever noticed how he was growing. Then one day when he came in, he couldn't turn around. He wouldn't back up, butted the cook and broke her arm. We had to almost dismantle the kitchen to get him out. Being ostracized made him so unhappy we finally put in one of those doors that opens on the top half. Now he stands outside with his head in the kitchen and seems quite happy. At night he sleeps with the cows as if he's one of them.

"As much as I hate going to bed not knowing all of your story." Tante Nina picks up her teacup. "We'd better retire now. We believe the other servants are loyal, but one can never be sure. Let's go before they come home. Just tell me one thing while we clear away the evidence of our celebration . . . why were you arrested? I would have thought with Kurt being in such an exalted position you would have been safe."

"The dungeons at Ostatetcznie were ideal for hiding partisans waiting to escape. Kurt wasn't at home much and, even when he was, neither he nor the servants who were loyal to him ever went down there. Some of the partisans in the Ostatetcznie village had heard of a tunnel that once had been dug to the edge of the old moat. Gerhardt found its entrance to the castle in the far-western corner, just above what would have been the moat's water line. A small opening, adequate for only one person at a time. One supposed that in the former days of its use, whoever was trying to escape had to swim across the moat and dive into the tunnel entrance to freedom. Using the castle entrance at night, now just above the dirt line, we three began to help the Partisans. The servant's rooms were all on the other side of the castle so we felt perfectly safe. Sometimes our guests were there for several days before it was safe to transport them to a town where a small boat could take them north on the Vistula River to the Baltic Sea. I did so want to go with them.

"There were so many that disappeared, Kurt would never have given up until he discovered what we had been doing and how it was done. We were so busy saving others we didn't have time to save ourselves. The time never seemed right. Five years . . ."

"But he did find out, didn't he?" Tante Nina catches Oncle Karol's arm, "We can hardly go to bed now without hearing the end."

A car door slams. Our host and employer quickly picks up my cup. "Too late now. Run upstairs, Caro. We'll explain you to Inge and Oola in the morning. Run."

My room is small, clean, and comfortable. There is no bathroom on the top floor, but there is a pitcher and bowl on the wash stand and a chamber pot will take care of my other needs. I'm sure Tante Nina would not leave the servants with no way to bathe. That explanation will come tomorrow. As tired as I am, I'm disappointed that the evening ended before I had time to tell everything. Safe here, in a clean bed with no fears for this night at least, I turn out the light and let myself drift.

As I do every night, I see Alex's baby face as I last saw it. When I pray, I am sure he's alive and that I will someday hold my little boy in my arms. But when?Then the terrible pictures come. I begin to see those who sacrificed so much for me. Was it only a few days ago that animal carried my dear Countess's tiny body out onto the square? And Major Metzgar? What grief his family must be feeling. I feel so guilty. Are my parents alive? Have they just abandoned me, or is it truly Kurt's vicious control that's kept their letters from me all these years? And when can I talk about Alex? Is it better if I don't mention him? Suppose someone made a slip and Kurt found out he had a son? Is it true that the end of this war may be near? I know now that I am near Poznan. If I run away, it will surely get the Donimierskis in trouble. I'll talk to Oncle Karol as soon as possible. He'll know how and when to help me. "Our Father which art in heaven, please Help Onkle Karol. Please help me.

The next morning I am setting the breakfast table when, without warning, the Polish radio interrupts the news. A man's voice, almost inaudible, says "We think we've just heard that Germany has surrendered. Stand by."

Hardly daring to breath, and like the newscaster, afraid to believe what I have heard, again the radio leaks out. "It has been confirmed, THE GERMANS HAVE SURRENDERED."

"Come quickly, everyone, come quickly," I yell. "Germany has surrendered."

"Did I hear correctly?" are Oncle Karol's first words. "Did you say that Germany has surrendered?" Then we all hear the announcer as he repeats his words over and over. "God be praised, God be praised."

"Thank you for answering my prayer," I say softly. "Amen."

Inge, Oola, Panna Katrinka, the cook, and Tante Nina, gather with us in the dining room while Bill, the buffalo, lets his frustration be known at being left out by snorting loudly and kicking at the door to the kitchen. Finally, to be able to talk above his racket, we take the radio with us and join him. Oola and Inge are sent off to the village to spread the word. Panna Katrinka insists we all have breakfast and, when we are seated at the table, Oncle Karol turns at last to me.

"Now my dear," he takes my hand in his huge callused one, "How do we get you back to your parents?"

"Oh, Please, No. I have to go to my baby." There is silence.

"Your baby?" Tante Nina stares at me and says at last, "You have a baby? Where is it?"

It is the 7th of May, 1945, and now, with freedom before me, I can tell them the whole story. I begin eagerly . . .

Chapter 38

There was no more reason than usual for the desolation I felt on that sunny July morning in 1944. Maybe it was that writing another letter to my parents when there would never be an answer seemed so futile or that, now that the Allies had landed in Normandy, their progress seemed so slow. Anna and I had been overjoyed when Gerhardt's contraband radio had gleefully shouted to us in June that the Allies' long anticipated and hoped-for assault had been successful. With the news that the Allies were fighting their way toward Paris, we all had envisioned a quick victory that would make a prisoner of Kurt and provide an immediate way home for Anna, Deu, and me. That hadn't happened. By mid-July the Allies had only pushed as far as St. Lo in France and we still had refugees moving through our dungeon—not many, but too many to leave without support.

Those poor, forlorn souls always arrived in the dark and were moved out at night. If Kurt happened to be at home, or Otto or one of the other servants were prowling around, it was essential to keep them occupied on the other side of the schloss. I never had any contact with the refugees or the partisans, but Gerhardt, Anna and I each had a job that no one else could fill. Gerhardt was their contact with the outside. Anna let them in and out and made them as comfortable as possible and I was the one who kept everyone else from knowing they were our "guests." All information between the three of us was passed from Gerhardt to Anna to me during our afternoon walks with Deu.

After the Allies landed it was easier. There were fewer refugees and the German Army was too occupied on two fronts to pay attention to the small fish. There were still people like Otto, who, in return for favors, would turn in anyone, with only the slightest provocation. On this particular morning, I was without optimism. Sitting at my desk, still in my nightgown and robe, I wrote to my parents.

'Your letters are still not coming through so I can't comment on what you have told me about where you are and what you are doing. I only hope you are getting mine. I pray for the day we can be together again to talk, and talk, and talk. Deu, Anna and I love and miss you so much. I hope we can soon be together.'

Not daring to say more in case Kurt was reading my letters, loneliness took over. The last sentence was a lie. I was without hope. After I put the short note in its envelope, I went out to leave it on the table at the top of the stairs. Anna or Gerhardt would pick it up and put it in the post box. Before I could turn around my arm was twisted behind my back and I was being forced into the bedroom. I recognized the odor of Kurt's shaving lotion.

"What are you doing?" I managed to ask as he kicked the door closed and let go. "What have I done now?"

He was in such a fury his face was bright red with white lines bracketing his mouth. "How dare you use my castle to help that filthy treasonous scum escape?" He was yelling so loudly in my ear I was sure my eardrum would break. "Who do you think you are?"

My first thought was, who had told? Then I knew it didn't matter. Someone had and now he was accenting every word by jabbing me in my throat with stiff fingers. It hurt. and I struggled to get away. Deu, on his feet, didn't know what was happening either, but his ears flattened against his head and there was a low, ominous growl.

Kurt snatched the ever-present revolver from its holster on his hip. "Growl at me again, you cur, and I'll kill you."

"Platz, Deu." I cried out. My heart raged in my chest, thrumming all the way to my ears. I put my hand on the dog's head to calm him. Knowing Kurt, he'd follow through on his threat. I stepped in front of my protector. "Platz."

Deu stood his ground, the growl continuous. Kurt hurled me out of the way. "I told you not to growl." Kurt said and shot.

My dog, spurting blood and with a bewildered look in his faithful, brown eyes, fell. My arms caught him and we sank to the floor. With his beloved head cradled in my lap, his tail thumped feebly, the expression of pain and bewilderment left his eyes, and his own breathing stopped. Tears streaming, I looked up at the monster who stood above me. The gun was still in his hand and I didn't care whether he killed me or not.

"He deserved it," Kurt whined like a little boy caught in some minor infraction.

Like a wildly gyrating tree in a hurricane, I pounded him wherever my fists happened to land. With months of stored revulsion gushing forth in words I didn't know I knew, I screamed accusations. He yelled justifications. When he raised the gun, I flung my arm at his hand and the weapon flew across the room, firing as it went. We both rushed for it. I would have killed him as easily as he had killed Deu, but he grabbed me by the hair and threw me against the armoire. It stunned me. Catching me by one arm, he flung me on the bed like a floppy Raggedy Ann. I kicked, bit, clawed and screamed while he tore my robe and nightgown from me. To avoid his hands I slid to the floor.

"Well, the floor will do," he muttered as his body dropped to pin mine against the hard boards. "Too bad, just when she's committed a crime, the lady arouses me again." He tore at his belt buckle. "She will have to be punished for the rest of her life. But first she will pay for her insubordination today. Lie still, you traitor." He unbuttoned his trousers and then he performed one last vicious, painful act of humiliation.

As he rolled away from me, I found the strength somewhere in that hate and self-disgust to jerk my knee upward. I hoped I had stopped his whoring forever. While he was doubled up moaning and clutching his groin, I ran into the bathroom and locked the door. Old and fragile, it gave way as soon as he crashed into it. When I regained consciousness, I had no memory of why I lay on the bathroom floor. Kurt was gone and Otto stood over me with the inevitable smirk. The nearest thing I could grab was the bathroom rug to cover my nakedness.

"Get dressed," the man ordered as he snatched unsuccessfully at the rug. "I'm not interested in your skinny body."

"Leave and I'll get dressed." I clung to the rug. "I have to bury my dog." Scrambling up, I turned toward the door with its full-length mirror. My jaw was swollen, the bruise already colored. Then I remembered and didn't care. Having Deu laid lovingly to rest in the garden was all that mattered.

"The trash heap is good enough for the dog, but that's not my job. The gardener is doing it. Now put your clothes on. I'm not leaving." He pulled the dressing table chair out and sat down.

I knew better than to argue. "Where are we going?" I asked.

"Don't bother getting too fancy. You're going to the dungeon. You should know what it's like. You certainly have made use of it long enough." He made a funny noise that could have been a suppressed laugh, yet sounded more as if he were strangling.

In the bedroom Deu's precious body was already gone, but the blood was still there. I wanted to go to it to do what? Perhaps to stroke it as I could no longer stroke his soft fur. I didn't even get to say goodbye. Tears started again. Passing the bed was a reminder of my shame. How could I have been senseless enough to have ever loved Kurt? I felt loathsome inside and out.

When I stumbled on the stairs, Otto caught me and, with his hand gripping my arm, marched me along. The house was ominously silent.

"Where's Anna?"

"Waiting for you."

"Gerhardt?"

"Dead."

"Why didn't Kurt kill us too?"

"He's afraid of your father." That funny noise came again. When had he lost his respect for Kurt or . . . did he ever have any?

"My father? What does he have to do with it? Is he here?" I could hardly get the words out.

"He's wherever a General called Patton is."

"How do you know that?"

"From his letters." He smirked. "I'm not just a dumb servant."

"What else do you know about my family? Please tell me, Otto." I needed any knowledge he had, and he was eager enough to brag.

"What will you give me? The Baron gives me a lot to keep my eye on you. What will you give me?"

"If you're so loyal to the Baron, why ask me?"

"I'm loyal only to Otto, but I deliver what I'm paid for. Pay me or rot in the dungeon. It's no difference to me." He lit a cigarette, knowing how I hated the smell of them.

"All right, I'll bargain with you. When the Allies win this war, the Baron will be taken prisoner. I will tell the authorities that you helped us escape. If you do, that is. After the war we'll see what happens. Who knows, I might even give you this castle. I never want to see it again."

For the first time ever, he beamed.

"Of course," I continued, "if Germany wins . . . ?

"Hah. Russia and the Allies are like a pair of giant scissors. They are preparing one day to snap together to cut off Germany's head. Germany will not win."

We had reached the heavy dungeon door. "I will think about your offer," Otto said as he shoved me in and slammed the door. The bolt slid home.

From the shadows, Anna pulled me into her arms. "Oh, God be praised. I thought that demon had killed you. Oh, my Kleine." She stroked my hair and my face and covered it with kisses.

"He wanted to kill me, I think, but in his fury he killed Deu instead." It was hard to talk through the tears that came every time I thought of Deu's death, but I had to tell her. Between sobs, when my voice was still little more than a squeak, I described the terrible scene. We were both crying. "I don't know where he's gone. And Otto said Kurt didn't kill me because he was afraid of my father." I choked back the tears. I had to think, get away, save Anna. "Otto was the one reading my parents' letters. He says my father is with General Patton, who's an old Cavalry friend. They are somewhere here in Europe." I wanted to hope, but disbelief was still strong. "He could be lying."

"But he knows this General Patton's name?" Her assurance gave me hope.

Surprisingly it was still morning. The sun, as if it felt we needed encouragement, sent in a ray or two through the high grill in the wall to pierce the gloom. Anna took my face between her hands and turned it toward the light. "What happened to your face? It's bruised and swollen."

"After Kurt killed Deu, I fought with him."

"That son of the devil hit my baby . . . as if she were a man? You are lucky he didn't kill you. He killed Deu on purpose, because he knew it would break your heart. That pig."

In a tiny voice I managed to mumble. "That isn't all he did." Then I told her about the rape. "I'm so ashamed. How, when I'm so consumed with hatred for him, when he had just killed my beloved pet, when he had struck me and debased me in every way he could, how could I have let him near me? I wish he had killed me. Even if we find my father, how will I face him?"

We dropped down onto the dirt floor and, with my head in her lap, I covered my face and started sobbing again. She made soothing noises and stroked my hair until I was drained.

"I'm not very wise," she said. "But I think that, it is like the frail line between sanity and insanity. There must be such a line between love and hate. You loved him once, but today had nothing to do with love. It was an evil you didn't ask for. Nothing you did or could have done could have changed it. We have to concentrate now on how we're going to get out of here. When the Allies come, they will take care of that devil. The bruise on your face will heal and someday a proper man will come to heal your heart."

We sat quietly without moving, while I thought about what she'd said. At first her words simply repeated themselves in my mind. Like robots, they were words without substance or meaning. They marched around in my brain a long time before the first glimmer of understanding and acceptance came. When they'd erased the guilt, I was able to tell Anna that I hoped Franz had buried Deu in the garden. Then I remembered my brief conversation with Otto and we talked again about what he'd said.

"That one's not to be trusted." She stood up and walked over to the secret door and tested it. "Locked from the outside," she pronounced. "We'll have to make plans of our own." She sat back down beside me in the dirt. "Unless the partisans have to move someone in the next few days and can't find Gerhardt, no one will come near that little door. I don't really think Otto will do anything to help us. It would be easier to let us die in here and, when the war is over and Kurt is out of the way, to just take over the estate."

"I offered him freedom from prosecution and a gift of the castle if the Allies win or Kurt is killed. What more do I have to give?"

"Wouldn't you want it if Kurt were dead?

"Beautiful as it appears, it's too cold in every sense of the word. No, I will never want to see it again."

Chapter 39

By the time Otto brought bowls of soup it was dark. Sealed in as we were, we could see no way to freedom. Even Dieter and Sybilla would never guess what had happened to us. Our only hope was Otto. Trusting him was like expecting a lion to show us his teeth in friendship. When he came, he simply put the bowls on the dirt floor and left in silence, taking his kerosene lantern with him.

In the damp blackness we felt for the bowls on our knees and drank the thin, tasteless soup, huddled together, hungry and hopeless.

When a key turned in the lock, we clutched each other and waited. The lantern, held chest high, reflected on Kurt's face in a way that illuminated the evil demons of his soul. Gone was the handsome man of my childish dreams and in his stead, a malevolent being advanced toward us.

"Do the accommodations suit your Ladyship?" Kurt's sneering voice issued from the disfigured lips. His words and arrogant manner suited that damaged face. He lifted the lantern higher and the hellish visage was magnified."

I turned away, from him and from the images of the bedroom, all too fixed in my mind.

"You ought to know better than to turn your back on me." With one step he lunged at me, caught my arm and spun me around. When he raised the other hand with the lantern in it, I flinched at the impending hit. Anna stepped between us. He used the hot lantern to push her away. Kurt's face again became that of a grimacing gargoyle.

"Did he burn you?" I shrieked. She shook her head. I looked back at Kurt and laughed, though it shocked me to hear it.

"What do you find so funny?"

"You should never carry a lantern, Kurt. It only shows your true character." Conceited as he was, I hoped he would put the lamp down and leave it.

He spat. "Take a good look. You'll never have another chance." Swinging the lantern higher, he strode to the door. Then, as if he had been given stage directions, he stopped with his hand on the latch. "Just so you don't waste your time waiting for rescue, there is no one left to help you." When he stood in the open doorway and glared, he could have been a madman. "Since dancing is your life and your love, you can dance for eternity in this dungeon. Be assured, Princess Aurora, you will never leave here alive. The world you think you've conquered will never care. Only your imperious parents will ever give you another thought and they will go through their broken lives wondering what became of you."

The heavy door clanged shut. Isolated from the world, Anna and I stood frozen as his cackling laughter melted into the darkness. I pictured two skeletons in the dirt of the dungeon floor, one with her feet in first position and her arms above her head, and the other with her arms properly folded on her breast, a dying swan.

Anna's whisper brought me back to the present. "Do you suppose he has killed Otto too?"

"If he did, who else will know we're here?" A faint roaring noise rose beyond the walls. "That must be Kurt's car. He's left, but if Otto's gone too, what good will it do us?"

Before we had time to even contemplate the deadly future and, as if in answer to my question, there was a scraping outside the secret door to the moat. The bolt squealed as it was drawn back. "Your Ladyship? Are you in there?"

I couldn't speak. Anna answered. "Who's that?"

"Krista, the cook. Oh, Frau Meier? Is her ladyship with you?" With assurances from Anna, she struck a match so we could see her and she could see us. "You must come quickly. The Baron has driven away, but Otto says he will return soon. Bitte, we do not have much time."

Otto was still alive and was performing his part of our bargain. "Thank you, God," I said aloud.

Krista looked like an angel in her white apron and cape. Already on my feet, we hurried to the faintly outlined door. One at a time we squeezed through the small opening. In seconds we were following Krista through dark bushes and into the dim village.

"Do you know if the gardener buried my dog?" I whispered to her. If we will pass the spot, I would like to stop. Just for a moment."

"He did, Baroness, but we will not pass by that place."

Pale hands belonging to moving shadows pushed us through an open door of what, I presumed, was one of the cottages. Before I could even say 'thank you', I heard the cook whisper, "he placed a small cross on the grave." When I stumbled on the sill, the same hands righted me and led me a few steps until my own fingers touched the rung of a ladder.

"Hinauf," breathed a voice in my ear and I went up quickly. I could feel Anna climbing behind me.

In the cramped space, it was impossible to stand erect. We fell on, what felt like, a straw mattress. Someone lit a lamp below and the small bit of light that filtered up to reflect on the thatched roof showed there was nothing else up there with us except extra bundles of thatch. After the dungeon's hard dirt floor, the straw felt like a feather bed. Anna clasped my hand in hers and we lay still, our breathing, slow and matched in the dark. At least for a little while we were safe. I tried to forget the last black hours and to be hopeful about what daylight would bring. Mentally and emotionally exhausted though, I didn't think I could sleep.

When rattling sounds from below wakened me, gray light outlined the perimeters of our strange environment. My first gesture on awakening was, as always, to pat Deu's eager head. I reached out before memory shattered my dream for all time. I would never know that joy again. With my first sob, Anna, who knew me so well, reached over to let me know she was awake. I heard my father's voice saying, "don't be a crybaby." They were both right. The sadness would remain, but silence was crucial to our safety. I had to put tears behind me.

In a little while baking smells floated up to tantalize us. Soon a blond head appeared. Krista's daughter, Bette, smiled, with a finger to her lips. When she withdrew, she left behind a basket of warm brötchen, already slathered with butter and jam, two cups of tea, a note written on a slate, a chamber-pot, and a wet wash cloth. There was no towel, but we used whatever it was that had covered us during the night. The light was growing stronger and we could almost make out what it was.

The slate, when there was enough light to read it, said "The Baron came home and the Gestapo have started searching the grounds." They will come here soon. It will not be safe to move you during the daylight hours. Stay quietly where you are and we will protect you."

"They're sure to find us up here," Anna whispered. "There's no escape from the devils." She sounded so definite and so bitter.

After we had finished with the washcloth, we used it to wipe the slate clean. Soon, Bette climbed the ladder again to take away our cups, the wash cloth and the slate. She was back a few minutes later with a bowl of flour and a wad of rags.

"They've already searching the village," she whispered. "Lie very still, you are about to die of small-pox." She began to pat the flour into my hair and over my face and neck. I sneezed. Though I tried to stifle it, both Bette and Anna plopped hands over my mouth and nose. "Don't do that again," they both hissed.

"Don't get it in my nose again." I whispered back.

"I'm having trouble covering the bruises. It shows through the flour, but the swelling does change the shape of your face." When Bette was finished, Anna whispered she thought I looked pretty dead.

"If they come up here, hold your breath. They won't get too close to a corpse with small pox. I heard it worked during the Russian Revolution."

I wasn't convinced sharp-eyed SS men or Hitler's henchmen could be fooled like ignorant Bolsheviks, but I knew if we were caught again we really would be corpses. And yet hope is a hard flame to extinguish.

She'd hardly finished when we heard shouts from the lane. Handing Anna the flour bowl and rags, Bette pushed her in behind the pile of the extra thatch that was kept in the corner. Bette, herself, was down the ladder, moaning and crying with her parents before we heard the searchers burst through the door.

"Stop that noise," a man's voice snarled. "Where are you hiding them?

Franz, the gardener, and his family only mourned louder.

"Stop it I say. What's wrong with you? Why are you making that racket?" More sounds of people clattering through the door.

"My sister just died of small-pox," Krista let out a terrible yowl. I could just imagine her throwing her large apron up over her face in grief. "We'll all die. We're doomed."

"Where is your sister?" The German soldier had toned down, nervous perhaps.

"We had to put her in the loft, to keep away the contamination. They say it's not safe to breathe the same air."

"Don't try to fool me. You have the Baroness and her maid up there." The man was climbing the ladder.

I held my breath. My heart beat so fast I was sure it would give me away. I felt the cover lift. It dropped again in a fraction of a second. I could hear the man sliding down the ladder and his yelp of fear. "She's dead alright. Let's get out of here. They're all probably infected."

Once the shouts and footsteps had retreated, Anna crept out from under the thatch Flour sprinkled everywhere as we shook with silent laughter in each other's arms. "It worked. It worked." We mouthed silently.

Later we heard hammering on the front of the cottage again. When it stopped, Bette whispered, "They've put up a Quarantine sign. No one else will come in here."

The local carpenter and his assistant came in the afternoon, but wouldn't come inside. They just pushed a simple coffin through the door. When it had been silent in the streets a long time, Anna and I felt secure enough to peer through the floor cracks and we could see the long box now standing on end in a corner of the room below.

In the afternoon when the searchers had long disappeared, Krista whispered that I was to be moved to the town of Bydgoszcz. In the casket. Her cousin there would weight the empty coffin with stones and bury it near his parents in the local churchyard. Anna would be disguised as the wagon-driver's wife. The cousin had a house in the middle of town where we could live in his attic until it was safe to move to the city of Danzig on the Baltic Sea. When a neutral ship docked there, we would be on our way home. The Partisans had a larger organization than we had realized and we were grateful to hope once again.

I was re-blanched with the flour in case anyone stopped us on the way to Bydgoszcz from Ostatetcznie and insisted on checking the coffin. A sign on the back of the wagon said, Vorsicht:Pocken (Beware:Small Pox). Anna and the driver of the wagon, Wolfie, wore masks to protect them from the fictitious Pocken. It was three days before I climbed into the coffin and rode away from Ostatetcznie on the wagon. Although part of my heart will always be in that garden, I prayed never to see the castle again.

The ride from Ostatetcznie to Bydgoszcz over cobbled roads took the whole day. Because Hitler had paved no roads in Poland and the horses had to be watered and rested every few miles, we stopped frequently. Sandwiches and pickle-jars of water had been packed in the casket with me. Aside from the jouncing and the heat inside the wooden box when the sun shone full on it, I wasn't physically too uncomfortable.

The hole that Deu's death had left in my heart was so sore that even my relief at our escape couldn't erase the pain. Over and over I saw his bewildered brown eyes as the sparkle drained from them. As the coffin bounced and jumbled, I began to see him, free and happy, joyfully galloping up a road lined with flowering trees, toward God. Perhaps during what was to come we might have been separated, forced to live out our lives without knowing what had happened to the other anyway. That would have been more frightening for him. was then I recognized that grieving was a selfish process and that, while I would always miss him, I should stop feeling sorry for myself. Deu was with that higher power that created all of us. I told him I loved him and would carry him in my heart always. Then I whispered goodbye.

With the rhythmic clopping of the horse's hooves, we rumbled noisily along. I, in a sense, entombed with my own thoughts. Sometimes I listened to Anna and Wolfie's conversation, sometimes I slept. By the time they unloaded me in the churchyard, it was dusk and. Krista's cousin, Jacob, was waiting.

Once released I crowded together with Anna behind an imposing tombstone with chiseled sentiments from the man's wife. The grave having already been dug, Jacob and Wolfie buried the casket. It was an eerie feeling as we heard the clumps of dirt echo on the empty box, but Anna was beside me. We rode into Bydgoszcz on the floor of a tiny car, possibly one of Hitler's touted Volkswagens. After Jacob turned us over to his wife, Lili, he disappeared as soon as we were inside the house. Bathed and in borrowed nightgowns, Anna and I sat like queens on real beds on the third floor. I was starved, but the town was permeated with the sickly sweet odor of the sugar-beet processing plant and as soon as the delicious soup went down, it tried to come back. It was a hard fight, but I won.

Lili took my bowl away. "Wait a bit. Perhaps it is too soon after that bumpy ride. Sleep a little and I'll bring bread with jam before Jacob and I go to bed. Something sweet. That might be better," she said with finality, turning off the one hanging bulb. We heard her step carefully down the steep stairway.

"What do you suppose is wrong with my stomach?" I whispered to Anna. "I hate to be so much trouble to these nice people."

"We haven't eaten much in the last few days, if you remember. I

317

expect you just need to eat a little less and more often. If the soup you've eaten stays down and the bread and jam, then we'll know we have the solution. I'm sure that's all it is." She patted my hand and turned over.

For a week or more, I struggled with the nausea while we waited to move on. Worried, Lili called a Polish doctor who could be trusted. After his examination he made a flat statement to all three of us. "It's unusual. But not unheard of. Morning sickness so early in a pregnancy. I suspect that's what this is. I can see no other reason for the nausea. My guess, you will feel better in about eight and a half months. Are you married?"

"I was," I stammered, shocked by his diagnosis. "My husband . . . " I was going to say, "is dead," but my next thought was that, more than my continued existence, the fact of his baby's birth, if that's what this meant, must never reach Kurt's ears. The doctor seemed to be an understanding man, so without weighing the rights, wrongs, or dangers I poured out the whole story ending with a desperate plea. "If I am pregnant, no one must know."

He stroked his luxuriant, gray beard. "You may continue to vomit for the first few months at least. That will be a dead give-away that a baby is coming." He looked at Anna and Lili. "Can she stay here?"

They looked at each other. Lili spoke first. "We will keep her hidden because, even without the vomiting, if anyone sees her hair, they will know at once who she is. An opportunist would surely notify her husband. Even though we've had no ballet for several years, this young woman is still a legend in Poland. Soon everyone will know Aurora is missing and the opportunists will be as alert as the SS and the Gestapo."

"To be sure Germany is busy between the Russians and the Allies." The Doctor was eager to contribute to the conversation, if only to let us know he was on our side. "In the small towns there are still some like that Quisling in Norway who have no loyalty and no shame. You must keep this lovely young lady safe."

He put his hand on Anna's arm as if for confirmation. Anna covered it with her own and the three of them presented an impenetrable wall.

Anna asked the question I couldn't. "If you can let us live in your attic for a few months, we will be eternally grateful. After the upset stomach part is passed, I would think they could move us on, yes?" She looked hopefully at the Polish woman.

"Yes," Lili helped the doctor up. After a few words of comfort and instructions to eat a little something every morning before I got out of bed, they went out the attic door.

With this new responsibility, worry stayed with me. "Do you think it's wise, Anna, to stay here?"

"It will be all right, I think, for a short time. We'll stay until the sickness goes away, which it will, if you are pregnant. Or even if you are not. We can't do any better than that, unless . . ."

"Unless, what?

"Unless you want Doctor Pogonowski to 'take away' the baby."

"What do you mean 'take away' the baby?"

"Like that girl in the Warsaw Corps de Ballet did. The doctor just scraped it out."

I jumped up. "How can you even think such a thing? No, no, no. If it is a baby, it did not choose to be born. I did not choose this path, but I refuse to let it die." Talking and thinking about the baby, I danced around the small room. "Kurt may think he's had the last word, but the joke is on him. If there is a baby, we will love it and it will live and it will never know the father. He will never feel that joy and glory the child will bring us." I wave my hands at the imagined wonders. "Despite all that hate and ugliness, his intent to hurt me, he will have given me the most wonderful gift of all." I circled around her in our little room. "All this will be a burden on you and the Barolowskis. I'm sorry for that. But if it is true, for me it's wonderful news."

Anna stopped me by wrapping her arms around my shoulders and holding me close. "There, there, Kleine. It was just something I had to say. Of course we will go through whatever we must to save this perfect child. And, because of whatever burdens it adds to our journey, we will love it all the more. Sit, now, sit down or you'll be sick again. We have plans to make."

The nausea stayed and stayed. It came with every meal and sometimes I had to eat more than once to get something to stay down. Doctor Pogonowski wasn't satisfied with my condition and when there was some spotting, he immediately ordered me to bed and advised against travel.

"If, of course," he said, "you would prefer not to have this baby, it seems God is willing to give you a choice. In which case you may do anything you like." Anna and I looked at each other before either of us answered.

"We both are fully aware that, in the end, God will make his choice, but Carole and I want a good healthy baby to take with us. If the Barolowskis are willing to keep us, we'll stay here until the baby is born." Anna sounded very definite.

Lili was jubilant. "I would be miserable if you left before that baby came and I never got to hold it, to even know whether it was a boy or girl. Jacob and I have grown so fond of you. You're like the daughter we never had." Embarrassed at her confession, Lili turned her face away to hide the blush. Both Anna and I rushed to hug her.

It was a long eight months. Once I found the courage to go downstairs, we became a family, except when someone came to the door. Then Anna and I hid, but even that bit of freedom helped. Because I could not risk going outdoors, the Doctor had me lie on the floor in front of a sunny window. Both the baby and I could absorb the sun's rays. He prescribed tonics and vegetables. Other things that were in short supply in war-torn Europe, were hard for Lili to find. I worried because food was scarce and Lili was so insistent I eat the right things. We had no money, but we kept a record. Once home, I could take care of that.

"I think the Barolowskis must be giving up some of their food for me," I said to Anna. "But the baby needs it too. I feel God has given me this chance and I must do everything I can to help. Am I wrong?"

"Don't worry, they want to help you. And the baby." Anna put her arms around me and cradled my head on her shoulder. "Lili and Jacob will be proud to have the baby born here. We are all eager to give up whatever is necessary to that end. I've talked to them. I know."

Relieved, I promised the Barolowskis that, as soon as I was home in America, I would spend my life giving back to them all the comforts they had given to me.

"We could come to America. That's something we have always wanted."

"We'll all go together," I said and took on another adopted family.

Alexander was born on the fourth of April, 1945 in the Bydgoszcz attic. A long and painful birth, but Dr. Pogonowski and Anna hardly moved from my side. He was only two weeks old when we left for Grudziadz. It had been only those few weeks I had been able to hold him close to my heart before I let him roll away with Anna on Rudiger Brietski's wagon.

Here it is almost the fourth of May, and I don't know whether they made it to Hel or whether they're dead or . . . I can't finish. At last I am in a place where I can cry. Tante Nina takes me in her arms. Oncle Karol leaves the room without a word.

"Where did he go? Did I chase him away?" I can finally ask.

"Be patient. Soon we should have a telephone call that will solve all our problems of how to find your baby."

Chapter 40
May 6, 1945

In the kitchen I was communing with the cook and the buffalo whose name was Butch when I heard Oncle Karol calling.

"Jannina, Carole, come quickly. I have news."

Tante Nina and I collided as we rushed toward the front of the house through the long hall. Disentangled, we watched Oncle Karol hang his hat on the Victorian coat rack, his grin was broad as the Vistula River at its widest point.

"Sit down, both of you," he commanded when we were in the sitting room. He hardly waited until we were settled before he began. "I've spent the day running down rumors and my sources are sure that the surrender of Germany is now being negotiated. They say the Russians are holding it up. They are so afraid the Germans will throw what's left of its armies in with the Allies and that they will all turn against the Soviet Union. Although Patton's Army is poised to do the job, the Reds are demanding that they be the first into Berlin and that all points in Europe surrender at the same time. If agreement occurs tomorrow, as it should, and once the Germans surrender, we should be able to travel to Hel with no problems. How we do it will depend on the Russians who, at the moment, surround us."

He pulled me up and into his strong arms where I nestled in his embrace like a trusting bird.

When he said there's more, I put my head back and look up. What more could there be? The face that looked down at me showed nothing but elation.

"I've sent a cable to your mother and would guess she will contact your father wherever he is. As soon as the war is officially over, we should hear from him. I can't imagine how they will be feeling to know you are safe with us."

"Otto said Daddy was with the American Third Army." I backed out of the sheltering arms. "If Otto was intercepting their letters, maybe Kurt didn't even know that."

Oncle Karol shook his head. "Still defending Kurt, are you? Believe me, though Otto may have been an accomplice, Kurt gave the orders. I have to admit though that Otto's information is probably right." Oncle Karol was excited. "I have reason to think several American armies are not far on the other side of the Elbe. We'll know soon. In the meantime let us celebrate what we are sure of." He went to the samovar and drew us each a hot cup of tea.

"Do your parents know about the baby?" Tante Nina unintentionally interrupted my thoughts as she ladled three spoons of black-market-sugar and a good dollop of cream into her tea.

"No. I was so afraid my letters would fall into the wrong hands that I just continued writing my letters as I had before, full of sweetness and light with no real news at all. I hoped they would accept what I said as the truth."

"If they did or didn't they must still have been worried sick, but we're near the end now. All we need to do is to get rid of that Teufel Hitler and go to Hel." Having lived in the United States for a year or so, Tante Nina giggled at her little joke. Oncle Karol winked at her, shook his head, smiled, and made the tsk-tsk sound of shame that's the same in any language.

Most of my days living with Kurt have taught me not to count on anything. "If they're there." I said softly.

"They are safely where they are supposed to be." Oncle Karol reached out and shook me gently. "You know that and soon you'll be holding your baby." Then suddenly, as if he could contain himself no longer, he threw his arms in the air and in a booming voice sang, "Hooray. Hooray. Hooray. It's been quite a day." He gathered me in his arms and in a sort of galloping step we threaded our way among the chairs and tables, repeating his song.

Tante Jannina joined in until exhausted we fell to the sofa in a clump. Drawn by the noise, the cook and maids clustered at the door. "Come in, come in." Tante Jannina broke up our clutch and waved her arms. "I hope I'm not speaking too soon," she said looking at her husband for confirmation as she pulled the cook into the room. "The war should be over by tomorrow." To the other two she issued orders. "Run, tell everybody in the village to come and join us in celebration. Don't come without the prisoners though. God be thanked they can be set free. Oh. God be praised."

Once they're sure they had heard correctly, they ran out into the spring air, waving their arms and shouting their news. When the villagers came, they were dressed in their Sunday best and marched in with the same diffidence they must show at Christmas time for the tourists. Oncle Karol commandeered two or three of the men to carry up the wine from the cellar. After he told everyone his news and how he acquired it, the toasting was joyful but still subdued.

Confused, the prisoners clustered on the edge of the crowd as if waiting for a chance to bolt, but when Oncle Karol waved his arms and pronounced them free and the Donimierski gardener gave a vigorous handshake to the man from Poznan, all restraint vanished. They cheered and yelled and hugged each other, the Donimeirskis, and me, but with the villagers there was still that invisible line. There were only introductions, serious handshakes and a few curtsies.

After a glass or two of wine, the villagers thanked the Donimierskis and wandered back into their own surroundings where we heard them rejoicing into the night. The prisoners were another story.

Since they couldn't be released officially until the surrender was publicly declared, the prisoners ate with us. Rather than send them back to their straw pallets, they were bedded down all over the house. We learned that most are or were married to professional people who, like Sybilla's mother, managed to irritate some Nazi. They came from every part of Poland, Germany, and some from as far away as Lithuania. Wherever they came from, they were our fast friends now.

Onkle Karol, Tante Jannina and I were finally alone in the sitting room after dinner when the telephone in the hall rang. Oncle Karol held out the receiver to me. My only thought was that somehow Kurt had found me. Who else could track me down? Breathless and trembling, I take the receiver when he hands it to me.

" Caro?" I just stood there like a dummy until he repeated it. "Caro, can you hear me?"

It's a voice I haven't heard in six years. "Daddy?" It couldn't be true. It was a dream.

"Yes, Carole. I'm here." His voice broke up.

"Daddy. Daddy. Where are you?" I choked on my tears.

"Not too far away; just the other side of Berlin. Our voice sounds funny. Are you all right?"

"It's just that I'm crying with happiness. Oh Daddy, when, how can I see you?"

"You'll have to come to Berlin. I can't leave here. Try to meet me at the American Embassy here the day after tomorrow. I may be late, but not even a war can keep me from you."

"I can't wait that long."

"I'm afraid you'll have to get your travel permits from the Russians and they won't make it easy."

There was a slight pause before he said, "Caro, I'm on a field telephone. I'll have to hang up in a minute. Do you have your passport?"

"No. I don't have anything at all."

"Quickly then, let me talk to Karol."

I passed the receiver and heard Onkle Karol say, "I'll try first thing tomorrow morning, but the Reds are intransigent people. Can you call me tomorrow night to see how I made out? The Russians are getting milk from me so I may have a little leverage there. No, I won't let her come alone. Someone . . ." After a moment he turned to me. "The line is dead. I hope he heard all that."

Reluctant to leave my only link with my father, I stood motionless until Oncle Karol led me back to the sitting room. "I'll see him the day after tomorrow." I can hardly get the words out. "The day after tomorrow. Oh, I wish I could talk to Mother too." Arms outstretched, I was spinning around the room, bumping into furniture and tottering lamps.

Jannina and Karol followed me, steadying their furnishings and saving the lampshades. "If you can stop whirling a minute," Oncle Karol said. "We'll try to call her. It's only eight in the morning there, but I don't suppose she'll mind being awakened for this."

It took a second for his words to register then I raced for the hall and the telephone. He was slower, but at last he was speaking to the operator. "Yes, Operator," I heard him say. "Mrs. Jonathon Pierson, no p—i—e—r—s—o—n." He was spelling it all in Polish, of course. "Crawfordsville, no, Craw—fords—ville. No, let me spell it." And he did. He has had the same trouble with Indiana, but The United States of America she apparently understood. There was a long pause while he listened. Finally he said, "No chance at all? Yes, I understand, but when do you think the lines will be fixed?" Another pause before he slowly put the receiver in its cradle and turned to Tante Jannina and me. "Apparently the Reds are more anxious than we thought. Somebody has destroyed all the communication lines between here, England, and the United States. The operator has no idea how long it will be before they're repaired." He wandered into the sitting room. We followed. "I'm afraid we'll just have to wait until we get to Berlin. In the meantime, I'm sure your father will let her know you're safe."

I was disappointed, but at least it wouldn't be forever. I was nearer to my baby than I had been and tomorrow I would be even nearer. Because everyone was trying to help me, I couldn't burden them with my disappointment. To lighten the mood I said, "Why don't we have a toast to the first good news we've had since Hitler took over this country." I reached for my tea cup, which still sat on the table where I'd left it when the phone rang.

"Well, we can hardly toast in tea. Hold on. We have to do this right." Uncle Karol bounced up and returnedwith three glasses and a bottle of champagne. Having toasted nothing but the end of the war with the village now we could be more selective.

First we toasted what was left of the poor scattered Polish Army, then the American Army, then the French Army, and at last the British who have fought so valiantly through seven terrible years.

"We can leave out the German people," Oncle Karol said. "And even though they switched from being 'anti' to 'pro' when they decided which side could win, I suppose we should toast the Soviets, too. They're the ones we'll need tomorrow."

He poured the last glass of wine. We raised our glasses once more before Tante Nina announced that it was ten o'clock and time for bed.

If it hadn't been for the soothing affects of the wine, I was sure I would have been awake all night. As it was, I went to sleep hugging my pillow to me as if it were baby Alex.

Chapter 41

The next day is the seventh of May. The radio is full of Germany's surrender. A voice tells us that Hitler and his mistress, Eva Braun, have committed suicide. The Donimierskis and I drive excitedly into the town of Poznan. We need to get our necessary travel papers quickly, to join the celebration which is sure to have erupted in the town with the announcement of the surrender. Oncle Karol is more hopeful than I. I'm still unable to believe it's all over.

The streets are crowded with local people and Russian soldiers. Among the beleaguered Polish people there are only old men, women and a few youths. Those who still possess even a cigarette butt or enough coffee for a weak cup try to share what little they have with us, but we graciously refuse. They are not insulted, but one can see they are distrustful of the Russians who are on the streets. The townspeople offer them nothing.

Oncle Karol has told me how terribly the Russian peasant-soldiers have behaved since they have been in Poland. It's not surprising. Ignorant of all the niceties of living, for instance in-door plumbing, they have pulled wash basins off one wall and stuck it up it in a more convenient place. Some even thought they could take it home to Russia and plug it into a wall there. I don't know how they thought the water got in or out. I laughed until I saw them in Poznan today. In mismatched, threadbare uniforms they are a pitiful lot. They try to be friendly, but they don't know how and they stand around in little bunches like clots in an artery.

The Russian officers, on the other hand, seem to have plenty of their own foul-smelling cigarettes and an inexhaustible supply of something alcoholic called vodka. They, too, want to share their bounty with the Poles, but only a few youths make the connection. Having tried the vodka, those foolish boys have already wilted onto the streets and in the alleys. Still, the church bells peal, and, though nearly every Pole in the crowd has lost someone to the war, each

330

face wears a smile, and all hands are outstretched.

As I watch, my mind and heart are filled to the brim with acceptance. I feel confident my baby is alive. My father waits and soon I will hear my darling mother's voice again. Surely the communication lines when I get to Berlin will be in order. Poor Poland has been under Hitler's heel for so long. It will take a long time for those things that have been broken to be fixed. Most of all . . . the hearts.

Our real mission in Poznan on this wonderful day is to locate a consulate with a Russian officer in command who can issue the necessary papers to allow me to ride the train to Berlin, through all the stops between Poznan and the eastern part of Germany. It takes several hours to find the unwashed, despotic little Russian officer. When we do, he has a steel incisor proudly displayed in the front of his mouth. With a smug and sardonic grin, he discounts everything presented to him.

Oncle Karol has brought all manner of documents of his own, but, of course, there is nothing of mine. Discouraged, I recognize how Kurt has managed to keep me under control even when his war is lost.

Suddenly the subject of "milk" comes up. Staring at one of the papers, not even looking at Oncle Karol, the Russian says, "You are the farmer whose cows provide our milk?"

There is a slight pause before my companion starts to tow me out of the office. "Yes," he says, nearly to the door and quite obviously counting on the man's probable lack of knowledge about the dairy business. "Isn't it too bad there won't be any more?"

"We have ways of making you give us the milk."

"I can't give you what we don't have. If the cows don't give the milk, there won't be any for either one of us."

The Russian knows there's more coming.

"Cows are funny animals." Oncle Karol's hand rests on the door handle, "If they're unhappy—no milk."

"Unhappy?" The Russian's smirk has disappeared and there are perplexed furrows between his bushy eyebrows. Scrambling to the door, he puts his hand out to stop it from opening. I smother a laugh.

"If the people who milk them are unhappy, the cows feel it. They become unhappy, then-----there is no milk."

"Wait a minute, wait a minute. Are you saying that if I don't give you the papers you ask for, the cows will be too sad to give milk?'

"It's possible." Onkle Karol takes my arm.

"Wait. You can have your papers."

Back in the office, he orders a subordinate to prepare the documents that will get us to Berlin. My mentor gives my arm a little pinch. When I look at him, he winks and smiles. By the time Onkle Karol has the papers in his hands, we have only two hours before the train leaves. Racing home, he turns the running of the dairy over to the estate manager, grabs a few clean shirts in a small bag, and we are back at the Bahnhof in Poznan. Tante Nina and the driver push a great basket that contains enough to feed our whole crowded compartment aboard and we are on our way.

Too wound up to sleep, we watch breathlessly as Russian officials dissect and question our papers every time the train stops, which is often. Fortunately Oncle Karol speaks some Russian and even I, having lived with Katya, can help a little. Twice, they get off the train with our papers, but eventually bring them back. However, when we reach the German border and all the Polish officials disappear, we are left with nothing but Russians. When they don't return our papers, we are terrified. It gets worse. The new set of Bolsheviks, with no explanation, drags us off the train.

The other travelers in our compartment, German and a loquacious Frenchman, having shared their war stories and the food from our basket, are now fast friends. They yell at the Russians in a cacophonous mixture of languages. All the noise plus eight arms gesticulating wildly from the train windows so confuses the unworldly Reds they hustle us back aboard.

We arrive in Berlin mid-morning, tired, wrinkled and still minus our papers. As we step off the train, a smirking guard thrusts them into Oncle Karol's hands. Still too shocked to feel relief, and fearful that if he waits he may not get a return ticket, Oncle Karol hurries to the ticket window. With only his small bag and the empty food basket for luggage, when a ramshackle taxi drives up, we take it.

The only hotels we've known in the past are on Unter den Linden. The taxi driver tells us that part of the city has been taken over by the Russians. We ask about the American Embassy. Have they taken that over too? Though he's a German, he beams with delight and volunteers that his own apartment is near the American Embassy. He is glad because he never followed Hitler, and now he feels protected. Inside I feel very small stirrings of hope. The ending of the war has made everything come out the right way after all.

U.S. soldiers stand in front of the embassy. The magnificent American flag waves from a pole above the entrance. My spine stiffens, my shoulders straighten, and though tears are running down my face and splashing on the one dress I own, I want to hug everything and everyone I see. Stepping lightly from the taxi I hug myself and whisper, "I'm home."

In the building there is a long counter like a hotel desk and a sign that says "Information." Still bewitched, I stand by the revolving door and absorbing the scene. Oncle Karol goes to that desk. Afterwards he leads me across the large room. "We are to meet your father in the Post Exchange coffee shop, which appears to be . . . right here."

We step into an enormous room filled with tables and divided into two sections. A printed sign in the smaller section says 'Officers.' A larger reads 'Enlisted.' This is no surprise. Life in the Army has taught me that in a war, though the welfare of the men must come first, an Army cannot function as a democratic organization. Separation and discipline must be maintained for survival. The coffee shop is busy. Every table is full. By the time we get there a bit of my mind has begun to function. I see a soda fountain, but we haven't any American money. Still, when one of the few small tables clears, we put our possessions under it and sit down.

"Can I get you something?" A young soldier with a white apron over his uniform stands beside us. He is speaking English. With an open mouth I look up at him as if he were a god from some outer planet.

"We haven't any American money," I manage to say. The words sound strange.

"That's all right. What kind do you have?"

"Polish Zlotys." Oncle Karol reaches into his pocket for his purse.

"Today we're taking everything. But if you have change coming, you'll get it in script. Is that okay?"

Before I could ask what script was, he draws himself to attention and salutes.

"Caro?" The familiar voice comes from behind me. In a split second I am up and wrapped tightly in my father's arms. The missing years cannot squeeze between us in reality or in memory. There is only now.

We separate only when Onkle Karol says "Jonathon." The two old friends shake hands, but Daddy never lets go of me. He holds on even when he pulls a tall, young American Major into the group and introduces him as Clay Baxter. It isn't until he adds, "Clay is my Aide," that I break loose and see, on my father's uniform shoulders, the two gold stars of a Major General. "One in Africa and one in Italy. Anyone can get them in war time," my father says before I can ask.

"Only if they earn them," Clay Baxter interrupts. "Your father earned his the hard way."

Taking a better look at the speaker, I notice first that under quizzical eyebrows, the Major's blue eyes look at me with interest. His nose may be a shade too large, but laugh lines bracket his mouth and the whole face, while not handsome in the way Kurt's was, is good-looking. A brown lock of wavy hair falls across his forehead when he removes his overseas cap.

"This isn't the time to talk about minor details." My father pushes us toward a larger table where we can all sit down. "We'll have a lifetime to talk over the happenings of the last years. Now, I think we have to get to the matters at hand. Clay has found rooms for you at a little Gasthaus near here. Not elegant, but what is in this post-war city? Karol," he turns to the man who has gone out of his way to shelter me from harm and despair. "How long can you stay? Troop transports are leaving now from Bremerhaven and I had planned to get Carole and Anna on one of them and home as soon as possible. Where is Anna?"

Oncle Karol looks at me. "I think Carole has something to say that may alter your plans a bit. Go ahead, Carole. Tell your father where we think Anna is."

"We hope she is on Hel with your grandson."

There are two gasps, one from Daddy and one from Clay, each for a different reason.

"Hel is the name of an island," my father says to his startled aide. "A grandson? You've had a baby?" The question comes almost as an explosion when my words register. "Why didn't you tell us in your letters? And why aren't they with you?"

"They had to save Alexander from his father."

"Your father needs more explanation, Carole." His face is only inches from my own. "Remember, he obviously hasn't heard the truth from you for a long time."

Embarrassed and apologetic, I begin with Kurt's amoral delivery of his father to the Nazi's. When I arrive at that last, terrible morning, I can't bring myself to talk of the rape and the beating in front of Clay. When I hesitate, Oncle Karol has no such inhibitions. Speaking of Kurt as an egoistic animal he fills in enough to start Daddy pacing. When we end with the wagon rolling away in Grudziadz without me, there is a long silence For the second time in my life I see my father cry.

Chapter 42

It's painful to say goodbye to Oncle Karol. He and Tante Nina have given me love, safety and hope. They have returned me to the status of a human being and reunited me with my father. While I love them for themselves and for being the beloved grandparents I was lacking, they have produced more happiness than I ever hoped for in the last week. Will I find my baby on Hel? And if I don't, can I live without him? These thoughts are tearing me to pieces.

Daddy has persisted in attempting to get through to Hel by all the methods at his disposal, but the Germans or the Russians have destroyed most of the communications with that part of the world. There seems no way to find out if Anna and Alex are alive before I can get to that long narrow little strip of land that dangles down into the Gulf of Danzig from the Baltic Sea. It allows time for my fearful mind to dream up more possibilities. The boat could have tipped over in the Vistula. Or in that cold, gray Baltic Sea. They might have run out of milk. No, Anna would have found something for him, even if she'd had to get out of the boat and run through fields to find a cow. But if the SS found them? And as always, how can I stand to wait any longer to find my answer? Although I try to think optimistically. I don't voice my feelings to anyone else. They fester in my heart until I am sure that when we finally get there, we will find the Hel empty.

The three days wait for my replacement passport seems endless. Fortunately the American Ambassador, once he hears my story, is able to expedite matters. Still it takes several days.

"Kurt will no doubt be tried for war crimes," Daddy explains during that waiting period. "I want you out of the marriage and away from Europe before that happens." Without any argument from me, he makes a few phone calls. Something filthy seems to slither from my shoulders when the acting Polish Ambassador says, "You are free, Miss Pierson. Your marriage is dissolved. Good luck to you."

Fortunately Dr. Pogonowski has also made Alexander's birth certificate out in the name of Pierson as if I had never had a German husband. The Ambassador bends the laws a great deal in issuing a passport for my baby.

"If I should ever find him," I say softly. That heavy feeling of dread covers me with its loathsome shroud.

"When you find him." Daddy is giving orders.

"When I find him," I repeat dutifully as my spirits rise.

"When she finds him," the Official echoes, but turns to my father. "But if she shouldn't, please bring the passport back to me so I can destroy it and all the paperwork. I won't turn any of it in until you tell me the mission is accomplished."

Because Anna was born in Poland to a German mother and a Polish father, her situation is even more complicated. First, she isn't with us so we go from the Russian to the Polish to the German Embassy. In that office the last vestiges of Hitler's Nazi regime cling to the 'still-to-be-replaced' official. It isn't until Daddy has a German General paraded in, in handcuffs, guards and all, that the now unimportant little man has a clear understanding of what surrender means.

With Anna's papers in his capable hands, Clay leaves us to get whatever else she will need to travel with me to America. To celebrate we buy a WAC's purse and a passport case in the Quartermaster store, zip the passport in its case inside the purse and I swear never to let the purse out of my sight. Daddy gives me some script to put in with the passport and I feel like a responsible human again.

"While we're here," my father says, "we might just as well go whole hog. You can't go around forever in that ill-fitting thing." He approaches a WAC officer who is shopping in the small store. "Do you have time to help my daughter pick out everything she will need to become a Second Lieutenant in the Women's Army Corps?"

The poor young woman looks startled, but when a Major General asks a favor of a young Captain she almost has to agree. She drops her own purchases on the counter, turns, salutes." Yes, sir."

"Good. Go with the Captain." My father pushes me toward her as if I am a child. I laugh. He might just as well have said "Shoo."

"Sir, what . . ." the surprised Captain gets no further.

Daddy waves his hand airily, "I'll explain later and treat you both to a soda, wine or even dinner."

"I'm Carole Pierson," I say proudly and put out my hand.

"And I'm Constance Gavin," the young Captain answers. While she makes the selections, I try to fill her in on the reason for the whole thing. She picks out two uniforms, two extra shirts, sensible marching shoes, stockings, some olive drab underwear and pajamas.

"He didn't say how much we could spend," she says shyly. "But a Major General should be able to afford two of everything. The shoes might get wet, the uniform might have to go to the cleaner. Besides, the extra uniform, should be fitted .We can't have you disgracing the Women's Army Corps."

"I can't promote you above a Second Lieutenant." Dad is laughing when he returns and pays for what he carefully pronounces as my "war" drobe. "I have to trust you not to issue any orders to subordinates, but this is what's available on short order." He explains this unorthodox and probably slightly illegal situation to Captain Gavin, has the Quartermaster swear me in, and we all go into the small Bier Halle next to the Quartermaster store. No matter what else the Germans were lacking there seems to be a good supply of bier.

"Don't worry, Daddy. O.D. is not my most becoming color," I say as soon as we sit down. "I'll be happy to resign my commission as soon as I can."

That is my second day in Berlin. Each day, since I arrived in Berlin, I ask Daddy if we are ever going to get to talk to Mother. "Maybe tomorrow," he answered. But now, when we are sitting in the coffee shop on this last day, and I am working on a malted milk made with powdered milk and ersatz ice cream, he finally says, "O.K. Caro, with all our duties performed, we come to the most important time of this wonderful week."

My father takes my uniformed arm and hurries me through the door of the busy telephone exchange office. There are long waiting lines of service men who have been given specific call times to hear the beloved voices denied them, for some as long as four years. I am surprised they wait so patiently.

"Mother?" I am almost afraid to ask the question.

"If all goes according to schedule, we are going to talk to your mother." Stars on his shoulder or no stars, my father is not one to demand special favors because of his rank. He pushes me onto the end of the shortest line.

Being in the middle of all the salutes is sort of like being caught in a windmill. I wonder that Daddy's arm isn't worn out returning them. In less than fifteen minutes the loudspeaker calls his name and we are escorted to a room full of phone booths.

"Number three, General." A pleasant young woman in a WAC uniform jumps up and motions with one arm, while she salutes both of us with the other.

"Salute," Daddy says in my ear. I am too excited to think about anything other than I am about to hear my Mother's voice, but I salute. Later when I replay the whole unimaginable day I have time to wonder how many times in an hour that poor girl had to jump up and down.

"Hello. Mother?" I quaver.

"My precious one. Oh. Oh." Even that fades. Unless the sound of our happy tears can transfer over telephone lines, there is silence.

"Hello, Janice," Daddy grabs the receiver. "For God's sake, say something, we only have three minutes. Carole's crying too hard."

That jarrs me enough to let me speak. "I'll be home soon and we'll talk and talk and never stop. I love you." The words are choked, but she will understand. I want to tell her she had a grandson, but am still too afraid I won't find him. I hand the phone back to my father.

"Janice, we have a grandson, but Caro has to go find him." Apparently Mother asks where he is. "On Hel. She's going this afternoon. She, Anna and Alexander will take a freighter from Gdynia. Who's Alexander? Your grandson, Janice, our grandson. No, we don't have enough time. Clay's going with her. He'll take care of her, don't worry. We love you more than tongue can tell," Daddy says before he hangs up.

My Grammie's words bring a new flood of tears. I haven't said any of the things to my mother I wanted to say. Daddy told me just this morning that my Grammie died in her sleep over a year ago. She had always been there for me, but I hadn't been able to hold her hand in her last, important dream.

We spend the last few hours before the train departs trying to talk through everything we'd forgotten to talk about in our five days together. He's had to do his job and squeeze my problems in between, but Clay has been with me when Daddy couldn't. Last night they showed a movie called Casablanca. In the dark Clay reached over and took my hand. I tried to ignore the thrill that fluttered my heart. I told myself it was only comfort I was feeling.

When I see the lines on Dad's face that weren't there and shouldn't be there at his age, I feel selfish. How dare I feel comfort? I see a sadness that was never in his eyes before and in Clay's, I see an awareness of life he's too young to know. War is a horror and a lifetime burden to those who live through it. Soldiering remains one of the very few professions in which men train most of their lives for something they hope won't happen. Yet . . . it is a profession that will always be necessary as long as one man anywhere harbors hate and greed in his heart. Hitler proved that.

Here we are again. Daddy, Clay and I at the Berlin Bahnhof where I've boarded trains before, some in joy, once in tears. I give that only a brief thought as we hurry through this bombed out shell. In my eagerness I feel there is hope for all of us traveling toward our futures. For that moment I am sure that up there in the Baltic Sea, mine will be waiting in Anna's arms.

"I wish I were the one going with you," Daddy says. "This is a busy wrap-up time for us all. Clay has a good head on his shoulders and you'll be safe with him. He'll stay with you until you're all three aboard a freighter then he can tell me about the baby when he gets back here. I'm jealous, but I guess I'll have to wait to see my grandson at home. I hope it won't be too long."

When the train inches forward, Clay pulls me aboard.

"Don't let him grow too much before I get to hold him" are the last words I hear.

Chapter 43

Because of the crowded trains, even my father's rank couldn't produce a single compartment. Clay shares his with a young man from Sweden, Lars, and I share mine with his sister, Kerstin. They've been caught in France when Hitler took over that country and are now trying to get back home. Since neither one of us speaks Swedish we converse in a mixture of French and English. Their English is better than our combined French. We four sit in the "girls'" compartment with our feet on large cartons that take up most of the space on the floor.

Lars points to the boxes with a puzzled expression. "What?"

Clay laughs. "Because of all the civilians and Russian soldiers trying to sort themselves out and get to their homes, as you know, the trains are full and there is no diner. Those who can afford to brought aboard their own food, but many of the Russian soldiers have simply been cast loose with neither food nor money. I expect the ones on this train count themselves lucky to be able to ride. Most of the remains of their Army will have to walk back to Mother Russia." He takes out a boy-scout knife and opens the box under his feet before he continues his explanation. "I brought aboard a huge number of sandwiches provided by the Officer's Mess for us and as many great boxes of K-Rations as our two compartments can hold. This can is a K-Ration." He presents Kerstin with the can.

"No one with a conscience could let the Russians starve." Clay takes the can back from Kerstin.

I think of Kurt and his treatment of his own, much less foreign soldiers. He would never have shared anything with someone he thought was beneath him. To get rid of the impediments in the two compartments as soon as possible Clay asks Lars and Kerstin if they would like to help distribute the contents.

"We would like to help wiz zis K-Food and, if you are sharing your sandwiches wiz us, perhaps you will allow us to share our cheese and biscuits wiz you. We have, also, some wine."

"We would be delighted to share with you. The Mess made enough to feed the four of us for a week. Come on, let's feed the starving multitude and get rid of these boxes." He tucks one case under each of Lars's arms and hands one to Kerstin.

"What is zis multi somesing?" Kerstin looks perplexed. "I sink we give zis k-foods to ze Russian peoples."

"We do. I'll show you what a multitude looks like when we get into the next car. They abound in there." Clay gives the last carton on the floor to me and with a box from the overhead rack under each of his own arms we start out. "There are six more in our compartment."

Laughing, we jounce up and down the train, distributing the K-Rations as far as they will reach. Steel teeth or no teeth at all, the gaunt men grin at us as they tear at the boxes. It is only when we are back in the compartment and are talking about how we might help them further that I wonder how they will open the cans.

"Resourcefulness," Clay says. "Don't worry, they'll get them open. Like the Post Office, the American soldier manages to do it even through snow and sleet and dark of night." That is the closest either he or Daddy ever come to any discussion of the miseries of the war.

But it is because of that war, we four sit companionably munching spam and cheese sandwiches and washing them down with a bottle of wine. Before Lars and Kerstin leave us for a while, we are old friends.

In the last few daylight hours Clay and I watch the shattered remains of Germany roll by in companionable silence. After the last five days of frenetic activity together we don't talk. We cross a river. And burned pastures. I don't know which one it is, but according to the sun we are going in the right direction.

Deep in my own worries, at first I miss that Clay is talking. When his words intrude on my mental pictures of our arrival on Hel, he is describing his own family. I apologize.

"My mother could have been a concert pianist," he says proudly. "But she didn't have the temperament for it. She was too shy to appear in front of an audience. And yet, if she were already playing when the audience came in, she would never have known they were there."

I am interested. "Tell me more about your family." I move over beside him so I won't be squinting into the sun when I look at him.

His parents are in North Dakota, he tells me. I hear about his school days, his college days before he went to West Point, and that he loves to dance. He makes it easy for me to see him as a little boy, lying on the living room carpet after dinner listening to his mother play. "Absorbing the music," he calls it.

I like what he shows me of himself. Some of the kindnesses of the last five days re-occur to me and, though some were very small, they were thoughtful and of the sort life with Kurt had schooled me to forget.

"My father was strict, but just," he says. "In the summers, while my mother took my older sister to Europe, my father and I toured the United States and Canada by car. We two loved to sing and we drove across the western states singing all the parts of whatever operas we knew and laughing at our own silliness."His eyes crinkle when he smiles at the memory.

"One summer," he continues. "When I was eighteen, we went to

345

Alaska. I got a job, hauling in fish on the boat on which my father was a paying passenger. I thought I had fallen truly in love with a young, school, teacher, another passenger. Her name was Margie." He looks out of the window at a young couple in a passing station as they walk along a lane, hand in hand. "Margie was three years older than I was. When I begged her to marry me, she laughed. I was crushed. After the ship landed, she disappeared. It took a day or so, but I was grateful she had taught me the difference between true love and puppy love. That's when my father told me that marriage should be for all time. He said not to marry anyone unless I couldn't see spending my life without her. I hope I can give the same wisdom, standards, and morals to my son some day."

Here is the exact reason I am here, my early acceptance of Kurt and his lack of all of those things. I have to hide that I am a little shocked that Clay is married.

As he talks about his family and his own feelings, I realize he is the measuring stick I have been using for Alex's future father. Someday maybe I will find someone who will be to my little boy what Clay wants to be to his son. Then, when I tell my son about Kurt, he won't care.

"Tell me about your wife, Clay, and your little boy. How old is he?" I ask.

"Oh, I'm not married," Clay looks at me in surprise.

Does he mean he has a son without being married?

"I haven't found the right girl yet. I know my father's advice was right. So I'm waiting. I have no son yet either." Before I can assimilate that, he changes the subject. "Your father told me all about you. He said you were a pretty fine football player before those ballet people got hold of you. He also said it was a shame because they ruined a good quarterback."

He is not laughing, but I am. The thought of my father sharing the secret that I had been a tomboy with this man is funny. The terrible weight of all my lingering fears lifts a little.

By the time Kerstin comes back and he leaves us for the night, I know he is a man I can trust. As Daddy knows, Clay will never try to take advantage of our present situation. Kerstin and I talk long into the night. In love with a Frenchman, she is headed home to Sweden for the wedding.

"I like your Clay," she says. "He much same like my Louis. Bos gentleman. He take good care you, I sink. When you marry?"

I start to laugh, but something stops me, that funny thumping of my heart. "We hardly know each other." And I explain why we are traveling together on this train.

"I be sure you find your baby. I be sure too also you sink about Clay. He good man." She sounded so positive. "I see too also he sink about you now already."

"What makes you think that?"

"How his eye look to you all ze time. You watch. Pay attention."

I intend to watch Clay and my step. I don't want another involvement before the proper time. Asleep, I dream of wading through a field of flowers with my hand outstretched to a tall figure under a misty, blossoming tree. Near the figure a child and a dog are playing. The tall figure has no face.

Kerstin and I are happy to see Clay and Lars when they appear for breakfast. We vote on whether to have another spam sandwich, or one of Polish sausage. Sausage wins. Lars and Kerstin take theirs back to the other compartment. After the conversation last night I urge them to stay with us. But they say they have to work on the wedding plans. As the door slides shut behind them, Clay says, "Be home in time for lunch."

They nod and we all laugh. Looking out the window, through the gloomy, rainy day, parts of the land we travel through seem to be untouched by the war and other parts are devastated. Those sections are depressing to observe so we talk. We talk about Anna and Meier, the ballet and my love of dancing.

"I want to see you dance," Clay says. "I know you will dance again. How could that self-centered beast have denied you something that was like a breath of life to you? He was not a real man." He picks up a map from the seat and flaps it down on his knee in anger. After a minute or two of silence, he adds, "Tell me something more cheerful."

I tell him about my friend Katya and my life at Ostatetcznie. Oncle Karol has already told him about that last terrible day so there is no need to go into its sordid aspects. It's hard to talk about Deu, but when I do Clay reaches for my hand. It's comforting. Our hands stay together between us on the green, plush seat. I remember that whenever my parents are together they hold hands.

At last I talk about Alexander. "Some day," I say. "I will meet someone who can give him the sense of decency our parents gave to us." And then I can't help myself. "But I'm so afraid I won't find my baby in Hel." Unwanted tears come.

Clay dries them with his handkerchief and doesn't ridicule me as Kurt would have. With no words he pulls me into his arms and lets me cry against his shoulder. My heart thumps and though I want to accept the comfort and security I tell myself it's too soon. I've shown that my judgment in men is flawed. I need time to understand myself. Maybe someday. I pull away. When I look up at him, he has a strange expression on his face.

"Sorry," he says. "I guess I forgot myself, but I—"

Afraid of what he might say, I break in. "I'm sorry too. For being a cry-baby, I mean. I know I can be wrong, but sometimes I'm so afraid Anna and Alex won't be there."

"Carole, he will be right where you expect him to be. And if not, Anna will have left word somehow. Believe me, we will find him. I promise you." His voice is grim as he takes back my hand and straightens the fingers of my clenched fist.

"Thank you" is all I can say. Though I want to, I'm afraid to squeeze the hand that holds mine.

It takes us another day and a half to reach Gdynia and there are no further requirements for apologies, but he makes it a warm, companionable time. It's as if we had needed that one romantic "speed-bump" and now we're free to build the friendship or love or whatever comes.

In Gdynia we say goodbye to Lars and Kerstin and wander the town. Clay buys me a lovely necklace of amber beads with real bugs trapped in some of their golden depths and I get him a tie clasp of the same interesting material. "For our hail and never farewell," he says kissing me lightly on my cheek, very close to my mouth. "I wish—" He starts to say something, then straightens up with an off-hand "never-mind."

We start walking again. I wish I knew what he was going to say. Though it's a seaport city, Gdynia appears almost like a stage set.

"Clay," I say. "Do you get the feeling that this city is hunkered down, getting its second wind and that when all the troops have passed through and all signs of the war are over, it will spring up like a huge shaggy dog."

"That's a great analogy." He grins. "I can just see it shaking the Germans and Russians out of its fur. Soon, it will be restored to health and be a bustling seaport again."

When we step aboard the little boat bound for Hel that afternoon, though Alex never disappears from my heart, it's as if, under a magician's spell, I am transported back fifteen years to the first time I set foot on, I think, this same little boat. It was 1930 and we had been in Poland less than a week. The sea was rough and with the initial dip and tilt, Daddy had fought his way to the nearest rail where he hung like a limp rabbit for most of the hour-long trip. Mother had time only to tend to my father while I wandered. Once I reached the head of the companionway, the stench from below of cooking food mixed with its active rejection by unseen passengers caused my own stomach to heave. I, too, took my place at the rail. Was that only fifteen years ago?

Minds are incomprehensible things. During this crossing I play back almost year by year, those fifteen years. It brings Mother and Daddy, the von Wechslers and all those whom I love and who love me, close. They stand near me as I perform my ballet exercises, run in the Friedenau gardens with Deu, accept the applause after my first starring performance and all the little moments of my life that make me what I am. It's only when the boat whistle tells me we are approaching Hel that, afraid to look, I squeeze my eyes closed for a moment.

But I can't leave them that way. I have to see.

Opening my lids I look around for Clay. All my own defenses have deserted me and, when I realize how much I need him, I push the thought away. "I don't have time for that now," I mumble to myself. "Let me find Alex first."

Strong arms enfold me from behind. "I'm here for you." His voice is warm. He understands how I must feel. "Hang on. We're going to bump the dock and then you can look up. I can almost promise you they will be there."

I believe him. When the boat bumps into the dock, I open my eyes to the little hill on which the cottage should stand. I can't see it. My heart drops and I turn my face into Clay's chest.

"Look, Caro, look at that woman. She's waving. I think it's at us." Clay spins me around. "Is that Anna? Is that our Alex in her arms?"

As I look up, my beloved Anna is running towards me with a blue bundle in her arms. My heart lurches. Joyous tears start. Everyone is running. When we meet and I feel that small, warm, weight in my arms pressing against my heart, I know that heaven is a peninsula in the Baltic Sea named HEL.

ACKNOWLEDGEMENTS

Although my memories are strong and a great deal of this book is faction, it would never have seen the light of day had it not been for my wonderful critique group of Susan Ramos, Bonnie Holmberg, and Sarah (Sally) Honenberger. Sally, in particular, with her knowledge of this infernal instrument called a computer and her "how to get things done" abilities, has gone beyond the call in keeping me from throwing all of my thoughts and words over the balcony railing with said computer and into the trash.

Also, to my table-mates here at Branchlands who read the finished product and pronounced it ready for publication if I could find a publisher, "I am so grateful to you all! Thank you!"

MORE ABOUT THE AUTHOR: JEANNE ANN LAMBERT VANDERHOEF

The author is the 92 year-old daughter of an American U.S. Horse/Armored Cavalry Officer and a mother who wrote 54 best-selling novels for teen-agers from 1940 to 1973, Janet Lambert. When her father was sent to Poland in 1930 to share methods of equitation with the Polish Cavalry, Jeanne Ann was fortunate enough to be able to spend a great deal of time on lovely estate called Ostaczewo (Friedenau in her book) with a wonderful, German family and to study ballet in the elegant ballroom.

She did not remain to further a career, but came back to the U.S. A. with her parents in 1932. She had her schooling in many places. Grade school was mostly in Lexington, Virginia. She skipped the 7th and 8th grade while living in the city of Grudziadz in the Polish Corridor. Having become bi-lingual in German, she and her mother spent six months in France where she attended a French school, though barely proficient in French. Two years of college at the University of Missouri taught her about living in a sorority and having a good time, but she resisted cluttering her brain with academics. When her father was posted to Governor's Island in New York, she became one of the early John Power models.

While dating at the U.S. Military Academy at West Point, she met a First (Senior) Classman, Dean T. Vanderhoef. It was 'love at first date.' A year later in July 1940 when he graduated, they were married. Their first child, Craig was born in 1942 while Vandy (Dean) was overseas for three years during WWII. Their second child, a daughter Lee arrived in 1946 and a second daughter Christa in 1948. After the war they spent most of Van's 20 years of service in the Washington, D.C. area with three years in Garmisch Partenkirchen, Germany, '47 to '50 and two years in Bangkok, Thailand, '56 to '58.

Her first book, <u>Gibbons in the Family Tree</u>, is an outgrowth of acquiring two baby Gibbons while they were in Thailand. She maintains that one cannot live in a small town in Virginia with three children and two apes (Gibbons) without having a funny or touching tale to tell. After 63 wonderful years of marriage, Van passed away in 2003. Jeanne Ann lives in Charlottesville, Virginia where Hot Toddy, a Shih Tsu, and Fritzi, the cat, allow her to share their apartment and to grant their every whim. Craig and Lee live near-by. Christy is in Harrisburg, Pennsylvania.

MEMORIES

In the later years of my life it has often occurred to me to wonder what if. On the other hand, the alternatives I chose have colored my life with all the colors of the rainbow and taught me lessons I might never have been forced to learn otherwise. Does our God hold the proverbial carrot on the stick to test our gluttony or our wisdom as I do for Carole Pierson? Do our own choices add to or clear the stones in our road to Heaven as hers do? Somehow, I believe this is so. What if . . . ?